Into the Dark

Lisa Hofmann

Into the Dark
- a fantasy novel -

Text copyright © 2016 by Lisa Hofmann
Coverdesign: Magicalcover.de/Giusy Ame, images:
Depositphoto

ISBN 978-3-946618-02-7

Published by Elisabeth Hofmann Verlag, Netphen

This book is, again, dedicated to my husband and children. I'm so blessed to have your support. It's also dedicated to my friend, Dana Winslett.

Many thanks to Patti Geesey (editing).

Lisa Hofmann, November 2016

⚘ Prologue ⚘

Nothing good ever came from magic, and the Bible clearly stated: *you shall not allow a sorceress to live.* Still, Rebecca couldn't bring herself to abandon her sister's child. She was sure there was also something in that book about protecting those you love.

Love might have been a strong word for how she felt about Catherine, but Catherine was family.

Watching her niece light the fire in the hearth, Rebecca wondered if Catherine felt the same. She doubted it. Catherine would be out the door without looking back, when the time came.

It never ceased to amaze her how quickly Catherine managed to create a blaze from the frail, gray embers on the grid. Looking into the flames, she wondered if it had to do with the girl's Ability. She couldn't say for sure, so she kept her thoughts to herself. The Curse thrived on ambition, and Catherine's ambitions were fueled by other people's disapproval, as well Rebecca knew.

Besides, there were things far more terrible than encouraging a spark to breathe warmth into the house on a damp morning such as this. As long as Catherine could avoid displaying what she was in public, Rebecca didn't intend to bicker about little things.

They hardly ever saw other people nowadays anyway, and she had her own issues to chew over.

Her fear of discovery for having killed Laura Shearer was one of them, though it didn't gnaw at her day and night as she'd expected it might. Not being able to generate a proper income posed a more immediate problem.

She hadn't told any of their new neighbors she was a midwife. Not even the pleasant ones several miles down the hollow way to whom she'd sold their horse and wagon. The last birth she'd been called to had gone terribly wrong.

The infant she'd pulled from its mother's womb feet first and ashen-faced after two days of labor never should have survived the night. That little boy wouldn't learn to work his parents' farm. They could count themselves lucky if he learned to talk. No doubt his father would look for somewhere to place the blame when it became obvious; the other six children in the household were all girls.

She often asked herself if she could have done anything differently in either case, but nothing came to mind.

Screaming, wailing Laura Shearer had been a liability, so she'd had little choice in the matter. With the boy, however, she'd simply made a mistake when she'd underestimated death's pull on him.

Rebecca hadn't given up much by coming here, though she made sure Catherine believed otherwise. A little gratefulness on Catherine's behalf didn't hurt her position with the girl.

Catherine rose to start her chores while Rebecca finished getting dressed for the day. They needed water so she could make breakfast. Catherine didn't smile when she passed her by with the bucket. She rarely smiled at all, but she'd grown into a strikingly beautiful young woman just the same.

Rebecca didn't regret making sure this particular child would live the night she'd helped her into this world. Catherine was headstrong and reckless at times, but having her there dispelled Rebecca's own weaknesses, and her dread of being alone.

Chapter One

❧ First Impressions ❧

The guard eyed Lorcan Aurum with skepticism, as he did most of the people waiting in line to be let through Ironstone's southern town gates.

Lorcan handed him the leather-bolstered haversack that held his belongings. He'd strapped his blanket roll to it. There wasn't much in the bag, but it was heavy enough to warrant a search every time he came to another new town, so he knew the routine. All the big settlements along the main trading roads invested in fortifications and protection, and that investment was money well spent.

"State your business," the gatekeeper said, while his partner took the sack off his hands and rummaged through its contents.

Two other soldiers meticulously picked apart one of the smaller merchants' carts on the other side of the wide entranceway. Its elderly Dwarven owner complained about the time this was costing him and the likely breakages, but no one paid him any heed.

"I'm a journeyman," Lorcan returned. "I'm looking for work."

The guard snorted. "What guild?"

"Carpentry."

Remembering his last visit to Ironstone, he thought he'd received a friendlier welcome that winter, but he'd come on horseback in the company of a scholar then. Today, he was a young man on his own, walking in on worn-out shoes, wearing a threadbare cloak, and looking every bit the rogue he felt like.

"Arms?"

Lorcan smirked. "Two of them, yes." He regretted the words even as they left his mouth.

The soldier frowned and shoved him roughly up against the wall to frisk him. "Are you trying to be smart with me, boy?" he growled in his ear as he pulled the coin pouch from his belt.

Lorcan wondered if his coppers would still be there when he got it back, but decided not to protest. "No, sir. I'm sorry."

"A knife, a file, and a hatchet," the other guard told the man, presenting his findings.

Annoyed with himself, Lorcan stood perfectly still as the soldier finished searching him.

"Tools of my trade," he explained. He had to get into Ironstone before dark because he couldn't really afford another night at an inn. "You'll also find letters of recommendation from the guild masters of Leignsbridge and Shingelsforth in there."

A moment later, the younger of the soldiers confirmed that and showed his partner the Bible he'd also discovered between spare shirts and breeches.

Lorcan was afraid either one of them would open the catch that held the covers securely together around its pages and find the other letter he carried with him – Thaddeus' letter. Until now, no gatekeeper had ever thought to look inside the book, but even if they did, he'd destroyed the Tierney seal that might betray him, and most soldiers couldn't read.

"Where did you get this?" the guard asked, waving the book in his face. Bibles were expensive.

Lorcan straightened his shirt. "Family heirloom."

The older man fixed his gaze firmly to Lorcan's, studying him, seeking some tell-tale sign of the lie, but Lorcan held his own. Finally, the soldier pushed the book at him, slapping it hard against his chest.

"Listen, witling," he said, "we don't need troublemakers here, and we won't stand for thieves. Do you understand that?"

Lorcan nodded without breaking their contact. "I do."

"Good, because you'll be out on your backside before the sun's down if you make a nuisance of yourself." The guard backed off and tossed the unopened coin pouch to him. "On your way, then."

Lorcan tucked the pouch into his belt and gathered his things up off the ground. Sorting them back into the bag didn't take a minute. When he raised his glance, the guard had already moved on to the supplicant behind him. The Dwarve's cart had been thoroughly ransacked, but the little man was finally allowed to pass. For a moment, Lorcan watched the donkey that pulled the vehicle laboring hard on the steep cobble pavement. Then, he looked around, and he realized Ironstone was every bit as beautiful as he remembered it.

Sometimes, a heart's longing painted recollections of people and places more intensely than they should have been, but he hadn't expected to find he'd like what he saw here today this much. For months, he'd debated with himself on whether he should make Ironstone a halting-place on his travels, but no matter which direction he'd chosen to go, the roads he'd taken had always brought him another mile closer to where he now stood.

Many good images came back to him as he walked the sloping streets. He could almost hear the Master Sorcerer telling Dean and him this and that about the history of the citadel and the ancient palace that crowned the hill… the ancient *Fairypeople* palace. It was where they'd brought the Snow Globe for safe keeping.

He had no desire to return to the palace and make himself known, but it was a good feeling to be near where the Globe was, somewhere close to the magic it held. It was almost like being close to the man who'd created it. He didn't need to see it - knowing it was there was enough. As long as it was there, the Master

Sorcerer's dream was alive, and his people would be safe.

Evening neared, but both market places were still busy. Vendors had begun packing their carts with the day's leftovers, and drays rattled by on their way to the gates, but there was still plenty to see.

A small shop culture had become established around the Fish Market. The beginnings of it had already been visible when Ortus had brought Dean and him to Ironstone. Quite a few of the businesses that no longer operated from booths and barrows speculated on passers-by stopping into small shops on the lower levels of the houses that lined the squares, and success seemed to prove them right in having taken that step.

He didn't need, nor could he afford to buy anything, so he tried to concentrate on finding the local carpenters' guild master. Masons and carpenters usually lived in the oldest parts of town somewhere between the main marketplace and the castle, so he decided to start looking out for the crossed hammer-and-rasp symbols above the doors of the tall, slender hall-houses as he passed them.

Many of the buildings on either side of the narrow alleyways in this part of town had a rather small base area, but they stood two or three floors high. Not one was like the other, and they were all in good repair. Each had its own charm, and the cheeky envyfaces that were carved into the horizontal beams above the first floor to ward off evil contributed more than anything to that. Most of the doorframes and window shutters were adorned with ornate patterns that had been scored into the wood. Here and there, decorative designs had been painted on the whitewashed clay-and-straw vaults between the girders. People here took pride in where they lived, and Lorcan liked that.

Thaddeus' letter of recommendation had turned out to be worth ten times its weight in gold in getting him started. His old apprentice master had known whom to send him to with it. The Cine had human friends and helpers in many parts of the land, and he'd never been without work and shelter because of it, but here in Ironstone, he didn't want to make use of it. He finally wanted to stand on his own two feet.

He carried the documents he'd earned from the guild masters in Leignsbridge and Shingelsforth with him proudly, and they stood for new beginnings and a rebuttal to his father's convictions.

Jaden had claimed a Cine could never make an honest living among humans, but Lorcan was determined to prove him wrong.

Human imagination was fueled by the same things a Cine's was, and it wasn't just driven by the blind, consuming ignorance and hate Jaden had perceived whenever he'd looked at a human since the massacres in the Sudlands. Lorcan had seen a lot of ignorance and hate himself during that time. He'd lost just as much as Jaden had, but he was convinced there was more to human nature than destructiveness, and he'd come to know good people since he'd left The Fair.

Jaden had been firmly convinced a Cine would never be able to hide what he was. Being poor, as their family had been, made someone all the more of a target for hate, but that was true for humans as well. Rich people didn't have the kind of problems with staying out of trouble that peasants did, or most of the refugees at The Fair did. A putative pedigree and a well-filled purse could conceal any anomaly in plain sight.

Ortus had lived most of his life among humans, well-educated and in the local nobleman's employment. He'd been the teacher of all his liege lord's children, and he'd married a human woman. A man of some standing despite his Cine lineage.

The Queen of Ironstone had Fairypeople blood, but it was so well-diluted, no one remembered but those who refused to forget. A powerful woman with influence despite her descent.

Lorcan remembered the reverence Ortus had commanded wherever he'd gone because he'd simply been as charismatic as he had, and he recalled staring at Cassandra and thinking how radiantly her beauty canceled out every last question as to her nature. No human would have dared pass judgement on either of the two as easily as they would on a shaggy old Shapeshifter who could turn himself into a smelly, potentially dangerous animal at will, or an impoverished Cine who might have the Gift of changing human perception for a moment or two and rob him.

Beauty didn't look as threatening to humans as a beast did, and wealth could buy you time and space when your luck had run out.

That was why Lorcan didn't intend to stay poor. Anything was possible if you applied yourself properly. Yammering didn't help you overcome what life threw at you. Changing the course you were on did.

All things considered, he didn't think he'd done too badly so far for all the drama and prophesies of doom he'd been listening to since he could think, and he was determined to lead a normal life.

Ortus' strategy hadn't worked, in the end, because he'd followed the wrong path. He'd been *too* trusting. But, his own kind had turned on him, and that was worse than if he'd been executed by a human headsman. Lorcan had loved Ortus, but he didn't want to die like the Sorcerer had, nor like any of the people he'd seen burned, quartered, staked or decapitated as a child in the Sudlands.

He hadn't asked to be born a Cine. He hadn't asked for any of this. If the price of magic was always death and destruction, he didn't want the magic, and he could almost understand why so many people were afraid of it. A sword alone was nothing but a piece of metal, and it was never evil by itself because nothing made of this earth's materials could be either good or bad. Only the man wielding it could be one thing or the other. He'd never blame anyone for being afraid of a sharp blade, though.

There was no way of binding magic or expelling it from the flesh and bone, so he was determined to lock it away and make sure it wouldn't touch surface again, hurt or frighten anyone. It would never cease to be a part of him, but he could put it in a dark corner of himself where it would do no damage, whether intentional or by accident.

Spending time with Ortus had led Lorcan to believe magic was something you could control if you treated it with the same amount of straightforward acceptance that the Sorcerer had. Ortus had once told him that controlling a Talent was down to simply embracing magic for what it was, accepting it, and acknowledging the fact that you'd never be done learning how to handle it and assuming responsibility for it.

Since the day he'd found the Master Sorcerer's body by the roadside, however, probably killed by Jaden, the acceptance was gone, so he hoped knowledge and responsibility would suffice.

He wasn't going to let his Talent dictate how or where he'd spend the rest of his life. He was set on embracing reality as it was outside of the bubble the Sorcerer had dreamt for all of his kind. He was the master of his fate and no one else – not Jaden, not Ortus, not any of the Fairground people who'd assumed they'd have a say in what became of him, and certainly not any clergyman who had no idea what magic could and could not make a person do.

Only a few rays of golden light still glistened on the slated rooftops as the sun sank beneath the horizon in the west, and he realized it was getting late. The streets were emptying. He'd need to seek out a boarding house or an inn if he didn't find the local guild's emblem on any of the sandstone buildings soon. He'd been meaning to save his coppers, but he was no beggar, and he didn't want to sleep in some alley or doorway and appear as one.

Rounding the corner of a candlemaker's workshop, he bumped into the burlier of two dark-haired women coming out of the building without looking. She'd been chatting with the younger woman just behind her, who was balancing a fussy year-old infant on her hip. The topic of her heated monologue must have been so distracting, she hadn't looked left or right, but just come tumbling out in front of him.

She dropped the parcel she'd been carrying and immediately began having a go at him over not watching where he was walking. Her voice was gruff, and the range of names she knew for clumsy men astounded him. It spoke volumes on her opinion of men in general, though the expression on her companion's face told him that their similar features didn't extend beyond physical appearance.

Lorcan quickly bent to gather up the candles that had fallen on the street and into the gutter. Several of them had gone to pieces.

Though not entirely to blame, he mumbled an apology and offered them to her, but she shocked him again when she wouldn't take them. The small child on the other woman's arm was tired and started bawling outright at this point.

"You're going to replace every single one of those," she told him loudly, taking the girl from her sister's or cousin's arm, wagging a finger at him.

He sighed but didn't object, feeling defeated and wondering how much this was going to cost him. The younger of the two women smiled amusedly at this, as though she could guess what he was thinking, and finally took the candles off his hands.

"Calm down, Geraldine, you're upsetting Samantha, and you'll give yourself a heart attack," she told her sister.

"I'm *so* sorry," he repeated, "I really am. I was in a hurry. I seem to have lost my way, and I just didn't see you coming out the door."

"Well, I'm guessing you're not from around here," the younger woman stated pleasantly, and placed herself between him and her sister and the screaming child. She appeared to have made up her mind to defuse the situation. "I don't think it'll be too much trouble to fix them."

Frowning from behind her, Geraldine let out a snort and pulled her away in the other direction with her free hand, muttering to herself. "You mean *I'll* be doing the fixing – you never do anything," he heard her telling her sister. "As if I didn't have enough to do with the washing and the cleaning and the little ones..."

"I'm looking for the carpenters' guild master," he called after the two quite openly then on a whim. The younger woman stopped in her tracks, detached herself from her sister, and turned to face him again.

"You are?" She smiled somewhat gingerly as Geraldine's face took on a darker shade of purple.

"Perhaps you could point me in the right direction." He was quite sure she could, by the mischievous gleam in her eyes.

"You're in luck," she returned, and gestured him to follow her as she started walking away from him, "because that would be our father."

This, he hadn't expected. Briefly hesitating, he observed Geraldine, who continued to glare at him over her shoulder without slowing. She was ignoring the struggling, bawling youngster on her arm in favor of damning him to hell under her breath, and he couldn't blame her for it, considering the first impression he must have made on her. He hoped the one he'd make on her father would be a little better because he really wanted to live and work in Ironstone – even for just a while – and the success of that endeavor was dependent on the guild master.

Chapter Two

∝ The Guild Master's House ∽

By the look of it, the guild master's hall-house had probably been there a while before the cobble-paved street in front of it. Lorcan thought its foundations might well have been laid around the time when the castle had been under construction a short uphill walk away.

Its timber framework was painted in the warm northern red typical for all the lands Ironstone ruled. The straw-and-clay filled vaults nestled in between remarkably straight oaken girders and braces; over a hundred perfect trees had been felled to please the eye of its builder. Neither paint nor clay were flaking anywhere, as far as he could see, but the ground's settling beneath the structure had left a few cracks here and there over the centuries. Although the roof sagged slightly in its middle portion, it appeared to be sound. This was not the home of someone overtly affluent, but a man in easy circumstances who respected that time would have its way with anything, in the end, no matter what means you employed to delay its bearing on your life's work.

Smooth, worn steps led downward to the entrance below street level. He followed the two women inside. A small window on either side of the door and four larger ones along the south wall to the left would have let a good amount of light into the front room by day. As it was, the evening gloom still gave him a fair impression of what was obviously a spacious workshop on the lower floor of the house. It did not double as a living area, and it was not like any other workshop he'd seen before.

Most carpenters he'd found employment with hadn't even kept a workshop. Housewrights and cartwrights usually worked on site, and their choice of tools would fit in a hand cart.

He wondered where the guild master and his family ate and slept, but looking around as his eyes adjusted to the dim, he was detracted from the thought by the assortment of things they caught on instead of a hearth, bedsteads, and stools.

The workshop accommodated all the furnishings a good craftsman would need – and more – for any kind of job. The man who ran it had to have a great sense of orderliness. Even in the waning light, Lorcan could see how meticulously the floor had been swept. Not a single wood shaving lay about, and there wasn't so much as a rasp or a try square out of place on any of the tidy boards or workbenches. No doubt everything had its exact place here. Awe fed his imagination and drew vivid pictures of what was possible as he squinted at the different types of saws and braces arranged according to size on their wall fastenings, and the fitted shelves and uniform cabinets with numerals on the drawers.

A door at the back of the room opened up into a corridor just wide enough for a steep flight of stairs and the narrow passageway beside it. The stairs led to the second of the building's three levels, and Lorcan assumed the passageway would take them to the stable at the rear end of the house, perhaps, judging by the biting smell of manure that hit him from that direction.

The corridor as such was cramped, but practically conceived to both join and separate the work area from what could be the access to some storage area above the workshop, as well as the living rooms behind it. It was an unusual spatial arrangement, but he liked the idea.

New floorboards betrayed that this part of the building must have been added fairly recently. They were as yet unworn and of a different color here, and it suddenly occurred to him that this was where two adjacent houses may have been connected, maybe for want of more room for a growing family and more apprentices. He hadn't noticed it from the outside, but he hadn't known what to look for before he'd entered.

Crossing the corridor into what Lorcan now realized had to be the neighboring building, they came into a generous kitchen with curtains on the windows and knickknack on the walls.

A chunky table with benches along its sides and two comfortable chairs on each end dominated the middle of the room. The candles on the table were of the same make as the ones he'd broken when he'd run into Geraldine. He cringed at the sight of them.

Lorcan was sure this kitchen didn't only feed the guild master's family, but also his employees. A few of them probably had their night quarters on one of the sleeping benches near the fireplace. He wondered if he'd have that luxury, provided the man would take him on after his eldest daughter could now testify to his clumsiness from first-hand experience.

Several weak oil lamps provided little islands of light around the cupboards and the counter by the back door, and a good blaze in the hearth commanded shadows that danced around the vacant rocking chair near the mantelpiece. He wanted to sit down on the rocking chair and try it out, but he dared not.

He noticed the small rectangular hatch in the ceiling near the chimney and remembered seeing one like it in his grandfather's home many years ago. The old man had explained how it would be opened on cold nights to allow the heat to rise to the room above, so he assumed this was where the guild master and his wife's bedroom would be.

Geraldine smiled at a girl of about nine or ten who looked up at them from the pot she was stirring over the fire. It smelled gloriously of stew with leek and onions. The girl eyed him with curiosity, and then acknowledged his presence with a shy nod.

"Gracie, where's Father?" Geraldine asked her, pushing the infant at her and taking the ladle off her hands in return.

"Still at the castle." Gracie gently caressed the baby's cheek. "He said he and Frederic won't be back tonight because they'll be working until late, and drinking with the men afterward."

Geraldine snorted, a sound much like a hen sneezing, and turned to Lorcan, satisfaction written all over her face as she abandoned the stew in favor of showing him the door.

"Well, that's that, then," she said, resolutely opening it for him. "Come back tomorrow. Goodbye."

The younger woman frowned, placing her parcel on the table. "Geraldine, no! He's nowhere to go."

Lorcan raised an appeasing hand. "It's fine. Not a problem at all."

Geraldine huffed at her sister. "You hear him. It's not a problem." She made a shooing gesture, again reminding Lorcan of a mother hen, but Amelie put herself in his way and stopped him from stepping across the threshold and into what he assumed would be the back yard.

A purposefully pleading look crept across Amelie's face as she implored her sister. The sincerity of her concern may have been underlined by the poor light, but he decided that she was probably someone very much used to getting her way, as opposed to Geraldine.

Amelie was pretty, and she had the look of someone used to smiling. Her deep blue eyes were soft and ever so sweet, but there was a wild waywardness in them, and he guessed she'd be equally good at pouting as she was at talking people into things they normally wouldn't dream of doing.

"Come on," she continued stubbornly when Geraldine didn't reply after a moment. "Let's show some hospitality and at least give him a good meal before we toss him out on the street."

Geraldine sighed, rolling her eyes. She obviously didn't think this was a good idea, but finally made way and allowed Amelie to lead him to the table in the middle of the room, where Gracie was already waiting for him with a bowl of steaming food and a spoon.

"I'm Grace," she told him, "but everyone calls me Gracie."

"So I gather," he said. "Pleased to meet you, Gracie. I'm Lorcan."

Amelie sat next to him, and Gracie put little Samantha on her lap before she went to fetch some more of the mouthwatering stew. Lorcan didn't know whether to eat or wait, but the baby took the weight of the decision from his shoulders by fussing and trying to reach for the spoon, so he pushed the bowl at arms' length toward Amelie, handing over his spoon to her.

Amelie's smile broadened, and she immediately began blowing on the hot food, stirring it so it would cool faster as the baby struggled and fretted, making her growing impatience known.

Grace set three more generously filled bowls down out of reach of the infant's pudgy hands, and Geraldine brought a wooden cutting board with a hunk of white bread and a knife.

He could see she wasn't happy as she placed an earthenware cup and a jug of wine in front of him when she'd cut the bread, but she didn't say another word. Amelie and Gracie began chattering merrily as they shared the job of feeding the child together.

He had no idea whether the baby was Geraldine's or just another sibling, but he doubted it was Amelie's – at least some part of him hoped it wouldn't be – and he tucked into his own food, gobbling down his first helping hungrily without tasting it.

It was only when Gracie provided him with seconds that he realized how good that stew really was, and he soaked up every last drop of the rich broth at the bottom of the bowl with a piece of the white bread Geraldine reluctantly handed him.

The cool, heady wine Amelie was consistently pouring for him between feeding and entertaining the baby tasted like liquid sunshine on his tongue, and he emptied his cup in large gulps every time she filled it.

Only on his third cup did the effects of that hit him, and all at once, he became aware of how tired he was.

He swayed slightly when he stood up after he'd finished, smiling idiotically at the ladies who'd provided him with a meal he definitely wouldn't forget so soon. Geraldine made another attempt to usher him toward the door.

Once again, Amelie placed herself between him and the exit while Gracie went to wash the soup off of the infant.

"Oh, really, sis! He's got nowhere to go."

Looking at Geraldine, Lorcan thought she was going to start hyperventilating, and in all honesty, he couldn't blame her. They'd done more than enough for him already. He was a total stranger to them, and he could have been a robber or a murderer for all they knew. That aside, it would be highly inappropriate for them to give him shelter for the night with the man of the house gone.

"Well, he can't bloody well stay here," Geraldine yelled more at him than at her sister.

Muddle-minded though he was, he couldn't deny she was right.

"No trouble, Amelie," he told her again, shouldering his backpack. "Thank you very much for your kindness and the meal. I'll be on my way now, and I'll come back tomorrow to speak to your father."

"What, are you going to sleep on the street now?" She folded her arms across her chest before turning back to her sister. "Because he's not, you know."

Then, before Geraldine could object, she grabbed his arm and pulled him into the corridor, taking one of the candles with her. "He's sleeping in the stable."

"No, he's not," Geraldine replied firmly, and Amelie turned to face her.

"Don't *you* tell me what to do. You're not Mother, and this is not your house yet," she hissed. Lorcan was surprised to find that Amelie had it in her.

Geraldine shot him another nasty look, but stopped arguing.

"Lock the door, at least, so we'll be safe…" he heard the woman mutter behind them.

He couldn't help but grin to himself as he went ahead of Amelie. He had the feeling that if he lay down anywhere right now, even if it was in the stable, he wasn't ever going to get up again, never mind enter the women's rooms with base intentions.

The stable turned out to be more comfortable than he'd thought. Entering it, he didn't find the smell quite as obtrusive anymore as he had earlier, oddly, even though two pigs threw their weight around restlessly in one of the stalls and a cow stood ruminating in the other, while a clutter of hens roosted on perches near the outer doorway.

Amelie showed him a stall where they kept some loose hay. She used the flame of her candle to light the wick of a small oil lamp that was firmly secured to one of the cross beams.

"You should be alright here," she said. "Try not to puke on the fodder if you can't hold that wine, and don't pee in the yard. There's a bucket in the corner."

"I *am* housebroken," he assured her and plopped down on the hay.

Everything began to spin even more that way, and he briefly considered getting back up, but decided against it. It was simply too stressful.

"Well, goodnight, then," he heard her say, but he didn't want her to leave just yet.

"Who's who in your house?" he inquired, straining to see her, and she tilted her head quizzically. "I mean, what name does your father go by, and how should I address him in the morning?"

"Dermot Ember." She waited for his reaction, but he didn't catch on. "Not a good name for a carpenter, I know."

Then it dawned on him, and he chuckled, pushing himself up on his elbows. "Oh…! I see…!"

"And in addressing him, *Your Lordship* will be fine." Deadpan face.

He wasn't sure if he'd be giving her the impression of being completely dimwitted if he asked, but suddenly she erupted in fits of giggles, and he was somewhat relieved.

"No, silly! It's *Master Ember* to all of his apprentices."

"I'm not an apprentice," he corrected her. "I'm done learning. I've got letters of recommendation. I'm looking for wages."

She knelt down beside him, scrutinizing him. "Well, it's *Master Ember* to the journeymen as well. But you don't seem old enough to be a journeyman."

"I'm seventeen, and I'm a quick learner." Peering up at her, he wasn't sure if he looked it. Especially not in his present state with her hovering just above him.

She seemed to believe what he'd told her, though the words slipping from her mouth were teasing him. "You are, are you?"

"What, seventeen, or a quick learner?"

"Both." Her voice was so soft, he thought he might drown in it.

"I guess so."

"Then I'll leave you to get some sleep so you'll be up to scratch tomorrow."

She had to be at least two or three years older than he, and he wondered why she was still living in her father's house and not with a husband and children, a family of her own. He was sure she'd have plenty of suitors, and he envied them all.

Before she could leave, he clutched her arm, perhaps a little too tightly, and she flinched. Immediately withdrawing, he scolded himself, but then, she patted his hand, irritation turning to curiosity within an instant.

"What?" she inquired.

"You haven't told me who Frederic is yet."

"Best keep on his good side," she advised him. "He's Geraldine's husband. And, he's going to be the master guildsman one day."

For reasons he himself didn't understand, he was relieved, though there had to be someone else in her life, surely.

"Good night," she repeated, and this time, he nodded.

Her eyes lingered on him for a moment before she carefully put out the oil lamp.

"Wish me a good night, too," she quietly reminded him, and he blushed yet again, though she wouldn't see it.

"Good night."

Chapter Three

ಐ Cinnamon ಐ

Lorcan's awakening was less pleasant than he'd imagined it would be. A bucket of cold water was tossed across him. The fright nearly stopped his heart. He was on his feet and ready to fight within seconds, but when he resumed breathing, he saw that he couldn't possibly have gotten the better of the two muscular men standing some feet away, both with their hands on their hips, and both laughing at him.

One must have been over fifty. He was balding, sporting a sizeable paunch and his shirtsleeves were rolled up, looking as though they'd been made to fit that way.

The other was younger by a good decade, taller, and with a smugness about him that made it clear who'd thrown the water even before Lorcan saw the bucket at his feet.

"So, you're the *journeyman* my daughters picked up on the street," the older man mumbled, wiping his red bulbous nose with the back of his huge hand. He didn't seem happy, and Lorcan couldn't blame him.

Pushing his wet hair back from his brow, he tried to think of something clever to reply, but he was still breathing hard and feeling like he'd been caught sleeping. Which he had. What a sight he must be, he realized. He knew he shouldn't have taken all that wine, but one glance at the men in front of him told him that Amelie hadn't been trying to get him drunk – these two probably set a standard in this house. Considering the way his stomach was churning around what felt like a dead cat, he didn't think he'd ever want to measure up to it.

"I'm Lorcan Murua, sir," he offered, straightening his back. "I'm from the South, and I'm looking for work in Ironstone."

The younger man scoffed, picking up the bucket. "Who'd have thought it?"

Lorcan didn't know whether to be relieved or annoyed that he hadn't managed to keep the cynical fellow's attention, and he watched him leave the stable by the outer door, perhaps to fetch a refill for the pigs.

The guild master studied him. "And why should I consider offering you employment? You look like you couldn't nail a plank to a wall, though my Amelie seems to think differently."

Lorcan briefly looked at his feet before remembering himself. Thaddeus had always reminded him to quit doing that. His head was pounding. What a start to the day.

"I have letters of recommendation," he said firmly.

"You do, eh?" Ember looked amused, and Lorcan rummaged around in his backpack, wondering what, exactly, Geraldine might have told her father.

When he'd found what he was looking for, he handed the older man the letters he'd acquired in Leignsbridge and Shingelsforth.

A guild master named Ember hadn't been on the list Thaddeus had given him, and that meant Thaddeus didn't know him. Lorcan asked himself what kind of person Dermot might be, and whether he was a hater of his kind, or someone who couldn't care less about saints and sinners.

Unsure, he left Thaddeus' letter where it was, tucked safely between the pages of his Bible, but uncertainty wasn't the sole reason for that decision. He didn't want to be connected to The Fair anymore. Not by anyone, and not even if they were sympathetic to the plight of the Talented. If he found Ironstone was a place where he could settle down, he wouldn't want a past he hadn't chosen for himself tainting his hopes for a future he did feel entitled and free to choose.

There was a lot to be said for Ironstone, and the daughter of the man now scrutinizing the letters he had given to him, the daughter who was standing in the doorway watching him with flagrant curiosity, wasn't the least of that.

"This one says you've been building carts, and this one that you've experience in roofing," Ember stated, carelessly tossing the letters back at him. "I make furniture."

Lorcan drew a deep breath. "I can make furniture," he said, but the burly man had already turned his back on him and was heading back inside the house. "I mean, I could," he called after him, not ready to give up just yet. "I'm good with my hands, and I'm a fast learner."

"And you said you could use another man," Amelie argued as Ember pushed past her, and then looked at Lorcan. "Breakfast is on the table, if you want it."

Lorcan did.

Hurrying to catch up with Ember, he brushed her as he entered the house, and if he hadn't been so nervous already about getting the job he so desperately needed, he would have been nervous about having touched her instead. Her cheeks glowed, and he pretended not to notice.

Following the guild master into the kitchen, he discovered that there weren't a lot of seats left at the table. There were several young boys sitting on the bench closest to the fireplace, laughing and joking, and he assumed they'd be the apprentices.

On the other side of the table, three men he gauged to be somewhere in their mid-twenties to early thirties wore more somber expressions on their faces as they took notice of him. Two of them brazenly looked him up and down before resuming their quiet conversation between spoonsful of food and whatever it was they were drinking.

Ember sat at the head of the table. Lorcan wondered if he should sit on the free place next to him so he could talk to him, but this was probably Frederic's place. Observing him, Amelie became aware of his dilemma and navigated him to the only other available seat beside the oldest of the boys at the other end of the table.

The lad stopped talking to his neighbor when Lorcan plunked down, dropping his backpack behind him.

"Who are you?" the boy asked.

"I'm Lorcan," he replied simply, not bothering to elaborate.

It wouldn't matter if Ember didn't want to take him on. Considering the disinterested demeanor of the older man, he didn't think he would. And why should he? He'd made a right fool of himself.

It was a shame because he'd have liked to work for Ember. He liked what he saw here, from the neat workshop to the well-kept house, and that wasn't all of it.

Amelie smiled as she set a plate of porridge down in front of him. He wasn't sure if he could eat all of what she'd ladled on it for him, but he was determined to die trying. This was normality. The smell of something deliciously exotic he'd never had before wafted up from the steaming oatmeal, and he quirked his eyebrows questioningly at her as he inhaled the smoky-sweet aroma deeply.

"What did you put in this?"

One of the boys spluttered in an attempt to stifle a laugh, but Amelie just slapped him across the back of his head with the rag she was using to dry some of the cups she'd already washed, and he settled down instantly, his face glowing while the others concentrated pointedly on their hands.

"I cooked it with milk, honey, and a little cinnamon," she informed Lorcan proudly.

He could only speculate what cinnamon might look like before it was ground or hacked, or whatever else the guild master's daughter did with it before she added it to the gruel. It tasted even better than it smelled, despite the dull ache last night's wine had infused his brain with. He emptied his plate completely but declined seconds because he could see everyone was finishing and stacking their dishes for Amelie to take to the wash basin.

Geraldine came bustling in with a basket full of fresh vegetables just as he was getting to his feet, and the look she gave him might have killed any other man, but he gave her his most pleasant smile before thanking Amelie and following the others out of the kitchen and into the workshop.

No one was paying him any heed, and he assumed that was the end of it. Ember hadn't even bothered to dismiss him, but, again, he didn't blame the man one bit.

There would surely be another master carpenter in a town like Ironstone, perhaps one who built houses or wagons. Also, he'd have to take another look at his list. He'd had a roof over his head that night and gotten a good breakfast, he told himself, and he hadn't lost a thing by coming here. He had nothing to do today but find another guild master to embarrass himself to, so he made for the door.

The apprentices immediately got to work unpacking the cases and boxes of tools that were standing around in the middle of the floor, and the older men filed out the door behind Ember. They unhurriedly commenced unloading a wagon that stood halted in the middle of the street, blocking all other traffic. There was more than a dozen grand high-backed chairs with luxuriously upholstered, but very worn-down seat cushions on it. The coachman waited patiently without getting off.

Lorcan stopped to look at the precious cargo more closely. He hadn't seen chairs like these before, aside from at the palace, but then it occurred to him that this was where they really might have come from. The armrests were carved to look like the claw-tipped paws of some vicious creature that lived in the far-off jungles of the uncharted Dark Countries. The backrest curved back near the top with ornately carved ears and a floral design on the rail, perhaps primroses. He found the detailing of the woodwork completely intriguing and tried to commit it to memory, though he didn't think he'd ever craft a thing like that himself. It was as Ember had said: all he'd been doing was fitting rafters.

"Well, what are you waiting for?" the master guildsman barked then unexpectedly. "You don't get paid for standing around here, boy. Move your arse and get those chairs inside. The queen wants new seat cushions. Let's see if you're as good with your hands as you say."

Chapter Four

❦ Pawns ❧

In the Sudlands, the Cine were referred to as *The Tainted*. Farther north in the Middlelands and in the Northern Territories, they were known as *The Cursed*. In Ironstone, Lorcan heard talk of neither one nor the other, although he saw the silver in the eyes of the people he passed on the streets or on the market places every now and then. It was weak in most of the men and women he encountered. He guessed that many of those who had it weren't aware it was there as living proof of their lineage; no more than they could see the telling aura around the soft brown of his pupils.

Ironstone had as many inhabitants of Cine descent as it had Dwarven, but he never once perceived the spark of recognition. He thought it interesting how the silver had survived all these generations of mixing blood without leaving at least that little Gift unaffected, and he often wondered why, but he supposed ignorance could be a form of blessing.

Ember knew nothing of silver or magic. He treated Lorcan as a member of his household with the same privileges and the same duties as everyone else.

The guild master made him work hard for his keep and the pay he received beyond board and lodgings.

Ember was Lorcan's first all-human employer, but he was no different from most Cine craft masters. He was as demanding as the housewright Lorcan had worked for in Leignsbridge and the cart builder in Shingelsforth, and he expected nothing but the best from his journeymen and apprentices, Lorcan included.

All of Ember's other orders had to wait while every available man worked on the chairs that had come in to the shop on Lorcan's first day, and the ones that were brought over the following weeks.

The queen owned a lot of chairs, as Lorcan remembered from his visit to the palace, and he deduced Ember had to be a busy man if he worked for the queen on some regular basis.

Even before they'd begun work on the second consignment, Lorcan had learned his way around the workshop and tools that were new to him. He knew how to take Frederic, and he could handle the other journeymen's humor, as well as Geraldine's dislike of him.

What he found more difficult to cope with was Amelie, although she was the reason he'd declined one of the other journeymen's offers of a room at his house in favor of sleeping in Ember's barn. Sleeping in Ember's barn wasn't the most comfortable of choices, but it ensured Amelie was the first person he'd see in the morning, and the last one he'd talk to at night, and that was what made sticking it out in the cold worthwhile.

Having Amelie around him was both wonderful and terrifying. He felt as though he was constantly making a fool of himself around her, and she bore witness to his every embarrassment, it seemed.

She'd laid claim to his heart the night she'd led him to Ember's house, and he was sure she was the most perfect girl he'd met in his life. He desperately wanted to take her for walks, bring her gifts, and tell her how he felt, but he didn't think he'd manage to say his piece to her face. Even if he did, he'd only make an idiot of himself again, because her father was bound to have other plans for her, plans that would secure her future. Lorcan was sure he had nothing to offer her. She was out of his league, and he believed she deserved better than him.

Still, as he went about his daily chores and she went about hers – so close, and yet always a world away – he liked to imagine how it would be to hold her.

Time flew by while he was busy and in love.

Every night after the journeymen went home, and when the apprentices had run out of things to talk about and retreated to their benches in the kitchen, he'd go back to the workshop. There, he'd chip away at the pieces of a chess set like the one Ortus had kept in his tent at The Fair. Ortus hadn't taught him to play, but Lorcan remembered the pieces and the board in all detail. He loved creating on his own version of it, carving and filing to sort through his thoughts and keep his hands busy after the house had gone quiet.

No two pieces were alike, and the sixteen pawns he made each received the same attention as any of the nobility did. The little soldiers were two inches high, but that was all they had in common. He gave their faces distinctive features, and spent hours detailing their clothes. He'd never understood why they all looked the same on Ortus' board. Any man who died for his liege lord in this world had scars that were only his own, a voice, a history, and a right to a name that would be remembered, so he crafted them individually with the utmost of care.

Sometime between the mid-winter and January, Amelie started bringing him tea before she went to bed, and she'd light-heartedly chat with him about this and that, keeping the topics of conversation easy to follow and remark upon. He was completely uncomfortable with that, but he found himself rapt in every little thing she had to tell him all the same.

"Who are you making those for?" she finally inquired over his shoulder one night because the big picture of what he was doing evaded her.

He smiled.

He knew she was a secret master of dices and Kahala despite her father's opinions on her engaging in those kinds of games. She and Geraldine and the apprentices played in the kitchen for odds and ends until the wee hours of the morning on Thursday and Saturday nights when Ember was away, and Amelie was a lucky hand at both. Chess seemed like a game that had nothing to do with luck, but he was sure she'd be good at it, too.

"No one in particular, yet," he answered, briefly glancing at her sideways. "But, maybe the queen or the prince consort would take a fancy to one of these, and if they had one, all of their friends would want one, too. I'd be a rich man in no time."

She chortled a laugh, cocking her eyebrow at him. He pretended not to notice the incredulity in her glance. He felt like a fool again, and he pointedly kept his focus on what he was doing.

She took the dark king and one of the pawns from the worktop and weighed them in her hands, studying them closely.

"I doubt the queen would want to buy a game where the pawns look healthier and wealthier than their regents."

"Oh, do you now?"

He set down the rook he'd been polishing. Crossing his arms over his chest, he looked first at the pieces in her hands and then at her face.

"Maybe she should be glad for that – if it weren't for her pawns, the king would be pretty defenseless, wouldn't he?"

"I don't think so. Look at the queen by his side." She put the pawn down, picked up the four-inch figure of the dark queen and compared the king and the queen.

"She seems so sure of herself. So strong. I'll bet that a king with such a queen at his side would be undefeated for all the days of his life."

He reclaimed both figures from her hands and placed them on the work surface.

"What a shame we're not royals, then."

"It is," she confirmed softly. "Or we might be more at liberty in the choices we make."

He wasn't so sure of that, knowing what he did about freedom of choice. It wasn't so much the social standing as the nature of the society you were a part of.

Unexpectedly then, she stood on her toes and stole a lingering kiss from the corner of his mouth. Breathing in the scent of her hair, he instinctively pulled her close before she could step back from him, knocking a rook that sat near the edge of the workbench to the floor. It rolled underneath one of the shelves, but he didn't notice.

Lorcan wasn't savvy on kissing, but he decided it was now or never, and kissed Amelie anyway, deeply and thoroughly. She responded to him as though she'd hoped for this moment as much as he had, and she tasted of honey and cinnamon.

When he was almost breathless, she shocked him by tugging at his shirt, undressing him, but he didn't object because he didn't want her to stop caressing the bare skin of his chest with her lips. He didn't want her to *ever* stop stroking him, holding him, kissing him.

When she finally did, it was only to bolt the door that led to the house corridor so no one would walk in on them.

Lorcan was sure the family and all of Ironstone had to be asleep by now, but while she was away, he took the time to blow out the candles he'd set around the workbench, lest any wakeful soul passing on the street outside should happen to glance in the window. The subtle red glow from the dying embers in the hearth would be enough for the two of them.

He asked himself what on earth he was doing as he cleared aside the other chess pieces on the work surface and lifted Amelie to sit in front of him. Her eyes never left his as she wrapped her legs around his middle, and he found no answer beyond his desire to lose himself in her embrace. Exploring her mouth with his tongue, he immersed himself in her warmth, relishing her touch.

His hands wandered her body freely, trembling when they brushed her breasts, shaking when he pushed them up beneath her skirts to find she wasn't wearing anything underneath. He froze, almost terrified that he was going too fast and too far, but she held his gaze and guided his hands from her hips into her lap to explore the soft curls that covered her sex. She showed him exactly what she wanted him to do, and then she helped him undress her.

He kissed every inch of her body as it was revealed to him, working his way from her neck to her firm breasts and downward as slowly as he could. Her fingers tangled almost painfully in his hair when his mouth reached her most sensitive folds and he burrowed tenderly into the sweetness he found there. She gasped, and he stopped because he thought he'd hurt her. He worried when he looked up and saw the strained expression on her flushed face, but she just slid off of the bench and undid the tie fastening of his pants. She made certain to show him how hungry she was for him, and he nearly lost control.

Gently gathering her up in his arms, he lay her down on the bench, amid the figures he'd been carving and joined her there. The last cognizant thought that entered his mind before he buried himself in her was that he might never be able to work at this bench again.

It got chilly in the workshop during the night, despite the old blanket Lorcan fetched from one of the cabinets, and their work-surface bed was too hard, but Amelie didn't seem to mind. She clung to him as he did to her.

Lorcan couldn't remember ever having been this happy, and he wanted to tell her how much he was in love with her, but he couldn't. He didn't believe he'd get the reply he'd hope for if he said it out loud, but he told himself it didn't matter. Nothing did when they made love between one nap and the next. She was his tonight, and he was hers for as long as she would have him.

She had to feel *something* for him, too, or she wouldn't have come to him like she had.

Would she?

"Would you miss me if I went back to the South?" he asked her when it was almost time to face the new day.

"Of course I would, silly," she replied, and pressed one last kiss to his lips before she rose and searched for her dress on the floor. "But I hate being lonely."

He sat up and watched her by the pale shafts of light the waning sickle moon cast in through the windows, mesmerized. She was graceful as could be, and he realized she'd *never* be lonely. It didn't matter, he told himself again, because he'd make sure she wasn't.

"Come on," she told him then, taking him by the hands and pulling him to his feet. "We need to get out of here before the others wake up. God help us if anyone found out."

Chapter Five

∝ Originals ∾

Lorcan carried his chess set in his satchel as he walked toward the Lower Palace Road in the wet February sludge. He hoped to find a Dwarven-run business Amelie had told him about there.

The owner, Seoid Abhac, was a specialties merchant who did a lot of his trade with the queen's court. Lorcan thought Abhac might be interested in adding the set to his stock if he offered it to him for free. Chances were, it would get some attention that way and there might be orders for more.

Lorcan had carved his initials in one corner on the back of the board before he'd oiled it. The intertwining letters wouldn't mean a thing to anyone who didn't know what they stood for, but if he ever made a name for himself, they'd stand for his work like the mark of a tradesman. He was rather pleased with himself. He was no master craftsman, but he would be, someday. Carving chess sets wasn't what he'd dreamt of doing with his life a year ago, but he found that he enjoyed it, and it was one possible way of laying the foundations for a good, and perhaps even comfortable existence. If he could manage that, Ember would surely consider letting him marry Amelie, if she'd have him.

The merchant he was looking for dealt in novelties and glassware; things that were beautiful and expensive. Amelie knew all about *beautiful* and *expensive* and where to obtain either or both in Ironstone. Much to her father's vexation, her dreams were made of pearls and velvet, but Lorcan wanted her to believe in them and he wanted to be the one to lay them at her feet because she was *his* dream. Perhaps this chess set was the key to all of that.

Amelie had described Abhac's house to him. The building had to be near the beginning of the street. Searching for the small, oval stained glass window she'd told him to look out for in the front door in a street full of doors with little stained glass windows of all shapes and sizes, he thought he'd have found it quicker if she'd come with him. She could have told Geraldine she was going on some errand or other, but she'd refused.

She was right, of course. There was no point in taking risks. It wouldn't do for her to be seen alone with him in public. People would talk, and Ember would be furious.

At times, Lorcan wished there would be some manner of talk so their little game of hide and seek might find an end. Ember might not be entirely against the idea of them being together even as things were if Amelie said yes.

If.

Oh, the dreams he had.

A Cine in a human world.

A poor journeyman wanting to wed the guild master's daughter.

That was about as likely as Jaden Aurum's son helping Dean Greenleaf manage The Fair.

Lorcan pushed the thought right back out of his mind. He was fooling himself. Ember would never consider it.

Not *yet* anyway.

Looking around, he discovered he'd now passed the same building for the third time. He needed to concentrate, but it wasn't easy with Amelie on his mind the way she always was.

In his head, he went over the conversational strategy he'd planned out for Abhac again. It wasn't making sense anymore because he'd thought it over a few times too many the night before. Either the set caught the Dwarve's fancy or it didn't, simple as that. He needed to focus on finding the right house, or he'd never know. Dwarven were said to be shrewd businessmen and keen observers, so he was wearing his best clothes, and he'd taken a bath and shaven so as to make a good impression.

Unlike in most of the towns Lorcan had seen on his travels, the Dwarven jewelers, money lenders and specialty merchants of Ironstone didn't live separate from the other townsfolk, and they didn't keep to themselves. They'd built or acquired their shops and houses in every quarter and with neighbors from every walk of life, but Abhac had his shop in one of the wealthier parts of town.

Lorcan had seen that the Dwarven goldsmith, Orry Misneach had his workshop on Baker Street. The four feet tall fur merchant, Greim Easog, did business right across from the weavers, within a stone's throw of the poorhouse. A Dwarven scribe called Muinteoir lived next door to the candlemaker, and a portrait artist named Breacad worked opposite the sewing women. Abhac certainly had the best address of the Dwarven Lorcan knew of in town.

Ember had no liking for the Dwarven. He claimed they took away from his business, tricked people into bargains they didn't want, cheated little old ladies out of their money and benefited from the queen's favoritism, but he had nothing to say against the quality of their work and merchandise. Lorcan didn't quite understand why Ember would think the Dwarven took away from his business, but he thought he'd form his own opinions on the rest of it today.

If he ever found Abhac.

After he was sure he'd looked at every house in the street, Lorcan finally admitted defeat and stopped a boy in passing on his way from the market with half a bale of hay on his back.

"Can you tell me where to find Seoid Abhac's shop?" he asked, and the lad grinned.

"You're standing right in front of it," he returned, gesturing at the house to their right before he was on his way again.

It didn't have a stained glass oval in the door. That was why he hadn't considered it, but then he realized that someone had boarded up the hole from the inside where the window should have been, so he supposed the boy could be right.

Aside from the provisional fix of the window, the house as such was neat and well-kept. There was nothing pretentious about it. Four envyfaces on the horizontal bearing beam of the first floor outer wall were its only extravagance. The beam itself was likely to be one of the few straight ones keeping the tall, narrow building upright. Lorcan guessed this was one of the oldest houses in the street – perhaps in all of Ironstone.

He wondered what had happened to the glass in the window as he opened the door. A little bell tinkled, announcing him to the proprietor, though Abhac was nowhere to be seen.

The shop premises were cluttered from floor to ceiling. Lorcan saw no manner of order in the dark shelves that lined the walls in the front of the room. He wondered if the boy had been mistaken, but then he had a closer look around.

Fine tableware and cutlery made up the bulk of what used up space on and under the tables near the door. Silver spoons and horn-handled knives lay in wooden display boxes that nestled between stacks of plates and exotic vases of all shapes and sizes. The pictures painted on the vases told of faraway places where terraced landscapes flowed in crimson rivers, and flightless birds built their nests on the ground. Sheaf gold lined the rims and handles of delicate porcelain cups that balanced on the plates and vases. Lorcan realized just one of those almost negligently piled cups was probably worth a month's wages for him, and he tried to avoid touching anything.

Farther into the room, shallow cases overflowed with shiny glass trinkets that reflected the light; there were beads and finished bracelets, figures to decorate mantle shelves, and keepsakes to put on a window sill. Polished daggers with hilts of ivory hung on leather straps from the backs of chairs, useless in battle, but perhaps capable of lending a dramatic touch to an empty wall above some fireplace or other.

"Hello?" he called at the top of his voice when he still couldn't see the shop's owner. Amelie had told him Abhac was deaf as a doornail.

"Here," someone called from behind the curtain at the far end of the room.

Carefully, Lorcan edged past piles of journals and books on wobbly stools. Boxes and crates obstructed his path as he tried not to step on any of the cats that slunk around his legs. He had to wonder how this could possibly work out as he pushed back the cloth drapes and peered behind them.

The novelties merchant sat at a full-sized work table and didn't even glance up from what he was doing. An oil lamp provided light in the gloomy section of the disorderly chamber, but the table itself was surprisingly tidy – an island of tranquility in the stormy seas surrounding it.

The legs of the Dwarve's stool were long enough to accommodate the small man comfortably at his work place. He sat with his elbows resting on the wooden board as he repaired the fastening catch of a music box. The other stools around the table were meant for humans and not as tall, but they were mostly stacked with even more boxes of knickknacks.

Age had bent Seoid Abhac's back. His hair was still full, but white, and he needed a huge magnifying glass to see what he was doing. Amelie hadn't been joking when she'd told him the merchant was old.

"Master Abhac?" Lorcan called out again far too loudly.

This time, the bearded little man looked up at him, his eyes briefly lingering on Lorcan's face before he returned his gaze to the music box. "What can I do for you?" he inquired softly.

"Are you Master Abhac?" Lorcan insisted, just to be sure.

The Dwarve sighed. He set the broken toy aside and tented his fingers, focusing on his visitor amusedly. "Do you see anyone else around here?

Would I be asking you what I can do for you if I were not the owner of these premises?"

Lorcan had to chew on that for a moment but decided to accept it. He set his satchel down on the floor and untied the cords that held it together.

"I was told you're the merchant to see about novelties for the palace," he said. He didn't quite believe that anymore, but appearances could be deceptive, and he had nothing to lose.

The expression on the old man's face turned from amusement to annoyance. He straightened his back and gesticulated at the boxes and crates all around. "You know, I have people coming in here every day wanting me to buy their things and sell them to the queen's household."

Lorcan stopped unwrapping his chess set. He was uncertain if he was still welcome, but the old man didn't look like he was about to throw him out.

"I don't want to sell you anything," he said. "I don't want your money."

Abhac tilted his head to one side in a quizzical glance. "You don't?"

"No. I want to *give* you something." Lorcan turned his attention back to his satchel, all fingers and thumbs.

"I don't understand..."

Without further ado, Lorcan pulled forth the chess board. He set it down in front of the Dwarve. Then came the pouch with the pieces, and he carefully positioned them on the board, one by one and each in its right place. He might not know how to play them, but he remembered where to put them.

Abhac rose from his stool, his eyes narrowing as he picked the dark queen up to inspect her more closely. He also looked at several of the other figures. The Dwarve's mien was unreadable when he turned his gaze back to Lorcan, and Lorcan's heart sank.

"Well, this is fine work," Abhac stated at last, his stare piercing as though he was trying to decide what kind of person Lorcan was. "Your own?"

Lorcan nodded, feeling as though he was standing on a crumbly ledge. "Indeed it is."

"And you want to give this to me?"

"Yes."

"Just like that?"

"Yes. You could call it a sample. I can make more, if there is a demand, and I could carve the figures to the taste of any customer willing to pay a reasonable price that would accommodate both my needs and yours. Now, if the queen had one like this, other people might also want one. She has a lot of wealthy guests, but I could make simpler versions for a smaller budget as well."

Abhac scratched his chin. "Sounds like you have this all figured out."

Lorcan smiled.

The old Dwarve offered his hand to seal the deal. "Fine, that's settled, then," he said. "I'll see what I can do. There is a royal birthday coming up in a few weeks, so people will be looking for unusual gifts. Where can I find you?"

Lorcan couldn't imagine what Ember would say if Abhac turned up at his house. He picked up his satchel and shouldered it. "Oh, that's alright, I'll just come by again."

The Dwarve studied him, hummed, and then accompanied him to the door. Lorcan felt uncomfortable. He wondered if Abhac guessed why he wasn't inclined to tell him where he lived, but then his eyes caught on the boarded up window.

"What happened to your door?" he asked.

Abhac laughed. "Just a few boys playing a prank the other night. It happens."

Lorcan wasn't sure about that. A stained glass window was a costly thing to have broken, even if it wasn't big, and even if Abhac was sufficiently well situated to replace it.

He could see there was still something else on the Dwarve's mind, and he waited, giving the old man some space to voice his thoughts.

"It's odd, but I could swear I've seen a chess set very like yours before." That piercing gaze again. "I know it's not the same, but it's similar to one I sold to an old friend a long time ago."

Lorcan felt his smile fade for an instant, but then he told himself that Ortus Greenleaf wasn't the only man in the world who'd ever owned a chess set. That aside: this part of his life was over, buried beneath frozen earth, leaves, sticks, and rocks along with his father, along with Ortus, somewhere in the Northern Forest. He didn't need to share on it here and tried to shake the chill of the memory.

"Really?" he finally returned. "And here I was, thinking I'd created something original."

Chapter Six

ରେ Discoveries ୭୦

Lorcan shifted his weight uncomfortably as he waited with Ember's little troop for the gatekeepers on night watch to open up and let them back into the town.

His breath hung in ghostly wisps in the icy night air of mid-March, and his threadbare cloak didn't offer adequate protection from the biting cold. It seemed he hadn't had enough to drink at the alehouse. He was the only one shivering while the watchmen struggled with the mechanisms of the huge gate. They weren't in the habit of letting anyone in after sundown, but they made exceptions for paying travelers, and Ember didn't mind being a paying traveler.

Frederic, who was holding Ember up with some effort, handed Lorcan Ember's coin pouch, and Lorcan counted out the last two remaining coppers from it for the soldiers.

"Better get him home to bed, then," one of the guards remarked.

Frederic laughed. "I think it's past bedtime for the lot of us now," he said to the man, and reclaimed the coin pouch from Lorcan. "Come on, lad, give me a hand. The old goat's getting heavy."

"Watch yer tongue, boy," Ember mumbled, inelegantly patting the other man's cheek before he wrapped his free arm around Lorcan's neck and shoulder.

Although Lorcan was sure the guild master had a heap of expenses to cover from his income, Ember tended to squander his money very easily on drinking and gambling in various taverns and inns around Ironstone.

They'd spent the evening at the *Blue Heron*, the tavern farthest from town, but closest to Ember's heart. He went there two or three nights a week with Frederic and some of the other journeymen in tow. Lorcan couldn't help but admire the old man's stamina.

It was only recently that Ember had started encouraging him to come along at least on and off. Lorcan had been reluctant to do so. He generally didn't drink for fear that the ale would make him betray what he was. One thoughtless word or action would be enough.

Amelie couldn't know that, and she'd talked him into going as often as he possibly could because it was the smart thing to do, she'd said. She was right. He needed to fit in if he intended to stay in Ember's employ. He didn't want Ember to think he was too shy or too up himself to drink with his boss.

Ember claimed that the walk to the *Blue Heron* and back was good to clear the head, but getting home safely posed a challenge for everyone involved at some point in the night, depending on the quality of their outing and the quantities they'd consumed.

Lorcan guessed the real reason Ember had chosen the *Heron* for his preferred locality was that it was just far enough outside of town to get properly drunk without all of Ironstone witnessing it. Ember wanted to believe no one would catch on, but that was an illusion. People weren't that gullible, and they smiled at his face and talked behind his back. Fortunately, Ember's neighbors weren't the people he worked for.

The evenings Lorcan spent in the carpenters' company at the *Heron* were long and cold, as this one had proved to be. Those who weren't at the tavern just for the drink played games of dice or sought the company of one of the whores who rented rooms from the brewer. Lorcan was intent on saving his money. He clung to his pint for hours until it had gone stale, and he didn't need a whore.

Picturing how Amelie would be waiting for him in the workshop or in the stable, he had no desire to be with other women. Fitting in was one thing, but there were limits to what he was inclined to do. Ember kept asking him if he wasn't paying him enough, but Lorcan observed that Ember himself never left the bar room with either of the two women who offered their services there. The old man was a drinker, but he had his morals.

Morals or no, Ember was a mystery to Lorcan. The guild master drank so heavily at the *Heron*, it was a wonder he could get up in the mornings, but he always did. He'd come into the kitchen for his breakfast looking as though he'd had a whole night of restful sleep even if he'd been completely wasted only hours earlier.

More dragging Ember than helping him walk through the lower east side of town, Lorcan thought he was going to crumple under the singing, jabbering man's weight and drop him before they got anywhere close to home. The smell of the tanner's work pits hit them like a punch in the gut as they staggered passed them, and the other two journeymen took their leave of Ember before vomiting in the sewage.

Amelie had told him that her father hadn't been like this before her mother had died. He'd been a model of diligence and virtue in her eyes, but Lorcan knew children often saw what they needed to see when they looked at their parents. He'd wanted to see only the good in Jaden, and, as a boy, he'd loved Jaden deeply no matter what he'd done *to* him or failed to do *for* him.

Lorcan gathered Amelie and Geraldine's mother had been the love of Ember's life. A brief, but severe illness had claimed her during her last pregnancy, and he'd started trying to numb himself so he'd forget his wife and unborn child. His work and the drink were the only things that could take his mind off the loss, and so he drank when he wasn't working, and worked when he wasn't drinking. Amelie had confessed she was grateful he still had the sense to do one thing after the other, though, or the family would have been lost.

Stumbling through Butcher Street, Lorcan breathed a sigh of relief when they finally rounded the corner to the house.

All at once, Frederic loosed a roaring tirade of his finest swearwords, and Lorcan saw that he'd stepped in the sewage, breaking through the thin coat of ice over the urine and feces. He wasn't done cursing before they reached the door, and Lorcan had to bite his tongue to keep from laughing. That was the second time in one week.

Between Ember's off-key warbling and Frederic's cursing, the two men had managed to wake the entire quarter. Window shutters clattered, and sleepy neighbors yelled at them to stop making a spectacle of themselves. Keeping the guild master on his feet as he yelled back at them was a hilarious challenge, but they made it inside without any further embarrassments.

Frederic kicked off his stinking shoes in the workshop. "I'm done in," he told Lorcan, and left Ember in his care.

After Lorcan had maneuvered Ember up the narrow staircase and onto his sagging bed with some difficulty, he dragged the old man's boots off. It was freezing in the room despite the open vent from the kitchen below, so he covered him up with a blanket from the foot of the bed and made sure he had his bucket within reach.

"You're a good boy, you know that?" Ember slurred, half snoring already just as Lorcan was closing the door behind him.

Lorcan didn't answer, but smiled, feeling slightly guilty at the thought of where he was planning on going from there.

He could hear Geraldine scolding Frederic, and an argument ensued across the narrow landing. He knew they'd be busy for a while when he softly opened the door to Amelie's room.

She was waiting for him, lying naked beneath her blanket, and welcomed him into her bed wordlessly.

The evenings with Ember were long, but life was great.

"Would you ever think of becoming my wife?" he whispered into her hair as he held her after they'd made love.

She looked up at him, somewhere between bewildered and mildly amused, and that made him wish he'd held his tongue. "Lorcan..."

"You don't have to answer right now. You could think about it."

She raised her hand to his cheek and pressed a warm, lingering kiss to his mouth. He had hope, but then she crushed it. "No."

"No...?"

He thought he'd misunderstood, but the expression on her face told him he hadn't.

"Why not?"

He'd been too rash. He'd messed it up. He shouldn't have pushed his luck so soon. "You know I could provide for the both of us, somehow," he stammered and realized she was getting impatient with him.

"I'm not going to marry a *boy* who wants to carve chess figures for a living," she returned as though the mere thought would be ridiculous.

She sat up, and he did likewise, startled by the bluntness of her statement, but she wouldn't look at him.

"I'm not going to marry a boy who can't offer me at least what I'm used to. Don't get me wrong, I do enjoy being with you. You're smart and you're witty, but don't think I'll ever fall in love with you. I'm going to marry a rich man."

Lorcan concentrated on breathing, trying to decide if she wasn't just testing him or making fun of him. "Are you, now?"

She didn't reply right away, and her skin felt cold to the touch all of a sudden. He put as much physical distance between them as her narrow bed would allow.

She'd made up her mind to reject him, and he couldn't think of anything to say. Whatever words came to mind would sound angry or mean if he said them out loud, and he didn't want that, but he couldn't look at her anymore either, so he turned rigidly to sit on the wooden edge of the bed. The board cut into his thighs.

"What, exactly, am I to you?" he finally asked her. He couldn't keep the bitterness out of his voice, though hearing himself was like listening to someone else.

Kneeling behind him, she wrapped her arms around him and tenderly kissed his shoulder. "Lorcan, don't do this..."

At that moment, Geraldine walked in, a candle in her hand. She was a mess in need of her sister's comfort, but seeing Lorcan there halted her in her tracks.

He thought she was going to start screaming at him. When she didn't and just kept staring, he had no idea whether he should be grateful or afraid.

"Please..." Amelie mouthed behind him as he pulled his shirt over his lap and began looking for his pants to avoid her gaze.

Geraldine shifted her stare from Lorcan to Amelie, and what seemed like an eternity passed in silence. He couldn't for the life of him tell what she was thinking.

All sorts of things went through his head. He wished she'd say something, even if he didn't want to hear it, or at least shut the door in case anyone else decided to wander around.

It was only when the baby started crying and Frederic began swearing and calling for her that she snapped out of it. Wordlessly, she retreated back the way she'd come, and as soon as she was out of sight, Lorcan tugged on his clothes while Amelie slipped into her nightgown. Carrying his shoes and cloak, he peeked out the door, and when he found the corridor devoid of angry kinsmen out for his blood, he cast one last glance at Amelie.

"Can we talk about this tomorrow?" he whispered.

She huffed, pulling on her slippers before she followed him out of the room and into the corridor. "There's nothing to talk about. It's Geraldine I need to speak to."

He didn't want to argue and left her. Tiptoeing down the stairs, he heard Ember snoring, the baby crying, a door opening, and he could feel his heart hammering in his head as he stepped through the door into the kitchen where one of the apprentices had awoken and looked up at him.

"Rough night?" the boy grinned.

"Shut the hell up," he returned and went out to his booth in the barn. He thought it might be wise to start packing.

Chapter Seven

ೞ Secrets ೮

Lorcan woke with a start. He'd drifted off sometime before dawn. The sun was already up, and there was movement about the barn as one of the apprentices milked the cow while the other rummaged around for eggs. Neither of them were concerned with him, so he assumed he still had a job.

Normally, milk and eggs were Amelie's chores. Rising to face the new morning and whatever it might bring, he was glad she'd dispatched someone else today.

He wasn't hungry or feeling particularly sociable, but he slunk into the kitchen after the boys when they were done with the mucking. Quietly, he sat down at the table and waited. He didn't know what exactly he was waiting for since no one paid him any heed, but he was sure he had something coming after last night.

Agitatedly, Geraldine slapped a bowl of burned porridge down in front of him, sloshing a part of the content. It looked as though she'd scraped it from the bottom of yesterday's crock, and she probably had. She said nothing.

The lanky boy next to Lorcan snorted a laugh and nudged him with his elbow. "Got in her bad books, have you?"

Without looking at the lad, Lorcan casually traded the bowl he'd been eating from for his own. The porridge in that one didn't look much different to the slops Geraldine had given him, but the boy got the message. He knew better than to protest and began stirring the tepid goo.

No one was having cinnamon today because Amelie wasn't there.

Lorcan didn't dare ask after her. She was either avoiding him or Geraldine – or the both of them – and perhaps she was right to.

Lying awake that night, he'd decided she couldn't have *meant* what she'd said, but the words kept bouncing around inside his head even now as he forced down a spoonful of his food without chewing.

He was sure Geraldine hadn't told anyone what she'd seen, or he'd have had Frederic or Ember to answer to long before now. Either one could have beaten him to death in his sleep. Perhaps Geraldine was saving the news for a better moment. He supposed he'd have to expect that *better moment* from here on in, but he doubted she'd choose breakfast for it with all of the household present.

Ember was his usual cheery self when he came in, clean-shaven and dressed for his work day. Settling down at the head of the table, he looked about, sniffing the charred gruel, and his mien darkened.

"Where's Amelie?"

Geraldine set a bowl in front of him, more gently than she had the others. "She's not feeling well."

Again, the boy next to Lorcan began guffawing. "Got herself the runs or something. Woke me and Jamie at the crack of dawn, barfing all over the floor, she was."

Whacking him on the back of his head with the flat of her hand, Geraldine took away his bowl and his cup, leaving him with the spoon still in his hand and wondering how he was going to get through the day. Lorcan was wondering the same thing, but, despite himself, he worried. Amelie never got sick.

"Great." Ember grumbled, bravely swallowing his first mouthful. Pulling a face, he pushed the bowl away. "I hope we don't all get what she's got now. Busy times ahead."

Frederic was last to trudge into the kitchen. He plunked down on the chair beside Ember, not looking quite as smart as his boss just yet, and he stared at what Geraldine set in front of him, eyebrows arching.

"With my wife doing the cooking, I guess we won't be eating much today anyway," he remarked, and ignored the dirty look she gave him.

Lorcan barely followed the rest of the conversation, and he didn't catch the day's planning that included taking measurements in one of the merchants' houses on the Upper Palace Road. Observing Geraldine as she went about her kitchen duties, he distinctly caught that she wasn't just mad at him, or upset. She was really troubled.

Understandably, she'd be concerned about her sister's virtue, and she probably blamed him for corrupting it. Geraldine couldn't know he was in love with Amelie, or that he'd asked her to be his wife. Perhaps she assumed he'd been forcing himself on her, though recalling her reaction the night before, it was rather unlikely she'd really believe that. She'd been shocked, yes, but she hadn't misinterpreted the situation, and she hadn't called for help or woken anyone, or even told Frederic, obviously. She loved Amelie too much to put her in such a position.

Considering how little Geraldine had thought of him before finding out he was her sister's lover, he hoped she wasn't intent on making his life a nightmare even if she didn't betray them. She'd find a million ways to give him hell, he was sure, but if that was all, then he guessed he'd have to count himself lucky.

Lost in thought, he scraped his leftovers into the pig bucket and cleared away his bowl.

When Ember had finished the eggs Geraldine had cooked for him, he ordered Lorcan and the two apprentices to pack a few things and come with him. Lorcan had no idea where they were going, but he didn't really care. Trailing some distance behind Ember as they headed across town, he tried to wrap his head around the last twelve hours' events and nearly bumped into half a dozen people.

Not knowing where he was at with Amelie was almost worse than having to expect he'd lose his job. Everything was wrong, and he didn't know how to right it.

Ember whistled as he went, nodding to everyone they passed on their way uphill and wishing them a good day. Lorcan found the old man's zest irritating.

Finally, the guild master sent the apprentices ahead and waited for Lorcan. "You're awfully quiet today," he said. "You're not getting ill, too?"

Lorcan shook his head and forced a smile. "No, sir. I don't think so."

Ember didn't seem convinced. "Let me know before you throw up on anything expensive in that house, will you?" He motioned at the estate behind the whitewashed walls up ahead. The apprentices had made halt at the impressive iron gates dissecting the walls, looking rather puny in front of them.

Lorcan had passed by this house several times while running errands for Ember, and he'd caught a glimpse of the courtyard. It somewhat resembled a peristylum, at least on one side. Winter-hard shrubs grew in the flower beds that lined the square, and there was a fish pond right in the middle of the paved yard. Hard, angular lines dominated the structure of the main building that seemed like a merciless, rigid weight on the hillside. Its sheer size was impressive, but Lorcan found it horrifying to look at. This wasn't a home. It was a cold chunk of rock. He wondered who would live here.

His lips felt far too tight as he forced another smile. The two other journeymen arrived. Ember had a key to the gate and led them all inside. A maid welcomed them at the door.

Entering the Romanesque building, Lorcan discovered it was colder inside than out, despite the blaze in the huge fireplace on one end of the main room, as though no one had lived here for years. Perhaps no one had, though everything seemed well enough tended.

"Can you all imagine my little Amelie as the lady of the house here, boys?" Ember declared chirpily as he put down the toolbox he'd been carrying.

The older of the journeymen, Harald, thumped the guild master on the back, and there was a hearty murmur of general consent.

Lorcan didn't understand. He thought he hadn't heard right.

"She's going to be very happy," Harald said. "Especially since she isn't disinclined toward the arrangement."

"That's right. She's a good girl, my Amelie, and she deserves to be happy, so let's get to work on those measurements for the new cabinets here and the wardrobes and dressers on the first floor so she'll get all that dowry of hers moved over here in time for the wedding. It's costing me a fortune!"

Lorcan's mouth fell open. He felt like he'd been doused.

"What?" he asked, incredulously looking around. "Have I missed something?"

Ember bellowed a laugh. "Didn't she tell you? Amelie's betrothed is back from his travels to the South, and they're going to be married next week. This is where she'll live with her husband, the cloth merchant Brandner. We'll be building some new cabinets for the happy couple."

Lorcan felt beyond stupid all at once because he was the only one who had no idea what was going on. "Betrothed?"

Ember's face froze. "Yes. Brandner. Didn't I mention this morning over breakfast how busy we'd be this week?"

Lorcan's chest clenched. When had Amelie been meaning to tell him this? Their conversation from the night before suddenly gained another dimension, but he doubted she would have told him then even if Geraldine hadn't walked in on them. Had she *meant* for him to find out like this? Just for the sport of it?

He felt Ember's eyes on him. "Oh! Yes, of course," he said, "I didn't think... I mean, I'm impressed. This is a big house."

Ember's mien relaxed into an amused grin. "Well, there's twelve rooms here for her to fill with my grandchildren." He turned to the other men. "I think she should manage that, eh?"

Everyone was in hearty agreement with him.

"I'll make sure she does," a boisterous, melodic voice unexpectedly boomed from behind them.

Descending the spiral staircase at the back of the hall, the man it belonged to was a sight to behold. He wasn't much above Lorcan's height, of slender build, and a good fifteen years older with sharp features and receding dark hair. He was a handsome man, and one who liked to get attention; a ring adorned his every other finger, gems glittered on his earlobes, and the way he dressed and his choice of colors reminded Lorcan of a peacock in mating season.

He felt the bile rising in his throat when he smelled the flowery scent of the man as he passed him by to greet Ember.

"I hoped you'd be early," Brandner said. "I've got business at the palace now, but I wanted to ask your permission to visit Amelie this afternoon and take her for a walk, if she'd like that."

"Of course, of course." Ember beamed. "She'll be thrilled when I tell her."

Brandner flashed him a smile and took a small wooden box from a pouch he carried on his belt. "I'm sure she will. I brought this back from Wenetoi for her and thought today might be a good day to give it to her." He opened the box and took a diamond ring out.

Lorcan had never seen anything of the like, and he observed the old man's face light up.

"They have excellent goldsmiths in Wenetoi, and I thought she'd like this, since I never got round to making her an engagement present before I left in autumn. I didn't want to give her my deceased wife's ring. It didn't seem right. I hope it fits."

Inspecting the ring Brandner handed him, Ember nodded. "And if it doesn't, we have a goldsmith who can rework it here."

Brandner took the ring back and sighed. "Yes, but he's Dwarven. I don't have dealings with the Dwarven."

Lorcan hated Brandner more by the minute.

The merchant tucked the box back into his pouch. "In the South, regents are so much more supportive of the guilds than they are hereabouts, especially the smiths and the merchants. Did you know they have laws there prohibiting the Dwarven from carrying on their trades in favor of putting humans first? That's how it should be, not the other way around."

"You're right," Ember replied. "But, trust me, people are waking up here, too, and things are soon going to change in Ironstone."

Brandner patted him on the shoulder. "I *know* they will."

Lorcan bit down hard on his lip, his glance wandering from the cloth merchant to Ember and back.

He had a feeling Abhac and his people were in for more than just broken windows in the years to come.

Brandner turned his attention to the laborers he'd been ignoring. "Thank you all for coming, everybody. I'm certain you're all going to do a fine job here for Amelie and me. Please let my servants know if you need anything."

Then, he shook Ember's hand. "I'll be off now. I have a busy week ahead myself."

Ember grinned. "Well, who could have known my fussy little Amelie would want to set the date so soon after your return?"

Brandner threw his head back and laughed. "Perhaps absence really does make the heart grow fonder," he said. "I must say I was surprised, too, but if that's how she wants it, that's how we'll do it. Anything Amelie wants is fine by me. Three years after the passing of my Elizabeth and our child, I'm ready to move on and fill this house with life – lots of it!"

Lorcan's stomach churned. Amelie couldn't wait to marry this braggart. Whatever was she thinking? But then he knew it: the house, the ring, the clothes… All her dreams of pearls and velvet, and he was the right man to provide them.

A part of him wondered if Amelie could ever really come to love Brandner, or if that wasn't so important with everything else she'd be getting. He was obviously intent on pleasing her.

Doing the math, it dawned on Lorcan that Amelie must have known the merchant before she and he had met in front of the candlemaker's shop. Perhaps Brandner had already spoken to Ember then and asked for her hand – before she'd lain with *him*. *Why* had she made *him* fall in love with her, if she'd already consented to marry her dream?

Lorcan didn't notice Ember's stare after Brandner left.

"What's wrong with you? You look terrible," the guild master remarked. "Are you going to make me send for the cart, or can you get home by yourself?"

"I can get home," Lorcan returned weakly. Ember eyed him for a moment before gesticulating at the door by way of a dismissal.

Lorcan gladly left the icy building.

He had to speak to Amelie, but he had no idea what he was going to say to her. Even taking a long detour through the stink of Butcher Street and past the Hay Market didn't bring him any closer to what he was going to tell her, but by the time he'd reached the house, he was so miserable, he was ready to beg. He'd never begged for anything in all his life, but he was sure he could now, if it came to that. She could still come away with him, and he'd find a means to make her happy and give her whatever she thought a good life would require – at least a part of it.

He found her in the kitchen with Geraldine's daughter, sweet loaves baking in the nooks of the hearth. He could tell by the aroma that she'd added cinnamon.

The smile she was wearing for the child she was entertaining at the table with finger-pictures in the flour faded when she saw him.

"How are you feeling?" he asked, closing the door quietly behind him.

"Better." She got up, set the tot on the floor and went to check on the bread. "Why are you home?"

He sat down. "We need to talk."

She released an impatient sigh. "Look, I've got work to do, and Geraldine and Gracie will be home from the market any minute."

"Well, they're not here yet, and I think you owe me that." He brushed some of the flour away from the table's edge.

"*Owe you that?*"

She was laughing at him, the tone of her voice hurtful and not at all as it should have been, not like he was used to hearing from her.

He tried to guard his expression, guard his voice, and guard his heart. "I think so."

Having found the bread not quite done yet, she seated herself next to him. Samantha reached up to her, wanting up on her lap again.

Lorcan stroked the child's face, leaving some flour on the nose, and Samantha reached up her little hand to rub it off, chortling.

"I met your future husband this morning," he said.

Amelie didn't reply. Instead, she said, "You know, Geraldine could have told Father about us last night, but she didn't."

"She knew. I didn't. Can you blame her?"

"Would it have changed anything between us?"

Lorcan closed his eyes for a moment, unsure. He'd have fallen in love with Amelie all the same, although he wanted to believe he wouldn't have let things go as far as they had.

"Yes, it would," he said. "I wouldn't have made a fool of myself."

Amelie half smiled. The child began to fuss, and Amelie irritably shifted her over to Lorcan.

"You didn't make a fool of yourself. If that's how you feel, then that's what I've made of you, and I'm sorry, but I don't have any regrets."

She might not, but he did. He hadn't wanted this, but he knew he only had himself to blame.

"You're really going to marry that man, aren't you?" It was more a statement than a question.

"Why wouldn't I?" She tried to take his hand, but he withdrew from her. He didn't want her touching him right now.

"Look," she continued, "he's attractive, he's rich, and I'd be the true fool here if I didn't."

He couldn't believe how that bothered him. "Amelie, you don't need that house or Brandner's gold. I would have taken care of you."

"Let's not go there again. You have no idea what's at stake here."

Unexpectedly, anger broke through where hurt and defeat had nestled only seconds before. Lorcan put Samantha down and rose, raking his hair. He tried to calm down, but he couldn't.

"Then tell me how living in a mausoleum is going to make you happy," he snapped. "Tell me how gold and silver will buy you love while Brandner is traveling the world. Tell me how a man who smells of lilacs and wears jewelry in his ears is going to stand by you when the going gets tough."

Again, Amelie didn't answer him.

Samantha, ignorant of their discussions, found a wooden spoon on the floor beneath the table and presented it to her proudly, laughing into the silence as though she'd defeated a bear. Involuntarily, both Amelie and Lorcan had to smile.

"You should have known Geraldine a year ago," Amelie said after a while. "Frederic made her really happy. They never argued. Then his vision became blurry, and he went to see the barber surgeon down by the smiths. Turns out he has cataracts."

Lorcan wouldn't have guessed, but some things became clearer to him. "I didn't know."

"No one does. Not even Father," she said insistently. "And that's how it's going to stay."

Lorcan thought Ember would hardly throw his son-in-law out.

"But how is Frederic going to manage?"

"He's not. The barber surgeon says he'll have another three or four years at most before he'll go blind."

He'd guessed as much. "I'm sorry to hear that."

"Yes. I was, too. You know, my father has drinking and gambling debts in every inn around Ironstone, and he owes every lumberjack between here and Leignsbridge for a year's worth of timber. Do you understand what will happen when my father gets too sick or too old to work?"

Lorcan needed a moment to digest that, but now it all made sense. Ember was going to leave shambles to a blind man.

"But, what if someone else was to manage the workshop? What if one of the other journeymen bought in, or…"

"No." She stood up. There was so much conviction in her voice, Lorcan knew her answer was final. She'd thought this through. "Frederic doesn't want that. He's just as proud a man as my father. He thinks he can still handle everything even if he is blind, but we both know that's not going to work, and Geraldine does, too."

"So he'd rather ruin the business than sell it."

She walked to him and stood beside him, folding her arms. "The business is already ruined. There's nothing to sell because when he closes shop, everyone will want a piece of what's left. Lorcan, I'm not only marrying Brandner to save my father's inheritance. This is for me, first and foremost because I meant what I said: I want the good life. But, it's also for Geraldine and Samantha, because it's the only way I'll be able to really help them when all is said and done."

"I still think there's bound to be another way to deal with this."

She smiled at him coolly. "Maybe, but right now you have to understand that I think this is what's best for me and my family."

He was about to argue, but she raised a finger to his lips. "I don't love you, Lorcan. Get that into your head. We had a lot of fun, but this has to stay between the two of us for so many reasons."

Geraldine entered the kitchen just in time to hear the last thing Amelie said. She paled, and Lorcan didn't get a chance to reply. His insides were churning, and she was the last person he wanted to see or share grief with.

"You didn't tell him, did you?" Geraldine asked, shooing Gracie back out the door before setting her basket down.

Amelie looked at the floor, taking a deep breath.

"You silly goose, you're about to get married to another man and you tell *him* you're pregnant with *his* child?" Geraldine went on agitatedly. "You have no idea what you've done, do you?"

Lorcan had to process what he'd just learned.

Facing Amelie, her sister's baby cawing at his feet, his heart skipped a beat. It was too much. "You're pregnant?"

Amelie shot a spiteful look at Geraldine, shaking her head. Then, she told him, "This is *not* going to change anything."

But it did. She had no idea how much this could change things.

Geraldine crossed the floor to pick her daughter up. "If you're smart, you'll go back to wherever it is you came from."

"Stay out of this," he told her from between clenched teeth and went after Amelie, who was on her way out to the stable.

He found her in his booth. "How long have you known?"

"Not long. A few weeks."

"And you're *still* going to marry Brandner?"

"*Of course* I am, Lorcan! And don't you dare stand in the way of this, do you hear me? It's *my* decision, and unless you want the both of us flogged and run out of town, you're going to go along with it."

He stood staring at her wordlessly until she'd had enough of him, and he didn't follow her when she went back in the house.

He had to think.

Chapter Eight

☙ The Peacock ❧

The sour smell of stale ale and last night's sweat invaded Lorcan's senses as he entered the gloomy tavern. There was only one other man in the room besides the brewer, and he snored, fast asleep in the corner.

The brewer was a stout, balding man in his forties and looked like he was as much a part of the place as the stool he sat on or the fellow in the corner. He was still busy drying mugs off from the night before. Whether he'd washed them or not was questionable, but Lorcan didn't care.

Curtly nodding at him, he chose a seat near the open window with no intention of leaving it again until the brewer was ready to throw him out that night. He'd chosen this particular tavern because he hadn't been here before with any of the other furniture makers. He was nearly sure he wouldn't encounter any familiar faces here. There wasn't a soul on this earth he wanted to talk to right now.

"We're not open yet, and we've no food, laddie," the brewer told him.

Lorcan hated being called *laddie*. It was a label, not a name, but his father hadn't seemed capable of finding any other way to address him.

"I didn't come here for food," he replied, barely glancing up. "And I can pay for drink if you'll serve me all the same."

He tossed some coins on the table, evoking a hum from the man that could have implied either pleasure or irritation.

The brewer sauntered over and picked the coppers up, studying them to see whose image was depicted on them. Satisfied that they all bore his queen's likeness, he closed his meaty fist around them and smiled.

"I guess I can make an exception today if you're really so thirsty, laddie."

Lorcan tried not to let his annoyance show. Perhaps he just didn't look his age, or the brewer *labeled* everyone who came into his tavern.

For Jaden, calling Lorcan by his name had posed a problem in some way. Lorcan supposed it might have evoked recollections of his mother and a past that hadn't suited him, but he'd never know. Every single member of his family was dead, and there was no one left to ask how accrediting a boy the simple right to a proper name could have been so difficult. Maybe it was easier to ignore and mistreat an unwanted offspring that way.

He asked himself if this was what Brandner would do with Amelie's baby if he found out it wasn't his own.

Some form of Talent was bound to emerge in the child sooner or later, and when it did, it would be in grave danger. Lorcan couldn't imagine Brandner would be inclined to raise a Cine in his house when he refused to even *"have dealings with the Dwarven"*.

The brewer returned and set down a large mug of murky ale in front of Lorcan. He drained it in a few drags without much noticing its watery quality.

Trying to drown out his restless heart's constant murmurings with cheap ale might not have been clever, but if it worked for Ember, it might work for him too, just this once. Things kept going from bad to worse for some reason, and he'd need to do a lot of forgetting before he was ready to move on from this.

For one crazy moment, he imagined going home and telling Amelie what he really was, and what the child growing inside of her was going to be, but he quickly realized this could be the worst possible choice he'd ever make. Something told him she wouldn't want the baby if she knew it wasn't human. She'd want to get rid of it – but he wanted his son or daughter to live.

Also, there wasn't a doubt in his mind she'd tell someone. Geraldine, at the very least. The thought made his mind spin. There was no way Geraldine would keep this to herself. She'd take pleasure in having him hauled off, and he'd be tried and executed for sure.

He motioned for a refill. The brewer complied, and he kept refilling every time Lorcan bade him to.

By early evening, when the locals gradually started filing in, the adulterated ale had made his head heavy and his stomach queasy. The floor seemed to move beneath his feet like the planks of a barge on a river rapid, and people and voices were becoming too much to bear, but the tepid pints hadn't numbed the toppling thoughts cluttering up his mind. They'd added to them.

He'd spent all his money faster than expected, and when he left the tavern, he found that he was more troubled than when he'd come here, and certainly no closer to any concept of where his life was heading. Aimlessly, he staggered off into the growing shadows.

For the first time since he'd left The Fair, he realized he had nowhere to go.

He couldn't return to Ember's house. If he did, he'd say a lot of things he might regret, and he didn't want to part on bad terms with the guild master. Ember had been good to him, and in return, all he'd done was betray his trust. He thought he'd fetch his belongings some time during the next day when everyone was out and simply leave. Wasn't that what journeymen did? Come and go?

But then again, why should he go? Because it was better that way? Better for whom?

He was just starting to build a life for himself, and he'd somehow gotten it into his head he could make Ironstone his home. Ironstone stood for so many things. It stood for the best weeks of his life with Ortus and Dean, it stood for the Snow Globe, and it had stood for new beginnings. He may not have been able to actually sell his idea with the chess board, but he'd been making money from his employment with Ember, and he'd soon have been able to afford a lot of things for himself, including the family Amelie didn't want with a *boy* who carved wooden figures. The *boy* who'd been good enough to *bed*, but wouldn't do to *wed*.

Amelie was pregnant with *his* child, and *his* child would never know him if he didn't claim his right to it. To his mind, that wasn't better for *him*, and it wasn't how he wanted it to be.

Deep down, he knew that pompous Peacock would have more to offer this baby than he ever could, but Amelie had made her decision without him, and that wasn't better for *anyone*. Not even for the Peacock, who would be raising a bastard without knowing it. Lady Amelie was determined to have her way. Amelie *always* got her way.

Brandner mightn't know she was lying to him, but she knew it… and Lorcan did… and Geraldine did.

That made three people who'd have to keep a secret if Amelie's little plan for the good life she wanted for herself was going to work out. While he was sure Amelie would guard herself well, he didn't know about Geraldine.

Stumbling along Butcher Street, he wondered whether the Peacock would be any good at math – but he'd have to be, since he was *such* a clever businessman and all, traveling to Wenetoi and God knew where else in between building an ugly mansion and losing a wife. According to Ember, he had pots of money, and the merchant looked every inch the part, but would he be clever enough to count back forty weeks in the calendar when Amelie's bastard was born? Or would he suspect anything before then?

What would the Peacock say when he lay with Amelie on their wedding night and discovered she was by no means the chaste, unblemished girl he'd probably hoped to wed? That she wasn't the innocent maiden he'd be longing to take to the altar and aching to take to his bed?

She hadn't even pretended to be anything of the sort for Lorcan. But, then again, Lorcan wasn't rich and she'd had no plans to marry him and move into his imaginary palace in the sky. He was nothing but a poor carpenter of questionable pedigree with no past and no future in her eyes. He'd been the dumb *laddie* to pass the time and bring some excitement to her nights when it suited her.

Of course, he'd greedily taken all of her that she'd given him, giving back all of himself to her just as readily in return. He'd given her his heart, and he'd given her the child she was carrying, and she'd given him the benefit of her experience like no maiden ever could have. It hadn't mattered to him whom she'd shared herself with before they'd met because he loved her.

Nothing else had been important.

It might matter to Brandner, however, and she'd have to give him the acting performance of her life if she wanted him to believe in the story she was selling him.

Unless, of course, Brandner had been the man who'd taught her the things she'd shown Lorcan, the things he'd been so eager to learn.

As he made his way uptown, it occurred to him that this was how it could have been, and Brandner wouldn't be in the least bit surprised by *any* performance Amelie would give him.

Imagining her touching Brandner the way she'd touched him, held him, guided him inside of her made his insides scream. The thought of her whispering to Brandner even half of the things she'd said into his ear just before she'd come apart for him, shattering him when she did, made his stomach turn over.

He retched up the last two measures of his drink into the gutter. Wiping the vomit off of his chin, he was aware that he had no real control of himself, but it didn't bother him. Not tonight, while Brandner was undoubtedly drinking to his upcoming wedding, and

Amelie and Geraldine would be excitedly working on patterns for the dresses they'd be wearing.

He hadn't been aware of the direction he'd taken when he'd left the alehouse, not consciously, but the Upper Palace Road must have had a pull on him, because that was where he found himself when he next looked around properly.

Firmly locked gates barred the way to the walled garden of the Peacock's estate. Wrapping the fingers of his left hand around the ornate bars beside the lock as he placed his right hand on the closing mechanism, he saw inside of the lock. It was a marvelous piece, marvelous as anything that belonged to the Peacock, and he pictured how the tumblers inside would slide into place if the right key was applied.

The gate fell open.

It must have been open before, he told himself, swaying.

The smartest thing would have been to walk away, but he couldn't stop himself from putting one foot in front of the other nonetheless as he entered the garden.

Dreary lights illuminated the courtyard and the fish basin in its center. All that burbling water made him realize how urgently he needed to relieve his bladder. The basin seemed appropriate.

He didn't notice the servant emerging from one of the side entrances until he was right behind him. When the man incredulously inquired for the second time what he was doing, he pulled his pants back up and took his time before replying.

"Taking a walk."

"Through a locked gate?"

Another servant appeared in the front door, this time with Brandner in his wake. Several other men trotted along behind him. Lorcan couldn't place any of them. He supposed they'd be the buddies Brandner would be drinking with tonight, celebrating his return to Ironstone and toasting to his new bride.

He wondered if the merchant would recognized him. "It was open."

The servant paled and turned to his master, flustered. "I locked it myself."

They'd only met once, and Lorcan didn't think Brandner made a habit of looking too closely at anyone who was as far beneath him as he. The disdainful expression Brandner wore on his face told him he wasn't used to conversing with the rabble. Not unless that rabble invaded his privacy and urinated in his garden.

The merchant casually patted the servant on the shoulder by way of a dismissal. "It's alright. I'll take care of this."

Then, he hooked an arm over Lorcan's shoulder. "Do I know you?"

Lorcan hesitated, wary that he was now trapped between Brandner and one of his friends.

"No... I don't think so. But..."

Before he could continue, Brandner punched him in the stomach. The unexpected, painful force of the blow would have made him double over, had Brandner not caught him and dragged him upright with the aid of his friend, iron grip closing around his arms as the merchant and his buddy laughed at him.

"Well, I'm William Brandner," he said, rubbing his knuckles and twisting his rings. "So *not* pleased to make your acquaintance, boy."

The merchant forced him to look up at him, flashing his perfect white teeth. For a moment Lorcan could have sworn they were sharp and pointy, like those of a pike.

Glancing around, he realized they were all having such a good time with him, he'd be lucky if he survived this night. Panic took hold of him, and he struggled, straining against his captors to no avail. His mind was quite sober now, and it told him his own stupidity had gotten him into this.

"Alright, men," the merchant said pleasantly, "I think some more introductions are in order. We wouldn't want to be strangers here in this lovely round, so let's make this a night to remember for our unexpected guest, shall we?"

Brandner nodded at one of the men who'd come outside with him. The tall fellow told Lorcan his name was Michael before breaking his nose with one vicious strike. Lorcan's mouth filled with his own warm blood, and he couldn't breathe.

The next to have a swing at him delivered his fist twice, hitting him in the eye and grazing his cheekbone. His name was Vincent.

After a brawny guy named Darian punched him in the abdomen again, Brandner let go of Lorcan.

He dropped to his knees, the sickening pain of the blows he'd received cramping his gut. Someone sank a fist into his kidney from above, while the other man who'd been holding him up with Brandner kicked him in the face, the pointed tip of his leather boot cracking his jaw. More kicks to his stomach and side followed, and all he could do was curl up and try to protect his head with his hands, but the last shoe to connect with Lorcan's left temple sent his world into blackness.

"That should teach him a thing or two about form and countenance," the merchant smirked, straightening his shirt and briefly inspecting his hands. "Let's get him out of here. He's bleeding all over the place, and I've got the carpenters coming in the morning."

Chapter Nine

෪ Other Concerns ෨

Lorcan was cold.

"Look at him… A shame, that is."

He couldn't tell where he was, or who was talking.

"What are we going to do with him?"

The conversation he heard from afar might have been about him, but he wasn't up to taking part in it. The coppery taste of his own blood made him want to spit, but he couldn't even do that. Something was making it hard for him to breathe, and he vaguely remembered the kicks and the punches he'd taken. Broken ribs, maybe.

Someone began moving him from where he'd been dumped. The gentle hands that lifted him hurt him without intention where bones had been fractured and dislocated. Wounds that had only just scabbed over broke open as he was carried away on a coarse blanket, but there was nothing he could do about it.

All he wanted was to be left alone so he could sleep through the torrents of pain that raged behind his face. He couldn't open his eyes and wondered if they were still there. Too tired to raise his hands to touch them and find out, he slipped back into merciful darkness.

In his dreams, he saw the Snow Globe. He was sitting with Ortus, looking at the model he'd created from the light in his mind. He'd loved leafing through the book that had prompted the action, and he began reading it, page by page.

Images flowed from the words, taking shape, gaining solidity. He felt connected to the man who'd begun the work as well as the man who'd sought to complete it and never had. It was as though he could reach into the thoughts that had borne it and immerse himself in them. Going there was like being in a safe haven, away from where his body lay.

He was inside the Snow Globe, at The Fair in the Big Top and watching children in colorful sparkling clothes at play with diabolos of fire and blue energy in the ring. Some walked on tightropes and others above or below the ropes on nothing but air. They did acrobatics that made their audiences gape in amazement, laugh, cry, worry, and think.

For some reason, he assumed one of those children might be his own. Any one of them, but none of them were aware he was even there.

The Sorcerer appeared next to him as though he'd been standing there all along. "They are *all* a part of you," he said. "Every last one of them."

"I don't understand…" Lorcan began, but just then, the Sorcerer faded out of sight.

In his dream, Lorcan hurried outside to look for him, but he couldn't find Ortus anywhere.

He saw the bear-trainer working with his animals, Freya passing him by with her biggest boa around her neck and waist, the equestrians' proud black horses in the paddock, new caravans between raggedy tents, and an old woman looking right at him with eyes that could not see but perceived everything at once.

"You need to come home," the Seer said, taking his arm, pulling him around and drawing his attention to Dean and Thaddeus.

Neither the young man nor the old one could see Lorcan. They walked right past him, talking, though Lorcan didn't catch what they were saying. He could only hear the Seer clearly.

"He knows the devil," she said into his ear. "He's invited her in."

"Who has?" Lorcan asked absently, shaking her hand off and wondering which of them she meant. "Who's invited the devil in?"

But then, the Seer was gone, and he returned to the Big Top to watch the children perform. One of them *was* his, he was sure, but he still didn't know which. He sat down on one of the seats closest to the ring, studying their faces.

Beside him, the Sorcerer's book reappeared, and between watching the show and leafing through the pages, he was happy.

Angry consciousness plucked Lorcan's mind from its hiding place from time to time over the next days, bringing him back to the real world, but never for long. Whenever it did, he wished it wouldn't, and he fought it despite the words of encouragement he perceived on and off from his caregiver. Helplessness was an unaccustomed feeling – a feeling he didn't like one little bit. Being invisible inside the Snow Globe was so much better than lying on his back in the dark.

Finally, the swelling in his brain went down, and he opened his eyes. The screaming, sickening pain in his head had petered out into a dull headache, but he was awake and back outside the Snow Globe.

Focusing, he recognized the man who'd been taking care of him sitting at his bedside and realized it was Seoid Abhac. The old Dwarve was squinting and laboring over some notes in his ledger.

"How long have I been here?" Lorcan mumbled hoarsely over the waterfall in his ears.

His tongue stuck to the roof of his mouth, and swallowing was agony. He tried to lift his right arm and shift his weight, but discovered it had been splinted, and he couldn't budge.

Abhac looked up, the furrows on his brow deepening as he put down his book and quill. "Easy, now." He straightened the cushions that propped Lorcan up in an almost sitting position. "Nearly a week now."

"Why am I here?"

"Why are you…?" the Dwarve began, chortling a laugh, but instantly seemed to realize how unfitting that might seem. "I found you bleeding in the gutter a few houses down when I was opening my shop. That must have been some fight you got yourself into."

"My employer doesn't know where I am…"

"I informed Ember. I knew who you worked for when you first came to me." For a moment, Abhac appeared reluctant to go on. He paused, fixing his gaze to Lorcan's. Then, something swayed him toward straightforwardness. "Your guild master has no use for a housewright who can't work. He had one of his apprentices help me bring you here and he stopped by the shop once. He left this."

The Dwarve reached under Lorcan's pillow and pulled forth a small leather pouch. Coins jingled inside, and Lorcan wondered what he should be thinking or saying. Since he didn't know, he decided to save his breath.

"Your clothes, your Bible, and some other things are in the chest in the corner over there."

When Lorcan still didn't reply, Abhac took a bowl from the stool next to his and lifted a spoonful of water to his lips. Lorcan took what he could, but most of it spilled, running down the side of his face and onto the towel covering the cushion he lay on. Part of his jaw was still swollen and his lips were cracked. He'd never have guessed how getting a drink of water could be so arduous.

Abhac gently dabbed the moisture from his cheek and chin with a rag. Patiently, he continued giving him small sips from the spoon. "The barber surgeon was here, and Ember sent for a priest, would you believe?" the Dwarve told him while he was doing this. "The surgeon said you'd probably live if you woke up. The priest wouldn't come in the door, of course, but he did do all of his... well, you know..." He paused for lack of terminology. Then, he waved about with one hand as though to sign a cross before closing it to a loose fist and imitating the clergyman sprinkling holy water left and right. "Anyway, he said he'd pray for your soul."

Lorcan would have laughed if he'd managed it, but a cough stifled the attempt.

It was odd to think how a priest could be afraid of a Dwarve. Dwarven gold-and silversmiths made most every precious object in every church around these parts. Even the bishop's ring had likely been cast by a Dwarven craftsman. How could a centuries-old connection like this turn to what it was now becoming?

"A week..." he mumbled, his thoughts jumping from one thing to the next.

That meant, Amelie could well be a married woman by now. Ember would have walked her to the altar to become the Peacock's wife, and there was no going back.

"Who did this to you?" Abhac asked then, just as scattered.

Lorcan thought about it for a moment. "Alehouse brawl."

Abhac's mien told him he only believed half of it. "There isn't an alehouse you could have crawled from in your state anywhere near here."

He didn't want to seem ungrateful to the Dwarve, but what good would telling the old man what he'd gotten himself into be to either of them? Drunken-stupid, he'd broken into a wealthy merchant's yard, urinated in his pond, and gotten a beating for it. Who was to say Brandner hadn't been well within his rights to do what he had?

How he hated the man.

"I don't remember," he said. "I was drunk."

Abhac nodded slowly, doubt lining his eyes, as he put the spoon down, but he let it go. Gathering up his book and quill, he rose.

"Well, then rest now. I think I'll get some sleep myself. I'll leave the door open so I'll hear you if you need anything."

"Wait…" Lorcan tried to sit up and regretted it as soon as he'd shifted his weight.

Abhac winced. "Give yourself a little time."

"Why are you doing this?" Lorcan really had no idea and wanted to know.

Abhac would have had to pay the barber surgeon for his visit and whatever ointments the healer had left. He'd given him a bed, and he'd taken the time to care for him and sit with him. All that for someone he hardly knew.

There was a place near the poorhouse he could have taken him, or had Ember's apprentice drag him, and he'd have been seen to – not as comfortably as here, but they wouldn't have let him die. Lorcan was certain he'd never be able to repay what he owed the merchant.

The man looked first at his feet and then at Lorcan. "That chess set you brought me... I remembered why it seemed familiar."

When he was gone, Lorcan turned his head so he could see the window, but he couldn't look out. He had no idea what he was going to do now.

Chapter Ten

☙ New Shoes ❧

The light was gradually gaining a different, livelier quality as the sun rose higher in the sky every day toward spring.

Lorcan's headache was gone, his face had begun mending, and his ribs weren't giving him the kind of hell he'd had with them over the first days. He thought it was past time to leave Abhac's house. He'd intruded on the merchant's hospitality for too long. Depending on someone like this didn't feel right.

Abhac had refused to help him get the splint off of his arm the previous evening, so he'd used a little magic to do it for him before he'd gone to sleep, and he'd slept the better for it.

He was sure he'd find work again within a reasonable time. There were other carpenters besides Ember in Ironstone. He'd leave Abhac the leather purse with half of his last wages on the chest at the foot of the bed. The coins inside might not cover the sum total of the expenses Abhac had taken on, but Lorcan thought he'd pay back the rest as soon as he could. He badly needed shoes because he'd lost his the night he'd made an idiot of himself, and even used ones were costly.

Lorcan hadn't spoken to his former employer yet, but he knew he'd have to do that before he started knocking on doors. He wanted his hatchet and his other tools from the stable where he'd slept – a hammer, a wedge and a knife he'd sorely miss if he didn't get them. The apprentice hadn't thought to pack them for him – or *meant to* pack them for him. He didn't know which.

He also wanted a letter of recommendation from Ember, if Ember was willing to give him one. Stuffing his belongings in his threadbare backpack, he supposed he'd just go to the workshop and ask. The worst thing that could happen was that Ember would refuse to write the letter and hand over the tools. Lorcan thought he'd only do that if he'd learned about his relationship with Amelie, and hadn't simmered down yet, but Amelie was safely married now. He didn't believe she'd have told anyone else about the baby.

Quietly opening the door that led from his room out into the corridor, he looked about, hoping for a quick getaway. He nearly tripped over a pair of shoes that hadn't been there the night before. Despite the gloom, he saw that they were new. The door across from his opened, and Abhac peeked out.

"It's too cold to go without," the Dwarve said, emerging fully from his room and pulling on a shirt.

"I can't take these…"

Abhac looked at him as though he'd just slapped him in the face. "Rubbish. I can't stop you from leaving, but I won't have people saying I'm not good for a pair of shoes."

Lorcan looked down at his bare feet. "I don't know when I'll be able to repay you."

"You would if you decided to stay on and work for me."

Lorcan almost laughed, but he could see the man wasn't joking. "I'm a carpenter, Seoid. You don't need a live-in handy man around your house, and I don't need charity."

"I know that. But you're an excellent craftsman. I was going to tell you over breakfast, but I guess now's the time... The queen took that chess set last night, and I got four orders for more by January. I think we could come to an agreement here."

Lorcan didn't know what to say. He thought he might have to sit down, and he did. Right next to his new shoes.

Chapter Eleven

ভ Merchants and Scoundrels ১

The Dwarve's nose nearly touched the table as he looked at Lorcan past the chess board. "Tell me, why is it again that you can carve these beautiful figures but don't know how to play them?"

Lorcan didn't look at the merchant until Abhac cocked his head in that odd fashion of his that told him he wouldn't stop asking until he'd gotten his answer.

He wasn't prepared to answer just yet and pushed one of his pawns a square onward in front of the rook. The moment he'd done this, images of Abhac's new choices became visible to his mind's eye. He wished they'd appear *before* he made his moves.

Abhac sighed. He took Lorcan's bishop with his knight and set the piece aside.

Lorcan hummed in disapproval. "You really meant it when you said I'd have to learn how to lose at this game to be able to win some day."

"I did. Why did Ortus never teach you that?"

Lorcan folded his arms and rested them on the table in front of him. "He wasted enough of his time and energy on teaching me to read. My father and I came from the Sudlands with the clothes on our backs, and Ortus took us in when we had nowhere else to go. My father was a thief and a liar, and he never worked a day in his life, not when I was small, and not at The Fair later. I never asked for anything because I was always afraid we'd be kicked out, in the end. I honestly don't know what Ortus thought he'd seen in me."

He was surprised at himself. He'd never been this forthright and honest about himself with anyone before. The old Dwarve had a way of extracting the truth.

"I can understand why you're not good at accepting help or advice. Tell me more about your father."

Lorcan looked at the chess board. "They should call this game Dwarves and Scoundrels." He moved his remaining bishop to a better position, and Abhac raised an eyebrow at him before taking another of his pawns.

"Well? What was his Talent?"

"He was an Illusionist."

"Is that what you are, too?"

"No." Lorcan had learned a few things about himself over the past years. They didn't match with what he'd assumed would be Cine magic. There was no denying what he was, and no matter how hard he'd tried to renounce and avoid using his Talent, it was always there, and it would always be a part of him – but it wasn't in any way like his father's.

He looked at his queen, and she moved toward Abhac's knight as though an invisible hand was guiding her. Abhac smiled mischievously when he saw he was going to lose the piece. Lorcan levitated the knight off the board and set it down on the table.

Chortling a laugh, Abhac took the queen with his bishop. Lorcan used the opening that gave him to take Abhac's rook with one of his pawns. Pawns were easily underestimated, it seemed, but, he'd lost his queen for the sake of showing off. That, again, was Jaden's blood inside of him, he realized.

After he'd put the rook to one side of the board with his mind, he unexpectedly began seeing a whole network of possibilities before the merchant had even touched the next piece he intended to move.

"Is there anything else you can do?"

"I can see what things are made of and how they work, or what they could be when they're finished."

Abhac's smile widened. "Ortus wanted to see the good in people, not just the Cine, but everybody. Unfortunately, that was always just guesswork. Perhaps he saw that you wouldn't have to spend your life guessing. Perhaps he knew you had the Talent to see not only what things are made of, but the decisions that lead to their completion."

He pushed his queen into position between Lorcan's knight and a pawn, ready to move in on the king.

Lorcan knew he'd lost, but he wasn't going down without a fight. He leaned back and pondered his options as well as what Abhac had just said.

His remaining rook moved to take out Abhac's remaining rook. The queen had left it unprotected. There was only a bishop between him and the merchant's king.

"You're getting good at this," the Dwarve muttered, taking a moment to think.

"My father was involved in Ortus' death."

Abhac let that stand without commenting. He moved his queen. "Check."

Lorcan moved his king. Abhac repositioned his queen. "Check."

Lorcan took Abhac's queen with his remaining bishop.

Abhac grinned. "I didn't see that," he admitted. "Do you think he killed him?"

"No. I believe it was his girlfriend. But, he was in on it."

The merchant moved his king out of the immediate danger zone. "Why did they do it? He never had much money on him, and that old horse of his wasn't worth a pair of boots."

The merchant's bishop was Lorcan's.

"Ortus had a very special book. He took it with him wherever he went. It was missing when I found his body."

Abhac lifted his remaining pawn and set him back down after a moment, reconsidering. "And you think your father and his woman stole that book?"

"No. My father is dead, and he didn't have it. The woman he was with was gone, but somehow I don't think she had it either. I believe they were going to steal it, but something didn't go the way they'd planned it."

"Did they..." The Dwarve paused, and then pushed his remaining bishop all the way across the board. "Did they use magic to kill Ortus?"

Lorcan saw through the baiting maneuver. "Yes. I think so."

This time, he decided against the use of *his* magic to corner Abhac's king with his knight. He picked it up and played it toward the merchant's rook.

"Check."

"Why did you not return to The Fair?" Abhac moved his king one last time.

"I did." Lorcan countered by closing the trap with his rook. "Checkmate. They weren't very happy to see me. They thought I had something to do with it."

Abhac laid his king down on the board. "You win," he said. "But how did you do that? Did you see how winning this would work?"

Lorcan looked down at his hands. "Honestly? I can't turn it on or off as I please."

"Not yet," the Dwarve said. "But Ortus couldn't do that when he young either. Learning is always about making choices. I think you had a lot of your decisions made for you in the past. This is the future, though. I'm not saying don't use your magic, but you should learn to work it and use it wisely. You get to make your own choices now." He crossed his arms and fixed his stare intently to Lorcan's. "Make smart ones from here on in."

Chapter Twelve

⊙ꜱ Flames ꜱ

The door to their little house was open when Catherine and Rebecca returned from the market. Catherine noticed that someone had left the catch up. It was always a little tight, and she distinctly remembered her aunt pulling down hard on the brittle wooden wedge before they'd left in the morning.

They had no way of locking it from the outside, but they'd never thought about this too hard. Being able to lock it from the inside had seemed more important.

She motioned Rebecca to stay back. The older woman's eyes widened in alarm as Catherine quietly set down the heavy sack of flour and beeswax she'd been carrying.

One of Rebecca's customers might have stopped by looking for her. Perhaps he'd decided to take the liberty of helping himself to his ration of the good stuff, thinking he wouldn't have to pay for his drink this week. They didn't usually keep the poteen in the house, especially when they were going to town, but there might have been a few bottles and jars in the cupboards somewhere, and Catherine could see this was the scenario playing in Rebecca's head as she put her own sack down.

Aside from the still and the equipment that went with it, they really didn't own much worth stealing. Someone could have taken it in hopes of either selling it or figuring out how to work it. The pot and the standpipe as well as the coil were made of copper, and they were quite good for the years they'd seen. It would be a costly loss to replace, if they could replace it at all.

Catherine ducked below the tiny window to the left of the door and peered in. The light was so bad she could hardly see in the gloom of the sparsely furnished room where they lived, worked, cooked, and slept.

Two mismatched chairs stood at a table behind the open timber framing that held the sagging middle section of the roof in place. Several of their overgarments hung from the beams. A rickety ladder leaned against the girder. It led to a small platform under the thatch where they stored the things they didn't need every day. The impenetrable shadows beyond the ladder absorbed the hind portion of the little house where the fireplace had gone cold and black. Someone could be lying in wait for them there, ready to slit their throats, but Catherine was almost sure their visitor was already gone. Almost.

She wasn't afraid because they were capable of dealing with some impoverished drifter who'd eaten the rest of last night's barley broth, a despondent crofter with more worries than hair on his graying head, or a few village boys looking for a free sample of either the poteen or the women who brewed it. They'd handle it because they weren't helpless. *She'd* handle it, with or without using her Gift, because *no one* entered her space to steal from her. Still, it was always wise to be careful.

Going around the house on one side while Rebecca went around the other, Catherine was relieved to find their chickens still there, scratching chirpily in the dirt. They chortled as soon as they became aware of her, and the racket they made would have awoken the dead. She tossed the hungry birds a few crumbs of the leftover bread she had in her apron, and they lunged at the morsels.

Couldn't hurt to be on her toes when she went inside, she told herself, so she took the ax from the chopping block by the wood pile and weighed it in her hand. Rebecca armed herself with a thick hazel stick.

When they'd rounded the cabin and were back to where they'd started, she signaled Rebecca. Rebecca pushed the door all the way back on its hinges while Catherine positioned herself in the entranceway to get a good look at what they might be faced with.

Cautiously entering the little cottage, they expected to find it askew, but it wasn't. Only a few cupboards had been searched.

Several empty earthenware jugs were lined up on the table. A whole week's worth of drinking all done in a single day by the raggedy man who lay on his belly beside the cold hearth, Catherine realized, and he was sleeping it off in a puddle of his own vomit. It was nothing short of a miracle he was still alive.

"Never could take his liquor," Rebecca remarked sharply, nudging him with the tip of her boot. A strange mixture of sympathy, annoyance, repulsion, and several other things Catherine couldn't make sense of reflected in her eyes as she took in the sorry form at her feet.

Stooping down to get a better a look at the filthy beggar, Catherine needed a few seconds longer to comprehend that the mess before her was her father.

She'd been right; they'd been robbed by a drunkard.

Life hadn't been kind to the gravedigger, but he'd never given it reason to be. He'd been drawn to death all these years, and the sickly color of his skin didn't withhold how very close he and his friend had gotten over the past winter. She supposed this was how it all came back to Caleb, but she felt no pity.

She felt nothing.

"Would you look at yourself?" Rebecca went on more softly, speaking to her brother-in-law as though he was her biggest letdown and a child in need of compassion at the same time. "You're a complete disgrace."

Telling people they were a disgrace seemed to distract Rebecca from her own stains and tarnishes sufficiently to make a bad moment more bearable, and

Catherine knew better than to tell her that he couldn't hear her.

Suddenly acknowledging that her niece was beside her, Rebecca regained herself. Her lips thinned and pulled into a straight line as they tended to do whenever she was upset, and she grabbed Catherine's arm, shoving her back out the door before there could be any discussion about it.

Catherine wasn't sure she *wanted* to discuss this, but she hated being *pushed*. She hated being touched, whether by her aunt or anyone else.

"Go fetch some water," Rebecca told her agitatedly as she pulled free of her grip and moved away. "We'll have to clean *that* up."

That. Her father.

They were forever cleaning something or other up, it seemed, and today it would be him.

She scowled, but reluctantly started to do as she was told, deciding she was going to take her time about it. *That* wasn't going anywhere too soon, and she wasn't looking forward to when he'd be awake and she'd have to endure his idiotic babbling.

The low, crumbling stone-walled well in the yard wasn't within sight of the house. Its water was murky, especially after a heavy downpour, and it smelled foul during a dry spell, so Catherine usually went to the river for their supply. She was aware that Rebecca expected her to go there now, but she didn't feel like making the long trip after they'd already been on their feet since before dawn to go to the market. Her feet and legs ached, and so did her shoulder from carrying the sack.

She picked up an empty wooden pail from the table behind the cabin and decided the water from the well would do for Caleb, no matter what it looked or tasted like today.

Making sure Rebecca wasn't watching which direction she was heading, she swiftly crossed the backyard. The older woman had probably busied herself lighting a fire in the hearth, and she was likely to stay inside with Caleb to see he didn't choke or stop breathing as he lay moaning on the floor.

Buying the chickens' silence with another few crumbs of bread, she tied the bucket to a length of rope fastened to the simple hand-driven spool under the roofed construction. She let it down into the depths of the well, hoping it wouldn't make too much of a racket by clattering against the flat stones that lined the hand-dug vertical shaft. When the pail was full, she didn't even think of using the pulley to haul it back up again. There was another, less arduous way.

Warily squinting about at the surrounding fields and the edge of the woods that began just beyond, she employed her Talent to do it for her. It only took a few seconds of real-time for the pail to reemerge, hovering an inch or two over the rim of the well next to her. Manipulating gravity within a confined space wasn't the hardest thing to do; it wasn't difficult to imagine a world where nothing was pulled to the earth anymore and particles were free of their attractions – not like physically lifting the weight of a bucket would have been.

Immensely enjoying her small defiance of Rebecca's rules, she pulled the bucket to her, set it down, and untied the rope from the handle as the small pebbles, grit, sand, and droplets of water that had come out of the shaft along with it tumbled back to where they'd been, splashing down a good thirty feet below.

The skills Catherine had been working on almost daily had escaped her aunt's attention all the months they'd been living together, and that was a source of tremendous satisfaction for her. Her magic was bound to the things she did, and it came effortlessly and naturally most of the time, bridging gaps and knitting fissures in her reality. It never wore her out or took away from her time, and so Rebecca had only seen what she'd been meant to see – or sometimes what she'd expected to see.

This particular little trick and others like it kept bringing smiles to Catherine's face over and over.

Daylight waned as she walked back across the yard with the pail. She briefly paused to observe the hens filing into their ramshackle dwellings one by one, and she couldn't help but hum a merry little tune as she gathered enough of the cool evening breeze's momentum to push the door of the shed closed so the fox wouldn't get in during the night. She'd lost several of the silly birds to a vixen and the growing appetite of her hungry cubs recently.

Fastening the carved wooden catch by hand with a soft, scraping noise, she made a mental note to set new traps in the morning. Although she respected the fox and liked to watch the cubs playing out in the sun near their den – it hadn't been hard to find – she wasn't willing to share one of their most reliable food sources with it.

Life was tough all around.

When she got back to the house, she could see Rebecca had already lit the candles. The window out back was open wide, and she heard Rebecca's and her father's voices.

She leaned against the wall, just out of view, but she was confident she would not be seen in any case.

It might be entertaining to hear what Caleb would have to say to her aunt in private. He and Rebecca were talking in what seemed like a civil tone, which was unusual for them.

"You're not supposed to come here," Rebecca was telling Caleb in a low voice, calmly, but not unkindly. "It's too dangerous."

"You have no idea what's been going on back home," he returned, slurring the consonants. "They've arrested the miller's wife because she had another one of her fits. They're saying it's the devil inside her."

Catherine smirked. There was no devil inside the miller's wife. When she'd been younger, she'd often thought this woman *was* the devil. Other than that, the miller's wife had been having dizzy spells and seizures since the day Catherine and Caleb had been there to pick up straw for their leaky roof, and that had nothing to do with the devil. It had to do with the fact that they'd both been cold and starving, and taking some barley right from under the miller's wife's nose hadn't been possible without a little distraction. The mere thought of a headache had sufficed to make Mrs. Miller throw up and take to her bed for a week. Need had priority over ethics, and Catherine hadn't been in control of herself then as much as she was now.

She briefly wondered what they were going to do with the old biddy, but came to the conclusion the world wasn't going to miss Mrs. Miller one little bit; whether she was hung, beheaded or burned, it was all the same to Catherine, and it would be all the same to anyone the miller had cheated in the course of the past decades.

Hollowed out weights, faulty measures and all of his fast talk had made him a wealthy man. His brashness was admirable, but the world was full of mean and stingy people. As far as Catherine was concerned, it would just be one less of them when the headsman's sword met its mark. The irony that the miller would have to remunerate the Inquisitor for his troubles because of his ill-begotten wealth didn't escape her, but she doubted he'd understand.

What did strike her as odd was that the clergyman was actually going after a person of some standing. This meant the good Father wasn't afraid of stirring up dust.

Rebecca shifted about uneasily, staring through Catherine who'd moved into what should have been plain sight outside the window. Catherine straightened her back as she folded her arms across her chest, watching her without being noticed.

"Who else?" Rebecca inquired curtly.

Caleb cleared his throat and sniffed, wiping his nose on the back of his hand. "Greg Shearer, his wife, and Brenda Long."

Catherine could both see and hear Rebecca draw breath. The Shearers and the Longs were guild members, and Catherine didn't think they had any Cine background. She realized if their membership and their reputation hadn't saved them, then no one would be safe anymore. The Inquisitor was a threat to every man, woman, and child who'd falsely assumed up until then that their life's biggest problem would be a greedy miller and his bickering wife.

"What about the Fletchers?" Rebecca whispered then, her mouth voicing the thought that had just formed in Catherine's mind.

Caleb slouched forward in his chair at the table with his back to her, but Catherine could see her father's face through her aunt's eyes for just a moment and caught a whiff of the vile stench of him — sweat and weeks-old grime, unwashed clothes, sour bile, and drink.

She didn't know how Rebecca could stand being in the same room with him for any length of time. It was enough to turn her stomach. She didn't think she'd ever been repulsed by him like this before, but she hadn't seen him in a while, and perhaps that was the reason: absence made the heart grow fonder. To an extent. Not being forced to look at him every day had made him seem slightly less deplorable than he really was. Seeing him like this brought back why she'd grown to despise him.

"The Fletchers packed up and left right after you did," Caleb informed her. "Their boy stayed behind another few days, but he's gone now, too."

He sat in silence for a moment, and Rebecca pulled a face, perhaps wondering why she'd asked.

A knot formed in Catherine's chest. It was made from the dull, burning ache of loss. Knowing where to find Dean if she felt it was safe to look was the one thing that had made the past year bearable. Not knowing where he was now or if he was all right slew a quiet, timid hope she'd been nursing.

Irritated by the power of her own emotion, she tried to wrestle the sentiment down. She told herself the gangly red-haired boy she'd developed something akin to affection for had never been hers to lose in the first place, but it was crushing after all the months she'd lain awake at night asking herself if he was looking for her, or if he'd even remember her now.

"We can thank the stars no one's put two and two together yet," Rebecca was saying when Catherine woke up to herself at the wilting sound of her aunt's voice. "Your daughter is only alive because of me."

Caleb raised an eyebrow at her.

There might have been some truth in that, though Catherine wasn't entirely convinced she couldn't have dealt with the situation on her own if it had come to that. Recalling the day she'd killed Cooper, she didn't believe anyone would have connected her to the man if the Shearers' daughter hadn't been there. An unfortunate turn of events, but nothing she couldn't have managed to take care of by herself. Rebecca's actions had been very rash and shown her a side of her aunt she hadn't been aware of.

"Oh, I know. I really appreciate what you've been doing," Caleb eventually admitted after he'd obviously realized this was what Rebecca wanted to hear from him.

The phoniness of his claim rang through like a chorus of bells on a Sunday morning. Rebecca was many things, but she wasn't stupid. Still, Catherine wasn't certain she saw through him.

"Caleb, what is it you want? I just don't know why you're here. Are you trying to get us *all* killed?" Rebecca sat back, her arms folded over her flat chest.

"Dear God, no!" he replied, sounding genuinely shocked this time as he jumped up, raking a trembling hand through his sparse greasy hair as he moved about the room. "I came here to warn you. You see, there are rumors."

Rebecca huffed. Catherine thought they'd probably heard them all by now anyway. They weren't all *that* far from home. Rebecca's sudden urge to leave the village hadn't gone unnoticed, and there were various speculations as to why she'd left, but all of them quite harmless.

Catherine's disappearance, however, hadn't really come to anyone's attention the first few weeks. No one's except perhaps Dean's. When she hadn't been seen around the woods, someone had started telling everyone Catherine was dead. It wouldn't have been unlikely she'd been killed by robbers with things as they were. There were more outlaws than ever scouring the lands, and no one went into the forest on their own without protection and got away with it for long. Not unless they knew how to keep out of sight.

"What rumors do you mean?" Rebecca inquired nonetheless.

Caleb placed both hands on the stone mantelpiece of the hearth at shoulder height, leaning against it rigidly. He didn't seem to know where to start.

"They're saying the Shearers confessed." He paused awkwardly, and although Rebecca probably guessed what he was going to say, she pressed her lips firmly shut, while he searched for words. Catherine was sure they'd have affirmed many things whether they were true or not – they would have been tortured – and her throat went dry. Maybe they'd found the bodies; the Shearers or someone else.

"They accused Cooper of sorcery. They said he'd been teaching their daughter magic for over a year before she disappeared, and they suspect she ran off with him."

Catherine had to suppress a chuckle. Laura and magic, that was like imagining pigs could fly. Laura hadn't had any manner of Gift. Cooper might have tried to teach her to read, at best, but he couldn't possibly have taught her magic. You couldn't *teach* magic. *He* couldn't teach magic. A Talent was either there, or it wasn't, and Cooper had been intelligent and able to read, but the only thing he could have taught buck-toothed Laura Shearer besides letters and words would have been his anatomy.

Her parents suspecting she'd run off with him meant they still didn't know what had really happened. The bodies hadn't been found, and that was good.

"I mean, everybody knew Cooper was into young girls – and magic," Caleb stumbled on then, as though this had been a fact when she thought it hadn't.

If anyone had doubted the farmer's integrity to that degree, then why had no one spoken up against him? There was a defensive tone to Caleb's voice

Catherine couldn't gauge, but the information as such didn't seem to disquiet Rebecca. It occurred to Catherine that her aunt had never asked her why she'd killed the man, and she'd never felt obliged to offer an explanation.

She supposed it was irrelevant now. Just as it was irrelevant whether they accused Cooper of being a sorcerer, a shapeshifter or a troll for that matter – the man was dead and buried, along with Laura and her overbite, and the world was free of him. Perhaps Rebecca's thoughts went along the same lines.

Caleb distractedly tapped his toe against the loose iron grate of the fireplace, rattling it and disturbing the embers.

"There's more," he went on. "They said their daughter told them about Catherine. She told them Catherine had powers given to her by the devil himself. And, Laura said she'd seen Catherine around Cooper's place without her knowing. She watched her practically force herself on him, do sinful things with him that weren't right."

Rebecca's face derailed, briefly making her look like a diseased horse with nostrils flaring and her mouth opening and closing but not forming sounds before her lips pressed together to a thin line once again.

Catherine had to suppress another snicker. Poor little peeping Laura must have been soft in the head to interpret whatever she'd seen or imagined she'd seen like that.

But there was more, still. Caleb was only warming up, it seemed. "She said she saw Catherine talking to people who weren't there, dead people or ghosts. Whatever. She asked Cooper about it, and apparently, he told her *everything*. He told her she was a Cine."

A small, but highly amused chortle nearly gave Catherine away, and Rebecca crossed the floor to close the window against the evening chill, frowning.

Striding around the front of the house to the door, Catherine remembered the stories Caleb had brought home from the alehouse the night she'd killed Cooper, and she had to press a fist to her mouth to stop herself from breaking out in hysterics.

She'd never have used her Gift in front of anyone but Dean. Cooper had been testing her all these years, but she'd instinctively never, *ever* given him what he'd wanted. What on earth would Cooper have told Laura, if in fact he'd talked to her about their relationship at all? That she was Lord Tierney's illegitimate granddaughter and flew on a broomstick by full moon? The look on the old man's face when she'd finally shown him the true nature of her Talent had been absolutely *priceless*.

The rumors Caleb was talking about had probably been doing the rounds since before she and Rebecca had left, but with the Shearers' daughter missing and them so talkative, there would be lots of fingers pointed in her direction now if they got a hold of her. The Inquisitor would be looking for other witnesses against her, and who'd be fool enough to deny that she was and always had been different? She was dirt to most people in that nameless village, and no one would be in the least bit interested in her welfare while their own was in danger. They needed a scapegoat, and no one would even have to look her in the eye while they told their lies. She'd be a juicy bone to keep the Inquisitor's rabid dogs busy, taking the pressure off of everyone else. A scary thought.

The Shearers didn't know for a fact what had become of their daughter, but Catherine had no sympathy whatsoever for them. They'd told the Inquisitor both Laura and she were magic users in exchange for a more merciful death.

Catherine hoped the headsman would miss his mark by an inch every time he struck. She hoped they would rot in hell. Her knuckles were white from holding the handle of the pail so tight that it hurt, but she found solace in the pain. Pain meant relief would follow, and relief that was hard begotten was sweet.

"So... they'll be out looking for Cooper and Laura. But they'll also be looking for Catherine," Rebecca observed, seating herself again opposite Caleb as Catherine opened the door a little way.

Caleb licked his lips, rubbing his stubbly chin so the scratching sound was audible out where she was standing. She hated that sound. "They'll *never* find the bodies, don't you worry."

"But they *will* find *us*," Rebecca snapped breathily, losing composure. "Do you realize you might have led them here yourself?" She rose abruptly, shoving back the chair she'd been sitting on. Wood scraped hard against wood, and the chair almost fell over. "Someone could have followed you, you idiot!"

Caleb sniffed again nervously, spinning around in time to see her grab one of the earthenware jugs from the table. She weighed it in her hand and launched it at him. He raised his arms to protect his face. The jug only just missed its target and shattered on the mantel shelf beside him. He ducked sideways when he saw she was going for the next.

"I wasn't followed, I *swear* I was careful. I didn't see anyone!"

"How can you be sure?" She flung a new jug at him and didn't miss this time. He yelped and clutched his hip where she'd hit home. The third fell short again, and he lunged himself at her, developing an astounding velocity.

"Stop it," he yelled, seizing her by the arms. "Are you crazy?"

"You're the one who's crazy here," she spat, pitting herself against him furiously, her face a fuming mask of loathing.

"No," he said assertively, holding her elbows firmly by her sides. "I think I'm the only sane person here, and that's how it was from the start. You and that sister of yours, you *ruined* my life." His voice was so low, Catherine didn't hear the resentment in it, but she could *feel* it radiate out toward her aunt. "How long do you think it's going to take for the Inquisitor to come after me, too, now? I couldn't stay there. Do you have any idea how much I despise you for that?"

Pulling free with a growl, Rebecca waved a finger under his nose. "You brought this on *yourself*. I loved you, and you chose my sister over me. Everything could have been different, but you didn't want that."

Catherine couldn't believe what she was hearing. Who would have guessed? She had trouble picturing it; she had trouble picturing *anyone* harboring anything but hostility and indifference toward the wayward gravedigger, never mind a woman finding it in her to freely *choose* to sleep with him.

"How would anything have been different?" she heard her father ask then. "Charlie was a good man."

"Do you think that's enough to make a commitment work? *He was a good man?* I never loved him. You and I, we could have left and never looked back, and none of this would have happened. Not to us."

"And you really believe that? Maebh was pregnant! And with Charlie sick like he was…?"

"Maebh was *always* pregnant," Rebecca returned snidely. "Whether by you or some other fool.

And, it took Charlie *years* to find the courage to end his own suffering. *We* could have been happy then."

"Do you really think we could?" He snorted, glaring at her. "Charlie was my best friend."

Catherine knew that Charlie had been his *only* friend. He'd told her late one night in a stupor, complaining about how lonely his life had become.

"Do you really think we could have started over on those grounds? That *your* curse would have skipped the next generation and spared any children we'd have had? That we wouldn't have been faced with the same problem we're stuck with now?"

Rebecca's face went blank for a moment, and thinking about it, Catherine suddenly knew why she'd never had children of her own.

"I should have suffocated Catherine in her sleep while I had the chance," Caleb mumbled, and Catherine didn't doubt that he wished he had. She had regrets of her own when it came to him.

"Maybe you should have," Rebecca conceded slowly. "It's what I told you to do when Maebh left, but you didn't have it in you. None of this would have happened if you'd done what I told you, but you were too soft, and I'll admit I was, too. Now, we're all going to have to pay for it."

Catherine discovered that she also had regrets concerning Rebecca, and her grip on the handle of the bucket she still held tightened once more. Observing herself, she might have been surprised to find that her lips thinned in much the same way her aunt's tended to do when she was upset, but she was nothing like Rebecca. The fact that they had no common ground beyond their blood ties and the murders they'd committed had just become blatantly clear.

Caleb remained silent for a moment before answering without acknowledging what she'd just tossed in his face. "We've been doing nothing *but* pay these last fifteen years, and this *has* to end."

"So what do you suggest?" Rebecca murmured resignedly, rubbing her tired eyes while Catherine was considering her options.

She watched her father sit back down at the table and offer Rebecca a chair, but her aunt chose to remain standing. He uncorked two of the bottles in front of him and raised them to his lips in turn, draining the last remaining drops they'd surrender to his craving.

Rebecca eyed him in disgust, resting her weight on one leg the way she did whenever she was growing impatient. Finally, she walked over to the one cupboard he hadn't raided and took out one of her rare glass bottles. She sold them at double what she charged for a clay jug because glass was so expensive and hard to come by. It was beautiful, but he had no eye for the packaging. He only wanted what was inside, and he reached for it greedily as she set a cup in front of him, seating herself next to him. She brusquely swatted his hand away and poured him his drink while he waited until she'd filled it about half way. Then, he gulped down the fiery, smooth liquid in one swallow.

Grimacing from the burning sensation in his marred esophagus, he wiped his mouth on the back of his hand and cleared his throat, or tried to. Expectantly, he pushed his cup in front of her again. "I've heard of a priest who can cure what Catherine has."

Rebecca tilted her head incredulously, her mouth dropping open again. She ignored his silent plea and recorked the bottle, much to his disappointment.

"I know it sounds improbable, but what if he can?" he went on nonetheless, quivering fingers moving for the poteen, but she resolutely positioned it on the far end of the table with a loud, final thud. Irritated though he was, he seemed to make his peace with that for the time being.

"They say this priest can take away the magic surgically, sort of cut it away like a wart. It *is* an evil, and it would grow." He fumbled about his nose, rubbing it nervously. "I mean, we both know she'd be so much better off without it, and he's done it a dozen times with some success."

"Really!" Rebecca returned.

Caleb nodded enthusiastically. It didn't seem to occur to him how ludicrous his proposition was, and he didn't hear the undertone in Rebecca's voice.

"*Surgically,*" she muttered, as though to herself. "Well, *what on earth* would he cut *off* or *out*?"

Caleb smiled, all gaps and foul teeth, looking every bit the idiot he was.

Catherine's jaw clenched painfully as she studied him briefly through her aunt's eyes, seething at the sight of him. She found it increasingly hard to breathe, but she was sure it wasn't fear. Perhaps she should have been afraid, but she wasn't. She was angry. The antagonism and distrust that had been there before turned into pure, agonizing fury.

She had no idea what part of her body her father would assume guilty of harboring her Cine Talent, and she could but speculate what he'd have the priest remove.

Eyes?

Hands?

Her brain?

Her heart?

This was some piece of reasoning. If she'd had to put a location with the origin of her powers and pinpoint the source of her inert magic, she'd honestly have to admit she couldn't; it was *everywhere* inside of her. She was *steeped* in it as though she was made of it, created from its essence. It was the reason she was alive, and she was convinced there was no separating it from her being. It *was* her being. The only way to take her magic away would be to kill her. Rebecca had to know that, though Caleb might not.

If she turned and walked away right now, she could put enough distance between them and herself to never have to see either of them again, but her feet wouldn't move. It was then that she realized she didn't *want* to turn away. She didn't *want* to run away from this, run away from *them*. She didn't think she *should* run from anyone if she could help it. And she could.

"That priest..." Caleb plowed on, squeezing his eyes shut for just a second as though to sort through the tumbling pieces of what he was going to tell Rebecca. "Several of the people he's treated have survived, and they're *cured*." He seemed very pleased with this statement. "Let's take Catherine to him and end this nightmare, and maybe we'll be saved yet. He could take away her curse and tell the Inquisitor he's freed her of the affliction. They couldn't make a case against her then, or against any of us."

Rebecca's shoulders slumped, and she slowly shook her head. "I don't believe this – I mean, she's *your* daughter, but, there *is* no cure for being a Cine..." she trailed off. Again, Caleb misread her and cut her short.

"She is *my* daughter, and there's human in her, so this is what we're going to do." He looked like a man who'd unexpectedly had a run of good fortune, and a stiff dose of resolve poured into his spine, strengthening it after he'd heard himself say it.

All Catherine could think of was how she detested every fiber of his being, and it sickened her how incredibly, unforgivably dense he must be. He'd never been a very clever man, but he'd probably managed to drink whatever had been left of his wits to oblivion in the months of her absence. He really believed what he was saying, and as surely as there was no cure for being a Cine, there was no remedy for *his* kind of affliction either.

"No, Caleb, she's your daughter," Rebecca sighed finally, giving up, "and this is what *you're* going to do. Maybe the Lord will have mercy and she'll be among those who don't survive."

At that, Catherine dropped the pail without realizing she'd let go of the handle. It clattered noisily to the ground, alerting her father and aunt to her presence as the door swung open and the water pooled at her feet, soaking its way up and into her footwear. Caleb spun around and stared at her for a moment, seeing her because she chose not to remain *unseen* by Rebecca and him anymore. He didn't move, and Rebecca huffed, lowering her eyes.

Caleb rose and took a few steps toward Catherine. "How long have you been here?"

Her feet were rooted to the ground because she was beyond making sensible sane decisions other than the one she'd already made: she wasn't walking away.

"That's close enough," she warned him, raising a hand in motioning him to stop, but he didn't seem to understand.

He just kept coming at her, talking to her – or talking *at* her – but she couldn't hear a word of what he was saying over the gush of the blood rushing through *his* veins, distending the vessels and straining against the fissures. It was pulsing at twice the speed it should have been going, and she stopped him the only way she could: she added another few notches to the momentum of the building pressure within his intoxicated, damaged body. She didn't know how to classify the tsunami of restless, swirling cells that started forcing every flaw in the tissue to its breaking point, but she was both author and spectator of the tragedy at the same time. She was in two bodies, residing in one, intruding in the other. It was almost like it had been when she'd taken Cooper's life, but not quite. She wasn't going quite as far as she had with Cooper in the end.

It wasn't her intention to kill Caleb outright. Not yet. She wanted to cripple him the way he'd have had her crippled. She wanted him *just* capable of remembering the lesson she was going to teach him for the remaining helpless minutes of his life. The breathless, humming surge of power that engulfed her when he went to his knees canceled out the faint echo she perceived of the searing pain erupting behind his left temple as he clutched his head. She caught a momentary glance of herself standing there by the door, observing him with an impassive expression before Rebecca started screeching her name, bounding to her father's aid.

Startled at the sound of the older woman's voice, Catherine hastily returned to her own cognizance, gradually releasing the hold she had on Caleb. It felt right to place him in the hands of the only person who'd seemed to have the capacity to love him, but it wasn't an act of mercy. It was a way to keep Rebecca busy.

"What have you done?" Rebecca screamed hysterically, trying to assess the damage and drag Caleb to his feet with some difficulty, but Catherine knew it would have been pointless to elaborate.

A whole tirade of words rolled off of Catherine, but she didn't hear them because her attention was fixed wholly to the red-glowing embers in the hearth. The beautiful shade of crimson on gray never ceased to capture her fantasy, and there was a quiet conviction within that there was no limit to what her fantasy could do. Adding oxygen to the restless particles of energy that were in motion beneath the charred wood and ashes by adjusting the reality in which they existed, she observed as sparks began to fly and dance about in a firework of swirling lights, freeing themselves of the space they'd been confined to.

Some of them caught on one of the cloaks that hung from the beams, and some landed on the bedstead in the corner of the room. The flames of the candles her aunt had lit on the table flared up, spilling liquidly over onto the wooden surface, devouring the sewing yarns that lay there.

Rebecca looked up, and her breath hitched. "What...?" The initial confusion in her eyes turning into pure, unadulterated terror as the sparks settled into her thick, blonde hair and the fabric of her dress. She was ablaze and thrashing within seconds, trying to put the flames out with her hands, beating at them and writhing in agony, but she didn't have a chance.

Catherine smiled at Caleb, who could do nothing but watch from where he was cowering on the floor, mouth hanging crookedly, his own clothes and skin burning unhindered because his hands would not obey him and his knees wouldn't hold his weight. There was no remorse, but the overpowering smell of charred flesh that soon mixed in with the biting smoke made her stomach queasy, and so she knew it was time to go.

"Goodbye," she told them both simply.

Her smile widened as she turned to close the door on this part of her life firmly and irrevocably, utilizing the breeze that had been picking up remarkably in the last minutes. A gust of wind banged the window shutters closed and pressed hard against the timber of the little house, whistling in through the cracks in the boards until the entire structure was a scorching inferno.

Eventually, Rebecca's shrieks subsided.

Putting one foot in front of the other as she tried to clear her mind, Catherine walked around the back of the cabin and straight to the hen house. Opening the narrow door to release the chickens to their own fate, she was dead certain she'd taken care of both the hobo

and the vixen forevermore, and she'd never look back.
Why should she?

Chapter Thirteen

❧ Sketches ☙

A year and a day since the Master Sorcerer had died, and Dean Greenleaf still didn't know what he wanted to do with his life. He knew what he *didn't* want, and that was the house he'd grown up in, so he'd come back a month ago to sell it. The money would tide him over for a while; he'd found that the kind of labor he could do for a day's wages wouldn't feed *and* clothe him.

The new owner of the house was giving him a few days to clear out what he was taking with him, but that wouldn't be much. It would have to fit in the bags he could strap to the saddle of his horse.

Having already destroyed the equipment he thought he wouldn't need from Ortus' workshop, he'd packed some bags with a few books and other things he couldn't bring himself to leave behind or burn. This was to be his final night in the home where most of his childhood memories had been made, and he sat in the living room, absently flicking through a folder with the sketches he'd made over the past years, some of them from before, but most of them after his father's death. He didn't think he needed them all. He'd lit a fire in the hearth – something Ortus would have done with a mere thought and a wave of his hand – and now he had to decide which of the drawings he'd keep and which he'd add to the flames.

He picked out two of his mother, comparing them. One had been done a few months before her death, when he'd been young and his hand untrained for the task of setting her likeness down on paper. The other he'd done in his travels when he'd tried to remember her pale blue eyes and the copper hair only a few shades lighter than his own. Pain rippled through him, and he set them both aside. Then, he took up one of his father. He'd captured the old man's toothy grin and the crow's feet that framed his eyes whenever he smiled.

There were drawings of tadpoles, frogs, and mongrels he'd done the previous summer, a lot of them keepers, and one of a firefly that was so smudged he tossed it in the flames without giving it another thought. A quick study of the ruins of the old Tierney castle held his attention for a moment, evoking memories of walls crumbling into the landscape and the mysterious mosaic on the floor of the hidden chamber. And, of Catherine. Beautiful, perfect, broken Catherine. She'd never wanted him to draw her, but he had, one day, when she'd been dozing beside him on the river bank. He fingered the parchment with the rendering and knew he hadn't done her justice.

A timid knock on the front door interrupted his thoughts. Assuming the new owner was a bit early, he walked to the entry and opened it.

To his surprise, he found the widowed alewife there in the dark. The old woman who ran the tavern on the other end of the village hadn't brought a lantern and stood in a thick flurry of snowflakes next to a skinny girl about his own age and height. The girl was shivering. Her miserable shawl offered next to no protection against the weather.

He stepped aside for the two right away, motioning them to come in. "Missus Brewster, what are you doing out in this weather?"

"Dean, I'm sorry to come at such an hour, but it's urgent we speak with you."

"Sit by the fire and warm yourselves," he told them, leading the way.

He set about pouring tea from the pot he'd just made for himself, and handed the steaming cups to the frozen women.

"What's going on?" He could guess already, but he hoped it wasn't what he suspected.

Missus Brewster blew on her hot drink, wrapping her hands around her cup. "Margarete here needs help."

Dean licked his lips, his mouth had suddenly gone dry. Was she asking him to take in a refugee? He could barely take care of himself, let alone a hunted Cine. His eyes wandered back and forth between the old and the young woman, and he noted how uncomfortable the girl was.

"I'm not my father, Missus Brewster. I don't know how *I* could help her." The girl was now on the verge of tears. He almost expected her to jump up and run to the door before he'd finished speaking.

The alewife huffed impatiently, rising. She set her cup down on the mantelpiece and took his hands in her own, like she'd done when he was small. He felt like a sulky little boy again.

"Of course you do, lad. You've been hiding in this old house and God knows where else for too long now. What would your father say to that? It's time you got back to your people, my boy, time you took your place like he wanted you to. Step up to your responsibility, Dean."

"But Missus Brewster, I–"

"No *buts*, Master Greenleaf." The old woman adjusted her shawl over her head and walked away from him, motioning the girl to remain there with him. "The steward from Pinebach is on his way here with a warrant for Margarete," she said, not looking back at him. "He'll be here tomorrow. Take her with you when you leave." With that, she slipped out of the door, closing it firmly behind her.

Dean gaped at the girl left in his care. She'd already pulled her gloves back on, but she was shivering harder than before even with the hot tea inside of her.

"I can find some other place to be," she told him. "I don't want to be a bother to you."

She'd walked almost back to the door before he stopped her, putting himself in her way. "No, don't. Look, you can stay here tonight, and we'll leave before the first light in the morning. I'll take you to The Fair."

She eyed him skeptically. Some of the color had returned to her pale cheeks, and he saw that her hair was drying to a soft shade of gold. He was pretty sure there wouldn't be any silver in her eyes, though, because he couldn't *feel* it, and he wondered about that. She didn't have any traveling clothes with her, but he'd hardly be able to take anything with him if his horse had to carry the both of them. It was more than a week's ride to The Fair as it was, the snow would slow them down, and he'd have to buy lodgings and provisions for two now.

"Are you sure?" she asked.

He nodded, barely able to hide his frustration. Whatever had the old woman been thinking?

"Have you eaten yet?" he asked her, trying to sound pleasant.

She shook her head and he threw her an apple. She caught it easily and returned to the hearth with him.

"Did you do these?" she asked, watching him riffle through the remaining drawings scattered about the table. She refrained from touching any of the parchments, but studied the sketches closely. There was genuine admiration in her mien, and it softened the lump that had formed in his stomach, somewhat.

"Yes." His gaze caught on a drawing he'd done in a field where Catherine had gathered poppy seeds for Rebecca one day. They eased pain, and he'd loved the color of the petals that cupped them, swaying in the breeze on long stems. He'd wished he had oil paints to capture the magic of that particular summer's day, but all he'd had was his quill and the last of his ink.

"They're beautiful," Margarete said.

Smiling, he reached down at one parchment, plucking one of the poppies straight from the page. Margarete gasped as the flower, all black lines, floated in the air before her eyes, slowly turning. Bright orange-red began to bleed into its petals as the stem and leaves greened and a faint fragrance filled the air. She reached for it, and it vanished as her fingers brushed the illusion.

Dean could see fear and uncertainty warring with hope in her brown eyes, and he was startled to realize that the hope was placed completely in his hands.

"You're not Cine," he said quietly. "Why do you think they mean to harm you?"

"My mother was Cine. I take after my father."

"Where are your parents?"

"Dead." She kept her composure, but a single tear slipped over her cheek.

"I'm sorry," he whispered.

"My father was a thatcher. He fell off our own roof and died of his injuries a few years ago. Mother was a midwife. She had a way with bringing babies into the world, even though I was the only one she ever delivered of herself."

Midwives were always targets, as well Dean knew.

"Last month, the smith called on her," Margarete continued. "He said his wife had gone into labor and was having trouble. She was late, you see, so we went with him. His wife was in her pains all night and into the next day, and the baby wouldn't come. It was breach. Mother was going to lose both of them, and Maddie kept fainting, she was so weak." Margarete was trembling and he held out his a hand. She accepted it. Her fingers felt gentle, and he liked being able to offer her a measure of comfort.

"She sent Samuel out to fetch water, to get him out of the house. Then, she used her Talent to turn the child. It took quite a bit of time and Samuel came back before she was finished. He dropped the pail when he saw my mother standing over his wife with her hands stretched out, willing the baby to get into place, and he just started screaming at her to get away from Maddie. He grabbed her and hit her and pushed her out of the door. Maddie and the baby died."

She paused, and Dean looked at his feet for fear of intruding on Margarete's sorrow as she searched for the words to go on. All he could do was hold her hand.

"He went to the steward, didn't he?"

She nodded. "Yes. He accused my mother of being a witch. He said he had caught her cursing the baby. She was tortured, but she didn't confess, and she was sentenced to be burned alive."

Margarete was sobbing outright now, and Dean instinctively drew her to him, cradling her head on his shoulder as she gave into her grief.

"Were you there?" he asked, hoping she hadn't been.

"No." She shuddered, and he wrapped his arms around her tighter. "She knew they'd be after me next. *Blood is blood* they say in my village. She told me to come here, and to find the tavern and ask for help. It took me a week to make the trip through the woods, but when I got here, the heralds had already posted the accusations against me."

For the first time in his life, Dean understood what his father had tasked him with. This girl had no Talent of her own, but she was one of *his* people just the same. Blood *was* blood, no matter how you looked at it, and Cine blood flowed through her veins as it did through his. She was fragile and alone in the world, but he had the power to change that.

"Well, you don't have to be afraid anymore," he told her. "You'll be safe at The Fair, I promise."

They'd both be safe there. It was where they belonged. He hadn't known what direction to take when he'd awoken that morning in a bed too small for him, but he knew now. The legacy his father had left him was one he had to choose, but if he didn't choose it, he knew he'd spend the rest of his life wondering what would have been different if he had. He'd make a home for the fragile woman who dared to believe in him at The Fair, and he'd show Ortus he'd live up to and beyond his expectations all on his own, even without Lorcan. With all three of his grandfather's books, he wouldn't need Lorcan. He wouldn't need anyone, really.

Chapter Fourteen

❧ The Woods ☙

Leaving the cottage behind was leaving behind all of what she no longer had a need for. To her own astonishment, Catherine felt liberated. She'd been waiting for an onset of some form of remorse in the wake of what she'd done, but she didn't feel that proverbial weight of her own actions upon her shoulders. The adrenalin prevented it, and as she made her way through the forest in direction of the Trading Road, she discovered there wasn't an ounce of guilt on her shoulders or anywhere else for that matter.

She didn't perceive the chill of the cool night air, and everything seemed eons away from her as soon as she'd gotten out of the smoke. It was like she was stepping out of her own skin and into a new age. Perhaps she should have been frightened, but she wasn't.

The coming days were going to be tough because she had taken nothing from the house. She had nothing but the clothes on her back, but it didn't matter. She'd get by. She always had before.

Rebecca had betrayed her in more ways than her dimwitted father had because she'd been the clever one of the two, so Catherine didn't want any of her aunt's belongings anyway. They'd only have reminded her how she'd let someone take control of her life a second time after she'd already allowed Cooper to violate and deceive her. That would never happen again. *Never.*

A full moon bathed the forest in a silvery light, and the ground started cooling, making a haze rise just above the earth.

The old Trading Road led through several villages and towns from east to northwest, and she reckoned it would be as good a place as any to start putting some miles between her and the Inquisitor – and the local punters, when they discovered what remained of the cottage. She wasn't sure what they'd still find in the remains of the house when the flames had finished gorging themselves on the treat she'd given them.

The drunks who bought their poteen from Rebecca might think to inform the lord's steward, and he might ride out to take a look at the ashes at some point. He might even find the bones of two people in there somewhere. A pine wood fire didn't get all that hot, even if it was born from anger. Bones were harder to burn than flesh, and with any luck, he wouldn't know they were those of a man and a woman instead of those of two women. He'd inform the cleric that Rebecca Moore and her niece, Catherine Salt, had perished so the good Father could make a note of this in his church register. Trust a cleric to keep count.

If that went as she hoped it would, she'd be off the hook. Unless, of course, someone else had knowledge of Caleb's intention to come and see them. She had no way of finding out whether or not someone did, but it was a gap she had no means of bridging.

A whole new life lay ahead nonetheless. If she could put a fair distance between herself and her old one fast enough, it was hers for the taking, she was sure.

The only loose end she really wanted to tie up before she left the area for good was fetching the book she hadn't yet managed to retrieve from the castle. It was quite safe there, and she didn't think any ordinary soul could extract it from its hiding place, but she wanted it back all the same. She wanted it with her.

The two books she'd found in the ruins were the only things of real value she'd ever possessed. With one of them gone because of her own stupidity, she was left with only half of what she'd started out with as it was. She couldn't lose that, too. Going back for it was a risk she'd have to live with.

The detour to the decaying stronghold would take her well out of her way. The Trading Road bypassed the nameless village to the west of the castle. She didn't want to leave the cover of the forest for too long, so giving the settlement and the sprinkled homesteads around it a wide berth meant walking three or four days in the wrong direction. She'd have to face another week's march northwest to meet up with the road again after she had the book.

It would be worthwhile, though. There were some other things in the chest and the hidden chamber she wanted besides. The dagger, for one thing. She was a woman journeying alone, and it would definitely be a good traveling companion. The blanket she'd brought down to the hidden chamber would keep her warm at night, if it was still useable, and she'd be glad to have the candle stumps for light at night if the mice had left them alone.

She also recalled a few bits of plunder she might be able to trade or turn to currency. She'd need some funds to get her started off on the long road toward the coast and the harbor town of Saint Aeden that lay at its end.

The strange ivory figurines Dean had admired because they reminded him of something or other of his father's would fetch a few days' worth of bread and some fruit. And, there was a ring she could sell very judiciously, as well as a few coins she'd never touched. She'd meant to save them for a time like this, and she was glad she had. A year had passed, and she hoped everything was still where she'd left it.

Saint Aeden was the place for her, she told herself as she walked. She tried to imagine what it was like by recalling what Cooper had told her about the growing town on the coast. He'd boasted having done business there as a young man. With all the revelry he lost himself to describing the markets and alehouses, she doubted he'd have left if he'd been successful.

Apparently, he'd tried to sell winter-hard fruit tree seedlings to one of the merchants shipping supplies to the Tribelands. The merchant, he'd told Catherine, had ordered a hundred trees, but the trees hadn't outlasted the journey, and neither had the profits Cooper had made.

He'd spent a good week in the town centered around the busy port that harbored up to five big trade ships on one day. They took goods from all over the lands across the ocean to the new settlements in the Western Tribelands and to Sutrailia, and brought exotic spices, strange vegetables, and even animals back with them. Some of them were rumored to return with their hulls filled with gold and silver.

Over the last few decades, old Cooper had told her while on a roll, some of those ships had started taking more passengers to the Tribelands than they had goods aboard, and they came back with hard timbers that made good material for construction rather than sail empty.

Whalers and fishers also earned a good living in Saint Aeden. Craftsmen's guilds like boatbuilders, smiths, and weavers thrived. Carpenters, soapmakers, and even a women's cooperation of seamstresses had established their businesses on the outskirts of town.

Cooper had assured her anyone prepared to work hard could become rich there. She'd never wondered why he hadn't. The man had been all talk, and his only real ability had been raping little girls.

Whatever.

That was behind her now.

She was convinced Saint Aeden was *the* place to start over. Making her way toward the Trading Route, she dreamt of the ocean and of the interesting things she'd see along her way, dreamt of Dean and meeting him somewhere between here and there, how he'd smile at her and tell her he'd missed her. She'd smile right back and make sure to kiss him properly then.

She was smart, and she knew she'd survive, no matter what. She just had to keep putting one foot in front of the other, and if she got to the castle, she'd also get to Saint Aeden. She'd think about what she was going to do there when the time came.

Chapter Fifteen

ଔ Betrayal ଥ

Drenched to the bone, Catherine scurried through the hole in the wall where the gate to the inner courtyard had once stood. It always seemed to be pouring when she came to the castle after a longer absence, as though the old stronghold bore grudges against those who went back on their promises. She'd never been away for as long as this since she'd started coming here.

Dean was nowhere to be seen. She didn't know how she could have hoped to find him here. Some small part of her wanted him to appear from behind one of the buildings. She'd pictured him staring at her in disbelief, overjoyed at her arrival, and she'd run to him, wrap her arms around him and kiss him. She'd kiss him properly, this time.

He'd tell her he'd been waiting for her because he'd always known she'd return. But, she'd given him no reason to believe that, had she?

Storms, the weight of heavy snowfall and ice in the crevices between the loose stones had shared the task of toppling one of the towers beside the keep over the winter. Her heart sank as she searched for the Great Hall's main entrance in the wreckage, hoping it hadn't been completely buried beneath the broken limestone blocks.

Scaling the mountain of rubble, she found an opening near the top of the doorway that was wide enough to let her in once she'd cleared away some of the crumbly debris. She slipped through, belly down and feet first, without giving it a second thought until she started skidding out of control when she lost her hold and the sandstone turned to dust beneath her hands. It happened so fast, she didn't have time to panic.

Winded and dazed, she landed on the other side, grazing her knees and elbows but otherwise unhurt. It was darker in the crypt-like cavern than she remembered it, and warmer than it should have been. Mold and the sickeningly sweet smell of Death wafted toward her; faint, but unmistakable.

All at once, her chest closed up, and her skin was crawling. A whimper escaped her before she could swallow it. What if it was Dean?

Powerless against herself, she searched the darkness, beating at her wet clothes with hands that felt sticky, trying to brush any number of writhing, squirming little bodies off of her dress, her hair, her face before…

… before they began burrowing.

A few of them got in her nose and mouth, spreading the syrupy taste of honey, and her stomach heaved. Unable to breathe, she gagged until she had nothing left.

The thought of finding Dean's remains and being trapped here if the building started falling down overwhelmed her. She wanted to climb back out the way she'd come and run, but blind terror's ineptness defeated any attempt to clamber up to the waning patch of daylight seven feet above her.

She'd clawed at the wooden board over the hole in her father's house until her fingers had bled. She'd scraped them to the bone, making deep, crimson tracks like miniature hollow ways in the forest, and still the maggots had crawled and wiggled and writhed...

She dug and pulled and beat at the rubble blocking the door, and still...

... still the worms burrowed.

She could hear them feeding on her.

Finally, with nightfall came something bordering on sanity. The moon stood high in the sky, unobscured by the thick clouds that had been hiding the sun all day.

She forced herself to listen for the sound of her heartbeat. She couldn't hear it, at first. It wasn't beating, following the steady rhythm of a drum; it was roaring like an angry waterfall. She ordered it to calm, taking even breaths, and *commanded* it to obey her and slow its pounding against her aching chest. By the time it did, her eyes had already adapted to the gloom.

She made herself look at her hands and down the front of her dress. There was nothing there but dust and dirt.

Swiftly scanning the hall, she found Death lurking in a corner to her right, where a small corpse lay decomposing.

A wave of relief washed over her when she discovered it to be the body of a child, not that of a nearly grown man. She couldn't tell in this light whether it was a boy or a girl, but its life had expired not much older in years than she'd been when she'd first come here. The little one had probably been shut in when the tower had collapsed, and perhaps it had been hurt, or simply not strong enough to climb out.

Briefly wondering if the child had been one of her kind, *or even the other Catherine*, she asked herself if the fortress had revealed its past to the *bairn* as it had to her, but then she told herself to stop being stupid.

The other Catherine would be older now, if she'd ever existed, and she hadn't come this far to mourn a stray dumb enough to have gotten itself buried alive, or to lose herself in recollections and silly dreams. Better the child than her. She had to get a move on. Playtime was over. She wanted what was in that chest, and that was all. The chest was the only thing *real* about this place now, and its contents would help her survive in the *real* world.

Her feet instinctively found the way to the stairs.

She'd left some candle stumps in the nook next to the bottom treads just over a year ago, and she began feeling around inside. Her fingers found nothing but cobwebs and dust.

Perhaps the child had ventured down here and taken them and the blanket to have a little light and warmth in its final hours. She would have done the same. *So what?* She'd expected this, and she tried to stay optimistic. The candles would have been half-eaten by mice or some other vermin now anyway, and the blanket rotten.

Envisioning the torches mounted on the walls when her ancestors had lived here, she made them appear. Golden light bathed the chamber in shadows, and she could see as much as she needed to.

She stopped half way across the mosaic floor to the wall that held the chest. Her eyes caught on the letters that spelled her name. One day, the ceiling of this room would collapse, and it would be buried here. Perhaps that day had come. She'd be buried here along with it, and no one would ever know, just as no one knew of the child that had died upstairs. She had to make herself look away and refocus, concentrate on what was important and what was real. The sooner she did, the sooner she'd be out of here. Moping or getting angry over things you couldn't change wasn't going to help her.

Continuing on toward the far end of the room, she located the stone that stood out from the others. Not hesitating any further, she opened the hidey hole where the chest was stored and pulled it out. At first, everything seemed as it should be. The dresses were still there, the dagger, and the rings and other miscellaneous odds and ends.

Oddly, her locket was, too.

The book wasn't.

She yanked one piece of clothing and keepsake after the other out of the chest, not caring where she tossed the remnants of someone else's life. A strange heat took possession of her even as she did this, seconds before she had to admit to herself that the book was really not there. Her own helplessness spilled over into a howl of anger that echoed through the structure only to die unheard as the torches flared up intensely for an instant and then vanished.

In the profound darkness and the silence that ensued, sanity slowly returned.

The child.

She felt her way to the stairs and scampered upward to the ground floor on all fours. On her knees, she examined the body of the waif and the immediate area where it lay, reckless and ignorant of both the smell and the insects that were still feasting on what remained of the fouling flesh cocooned within the stinking, flaking shell of Catherine's old blanket.

Nothing.

Not even a burned-down candle stump.

She searched and searched.

Nothing but the bones of a dead rat, gravel, stones, feathers, pieces of wood, dead leaves, the rusty bowl of a spoon and some clay shards in the dirt.

Where was it?

She searched again.

Who would have suspected its existence?

Who would have known where to look?

Who... but Dean?

That was the only possible explanation. She'd brought him to this place. She'd shown him how to open the niche. He'd been her best – and her *only* – friend. And, he'd betrayed her.

Just like Cooper had. Only worse.

The book hadn't been his to take. He had no right to it.

Maybe he'd taken it because he'd thought she was dead, but she didn't think he could have heard of the fire yet. That, and he couldn't have been here anytime recently, or he'd have cleared the doorway to the keep at least a little way. No. He'd been here before the tower had collapsed, and that meant he'd taken that book without knowing if she was coming back for it or not.

He'd *said* he was her friend and she'd believed him.

Oh, how she'd *wanted* to believe him.

By the look of things, he'd stolen her book nonetheless, and she had no way of finding out where he was to get it back.

Dean was gone, and Cooper was dead.

She'd never get the only inheritance back *Catherine* had left her. The books were gone, and so was their magic.

The keep would collapse, and in a few years, there would be nothing left of the castle, nothing left of *her*. Not unless she began looking out for her interests more determinedly. She vowed then and there she'd make sure no one got the better of her ever again. She wasn't weak, and she wasn't stupid or defenseless. She wasn't *the other Catherine*.

There had to be a way to stop herself from being buried alive, and she'd find it.

She needed to get out of this tomb. She didn't want to sleep here. There would be some other dry place to hang her clothes and spend the night.

She returned to the lower chamber, imagined the torches into being again, and chose two of the dresses. She bundled them up so she could carry them more easily. They were frilled, fancy and far too big for her. Sneezing, she also realized how much dust the ancient pieces had gathered despite having been stored in the chest, but they'd keep her warmer tonight than she had been over the last few nights. Becoming ill wasn't an option.

She donned the locket and picked up the dagger, the ring, and the four small coins, but decided to leave the rest. Some of the ivory figures Dean had been mooning over had chipped when she'd smashed them to the floor, and there was only so much she could take with her.

The coins looked as though they'd buy a new blanket and tide her over for a while. The ring was something to be saved for emergencies. She tore a long, wide strip of fabric off of one of the other more delicate dresses that lay at her feet and folded it carefully around the coins. She'd tie it around her middle beneath her bodice in the morning like a bandage. If she could get hold of a needle and thread one of these days, she'd sew it to her underwear. No one would notice it there.

The dagger would call for another solution. She needed it where she could get at it quickly, but she didn't have any ideas for that yet. Ascending the disintegrating staircase, she was sure she'd think of something. She always did.

Chapter Sixteen

❦ Alone ❧

"Well, what have we got here?" she heard a man's voice saying, and she was awake and on her feet in an instant.

The vagrant revealed his foul teeth in a crooked smile. He was a mere ten paces away, and she realized just how careless she'd been in choosing her sleeping-place. She'd been ill the previous night and tired because of it. The long march and the driving rain had finally taken their toll.

Several more men came into sight farther back between the trees, obviously traveling companions of the first. They'd already spread out and were steadily closing in on her like a pack of grinning wolves slinking around their prey. She counted three and hoped she hadn't missed anyone.

The woods had always provided for Catherine. She knew her way around; knew what was edible and how to find water, and she knew how and where to make a safe place to rest for the night. She'd never been caught off her guard like this before. There was nowhere to go on the steep, slippery slope. It was four against one, and her rattling cough would leave her short of breath if she tried to run for it. She'd be far too slow because the raggedy drifter was close enough for her to smell the sour odor of sweat that clung to his filthy clothes.

Over the years, she'd learned that the best line of defense was attack, but she didn't want the man to guess she could take care of herself. She backed away until she felt the rough bark of a basswood tree against her shoulders, doing her best to look terrified.

He read panic into her retreat and lunged at her, but before he'd even gotten a firm hold of her, she drew her dagger from its scabbard and drove the blade into his abdomen. With one swift motion, she pulled the knife upward, twisting it as the cold metal sliced through fabric and flesh, and she watched his eyes widen in an almost comical mixture of shock and admiration. He didn't scream when she pushed him over.

Falling heavily on his side, he clutched at the fatal wound, but he couldn't stop the gush of warm blood, and it soaked straight into the dead leaves and soil beneath him. Catherine absently wiped her hands on the skirt of her dress.

Her assailant's buddies raced toward her, but instead of trying to run away, she made straight for the youngest of them coming at her from the left, a little downhill from where she was. He was a year or two her junior, and she found her way into his mind more easily than she would have thought. There wasn't much to keep her out, and she could feel the adrenalin pumping through his veins. Tiny red spots appeared before his eyes, and she didn't have to waste time going any further. The distraction was enough to make him stumble, and he lurched forward, straight into Catherine's dagger. She'd aimed for his jugular, and the blade cut through the tender skin of his neck like butter. He made gurgling sounds as he rigidly collapsed on the ground.

She didn't stop to find out what the others were doing and kept running downhill, sliding and nearly losing her balance with next to no breath left in her lungs. Risking a glance when she was back on the gravel bank of the river she'd been following, she noticed they weren't giving chase.

Four or five more people had arrived to the slope, men and women. Some carried bows, and some were armed with swords. It took her a moment to establish that two more dead bodies lay on the ground.

"Ye're alright," one of the women called down, her voice thick with an accent Catherine couldn't place. "They won't be botherin' no one again, these lads."

Her instincts told her to keep going, but her ribs hurt, and she didn't think she'd get very far. Not with the archer peering at her, an arrow at the ready.

"I haven't got anything of value," she called up, gulping for air, while keeping an eye on the bowman. "You can have whatever you find up where I slept."

"We've no interest in some moth-eaten ol' horse blanket and a firestone." The woman laughed. The sound of her voice echoed fearlessly through the narrow funnel valley. "I've no idea where ye stole those, but I do like the spunk o' ye. I'm comin' down, so put that knife away, luv."

She didn't, of course. Gripping the bloody dagger tightly in her hand, she waited. Beads of sweat trickled from her forehead, and she felt the chill of a passing fever, but she ordered herself to get a grip.

The woman descending toward the river bank was unarmed. Her friends kept their distance. Catherine felt their eyes on her.

"I'd really appreciate ye cleanin' that thing and puttin' it away," the woman repeated when she'd reached the riverside, straightening her dress. She motioned at Catherine's arm, where Catherine had tied the leather sheath to her upper sleeve. It was hidden beneath her cloak, but the woman was a keen observer. "Clever idea with yer wee scabbard, by the way. I like it."

Catherine thought the blonde might be in her thirties, and she had the look of someone to whom appearances had some importance. The traveling dress she wore was simple but elegant, and her long hair was plaited to a loose braid. The fragrance of scented soap carried on the breeze. Costly leather footwear peeked forth beneath the hem of her skirt. The only odd thing about her was the small yellow square of cloth tied to the laces on one of her expensive shoes. Catherine realized she was talking to a whore.

"I'd appreciate it if your friends put away their weapons."

The woman gave her companions a wave, and they did as they were told.

Bending a little toward Catherine, she smiled. "They're not actually me friends. We pay 'em to look after us a bit."

Catherine turned and hunkered down by the water to clean the drying blood off the blade and off her hands. "Who's *we*?" she probed, thinking she might be wrong.

"Me girls and meself." The harlot crouched down beside Catherine to wash her hands. "Those fellas that were givin' ye trouble? They were slinkin' around our camp last night, wantin' services for free, but we don't do free, and our boys sent them packin'. Ye did well protectin' yerself. I'd never have expected it of ye."

"They would have killed me," Catherine stated.

"O' course they would've. Ye had no choice. Very impressive how ye handled it."

"Thank you... for dealing with the other two." Catherine dried the dagger on her skirt and returned it to its sheath.

"Ye're most welcome."

Both women rose.

"Ye know, these is dangerous times. Especially for a woman travelin' alone, what with all the robbers and the thieves and the Cine runnin' round free. There's been sightings of werewolves in these parts recently." She paused, studying Catherine's face to see if she was hitting a nerve before continuing. "Even if a woman does happen to be good with a knife, she has to sleep *some* time or other. There's no tellin' what would've happened if we hadn't come by. Where is it ye're goin'?"

Catherine wasn't inclined to share on that. "Look, I'm grateful for what you did. I really am."

Again, she decided she had nothing to lose. She began walking away from the other woman, writing off the blanket and the firestone she'd taken from a farmer's cart while he was relieving himself behind a bush. She thought she had to be nearing Leignsbridge now, and she'd trade one of the coins from the chest for replacement.

"I didn't mean to pry," the whore said to her back. "I was rather thinkin' ye might like to travel a ways with us if we're going in the same direction. We've got a wagon, and we're headin' for Saint Aeden."

Catherine stopped. She wasn't used to company and she wasn't sure she wanted any, but that *did* sound appealing.

Chapter Seventeen

❧ The Harlots ❧

Nine very young women were traveling to Saint Aeden in all, every one of them fitted with a similar square of yellow cloth their leader had tied to her footwear. Catherine wasn't surprised to find two girls even younger than herself amongst them.

Deirdre, the woman who'd undisputedly saved her life in the woods, told her she could walk with them for as far and as long as she liked. What she couldn't do was share their meals, unless she paid for them. Catherine thought she could live with that.

The *wagon* the older woman had boasted about turned out to be a cart unworthy of the name. An ancient mule pulled it over the muddy roads. It was laden with tents and a dilapidated store of supplies. They'd make halt to restock those in Leignsbridge, Deirdre informed her, and then they'd go northwest from there in a few days.

Three armed men walked with them. One of them led the mule. They talked to the girls and jested with them, and the girls seemed very much at ease. Catherine wasn't. She felt the archer's eyes on her, and a mousy waif of twelve or thirteen avoided looking at any of them. She didn't speak the whole way to Leignsbridge.

Midday had come and gone by the time they reached the town. They stopped and unloaded the cart on a small field almost a quarter of a mile from the bridge and the town center. Catherine wondered why, but Deirdre told her to stay with the others while she went to speak to the town officials.

She was expected to help set them up while Deirdre was away. She did so without complaining, taking note of the good quality of the tents they quickly put together and the soft blankets each girl had to herself. There were more blankets on the cart than they'd need, but Catherine wasn't sure if she'd be allowed to take one for the night.

A dark-haired girl named Bridget with perfect teeth and a winning smile answered that question for her by handing her one of her own.

"You'll have to share a tent with Amber." She pointed at the little mouse. "She's new, too. Brendan and Saul were supposed to break her in last night, but she screamed like a stuck pig before Brendan even got started, despite the tea Deirdre gave her. Deirdre said she'd leave her by the roadside if she ever did that again. She'll frighten away the callers. She's to have a night's rest and think about it. She doesn't get to eat until she decides to start working, though."

Brendan was the archer. Saul was the swordsman. Catherine hated them both.

Deirdre returned with some eggs and a bag of red kerchiefs, one for each of them. "Not getting into town tonight, ladies. Silly me forgot that it's Sunday today, an' none o' yez reminded me either. I was lucky they didn't chase me off. But, I did get the eggs, and the new colors."

She handed out the kerchiefs. "For the hair. Pretty, eh?"

Most of the girls burst out laughing as they inspected their new *accessories*, trying on the latest fashion as they imagined an elegant lady of standing would do when she got excited over the newest addition to her wardrobe.

Amber just stared at hers, and Catherine chewed on her lower lip, trying to come to some conclusion about the invitation Deirdre had just extended.

"Do yerselves a favor," Deirdre told them, her tone harsh when she became aware of their lack of enthusiasm. "Wear 'em. Them's the colors here. Ye'll be dragged off if yez don't."

Back in the nameless village, no one would have enforced a law that stated how a whore was to identify herself in public. The alehouse generally had a girl for the backroom, but Catherine had never seen her wearing the yellow band in her hair that was mandatory there when she was out and about.

Yellow or red, in her hair, around her arm, on her shoes – it was all the same to her. If she put it on, she was a whore. Then again, she'd been one for years without wearing a colored band or kerchief anywhere on her, and it couldn't get much worse than Cooper.

Reluctantly, with all eyes on her and Amber, Catherine complied. It was official. Defeat rimmed the little mouse's eyes, and she followed Catherine's example.

After she'd given the eggs to Bridget to cook, Deirdre took Catherine aside. "Ye don't have to do anything ye don't want to, luv. No one 'ere does. Me offer stands. Ye get to travel with us for free, no matter what ye decide. The kerchief is for yer own protection. As long as ye're wearin' it, ye're with us, and no one can touch ye unless ye want them to. The townsmen here are obliged to pay for our services, and they're much nicer to the girls they pay than the ones they rape."

That made sense to Catherine, on some level. Cooper had tried to be nice to her, at times, but he'd never quite managed it. She wondered how other men would treat her, and how they'd want it from her, because she'd already made up her mind there was money to be made. Once they got to Saint Aeden, she could always take the kerchief off, but this was going to get her a decent start there.

"I usually pay our taxes in advance in the towns we pass through on our way to Saint Aeden. That means, we can set up shop for a few days here. Should make enough to tide us over till we get to Ironstone," Deirdre continued.

"We'll only be allowed into Leignsbridge tomorrow. Sundays are off limits in most towns cuz it's the Lord's Day. Wouldn't want the likes of us turnin' a man's head before he goes to Holy Communion now, would they?"

Deirdre grinned at Catherine. Catherine didn't believe most men would care what day of the week it was when the market came to town.

"Sunday or not, the first clients will be around before dark," Deirdre confirmed. "They always are. They look, and if they're willin' to buy, then it's up to ye to decide whether ye'll take a fella or not. By the king's law, ye have to take any man askin' for ye. By *my* law, ye decide for yerself. When ye have, ye get him to show ye what he's got so ye can see if he's got any disease on him. Send him away if he does. Ye can't sell if ye smell, I always say, and life's short as it is. Our boys'll look out for ye and make sure nothin' gets outa hand."

Catherine thought that sounded feasible. "What do I earn?"

Deirdre looked almost excited. "Ye get what every fifth man is willin' to give, and the rest is mine. I pay our travelin' expenses, I pay the boys for their help, and I pay for our food. You pay for a tent and for the blankets. When we get to Saint Aeden, I'll make arrangements with the brothel keepers and the hangman for everyone here. Most people in Saint Aeden are rich. The men there'll pay double and three times whatcha can earn out here." She looked around disdainfully and then back at Catherine, smiling. "A girl as sweet as yerself'll be rich in a year, too."

Catherine seriously doubted it. She wasn't stupid. "I get what every *third* man pays, and *you* get to keep the tent and the blankets after we get to Saint Aeden."

Deirdre's eyebrows arched right up to the hairline, and the creases on her forehead looked as though they might leave wrinkles.

"Well, I'll be darned. Ye've got spunk – I like that." She paused and let it sit with her for a moment until she'd arrived at what she obviously thought would be a good compromise. "Tell ye what I'll do: I'll give ye what every *fourth* man is willin' to spend on ye, if ye're willin' to do special jobs."

"Special jobs?" Catherine could have bitten her tongue for asking. She had a pretty good idea already.

Deirdre sighed. "I take it ye're not about to spread yer legs for the first time, luv. I have no idea what yer experience is. Maybe ye had the neighbor's boy out in the barn, or it was the other way around, and *he* had *ye* there. Or yer daddy did, or some other man that promised ye somethin' pretty in return."

Catherine held her gaze. She wasn't about to pour her heart out. It was no one's business but her own.

Deirdre's eyes narrowed. "Whatever. Ye'll have been lying on yer back when the neighbor or yer daddy forced himself on ye. That's all a lot of men know. But, some of our clients have... *other* needs," she explained. "They'll want ye to be nice to them in other ways."

Men had a lot of needs, it seemed to Catherine. Most of those needs had nothing to do with *nice*, and they involved hurting people – some more, some less, in the beginning. But, the needs you could satisfy below the waistline didn't get you killed, or permanently maimed. Pleasuring a man wouldn't make her feel half as empty as she'd felt when she'd discovered her book was missing.

It was all a means to an end, and nothing lasted forever. At least, Cooper hadn't, she thought wryly. The recollection of how she'd repaid him for what he'd taught her almost made her laugh, but she realized how inappropriate that might have struck Deirdre.

"There'll be men that'll want ye to suck their soldier," the whore went on, watching Catherine for a reaction. "But, remember, ye don't have to swallow the seed. That would be a sin."

Catherine wasn't even impressed. Cooper had loved to sin.

"There's men who'll want to use ye from behind, and that's a sin, too, but ye can say ten Hail Marys and an Our Father right after cuz it costs double, so it's very worthwhile."

She still wasn't shocked. She'd never said a Hail Mary in her life, and neither had Cooper, she was sure.

"It'll have to count double, too," she returned. "What else?"

Deirdre had a whole list of more sins that would have made the old farmer's eyes water, but Catherine kept her thoughts to herself.

The two women were done haggling over the terms of their agreement before the eggs were cooked, and Deirdre handed one to Catherine while Amber looked on hungrily.

"Welcome to the troupe."

Amber skulked away just after dark. Hardly anyone noticed. Of those who did, no one stopped her because, as predicted, the first clients began to arrive, and Catherine didn't give the girl another thought.

She had other concerns.

Chapter Eighteen

ଔ Leaving Leignsbridge ଚ

Leaving Leignsbridge on a sunny Thursday morning just as the town was beginning to stir, Catherine observed a burial east of the Trading Route and just outside of the regular graveyard. No clergyman was present, only the diggers. The two men tossed the small shrouded body they'd brought there on a barrow into the shallow pit and began covering it with earth just as the harlots passed.

Bridget nudged Catherine with her elbow. "Bright side? She won't have nothin' to fear no more."

Catherine frowned. She thought she might be a bit slow today because she didn't quite understand.

She'd been hurting most of the night and hadn't slept much. Her last caller had wanted *special*, and he'd wanted it several times over. He'd paid in advance. Looking back, she knew she should have turned him down. She'd seen it in his eyes. He'd been brutal, and she hadn't been at all in control of the situation and nearly panicked.

Having decided against calling for help nonetheless, she'd endured for as long as she could, but she'd finally had to do *something*. His sudden headache had made him feel nauseous, and he'd forgotten all about the other things he'd promised to do to her in the course of the night. Rolling over on his back, he'd moaned and pressed his hands to his temples. She'd been afraid she might have overdone it and lain there for a time, just waiting.

She was always afraid someone might suspect. How was it going to look if the men she serviced came out of her tent ill, or even feet first? There would be talk in either case, or worse. And, if she didn't perform, she didn't get paid. Simple as that.

"Who? Who are we talking about?"

"Amber," Bridget returned absently. "Deirdre says they found her floating in the river a bit downstream yesterday. She drowned herself."

That wasn't hard to believe. The way Amber had looked at Brendan and Saul had spoken volumes. Observing them, Catherine would have categorized both men as *pigs,* and she knew first-hand what it meant to have a pig between your legs when you were barely old enough to bleed. Amber hadn't been very strong. You had to be strong if you wanted to survive the pigs and all the other animals.

One of the men shoveling dirt on the little mouse's corpse was whistling a tune that seemed familiar, somehow. He reminded Catherine of her father, and she hastened to put Caleb out of her mind as quickly as he'd entered it.

Shrugging, she said, "She's better off like this."

Bridget nodded. "When I think of the troll *you* had last night on top of *her*, I'd say you're right. She'd have been just as dead, only she'd have gone out screamin', and put the rest of us out of work for the night."

Catherine didn't reply to that. An image of the waif in the hidden chamber at the castle crept through the door she'd left ajar in her mind after having evicted Caleb. The child suddenly had a face: Amber's.

Swathed in Catherine's old blanket, she'd lie there with maggots eating her corpse from the inside out. Catherine felt sick, but tried not to let on. Neither person had been nor was now any of her concern.

She wondered if Dean had known the girl at the castle. Perhaps the child had followed him there in the same way Laura had followed Catherine.

Who knew – if that tower had collapsed the winter before last, it might have been Laura in there instead of some orphan or bastard who'd been abandoned in the woods. Catherine would have more choices today than she did, but she couldn't say she regretted the outcome of what dear Laura had set in motion. Not all of it.

The Shearer girl had probably done her a favor because things were finally moving now. She was going places, and she was free of Cooper. No one would ever force her to do anything she didn't want again.

There was one thing gnawing at her day and night, though, but that had nothing to do with Laura or anyone else who'd obviously been out to make her life miserable. It was Dean. She'd never find him, or the book he'd stolen. Everything she'd truly cared for was gone, and she had no way of getting it back. Yet.

Dean's face haunted her mind, and a strange mixture of emotions filled her whenever she thought of him. Why couldn't he have been there waiting for her when she'd come for the book? Or why couldn't he have been the corpse in the corner? Then, at least, she'd know what had become of him, and she'd still have the book.

She'd dreamt of him that night. After the troll had left her, she'd even been too tired to go and wash. She hadn't moved except to reach for her blanket when he'd finally pulled up his pants and crawled out of her tent.

She remembered Deirdre looking in on her. The older woman had notched the tally stick Catherine kept by the flap, and she'd collected the money from the clay jar beside it. Catherine had turned on her side and pretended to be asleep. It was then she'd imagined seeing Dean.

He'd smiled at her sideways the way he'd often done, not knowing where she'd been or what she'd been up to before they met. She didn't think he would have guessed about her and Cooper. What would he have thought of her, had he known of the bargain she'd struck with the old farmer? It was all the same now, but it had mattered to her then. If she'd told anyone, she'd have worn that red – or yellow – kerchief a few years earlier, and although it hadn't mattered to her what people said, it would have mattered what Dean might have thought. Possibly he wouldn't have wanted to be around her.

He would have thought twice about trusting her with the knowledge that he, too, was a Cine, and he wouldn't have shown her his drawings. He certainly wouldn't have told her about his father or that crazy idea of his about bringing their people together someplace. Ridiculous, but that was sweet Dean. He was innocent in so many ways, she was certain, as opposed to her.

In her dream, she'd kissed him, on the mouth this time, and he'd kissed her back. She'd undressed him, and she'd made love to him lying beneath her, slowly, enjoying his hands on her skin. For the first time, she'd felt good moving with a man inside of her, almost magical, and she'd woken with her heart thumping in her throat. A second later, she'd realized she was lying in the sticky pool of another man's semen, and reality had hit her like a hammer to the skull.

"How long will it take us to get to Ironstone?" she asked Deirdre.

The older woman trailed along behind to accommodate the slower progress of the newest member of their caravan. A battered, puffy-eyed woman in her early twenties dragged her feet beside her. She'd been accused of infidelity and given ten lashes on the marketplace a few days earlier, despite being with child, and her husband had put her out on the street. Deirdre had already taken care of the baby growing in her womb.

"Another week to Ironstone," she answered, "and we might be taking a little detour along the way, but I'd say about six weeks in all."

Six weeks. She thought that was manageable.

Chapter Nineteen

↷ Going Places ↶

Ironstone was everything she'd hoped it would be. Deirdre had told her of the two marketplaces and the pretty alleyways in between, and of the palace on the hill.

No one at the Hay Market seemed to notice her walking from one trader to the next, inspecting the fine cloth on offer. Colored fabrics seemed to be more readily available here than in most other places she'd seen so far. There was wealth here. People held currency, and they could afford themselves the luxury of dyed and pattern-woven cloth. She could now, too, and she was determined to buy something good. She'd have to find a sewing woman to make a dress of it for her, though. The one talent she lacked was any ability to handle a needle.

A peddler selling cloth in the shade of green she liked best took notice of the yellow band in her hair. It was the whores' identification for Ironstone. She hated the looks it got her, and he obviously doubted that she could pay for the merchandise she was fondling. He raised an eyebrow at her in surprise when she asked him for the right length to provide for a woman of her size and build.

"How are you going to…?" he started saying, but a smile stopped his flow of words and softened his features when she absently held out what she deemed to be a fair amount of coins to him. "Never mind," he closed, and quickly got to work measuring and cutting the fabric.

She watched him bundle it, and then he handed it to her. "I think that'll make a fine garment."

"I'm sure it will." She held his gaze for a few moments, just long enough for him to give her back the coppers she'd paid, and for her to whisper into his mind what she wanted him to say so he'd believe it when she was gone.

"No charge. Beautiful women should have pretty things."

Seeing herself through his eyes, she thought a dress of this color would indeed be perfect on her. He kept right on smiling as she nodded a brief goodbye and turned to leave.

Clutching her bundle, she started to walk back the way she'd come when Deirdre grabbed her arm, hooking her own underneath. She acted as though Catherine was her best friend as she hurried her away.

"Beautiful, Catherine, I must say. Yer taste is absolutely unquestionable." She gripped her arm so firmly that it hurt as she steered her toward a quieter part of the market.

"Let go of me," Catherine hissed, trying to keep calm. "I can walk by myself…"

"No ye can't." The dangerous glint in Deirdre's eyes told her to shut up. "Ye're far from being able to walk alone, and I'm tellin' ye, I'm not lettin' ye out of my sight again anytime soon until ye've learned to behave yerself."

"What do you want from me?"

Catherine's voice was a pitch above where it should have been, and Deirdre's iron grasp tightened even further, nails digging into skin. She wasn't sure which part of her exchange with the merchant Deirdre had actually witnessed, but she had no intention of admitting to anything.

"I know *your* kind, dear." Deirdre marched her into one of the alleys where the stink of open sewer was so prominent, they were sure not to be disturbed. "I know what ye are. Ye're one of the Tainted."

Catherine didn't reply. Giving her one last shove, Deirdre let go of her. Huffing, the older woman straightened her dress and smoothed back a stray curl of hair from her brow. Catherine considered her options. She could run, but she wouldn't get very far if Deirdre decided to sound the alarm. Something told her that wasn't about to happen. Deirdre was smarter than that.

"So?"

"Ye may think ye're clever, but ye've got a lot to learn. I knew what ye was the moment I laid eyes on ye. I took ye in all the same cuz ye're a pretty face to look at and somethin' more, but I won't letcha ruin my business by givin' me a bad name, ye hear me?"

Catherine could see how upset she was. Red blotches had formed on her cheeks. She wondered if Deirdre had been watching her more intently than she'd thought, waiting to catch her red-handed. Did she know about how she'd manipulated some of her callers when they'd gotten too rough, or when she hadn't felt like pleasing the *pigs*?

"Ye and I both know ye stole that cloth, somehow. I seen how ye looked at that merchant, and I seen how he gave ye back yer money."

So there was no denying it. She still didn't feel like elaborating, but Deirdre was proving to be stubborn.

"Some o' yer people have a knack for manipulatin' what others see, I know that. A cousin o' mine was the half-bred bastard son of a witch, and he cheated at dice until they caught him. They always get caught sooner or later. Ye know what they did to him?"

Catherine could imagine, but she knew Deirdre was going to tell her anyway. Most people loved their stories of a good hanging, burning, or drowning, and they kept adding detail every time they told it.

Deirdre surprised her by not going there. Instead, she fixed her hands on her hips and looked at her feet.

"Now, I couldn't care less what they'd do to ye if ye were on yer own, but if *you* get caught, it'll fall back on *me*, and on all o' the girls travelin' with us. We'll all be questioned, and ye and I both know how that'll end. Do ye understand that?"

She did, oddly. She needed to be more careful. If Deirdre had been able to tell what she was doing, someone else might have, too. She wondered if any of the other girls knew. Not only would she have to be more careful, but she'd also have to put some thought into the new status quo. She didn't like the idea of *anyone* knowing about her Talent. It was plain dangerous. All of life was dangerous. She was putting her life at risk every day and every night, just like all the harlots were. But, Deirdre knowing about her wouldn't do. She'd have to give this some thought.

"What about this?" she asked, meaning the cloth.

Thinking about it, Deirdre wiped her lips on the back of her hand. "Keep it. Ye can hardly take it back, can ye? Buy more in red somewhere else and get one of the sewing women to do somethin' *really* good with it so I won't have to keep sendin' ye the pigs. Ye could do better than that. Eat once in a while. Ye never do, and ye're too boney. Ye won't last long like this. And, get one of the other girls to help ye with yer hair. It's too long. Ye're a mess."

That having been said, she turned and stomped off without glancing back.

When Catherine was done thinking, she went to buy the cloth and find a sewing woman. The rest was something to be tackled when the time came. She couldn't solve all of her problems at once.

On her way out of town, she took two wrong turns. Before she knew it, she found herself on the street below the palace walls. A small shop caught her attention because it had a display of goods set out on a table next to the door. Among the things on offer stood a set of wooden figures on a checkered board. She recognized the figures. They weren't the ones from the chest, they couldn't be, because these were new, but they looked so very much like them that they made her heart beat faster. She picked several of them up to inspect them more closely one after the other, and suddenly it occurred to her that she might find Dean here.

Bursting into the shop with two of the figures still in her hand, she looked around.

A slender, dark-haired young man further back in the shop looked up and stopped working on his carvings. He rose slowly from his chair, staring at her as though he was seeing a ghost, and she wondered if she should know him.

His nose was slightly crooked, as though it had been broken, and he wasn't very tall, but that didn't detract from his otherwise handsome features. She'd seen a lot of men lately, handsome and otherwise, but she was certain she couldn't recall this fellow.

Considering the figures and tools on his workbench as she drew closer, she concluded that the ones outside were his doing. She'd been mistaken, and she was making a fool of herself.

"I'm sorry," she said before he could recover his tongue, "I was looking for someone. I thought I recognized these." She held out the figures to him lest he think she was trying to steal them if she took them back outside herself. He hesitated before accepting them from her.

She wondered what was wrong with him. Maybe he was a half-wit. Fixing her gaze to his, she could tell there was something extraordinary about him, but it wasn't a lack of intelligence. All at once, she was clear on the fact that he was one of her kind, he was a *Cine*, and she didn't think it would be wise to linger. She'd had enough revelations for one day, and if she could tell he was a Cine, then he might be able to see who she was, too.

The man seemed to snap back when her fingers brushed his, and he shifted his weight from one foot to the other. "Well, I'm the only one here. My employer is Seoid Abhac. Is it him you're looking for?"

"No." She turned quickly to leave.

"You're not from here, are you?" he asked to her back, and she halted. Surely he'd noticed the band in her hair.

"No," she replied, pasting her sassiest smile to her lips as she faced back to him. "I'm here on a visit with a few of my friends, actually. We're lots of fun. If you're looking for a good time, come to the Hanging Field and see us. It's just outside the town walls."

He smiled back at her tightly. "I'll keep that in mind."

She knew he wouldn't. He wasn't the type.

She was back out on the street before he could say anything else to her. Pocketing the black queen she'd held on to without him noticing, she disappeared in the crowd.

Chapter Twenty

❧ Images ❧

Lorcan forgot to breathe when the whore came into the shop. She looked so much like Maebh, his heart missed a beat.

Telling himself it couldn't be her because the harlot was half Maebh's age, he followed her outside after their strange exchange. He meant to ask her where she was from, but he lost her in the sea of people. It was as though she'd blended in with the backdrop, and he assumed that was an Ability of hers. She was one of his kind; he'd known it the moment he'd seen the silver in her eyes.

He was about to start searching for her when someone else caught his attention. By that time, he was fairly sure this wasn't his day.

Aeden sat on the Peacock's shoulders, laughing as Brandner bounced him up and down. He was nearly three now, and he was so beautiful, it pained Lorcan just to look at him. He seemed to be a happy boy, and for that, Lorcan knew he had to be grateful, even if the man who believed he was his father had named him after a northern port.

Amelie walked beside her husband and child in silence, doing a great impression of her sister's sour-faced mien. She, as opposed to Aeden, didn't seem in the least bit happy. He hadn't once seen her wearing the same dress, and the house she lived in, so he'd heard, was filled with things fit for a queen. Brandner was away for months at a time, but when he returned, he always brought back presents for her and the boy. She had it all. Brandner had laid her dreams at her feet, but Lorcan knew she'd never be satisfied. Nothing would ever be enough.

With that realization had come a phase when he'd been angry at her, and after that, plain indifference. Sometime around Aeden's birth, he'd discovered he was over her.

The boy was another matter. He had a responsibility toward his son because Aeden would need him one day. He had the Cine silver, bright and clear, and he'd be in grave danger when his Talent emerged in a few years' time.

That was the main reason Lorcan was still in Ironstone. He would have to find the right moment and a suitable way to communicate with Aeden. Perhaps he'd have to bring him away from here. Ironstone was getting too quiet of late. The hush reminded him of the silence in the winter woods before ice and snow began breaking the overladen boughs. The queen had taken to her bed with a difficult pregnancy, and the prince regent's rule had divided the council in these last months.

Lorcan still had the chess figures the whore had returned to him in his hand as he casually turned away from the happy family. He knew he tended to stare, and that couldn't be good.

Placing the pieces back on the board, he noticed the black queen was missing, and he wondered if she'd stolen her. Perhaps she'd taken a fancy to her. There was no point in thinking about it. He'd never get her back, so he'd just have to replace her and that was that. He'd had figures stolen before, but that was the price of leaving them out here unattended. The Dwarven boy he'd been paying to watch the merchandise hadn't come to work today, and Abhac had taken the other boy he'd employed to learn his trade with him.

Lorcan felt a hand on his elbow and startled.

"Are you Lorcan Murua?" a slender Dwarven woman asked. "The human man who works for Seoid Abhac?"

She was lugging a heavy traveling bag. A girl half her height stood next to her, a sack strapped to her back, and her husband waited across the street, keeping watch and visibly irritated at having to do so.

Out of habit, he stooped so the Dwarven woman wouldn't have to look up at him.

"I am." It was half of the truth, at least. "What can I do for you?"

"Leave Ironstone. Do it now. And then find Abhac and warn him not to come back here. There's a storm coming," she told him in a low voice, glancing around for uninvited listeners. "We're leaving before it sweeps us away."

Lorcan frowned. "What are you talking about? What storm…?"

"The new Inquisitor is here. The papal bull is through, and he's sending soldiers for the Dwarven tonight. You are in danger, too – you work for Abhac, and that is enough."

The urgency in her eyes conveyed that this was no joke; he could smell her fear, and a portion of it became his own.

Lorcan had no idea where he'd start looking for Abhac. The merchant had told him he'd be heading east to stock up on glass bottles. Glass in any form was all the rage in Ironstone these days; the bottles were easier to clean than clay vessels and more pleasing to the eye for the way they captured the light. Usually, Abhac would be gone for just over a week, and he'd have been due back today or tomorrow at the latest.

He'd never accompanied Abhac on his trips, so he didn't know the way to the glass manufacturer. He'd always thought there would be time for that later. Perhaps there wouldn't be a *later* now. What had he been doing these past years? He'd been fast asleep.

Squeezing his arm, the Dwarven woman hurried off before he could ask her anything else, pulling the child along with her. Husband and wife took the girl between them and quickly scurried away in direction of the Hay Market from where they'd probably head on down to the town gates.

He slammed the shop door shut, though he couldn't quite say why he bothered, because he hadn't cleared the street-display away, and bounded toward the next alley that would take him to the goldsmith's house and workshop.

Lorcan wasn't fond of Orry Misneach. Misneach was a selfish old miser. For reasons Lorcan would never understand, he was Abhac's best friend. Aside from that, Misneach was also extremely well-informed, and if anyone could tell him what was going on, then it would be him.

Rattling the door, he discovered that the goldsmith had locked up his shop early. There was no sign of him or the maid he employed around the house. Perhaps they, too, had known to flee. It was that, or the storm had already swept them away.

Next, he tried the bookbinder. Leabhar was a cousin of Abhac's, and he was carved from much the same material as Abhac, but he was a family man through and through, and his business would have gone to his sons one day, not to some apprentice. He wasn't at home either, and his wife and sons were nowhere to be found. Lorcan hoped they had a place to go.

The sun's last minutes painted the sky orange and red. Although it wasn't the time for Mass or prayers, the church bells up at the palace, as well as those in the smaller chapel in the eastern part of town, tolled as though there was no tomorrow. Their rich, musical sound filled the streets, and people came out of their houses to see what was going on.

Lorcan looked about and saw one of the queen's heralds heading for the Hay Market and followed him there.

The man wore his finest tabard, and he carried a chunky staff with a dozen little bells attached to it near the top. They jangled as he walked, and he seemed irritated. He lost no time in climbing the steps that led up to the speakers' platform and brought down his staff hard several times to get attention.

"Hear, hear! Announcements for the ears of one and all from their Majesties, the Queen and King Consort of the Middlelands and Northern Territories! Hear, hear!"

When a sufficiently large crowd had gathered, he spoke. "In the early hours of yesterday morning, a new prince was born to our great queen and christened Eamon Oisin. He will stand second in line of succession to the throne of Ironstone after his sister, Princess Eavan Aoifa of the Middlelands and Northern Territories."

The Hay Market pulsed with giddy excitement, cheering and applause. There were still people pouring in from the five streets that led to the pentagonal market place, and the herald had to wait until the noise died down so he could continue.

"Secondly, their Majesties wish to inform that Pope Angelicus I has authorized his Grand Inquisitor, Terrence of Driesburgh, to investigate the unnatural death of his predecessor, Thomas of Ornoa. Furthermore, he is to take legal action against the Dwarven. The Dwarven have been found guilty of the capacity to enact magic because it is in their disposition. They are to be classified as Tainted alongside anyone of Cine or Fairy descent, and the Lost Peoples known as Shapeshifters. They will be questioned and tried, and they will be put to death if found guilty of the crimes they are charged with."

Lorcan thought he wasn't hearing right.

"His Holiness has also authorized Terrence of Driesburgh to name two bishops to act on his behalf throughout the kingdom in place of Thomas of Ornoa, who was murdered by a complot devised by Dwarven people. His Holiness has ordered the Grand Inquisitor and his bishops to employ any means they see necessary of bringing these criminals to justice. They have full procuration to crush the resistance Thomas of Ornoa was confronted with on the issue of the potential threat of the Dwarven to humankind and their presence in the Middlelands and the Northern Territories."

A murmur went through the crowd. The elatedness that had gone along with the first part of the announcement vanished in a haze of mixed reactions.

Some of the onlookers who'd applauded and cheered only a minute before became silent, while others began whooping. A very few brave men whistled in protest, as was the sign of disapproval here, and others just walked away.

From the perimeter of the market, soldiers observed the goings-on. Their comrades would undoubtedly be doing the same down on the Fish Market, and wherever else the queen had sent her heralds.

Only now did Lorcan begin to understand what was happening. The Dwarven woman was right, and he remembered the rumors he'd heard years ago. They were facing a storm.

He doubted the Inquisitor had been murdered. Ornoa had been a known drunk, and nobody had wondered when his bloated body had been fished out of the river near Leignsbridge a few months ago.

The Inquisition had all but wiped out the Shapeshifters and eradicated the Cine within the last hundred years, but no one had ever bothered with the Dwarven.

Not until now, and why should they have?

No matter how you looked at it, the Dwarven had no magic. None except for the kind they worked with their craftsmanship or the shrewd bargaining tactics they were renowned for. They weren't dangerous or frightening, and they didn't hurt anyone, and yet, they'd been eyed with skepticism for the longest time. There had always been persecution. Lorcan hadn't perceived it here as much as in the other places he'd been to. He hadn't seen any of the open hostility in Ironstone that he'd witnessed as a child in the Sudlands, but it had been there beneath the surface, and where the seed of envy, resentment or ignorance fell on fertile ground, hate would take root and grow.

The Dwarven dealt in costly goods like gold, silver, and precious stones, and they traded in furs and fine cloths. In doing so, they traditionally held portions of a market that might invite envy. They had their own networks, and they tended to keep to themselves, but here in Ironstone, they were an accepted and well-integrated part of community and public life. Or so Lorcan had thought.

His stomach was churning.

Particularly when he looked about and became aware of the steadily increasing presence of soldiers and guards appearing on the sidelines, wearing the Bishop's emblem on the tunic they wore over their leather armor. They were heavily armed and expecting trouble. Lorcan wondered if anyone would be willing and able to give them some. No one was. The herald was about to step down from the speakers' platform.

"The Dwarven don't practice magic, and we all know it," he shouted at the top of his voice then, startling himself.

The people in his immediate vicinity stopped talking in favor of staring at him. The damage was done, but he didn't regret being the one who'd stood up. Somebody had to.

"They don't have any magic and they never did," he repeated, addressing the herald and watching the guards dig their way through the masses toward him. "Wake up, and just ask yourself: who's going to benefit from this? Wake up!"

It became very quiet when he'd said that.

He searched for a gap in the soldiers' lines to slip through and realized it wasn't going to be easy to get away from them.

"Why would you defend their kind?" another voice boomed from somewhere by the walled well. "Bit short yourself, but you're not one of them, are you?" Bursts of laughter erupted. "Do you not trust in the Holy Father to be a better judge of the character of unnatural beings than you?"

Lorcan looked around until his eyes found the Peacock. He'd come around next to the herald and appeared to be beyond pleased with himself.

With the soldiers closing in on him, he knew he didn't have time to argue. The new Inquisitor's men weren't taking any form of protest. Terrence of Driesburgh meant business, and Lorcan knew the soldiers would be making an example of him if they managed to get a hold of him. It would be his tongue or his life, or both in that order.

He briefly considered doubling back to the shop, but decided against it when he overheard someone saying they were closing the town gates. He realized he had to leave Ironstone *now*, but his feet wouldn't budge. This was the place Ortus had vested so much hope in, and despite everything he didn't want to abandon the notion that had held him here all this time, even if it had turned out to be a lie. If he walked away from Ironstone, he might never return, and he'd never see his son again.

He'd be leaving for good.

Chapter Twenty-One

---

෪ The Wind in the Trees ๑

Catherine heard of the new prince's birth from the herald at the Fish Market. She stopped there just long enough to listen to the fat little man shout his news above the murmur. His second announcement didn't do much more to impress her than the first, but she had a bad feeling this was going to have some repercussions for the whores camping out on the Hanging Field.

Glancing around for any sign of trouble, she was glad the angry craftsman she'd deceived hadn't followed her this far, and she decided to go back to the sewing woman for her cloth. Who knew if she was going to see it again if she left it here now and they decided to lock down Ironstone. That fabric had cost her a fortune.

Clapping, jeering, whistling, and heated discussions followed the herald's proclamations on the square, charging up the atmosphere. The streets leading away from it congested as the crowd there dispersed, and she hated all the pushing and having people brush up against her as she walked back the way she'd come. The warmth of their bodies and the sour odor of sweat and grime mixed in with the smell of fresh horse dung and fouling fish. She thought she was going to be sick if she didn't get away from the writhing, undulating masses soon. They were maggots, she realized, all of them, and she was going to be eaten if she didn't protect herself.

Moving rigidly with the flow, she lowered her head and ordered herself to keep breathing. With her eyes trained on the street immediately ahead of her feet, she thought of the forest where she'd grown up. She saw it there in front of her, and she imagined that all those wriggling, burrowing maggots brushing up against her were trees. The gnashing noise of their feeding was nothing but the wind.

Clutching the chess piece tightly in her hand, she passed the dark-haired young man she'd stolen it from without noticing him. He didn't see her either. They were going in opposite directions, and they could have looked the other straight in the face if they'd had other concerns than they did, but she was determined to have what was hers, and he was determined to find someone else.

The sewing woman wasn't happy to call off their agreement. She returned the cloth to Catherine after some haggling, but insisted on keeping the coins Catherine had given her as an advance. It was half the price of the work. The woman thought this was fair to a whore who went back on a deal, but Catherine didn't feel inclined to share that opinion. She was no longer inclined to share *anyone's* opinions today.

With nobody in the house but the sewing woman and herself, Catherine smiled as she quietly closed the front door from the inside. She bolted it, and the woman protested, but Catherine was no more in the mood for protest than she was for opinions. It wasn't just the loss of her hard-earned wages, but the fact that some women thought they had a right to pass judgement on her.

Pins and needles seemed quite appropriate for teaching lessons in humility, since pins and needles were what Catherine was feeling all over her skin when she thought about all the women who'd been appraising and condemning her, telling her what she could and couldn't do.

She slipped inside the sewing woman's witless mind as easily as she might have inside one of her new dresses, and she began telling her what to do with those needles while working on the dress she had on the table in front of her. It was a joy to watch her pricking herself and see the fabric stain, so she did so for as long as she dared to. Not an inkling of remorse stood in her way as the woman sewed and bled, and bled and sewed without realizing she was stitching the cloth to the skin of her left arm.

Catherine found her coins and someone else's besides in a box beneath the work table and put them into the small leather purse she had secured to her thigh beneath her skirts. She couldn't stop smiling and pleasantly wished the industrious woman a good day before she left the shop with her cloth and her new funds.

She was down at the town's main gates by the time the sewing woman's daughter returned to her home from the Fish Market. The girl had a lot of news to share, but the sight that met her eyes made her forget everything she'd heard. She dropped the sack of beans she'd carried back with her and screamed at her mother to stop hurting herself until she was hoarse, but no one heard her.

No one except for Catherine, who'd been listening intently to the wind in the trees.

Chapter Twenty-Two

❧ Army of Fools ❧

The guards at the eastern gate hadn't left their posts, but they stood with their backs to the narrow passageway, facing away from anyone who was intent on leaving town.

One of them was singing the Queen's Anthem as Lorcan sprinted past him, following two Dwarven men heading for the field road that led between a meadow and a barley field toward the forest.

Oh can you hear the mountains and the valleys ring

With freedom's voices as they sing...

There was no one else behind Lorcan, and he could hear the creak of the iron hinges closing as he ran.

Hold faith through darkest starless night

When wrong is deemed as right, united we will fight...

He thought he might be the last person to leave Ironstone tonight, through this gate, at least. He had a hunch the Inquisitor's soldiers would be faced with a few obstacles while trying to give chase to the fleeing Dwarven. The Pope's new hound had underestimated the task of rounding up Ironstone's Midget population, it seemed.

The sound of fighting soon drowned out the clear voice of the gatekeeper. Swords struck armor, shields, and finally cut into living flesh, but the gate didn't open again until he'd almost reached the tree line.

Lorcan knew neither he nor the two Dwarven men would get very far if the soldiers who were coming after them were on horseback, but they weren't going to conveniently lie down and die for them just yet. The trees would give them cover, and they'd be harder to find in the dark.

Just at that moment, Abhac drove the Friesian pulling his cart out of the forest toward him at breakneck speed. He wasn't coming from the direction of the hollow way, so Lorcan assumed he might have been waiting somewhere in the brush. Despite the distance between them, Lorcan saw the strained worry written all over the old man's face as he labored with the reins. The boy wasn't with him, and the cart was empty although it should have been laden with goods.

Turning briefly at the sound of angry voices and commotion, Lorcan saw there was heavy fighting at the gate behind him, but a good dozen horsemen wearing the bishop's blue and green tunics moved out into the dusk nonetheless. Half circling around Lorcan and the two Dwarven, Abhac urged them to get in, and they scrambled onto the back of the cart.

"Anyone else?" the merchant barked.

"No," one of the Dwarven behind him replied. "We went through most every house."

"Good to see you, Seoid Abhac," Lorcan said and meant it, bracing himself against the front board behind the merchant as Abhac yelled at the horse to get a move on. "I was just going to look for you so I could save you."

The Dwarve smirked. "On foot and leading a garrison of the Inquisitor's men, I see. How thoughtful of you, my boy!"

"Well, I hadn't gotten round to dealing with those yet…"

The other two exchanged a bewildered glance and guffawed as the cart rumbled through the thicket downhill, bucking over roots and weaving in and out between the ancient beeches, elms, and pine trees. Lorcan's stomach turned as he imagined them breaking an axle or skidding out of control on the slope he never would have ventured upon with a hand cart, never mind the one they were sitting in now.

The forest to the east of Ironstone was wilder and more sparsely cultivated than the woods farther south, and there were rumors of wild beasts, wolves, and other creatures here. The further in they went, keeping well away from the hollow way, the darker it got. Lorcan strained to see any sign of the men following them, but he couldn't tell where they were.

"You do realize they're faster than we are," he told Abhac. "We're making a hell of a racket. We might be better leaving the cart and hiding in the undergrowth–"

"Ach, you worry too much," Abhac returned.

Lorcan couldn't hear himself think, much less see more than a hundred feet ahead into the narrow, trough-like valley they were heading for, but that didn't seem to bother Abhac. The Dwarve directed the Friesian right down into the foggy blackness.

"Almost there, they won't follow us much further," the old man shouted. "Those soldiers will be learning to fear the woods tonight."

Lorcan's heart hammered in his chest. "What do you mean *they'll be learning to fear the woods*? *I'm* in fear of these woods *right now*! You're going to get us all killed!"

Abhac ignored him, maintaining his speed while the other two Dwarven grinned, bobbing with every fallen branch and rotting stump the cart's wheels thudded over.

When they'd reached the bottom of the dingle, more sliding than rolling, the light suddenly changed. All at once, thousands of dancing pinpoints of luminescence swirled in the magic-charged haze around them. They emitted a golden glow so warm, Lorcan felt as though he was out in the brightest light of a summer's day instead of the darkest part of the woods he'd have avoided at any other time. His senses told him he smelled honeysuckle and sun-kissed cherries, and even though he knew they were lying to him, the knot he'd had in his stomach since he'd started running for his life began to melt away. A strange kind of peace took charge of him.

He was about to ask Abhac what was going on, but the Dwarve hushed him, old eyes telling a young man now was not the time for talk. The merchant slowed the cart down but didn't stop. He continued on patiently, letting the horse's instincts and the shape of the land be his guide. It was like they weren't in much of a hurry anymore and didn't have a concern in the world.

The lights cocooned them in their radiance until they'd safely made their way out of the gorge, and then vanished as suddenly as they'd appeared. A scrubby birch wood lay beyond, and the pale moon lent the ghostly trees its silver, but it wasn't long until they, too, began to wane, yielding to a small clearing where Lorcan saw another dozen or so carts and wagons of all shapes and sizes. He recognized a lot of the Dwarven waiting there, sitting on boxes and crates, on the ground, or on the loading areas and the dickey boxes of the wagons. They were all from Ironstone.

"We're here – let's move!" Abhac called, halting only briefly to pick up as many passengers as would fit in his cart, including his apprentice.

"Where are we going?" Lorcan asked, noticing the glass freight in the crates they were leaving behind as he joined the merchant on the front seat.

Abhac patted his shoulder. "To the Winter Mountains."

"What about the bishop's men?"

"They won't be a problem. The Fairyflies will be taking good care of them."

Chapter Twenty-Three

☙ Saint Aeden ❧

Having decided the Inquisitor might not be fully engaged with the destruction of the Dwarven population in Ironstone, the whores lost no time in breaking camp. There was no point in waiting for the focus to shift from the Tainted to the ordinary sinners. Catherine couldn't say she was sad about that. The only thing bothering her was that she hadn't gotten her dresses made.

A four week march took them to the northern port of Saint Aeden, just as Deirdre had promised. Catherine wasn't impressed with the town. The overcrowded, filthy streets bred disease, and the docks reeked to the heavens above.

Although winter was nearing and the sun's light couldn't spoil as much of the day's catch between the boats and the busy market nearby, Catherine was sure there had to be something wrong with the women who gutted and sold fish there. None of them seemed to have a sense of smell; caked from head to toe with innards, they peddled their employers' wares with an enthusiasm she'd rarely witnessed before, and Deirdre informed her they did it seven days a week from dawn until dusk.

The three-master lying at anchor in the harbor was a trading ship that went back and forth between Saint Aeden and Bharat, making stops along its route in Eberia and at the Cape of Faith. Catherine had to admit she was a sight to behold, but she couldn't imagine ever going aboard such a vessel herself. It frightened her, for reasons she couldn't explain, and she was glad they weren't getting a tour.

Deirdre did, however, take the time to show them the poorhouse on their way across town. The tumbledown building hardly seemed worthy of the name. The crowded cemetery next to it indicated that more people seemed to be dying there of causes other than hunger than could survive on charity and church welfare. The stink was almost as bad as down by the fish market. Two monks wearing scarves over their mouths carried a body out the front door on a stretcher between them just as the whores were on their way in.

Catherine wondered what on earth they were doing here.

Deirdre was greeted by a padre, and the two exchanged a few words. Catherine could feel the bald Dominican's wary eyes on her as she watched Deirdre hand the man a leather purse. He thanked and blessed her, and they were back out the door before any questions could be asked or answered.

"Not the place we want to end now, ladies, is it?" the blonde teased. No one bothered to reply.

Leaving the waterfront and the big Kontor's warehouses behind them, Deirdre led them up the streets of the merchants' district where rows of neat shops not unlike those in Ironstone sold a part of the goods coming into the port and provided essentials for the laborers and sailors who worked there.

Signs above the doors gave an idea of what each vendor specialized in, and the proprietors themselves stood outside to hawk their wares at the passers-by. Housewives haggled over prices and children darted about. Most people discreetly overlooked the little parade of road-weary whores shuffling past them.

Deirdre led the girls through an alley between a bakery and a shoe maker's workshop into a backstreet that housed other kinds of businesses – more the service type than the vendors'.

Noticing the generally poor state of the buildings, and how many windows were boarded up here, Catherine thought they'd entered an entirely different world. The odor of brewing ale hung in the air. Fewer people wandered about, but taverns didn't really attract business until the workday was over. She suspected this side of town would be quite busy come nightfall.

"Here we are," Deirdre sang out a bit too cheerfully in front of a house that was two stories high.

A long balcony stretched across the second floor. Ropes had been strung across the length of it and were covered with drying laundry. The sign on the balustrade identified it as a bathhouse. The older woman ushered everyone inside without much ado.

Weak light filtered into the main room from small windows set high up near the ceiling. A huge fireplace occupied the middle of the far wall, and several large caldrons on iron feet stood at intervals inside, steam twisting over the tops to seep into the room. A long table flanked by low benches ran up the center, and wooden, cloth-lined tubs ran along both sides at regular intervals.

Almost immediately, Catherine felt beads of sweat forming on her body from the moist heat in this place, and her dress clung to her damp skin.

A portly woman with graying hair greeted Deirdre and eyed the girls with unconcealed curiosity. She barked a few orders to a pimple-faced boy and two young women around Catherine's age before she drew the blonde into a backroom and closed the door.

The boy and the two women served them all bowls of thick fish stew and coarse bread. Hungry as she was, Catherine wolfed down the food without really tasting it, listening to the servers answering her companions' questions about what they did here, which was, of course, exactly what she'd expected.

When Deirdre finally rejoined them, she told the younger girls that most of them would be staying to work here or at one of the other bathhouses in the area. There were no tearful goodbyes as Deirdre turned them over to the Madame, telling Catherine, Bridget, and six others they were coming with her.

They quickly left the waterfront behind them and sauntered through one of the better parts of Saint Aeden, where well-kept houses and tended sewage reminded Catherine of the Palace Road in Ironstone. This was where she wanted to be. She wasn't going to live out her days gutting fish or washing smelly workmen and servicing them for pennies.

It took the better part of the afternoon to drop the other girls off at various alehouses and taverns. Some of those seemed like clean places, others didn't.

Finally, there was no one left but Bridget and Catherine, and Deirdre took them for a meal in an inn just outside of town. It was a welcoming house that looked as though its rooms might be costly. Catherine couldn't imagine they had whores here.

"This is where I stay when I'm in town," Deirdre informed them before she spent a time chatting with the innkeeper's wife.

Bridget was on her second helping of bread and milk by the time Deirdre rejoined them. "So what about us?" she inquired between bites.

"Well, I was thinkin' one o' yez would be good right here." She patted Bridget's hand. Then, she nodded to Catherine. "The other of yez a bit further down the road."

Catherine wondered what she meant by *down the road*. It wasn't that she was attached to Bridget's company, but she felt something was off.

"Don't look at me like that. Ye've nothin' to be worried about." Deirdre snorted, catching her gaze. She poured each of them a generous cup of strong wine. "I have just the place for ye."

"And where would that be?"

The older woman looked up with an amused expression, her eyes bright as the drink coursed through her veins. "An old friend of mine. He's the local hangman."

Catherine knew she was watching her for a reaction and merely shrugged. If the allusion to the executioner was intended to be a threat in light of her being a Cine, she wasn't going to bite. "Afraid of the competition?"

Bridget nearly choked on her beverage, coughing some of it up over Deirdre.

Forcing a smile, Deirdre cleaned herself off and shook her head. "No, dear, there's plenty of sinners to go around for everyone. Binns runs a clean house with a few girls what's been with him for a while; girls like yourself." She leaned across the table. "Girls what attract a certain type of sinner. I'm doing ye a favor."

Catherine couldn't help herself and erupted in a laugh. She hadn't been in this business very long, but she knew she alone had probably made Deirdre more money by her willingness to provide special services for her clients than most of the other girls put together. Deirdre was smart, and she guessed the hangman was, too.

"And how much, exactly, are you getting for me?"

The older woman raised her glass in a mock salute. "Nothin' that I wouldn't have earned for trainin' ye and gettin' ye a placement."

Catherine rolled her eyes. She didn't remember Deirdre providing any more training than to tell her how much to charge.

Growing serious, the other woman crossed her arms on the table and tried to look sincere. "I always take care of my girls, Catherine. Every one of ye will have a place to live and food to eat, and ye'll be able to make yer own money. Would ye rather I'd have said goodbye at the gates and let all o' yez fend for yerselves?"

No, she didn't. Catherine didn't think any of them would last a week on the street once the winter set in. Even if they did manage to earn a little money, they'd be targets for every jackal out there, and they'd never find affordable shelter by themselves. This was what their little visit to the poorhouse had been about, because the poorhouse was where they'd end up if they went it alone, at best.

There was no reason to resent the older whore for her business-smarts and making a little money off finding each of them a place. Strangely, however,

Catherine did, but the nearly seventeen years she'd lived in this world had taught her one thing: what went up, had to come down, at some stage, and this would apply to Deirdre as it did to anything and anyone else. It was all just a matter of time.

Chapter Twenty-Four

ଓ The Winter Mountains

ଅ

Early the next evening, the narrow winding road they'd been following petered out in the moors of the Winter Mountains. Shafts of light pushed through the leaden clouds above and moved across the mountainsides with the changing skies. The marshland that lay before them was sprinkled with Bog Stars and Hawksbeard.

The little convoy behind Abhac's cart continued its trek upstream along the river's miry bank until the path became too difficult to navigate a mile on into the next rocky, sloping ascent. Lorcan didn't think they'd get any farther, but Abhac simply jumped off the cart and led the Friesian through the shallow water a few hundred yards on into the boulder landscape. A small, barren gorge opened up to them, probably one of many here.

Walls of water cascaded from the sheer limestone cliffs to either side of them and ahead, pooling in a wide lake at the bottom. There was no other way in or out of the valley, and Lorcan cast a questioning glance at the Dwarven boy beside him. The lad just smiled.

Abhac led the old mare straight toward the largest of the waterfalls, as though he was determined to give them all a good shower. There was an electrical charge in the air just before they entered it, and it pricked painfully at Lorcan's skin and recollections. He knew the familiar tingle and what would follow the strange sensation, and he was somewhere between dumbfounded and alarmed as they passed through the curtain of icy water into the short tunnel behind it.

The passageway wouldn't have been wide or high enough for the heavy merchants' wagons that rumbled through the streets of Ironstone, but Abhac's cart was much smaller, and he had no problem guiding his Friesian inside. The mare had been here many times and knew there was no danger ahead. She trusted her master blindly and knew where to put her feet in the pitch-black underpass, trotting on toward the road on the other side despite the thick layer of magic that protected whatever lay beyond.

Lorcan recognized the make of the wards that safeguarded the place where Abhac was taking them. The momentary blindness and static that ensued as they transitioned assaulted his senses. It felt, smelled, tasted, and sounded just like the one shielding The Fair. He could almost read the hand that had crafted it, and he realized there was more than one common denominator aside from the man who'd created it. It was the Snow Globe.

This Haven was a part of the Snow Globe, too. Its fate was linked directly to The Fair by the same enchantment – he could see the glass and the hands that held it out for him to inspect on their journey to Ironstone a lifetime ago, and his fingers remembered the cool, smooth surface of the perfect orb. He could feel the knowledge stored within it; it hummed an ancient song, and the words were almost there within his grasp, but not quite yet complete. Then, the flash of clearness was over, and the emptiness it left behind tore a hole in his heart. It made him clutch at his chest when they emerged from the gateway to the Winter Haven.

"Alright there, Lorcan?" the old Dwarve asked.

He nodded silently, fixing his gaze to the wooded path ahead behind the rock shoulder that marked the end of the tunnel.

In the play of light and shadow, a forest of bearded century trees appeared, dense and huge and hugging the mountainsides ahead with as many roots above ground as below. Their enormous branches intertwined everywhere as though they were lovers holding hands over a world that was uniquely their own, creating a roof of clover-shaped leaves above steep paths that snaked uphill and down again across half a dozen terraced levels cut into the rock to accommodate dwellings.

Between their massive trunks, stone and root stairways led from one terrace to the next, from path to doorway, and between the paths. The paths and the Dwarven homes must have been carved into the limestone in decades of hard work, and Lorcan's breath hitched at the artfulness of it as Abhac halted the horse just below the first level of the Dwarven town.

The other twelve carts drew up behind them one by one around the walled well in the open space at the bottom of the combe.

Dwarven people peeked out of their windows, opened doors and came out of their houses. Most of them were old, but there wasn't a sour face or a scowl, or a distrustful stare anywhere to be seen.

Looking around at his rag-tag traveling companions, Lorcan realized they were a good eighty in all, and they were refugees. He'd been worried if they'd all be welcome, but his fears were soon put to rest by the Dwarven who came to help them unload their carts, offering blankets and towels to dry off on, asking for their story.

Some of the Ironstone Dwarven had no relatives here, no baggage to unload, and they were tired, especially the children. All they had was the clothes on their backs and their lives, but they were taken in before Abhac was finished speaking to one of the town officials.

Lorcan unhitched the horse and helped maneuver the carts so they'd be out of the way until a better place could be found for them. The boy helped him. When they were done, the lad was off to find a granduncle he'd visited sometimes.

Abhac had a home of his own here on the south side of the lowest horseshoe-shaped terrace. It had belonged to his parents. His sister still lived there, the Dwarve informed him. She worked for one of the glassmakers, producing fine drinking-glasses and creating delicate works of art. Glass was the Winter Haven's economic mainstay – at least up until now – and most everyone relied on that industry in some way or other. Lorcan wasn't sure how this was going to work now that the Dwarven would no longer be able to sell their goods.

Abhac's house, like most, was set back from the path and dug straight into the mountainside. Two supporting pillars of stone dissected the wooden ivy-covered front. Small pointy-arched windows sat in their frames to the left and right of the door, and a bench, formed from the roots of the century tree that grew next to the house, stood beneath one of the sets of windows.

Ruanna Abhac yelped in surprise when her brother walked through the door, followed by Lorcan. She was younger than Abhac, but had the same friendly eyes. There was less wariness in them, and she doted on the men incessantly, serving them bread and honey to eat until they were full. Finally, long after dark, when Lorcan couldn't keep his eyes open anymore, she showed him where he could sleep.

His bed was shorter than he'd have needed it, but it was warm and soft, and that night, his dreams were strange and full of things he hadn't thought of in such a long time. People who might as well have been lost to him followed him wherever he went, talking to him. There were so many voices, he couldn't hear what they were saying, and he woke up drenched in his own sweat several times before a more restful kind of sleep claimed him.

Chapter Twenty-Five

☙ Alliances ❧

Voices woke Lorcan, but they were not like the ones in his head that had stolen his rest the previous night. None of them belonged to Aeden, or the Peacock, and none of them were angry or frightened.

Abhac had a lot of friends in the Winter Haven, and most of them had already arrived by the time Lorcan had unfolded himself from the bed he'd slept in. He climbed down the sturdy ladder from the upper level to the living area and stood in the front room for a moment to get his bearings. The entire house was teeming with people, and he felt odd – too tall, too grubby, and all kinds of awkward. Also, he was imposing on Abhac's hospitality.

"Up already?" Abhac remarked in passing him on his way to the kitchen with a mug of fragrant tea.

The goldsmith behind him barked a laugh. Misneach hadn't been with them when they'd fled Ironstone, and Lorcan wondered when the man had arrived.

"Here already?" he directed dryly at him. Misneach decided to ignore him as he settled down on one of the stools around the little stove beside Easog.

Muinteoir was there, and half a dozen other Dwarven people Lorcan didn't know. He assumed they would be part of the council Abhac had told him about on the way here – the Dwarven Ortus had done dealings with over years.

The scent of sweet panbread baking made his mouth water, and Ruanna was at his side with a plate before he could say anything else.

"Sit," she commanded, ushering him toward the others. "There's a lot to discuss today."

"This is my assistant from Ironstone, Lorcan Aurum," Abhac told everyone.

"He's the Cine who made the chess set?" the town official Lorcan recognized from the night before asked. Abhac nodded.

"Aye. He's Ortus' boy. He's also the one who carved the Snow Globe's foot."

Lorcan swallowed his hot tea too fast. "I'm not, actually… I mean, I did, but I'm not Ortus' son."

The town official mustered him briefly. "You were a son to him. He trusted you with the secret of the Globe and its magic. That's good enough for us."

Abhac chewed on his bread, and there was a moment's quiet.

"Alright. Now, Seoid and Orry have already told me most of what's been going on in Ironstone, and we all know how bad it's gotten over in Leignsbridge and other towns in the Northern Territories. The queen can't help us any more than she's already done. Abhac tells me you came to Ironstone a few years ago. We haven't had contact with anyone from The Fair since Ortus was killed. Have you?"

All eyes were on him. "No, and I haven't been back. I don't have that kind of Talent, so I don't really know how I could help you."

Several of the Dwarven exchanged bewildered gazes.

"Could you still find it if we were to provide you with a good horse and whatever else you'd need?"

The question was if he'd want to do that. He wasn't entirely sure.

"I don't know. I'd have to search for it. Could take a while."

He'd been reminded of the fact that he could feel the magic of Ortus' wards just the previous night, but he wondered how often the community had relocated since he'd gone, and whether he'd recognize the markers – provided they still set them out when they moved.

"But could you find it *if you tried*?"

"If I knew roughly where to look, yes, but the only time of year we didn't move every few weeks unless we were forced to was winter. I mean, it could be *anywhere* now."

Anywhere could well be a place very far away from Ironstone and any chance of keeping an eye on Aeden. He took another swallow of his tea, grateful for the fresh mint taste of it in his mouth. His teeth had a pelt, it seemed, more now than they had ten minutes ago.

He wasn't the boy who'd left The Fair anymore. He wasn't sure he really wanted to look for it, even without Aeden on his mind. The boy was likely to be safe for another few years yet before his Talent emerged, but Lorcan knew he might not be welcome at The Fair, and he wondered what the town official was getting at. The man wasn't letting him in on his train of thought just yet.

"The queen says there's no need to relocate the Snow Globe," the goldsmith said into the silence. "It's still safe. The Winter Haven is still safe, and so is The Fair."

"Do you really think so?" Easog replied sharply. "What say you, Iarla?"

The town official was a thousand miles away. He scratched his nose. "I believe we should have faith in Cassandra. The Globe should remain with her."

"Cassandra has failed us," Muinteoir objected. "She's given the Inquisitor free hand in Ironstone. Who's to say she won't use the Globe to destroy the wards and betray us, if it'll keep her on the throne?"

"She'd die rather than betray us. What was she supposed to do?" There was anger in Abhac's voice. "That little boy of hers is very ill, and if he'd been born dead, the Inquisitor might well have demanded she stand trial for infidelity or deviltry. Driesburgh was just waiting for that to happen, and thank God it didn't.

If she'd refused to cooperate, *none* of us would be here now. We all got out, didn't we? We're all alive, and a dozen human soldiers might well hang for their loyalty to their queen, and for helping us."

Misneach shifted his weight on his stool. "The merchant Brandner whispered in Driesburgh's ear. She had to do something, or she'd have lost any chance to take influence on what'll become of Ironstone."

Lorcan nearly choked on his bread. "Brandner?"

"You know the cloth merchant," Easog affirmed sourly. "He's the master of the merchants' guild now, and he has his sights set on a seat in the council."

That shed light on a few things. Brandner had made a name for himself, and he was strengthening his position by sowing doubt. His cronies – and Brandner himself – would undoubtedly stand to benefit from weakening the queen and her tax and price laws.

"What charges did he bring against her?" Lorcan asked.

"He accused Cassandra of being an Unnatural. He claimed she was harboring the last Inquisitor's murders within the walls of Ironstone. Something about a Dwarven conspiracy."

"Is it true? I mean, was there a conspiracy?"

Misneach grinned. "Of course there was. In case you haven't noticed, there are humans trying to kill your people and mine."

"But the human who knocked Thomas of Ornoa over the head wasn't from Ironstone. Ornoa made himself plenty of *good friends* over in Leignsbridge without any of *us* having to meddle," Muinteoir said, winking.

"You see, one of those friends was the son of a rich widow put on trial for being a Cine. She'd been running the messenger coaches on the Trade Road between there and Saint Aeden after her husband's death, and she was a thorn in the eye of a neighbor who loved the idea of making a living from delivering letters and parcels. They paid Ornoa ever so well to have her questioned and burned when she wouldn't confess to being something she wasn't. The messenger coaches are still operating, by the way. There's a lot of money to be made in letters and parcels, and her neighbor decided it was his civic duty to continue her public service. Her son is currently on his way to the Western Tribelands across the ocean to save his neck."

"Maybe that's where we should be going..." Iarla muttered.

"No," Abhac said. "You couldn't be more wrong. This is our home. Some of us have lost everything – but we're not ready to give up just yet. Do you think it would be different in the Western Tribelands, or even Sutrailia? People are the same wherever you go, and they'll carry their plagues with them to the ends of the earth. No, we're staying right here, and we're going to stand our ground as best we can, in our own way and in our own time. We're not going to run and take our troubles with us to foreign lands."

Misneach accepted another piece of bread from Ruanna. "Ortus was wrong. We just can't win this. There's not enough of us left."

"That's why we need to stick together," Abhac replied.

Lorcan remembered how often Ortus had told him and Dean this on the road to Ironstone. That was what The Fair was about, or what Ortus had wanted it to be about. He'd been convinced the time would come when humans would learn to see more clearly, and the Tainted would help them to do that. They'd be free, some day.

To Lorcan, the idea had seemed a bit naïve even then. He didn't know if the Sorcerer's dream would ever come true, but he did know it was time to face his inner demons and make a stand of his own. Ortus had treated him like a son. Abhac had taken him in. It was time to give something back to the both of them, though he didn't quite know how yet.

Abhac rose and folded his arms across his chest. "We need to find The Fair and let them know we're on the same side. We need to forge an alliance. I think that would double our chances of survival."

Iarla was skeptical. "But do we even know if The Fair still exists? It's going to be hard to survive here on our own, but who's to say The Fair would be interested in cooperating with us? If it hasn't already been destroyed."

"I don't think so," Lorcan said firmly. "The Fair was Ortus' dream, and he did everything to make it come true. He created it not only to protect the Cine from the humans, but also to protect the humans from us and what we would become without an anchor in the real world."

There was another silence, and Lorcan didn't know if he was overstepping, but he felt a need to get his point across.

"Moving farther away from one another is not going to help any of us. We all breathe the same air–"

Iarla cut him off, barking a laugh that didn't have an ounce of amusement in it. "Only *they're* making us suffer, sending their henchmen for us, destroying our livelihoods and *killing our people.*"

Lorcan set down his tea mug on the floor at his feet. "I know, and they're not going to stop. There's not enough of us to win a war against them, but we can keep fighting for recognition by *not* giving up and shutting ourselves off from them, nourishing their fears. What every one of us, human or Cine, fears most, is the unknown. We need to stay in the light."

"Listen to him, would you?" Iarla scoffed, gesticulating before fixing his stare to Lorcan's earnestly. "How old are you?"

Lorcan grinned with a sting in his chest. "Old enough to have lost my home and everyone I loved," he replied, remembering that terrible last year of his childhood in the Sudlands, and other things he didn't want to recall.

"Do you think The Fair still stands for the same things it did when Ortus was alive?"

Lorcan took another deep breath and let his gaze wander. "People – and Cine – are the same wherever you go. You have to keep that in mind, but I'll find it for you, if that's what you want, and I'll let you know. I do think it would be clever to make sure you don't stand alone – that *none of us* stand alone." And, that Aeden wouldn't stand alone, one day. He would fight so his son would have a place in this world.

"But do you think they'd be interested in forging an alliance with the Dwarven?" Iarla asked again.

"I believe it's what Ortus would have wanted, or he would not have tethered the Winter Haven to the Outer Haven with his magic. I can't speak for whoever is in charge there now, but I'll be your go-between. Give me a few months' time, and we'll find out exactly what they want."

There was a murmur of agreement, and Abhac thumped him on the back. "Alright, son. That's what we'll do, and we'll see."

Chapter Twenty-Six

---

ca Back to The Fair so

Finding The Fair wasn't hard once he'd crossed the Middlelands and the kingdom of Wirtenberg. Not as hard as he'd have liked it to be.

A string of eighteen Cine markers led him from the place where he'd brought Ortus' body over three years ago to where he stood now on the fringe of a big field several miles from the town of Ravensburgh.

Many of the commoners here spoke in a tongue he didn't quite master – or *want* to master – anymore. It was very far south, and he had no affinity for the south. The Cine didn't have a lot of friends here, and he wondered who'd been so reckless as to move The Fair so close to the borders of the Sudlands.

He knew Thaddeus had left those markers specifically for him. The old carpenter hadn't made them from twigs and pebbles either, like he did for the stragglers they'd sometimes had to leave behind when they'd been in danger of being discovered before Ortus had created the Snow Globe.

Thaddeus had cut these new markers into trees and rocks, as if to make sure they would withstand the passing of time almost indefinitely, but there were additions to the symbols, and Lorcan wasn't completely sure the man was still in charge of the little community anymore.

He recognized the hammer with the s-shaped grip and the slanted cyphers next to it. The hammer stood for Thaddeus' work. It always indicated in the cardinal direction where Mary had taken The Fair. The cyphers next to it stood for an approximate distance and a prominent landmark. The new thing beside the hammer, though, was an oak leaf. It was on every single marker he'd encountered save for the first five, and it reminded him of the Tierney crest.

Perhaps it was Dean's mark.

Despite the pleasant hope of seeing his old friend again and the miles he'd traveled to get here, Lorcan still had doubts. He didn't know if he was making the right decision by just turning up out of the blue. If he hadn't promised Abhac he'd make the connection, he might well have changed his mind before he finally crossed the barrier into the Outer Haven.

He took a deep breath and began walking. Static and blurred vision briefly obscured his senses as he transited.

A sand-colored cat greeted him on the other side, purring around his legs. He bent to scratch her head.

"Who are you?" he asked softly, as if she could answer him. "Are you mistaking me for someone else? Or are you the new welcoming committee?"

She looked up at him almost expectantly. He smiled. There was something strange about her, but not in an alarming way. He'd never seen a cat like this before. Her ears seemed too big, her fur was extremely dense, and she was very stocky. For a moment, he thought he saw a hint of silver swirling in her dark eyes. Shapeshifters had threads of gold around their irises, but silver was unusual, and she didn't look, or *feel*, like a Shifter to him. The gleam vanished before he was sure he wasn't mistaken, and he dismissed it. He'd been on the road for a long time, and he was tired.

"Well, let's go take a look at what's become of this place," he told the cat.

Tail high in the air, she walked a few paces ahead of him, glancing back every now and then as if to make sure he didn't change his mind.

Things were different here, that much was for sure. The grounds were bigger by far than he remembered, and they had to be. There were so many more people than before, and so many new attractions and sales stalls.

A few people observed him with curiosity as he led his horse past brightly painted caravans and spacious yurts toward the heart of the fairground. Some of them he knew, but most he'd never met.

They'd built all kinds of wagons while he'd been away, and they were more beautiful than he'd imagined they would be when Thaddeus and he had begun building their prototypes. One kind had little porches, and another had real glass windows. Some were barrel-shaped, others arched. Open-sided wagons were fitted with square tents attached to them to make more room for the things their owners peddled.

Here and there, dogs lay dozing in the sun or wandered between the caravans, looking for someone to feed them, but none of the mongrels acknowledged the Sand Cat in his presence as Lorcan passed the candlemakers' workshop. One of the young men creating works of woven art in warm, golden beeswax nodded at him, and he tried to put a name with the face, but failed, and simply nodded back.

Not far from the workshop, several stands sold household items for the kitchen, scented soaps, oils, and combs. The glorious scent of the soaps made Lorcan light-headed for a moment, and he smiled, wondering what they were putting in the mixtures as he continued on his way in direction of a seamstresses' marquee he had never seen the like of before.

A whole crew of sewing women sat busy at their tables beneath the awning. An assortment of wooden racks huddled around them, bending under the weight of all sorts of fine clothing in colors only wealthy people would normally wear. The magic that was spun into the fibers of the fabrics almost glowed, at least to his perception, and he wanted to know more about it, but then remembered why he was here, and moved on.

Passing a large pavilion with a dozen man-high mirrors near the main tent, Lorcan noticed a few booths that offered games and gambling he was sure Ortus wouldn't have approved of. They blended in and seemed to belong, but there had been a time when the kind of people who earned their keep by cheating other people out of their hard-earned coins would have been asked to do their business outside of The Fair's perimeter.

He hardly had time to think about it before he reached the Big Top. The huge tent had been fitted with an impressive standard, and a rendering of an oak leaf on every other segment of the tarp.

A man with copper hair came out of the main entrance just as Lorcan was about to go inside. He was talking to a Firestarter Lorcan recognized as Rua Tine's brother, Bui. The smile on the Firestarter's face turned to confusion when he recognized Lorcan, and Dean fell silent for a moment.

"Good to see you, Dean," Lorcan said, ignoring Bui's sour mien.

He could tell life hadn't been cruel to Dean; the Sorcerer's son seemed well-nourished and in good health and spirits.

Demonstratively, Dean embraced him, heartily thumping his back. "Well, I'll be! I didn't think I'd ever see you again. I'm so glad you're here!"

Lorcan had hoped they would be all right with one another, but he hadn't counted on it, and a wave of relief washed over him. Dean hadn't changed, even if everything else here had.

"What the hell is *he* doing here?" Bui snarled, more in keeping with what Lorcan had been expecting.

Lorcan patted his cloak as though he was searching for something.

"So nice to know you're still your old self, Bui. I think I still have the map your brother drew for Jaden around here somewhere. It was very good, and I've been meaning to ask him about that for a long time now."

Dean's gaze wandered between the two men, and Lorcan could see Bui was seething. The silver aura in his eyes flashed dangerously, and he hoped the man was in control of himself, but then it dawned on him Dean didn't know about the map. He burned to find out if Rua was still around.

Tearing through the tension, Dean hooked his arm over Lorcan's shoulder and pulled him away from Bui.

"Come on, there's someone who's been waiting for you."

Reluctantly, Lorcan let Dean lead the way. Glancing around, he noticed the Sand Cat shadowing them.

When they were out of earshot of Bui, Dean said, "We have a lot to talk about. I know you had nothing to do with my father's death. We'll have time for that later. You're not in a hurry, are you?"

"No, I can stay for as long as you want me to."

Dean seemed genuinely happy to hear that.

He directed Lorcan to a caravan that stood a little apart from the others. Looking at the patterns on the shutters and the floral designs around the door, Lorcan could guess whom it belonged to. He was proven right when Dean pushed the door open. The cat elegantly slunk inside ahead of them.

The small room was flooded with warm afternoon sunlight. It was tidy and immaculately clean, but the smell of illness hung in the air. Lorcan's heart grew heavy when he saw Mary sitting on a stool by her husband's bedside, humming a song to him as she dabbed his damp brow with a rag.

She almost dropped the rag when she became aware that Dean wasn't alone and realized Lorcan was there behind him.

"My God, we were so worried about you," she told him, pushing past Dean to close the short distance between them.

She wrapped her arms around him like a mother, and he let himself fall into the warmth of the moment. He hadn't been aware of how much love the elderly woman's heart had held for him then and still did, and his ignorance struck him with shame when she released him and he could see the tears streaking her cheeks. She wiped them away hurriedly and traded places with him so he could see Thaddeus.

Lorcan bent down and took the old man's calloused hand in his own, but the carpenter clearly couldn't see him or feel his touch. His breathing was labored, and a sheen of cold sweat covered his skin.

"Hello, Thaddeus," he said softly, studying the man's face.

There were more lines and creases than when he'd last seen him. Ortus had left him with a lot of responsibility to shoulder, and Lorcan was certain he'd surpassed himself. Thaddeus had always dealt with things while Ortus had been away, but he'd been alone these past years, and he'd continued building this community on his own.

Lorcan pulled up the stool and sat down without letting go of his former master craftsman's hand.

"I think you'll be wanting to hear about the places I've been to and the things I've seen. No time like the present, is there?" A twitch of his free hand closed the door, leaving the horse outside to its own devices.

He looked at Mary. She was still staring at him. "Do you mind the cat being in here?" he asked her.

"What cat?" She turned to look at the dresser, where he'd directed his gaze.

Lorcan was at a loss. Neither she nor Dean seemed to perceive the feline sitting there, eyes half closed and smiling at no one in particular.

"Never mind." He didn't know what to make of it. The cat settled down, tucking her paws beneath her and began dozing, and he decided to let it go. The Fair had always been a place where strange and wonderful, or terrible things happened – he'd taken a liking to the Sand Cat and didn't think this was one of the terrible things.

Dean sat down on the chest by the small folding table while Mary poured them all some elderberry juice. Lorcan took the cup and savored the first sip, swirling it around in his mouth before he swallowed and began telling his story.

Starting at the end, he worked his way backward from the markers he'd found leading him back to The Fair. He left out a great deal, including the existence of his son, but he conveyed enough of his travels to prove his willingness to put his cards on the table. When he got to the part where he found Ortus' body by the roadside, Dean covered his mouth with his hands. He looked like a boy who was lost in memories of his own.

"I don't know whether it was Jaden or the woman he was with, but I'm fairly sure one of the two killed him. They planned it, but I don't know how they did it. My father lay a little way off from Ortus. A snake must have bitten him, and he was dying. He kept telling me to be wary of that snake, and I actually found it, but Maebh was gone."

"What did you do with the creature?" Dean asked. "With the snake, I mean. Do you think it could have been a Shapeshifter?"

Lorcan had already given this a lot of consideration. "No. I know for a fact that Maebh wasn't a Shapeshifter. She was a Cine. Maybe she just took off after Jaden was bitten. I noticed Ortus' book was missing – you know, the one he always carried with him – but I doubt she would have had much use for it. I brought the snake back with me and gave it to Freya. Maybe she still has it."

"I wish you'd stayed," Mary told him. "I wish you'd just told everyone all of this and stayed."

Lorcan got up and hugged Mary. "I'm so sorry, but I just couldn't."

She nodded, though she wasn't convinced.

He opened a window, and a cool breeze wafted in. Dean lit a few candles and placed one in the shelf above Thaddeus' bed.

Lorcan recalled the moment he'd reached the Haven with old Bessie and the Master Sorcerer across her back. He'd already made up his mind to leave before he'd crossed the barrier. The welcome he'd received had merely accelerated his departure. A tear worked its way down the side of his face, but he didn't feel it. It went unseen by Dean, but Mary tilted her head and Lorcan knew she saw what was inside of him. All of it.

"You were hardly more than a boy, and you didn't know what to expect here. I get that."

"And now?" Dean asked, watching Mary moisten Thaddeus' lips with a few drops of water from a spoon. "Why did you come back now? And, are you planning to stay?"

Lorcan faced Dean. "There's still a lot to talk about. You have to know that I'm here with a proposal from the Dwarven of the Winter Mountains. They're seeking to form an alliance, and they've sent me to negotiate. The question is, are you going to be the man I'll be discussing this with?"

Dean's eyes rested on Thaddeus, and he briefly deliberated before answering. "I've been here for a while now, and I think it's time I stepped up and did my part. There's no way I could ever fill my father's or Thaddeus' shoes, but I'll be damned if I don't try to walk in them and do whatever it takes to further this community, so yes. I believe I'm that man."

Doing his part – a sense of duty… Lorcan asked himself if that was why he'd agreed to come here. He did feel an obligation to Abhac, and being here reminded him of what Ortus had done for him. Thaddeus had believed in Ortus' dream unconditionally, and even though Lorcan had always been skeptical, he asked himself if he could find it in him to do so as well. Perhaps this was why destiny had brought him back here.

At that moment, the silence in the small room gained a different quality. Oddly, the Sand Cat had vanished into thin air. Lorcan was the first to realize Thaddeus' suffering had come to an end. His absence was palpable. It felt like a cog in the mechanism of time had gone missing, and the machine stopped, if only for a moment.

Mary rested her head on her husband's chest and cried softly into his blanket. Lost for words, Lorcan stood with Dean. Perhaps it was time for him to do his part now too, he thought, and keep the promise he'd given to the Master Sorcerer.

Chapter Twenty-Seven

✑ The Hangman's House ✑

The hangman was a giant with huge hands. They looked strong enough to hold any kind of blade-heavy sword or ax, and sufficiently calloused to prove they often did, but he walked with a limp as though his hip or back or both were causing him pain. The yellow discoloring in his eyes spoke volumes of his drinking habits, and he smelled of ale despite the early hour.

Catherine wondered if a constant proximity to death did that to men in general, or if it was only the weak ones who couldn't help themselves. If he was weak, she knew she'd have to watch her step around him.

"This is one of me best girls, Catherine," Deirdre told him when he led them into the kitchen of his house, and then faced back to Catherine. "Catherine, this is Matthew Binns, your new employer."

Catherine felt the stooping man's gaze brazenly roam over her body. He was so tall, he couldn't even stand up straight in his own home, but he belonged in this house like a bear did in his cave.

"Bit thin," he said, seating himself near the hearth where he'd been twisting strands of hemp into a thick rope. Deirdre took a chair opposite him. Catherine chose to remain standing.

A girl younger than she entered the kitchen. She startled and was about to head back out the way she'd come, but Deirdre jumped up and grabbed her arm, pasting her brightest smile to her face as if she was greeting a relative she hadn't seen in ages.

"Ellen, how nice to see ye!" she sang, and Ellen stopped in her tracks. The girl was pale and drawn. "Make friends with Catherine and show her to her new room while Matthew and I talk business."

Reluctantly, she nodded. Deirdre all but ushered them both out of the room.

A flight of narrow stairs dissected the spacious house that had been built for a large family. Half way up and lugging her bag, Catherine had to watch her head. She imagined Binns bending and twisting his heavy form to climb to the second floor, perhaps on his hands and knees when he was having a bad day.

"How long have you been here?" she asked the girl when they'd reached the top.

"Two years," Ellen replied without looking back at her or offering another word.

She pushed open a door on the right side of the corridor.

Looking inside, Catherine discovered it was tiny and filthy, and she wouldn't even have it to herself. A girl roughly her own age occupied the cot to the left of the shuttered window, cocooned in a stained and tatty blanket. The other bed was empty, but the sheet covering the sagging straw mattress was a mess.

"What is *this?*"

Ellen went rigid at her tone. "Your room," she offered timidly.

The other girl awoke, sat up and glared at her. "Get out of here," she mumbled, "I'm trying to sleep."

"I can see that."

Catherine turned to Ellen. "Show me the other rooms."

Ellen was about to protest, but Catherine took one menacing step toward her and she flinched. She reminded her of Amber. Little Ellen was scared of her own shadow.

"Show me the other rooms. Now."

Ellen stepped aside and motioned to two other doors toward the front of the house. The rooms behind them were no better than the first. There were two other girls besides, but they were both out. A fourth door led to a steep set of stairs that went up into the attic.

Ellen stopped her just as she was about to go and take a look. "Don't. That's Binns' room. We only go up there when he calls us."

Catherine freed herself of Ellen's hand and went anyway, each dusty tread creaking beneath her feet.

The attic wasn't meant for standing up even for someone of her height. A dormer window provided shafts of weak light. The odor of stale sweat hung in the air, and she was sure an unemptied chamber pot lurked somewhere beneath the big bed in the center of the loft. A dresser and a chest that matched the bed stood lost beneath the diagonal joists, and both looked as though they hadn't been cleaned in a long time.

Still, this would be *a lot* better than the rooms on the second floor, Catherine decided. Binns couldn't possibly manage those stairs very much longer, and she was already planning where she'd move the chest when she heard voices below.

"I tried to stop her, but she wouldn't listen," Ellen whined.

"That's alright, darling," Binns told her. "Might as well see what we've got. I've a hanging this afternoon, and I could do with some distraction for an hour or two while she's already there."

Catherine's breath caught as she watched him close the door behind him and heave himself up the stairs. She couldn't help but be just a little bit afraid of what was in store, but this was where she was at, and she didn't think she would be here for as long as Ellen. She was going to earn a lot of money until something else came along, and when it did, she would forget this ever happened.

Binns pushed past her without so much as a glance, and she watched him bend his crooked back to open the trunk. From it he retrieved a black hood, a pair of shackles, and some leather cords.

"Deirdre tells me you know what's expected of you," he said, tossing the things on the bed.

Catherine raised her chin and watched him stripping off his clothes.

"Of course," she said, hating him already, but there was nothing for it.

He grinned, looking past her. "Well, then what on earth are you still waiting for, girl?"

When he was done with her, he left her chained to the bed to go and manage that hanging he'd told Ellen about.

She waited until she was sure he was gone and then freed herself, though he'd never know how she'd done that. By the time he got back, she'd already started the girls on cleaning the house and found out where he kept his liquor and his silver. He didn't say a word to her, but asked Ellen to make his dinner.

Two weeks later, he'd grasped the logic behind giving Catherine the loft and having a carpenter make a bed for him on the ground floor. She shared with him most nights after the last of her customers had gone home, because there was a logic behind that, too.

Chapter Twenty-Eight

෬ The Merchant ౖ

A hard night had ended early for Ellen when Binns had to throw out a caller who'd known no measure. The girl was still asleep in her bed at noon the next day, but Catherine decided to leave her alone. She'd given her something to help her heal and forget, mixed with perhaps a little too much wine, but sleeping was going to help her more than any powder or ointment would.

Between what Catherine had learned from Rebecca and been taught by Deirdre, she'd already had a decent knowledge of anatomy and medicinal herbs when she'd arrived in Saint Aeden. The hangman's little library of journals on the workings of the human body and his lessons in precision and dosage of good and bad poisons had expanded on that considerably.

It was Binns, of all people – *the executioner* – who'd given her the benefit of his experience with pain and trauma and the means to deal with the whole spectrum of injuries a whore had to contend with. He had spent a great deal of time researching antidotes to all of the common afflictions a working girl was prone to, and that was the knowledge Catherine had drawn on these past three years.

Binns was at a hearing today, and she'd dispatched the others to scrub the floors, do their laundry, and then go to the market for carrots and parsnips, so she finally had some time to herself now. The occasions when that happened were rare and precious, though she'd grown accustomed to the givens of life at the hangman's house.

Her first months there had been tough, and she'd hoped it would all pay off soon, but she hadn't anticipated how much of her income would go toward costs Binns felt obliged to share with the girls who shared his house.

One year in fall, he'd said the leaky roof was Catherine's problem, since it was her room getting wet and moldy, and when a part of the chimney collapsed the following winter, he'd kept four weeks' earnings from all of them to reimburse the mason and his apprentice for the work.

Binns was a wealthy man, and although Catherine knew where he stashed his silver, she also knew he counted it daily.

Lying with him, managing his household and doing everything to keep him happy gave her a good standing with his other employees, even those who'd been there longer than she, but she couldn't see herself doing what she did until she got too old for it.

She was aware by now that she hardly stood a chance of getting off the treadmill she was on in Saint Aeden, but several ideas had lodged in her head. One of them was starting her own business when the hangman was too ill to run his sideline enterprise any longer. Unfortunately, however, she thought he might have a few more years left in him, so she was stuck with him, for better or for worse.

Unless, of course...

She'd played with the thought of ridding herself of him, but since his house would go to his brother's son when he died, she knew she'd either just be passed along, or out on her ear and lacking sufficient funds to support herself. She'd be forced to look for another employer or she'd be anyone's fair game.

The problem was churning in her mind when there was a knock on the back door.

It wasn't unusual to have customers during the day, but Catherine was annoyed by the prospect of having to deal with some smarmy caller just now while she was alone.

A narrow window on either side of the heavy wooden door allowed for a view of the man who was waiting outside.

He had his hat pulled down over his face, and that came as no surprise. Decent people wouldn't want to be seen visiting the hangman or the soiled doves nesting in his rambling house. Everyone liked to think of themselves as *decent*, and in her experience, the ones most convinced of themselves were the most *indecent* of them all.

She could see that his clothes were made of fine material, and he looked very clean. He knocked again, more impatiently this time.

She opened the door with a practiced smile. "May I help you, sir?"

He looked up, startling her with eyes as blue as the sky, fringed by dark lashes. She felt warm as they raked over her appreciatively, and she all but gawked at the clear beauty of them before she remembered herself.

He rewarded her reaction with a lop-sided smile that did very pleasant things to his face and stopped the breath in her chest. She'd been with more men than she could count, but she'd never seen one whose features neared perfection as much as this man's did.

"I beg your pardon, milady," he said, his voice smooth as silk. "I'm looking for Matthew Binns."

She was oddly pleased to discover he wasn't here for one of the girls, though she couldn't think why.

"He had business in town, but he should be back soon. Would you like to wait inside for him?"

She felt stupid the moment she'd invited him in. By the look of his attire and the way he conducted himself, she believed he might be a merchant or a member of the council. Surely he had legitimate business with the hangman and would be put off by the thought of being entertained by Binns' Madame. He astounded her by taking off his hat and nodding with a polite bow and a smile, and she moved aside to allow him in.

She led him to the parlor where the clients usually waited. The redecorating she'd done here shortly after she'd moved into the attic made a world of difference to how it had been before, and she thought it was now the nicest room in the house. Having him sit in the kitchen just didn't seem right.

She poured him a cup of wine from Binns' personal stock. He was probably used to better, but it was all she could do for him.

His fingers accidentally brushed her hands as he took the cup, and the sensation sent a shiver down her spine.

"You have a lovely home, Mistress Binns," he said, seating himself on the chair she offered.

She laughed before she thought better of it, wondering whatever gave him that idea. Shaking her head at his puzzled expression, she corrected him. "I am not Mistress Binns."

"I'm sorry – his daughter, then?"

"No."

A strange pain took root in the pit of her stomach and she suddenly felt embarrassed as he waited for her to elaborate. She was loathe to tell this stranger who she really was. She couldn't remember the last time someone had assumed the best of her, looked at her as a woman and not a whore. She'd rather liked this moment and his assumption. Steeling herself for his reaction, she made sure the smile did not slip from her lips, and that her shoulders were straight, but relaxed.

"I manage his house," she said, "and I manage the women in his house."

"Ah." His face told her he understood.

After a moment's silence, he raised his glass to her. "Well, I'm very glad to make your acquaintance. Won't you sit with me while I wait?"

She did as he asked, though less comfortable in his presence now.

Then, he surprised her again. "If I may not call you Mistress Binns, will you tell me your name so I'll know to whom I owe the pleasure of speaking with?"

He kept face, she had to leave him that. "I'm Catherine."

The easy smile returned to his lips. "Catherine."

She loved how he said that.

He went on to inquire about the town and its port, and he listened attentively to her observations, although she was sure by the manner of questions he asked that he knew his way around already. If he'd been discomfited by learning of her occupation, he didn't show it.

Aside from haggling with the vendors over purchases or the workmen about repairs to the house, she never had conversations with men that didn't involve their wishes and demands, but he seemed genuinely interested in what she was saying, so she bravely ventured to build on that. She was curious as to what business he could possibly have with Binns.

"If I may ask, what brings you to our lovely town, sir?"

He released a deep breath. She was about to apologize for her unseemly forwardness, but he leaned forward in his chair and cut her off.

"I am Master of the Merchants' Guild in Ironstone. A few months ago, I commissioned someone to bring a load of furniture and cloth goods to Lord Alster for his daughter's wedding."

Catherine knew the steward and she'd heard of the grand wedding he'd afforded his favorite child. Alster was a loving father, but he was also a harsh choleric. He liked to work his frustrations out on plump little Farren in the room right above this one whenever he could make time.

"Well," the merchant continued, "the boy made it a half-day's journey this side of Saint Aeden when he and the friend he'd taken along fell prey to a band of robbers. It isn't enough that they left him half dead and took his friend, and that the guild has reimbursed his lordship for the lost goods. No. Alster wants Willard punished as a thief. He claims the young man who accompanied him could have stolen the wagon, and he forwarded his allegation to the council's court here. The claim was heard and sustained."

Catherine shuddered. That meant at least thirty lashes, depending on the value of the lot.

Things like these were never pretty, but Binns was especially brutal with the whip. Still, the right amount of coin in his hand could alter the course of events and decide between life and death in its outcome.

"So you're here to intervene on the boy's behalf?"

The man looked at his feet, and then back up to her. "He's a good lad. His father pays his dues on time, and I'd hate to lose his trust and his support."

Everything men did was always either about money or politics, but she respected his honesty. In this, he was different from most of her callers, and she wondered why he'd told her. She was glad he'd come when no one else was at home. For a moment, she tried to imagine what it would be like to be as respectable as this man pretended she was, to *always* be spoken to the way he spoke to her. She knew she'd do *anything* to get that.

The front door opened with a crash, and Binns stooped beneath the lintel. "Catherine!" he bellowed. "Give us a hand, woman."

The dream was over. Catherine thought killing the old leech might not be a bad idea after all.

Her companion smiled sympathetically.

"Duty calls, I see," the merchant said with half a grin.

Offering her his hand, he helped her rise from her chair and followed her to the front door where the old man was busy shedding his cloak.

Binns reeked of blood. Catherine was never sure whether it was his own or someone else's.

"You have a visitor," she told him, helping him with the cloak. "Master– ?" She turned to the dark-haired man for a name, realizing she'd given him hers, but hadn't asked him for his in return.

He stepped forward and hinted a bow toward the hangman. "Brandner of Ironstone. We've had dealings before. Might I have a word with you, sir?"

Binns gestured for him to follow him back into the parlor and tromped ahead of him.

Brandner took Catherine's hand in his and bent over it like some knight from an old tale. "Until we meet again, Catherine."

She thought about that all the rest of the day, and pictured his clear eyes on her even as she lay with two other men that night.

The next morning, he sent a carriage for her from the inn where he had taken a room until the end of the month.

Chapter Twenty-Nine

❦ Unexpected Things ❧

Smiling, Catherine pulled the dress over her head and smoothed the bodice and skirt down over her waist and hips. Brandner lay on his belly, sweat glistening on his face and back. He rested his chin lazily on his arms as he watched her run her fingers through the damp tangles of her dark hair.

"You really know how to ruin a man, don't you?" he said.

"You've been telling me that every Sunday for the last five, and a summer's worth of them before that," she replied without looking up, her smile widening. "But you were ruined long before you met me."

He laughed, rolling onto his side.

"Maybe I should show you just how much next time."

She pulled on her sandals and cast him a wicked sideways glance. "Promise?"

Whores were forbidden to work on the Lord's Day even in Saint Aeden, but this was the one day of the week she could justify doubling her fee for a man she definitely knew could and would afford it. The extra income allowed her to put a little something away without Binns suspecting, and it was beginning to amount to something. William Brandner had become her best customer.

Binns would be furious if he found out she was withholding her earnings from him, but she'd been with him for so long now, she'd reached a point where she just didn't care anymore.

She met with Brandner at the inn down by the docks whenever he was in Saint Aeden – not the inn where he was staying. Discretion was as important to him as it was to her. He had a wife and child in Ironstone, and since he was the merchants' councilman both there and in Saint Aeden now, he had no interest in bragging to anyone about their arrangement.

His visits to the port had become more frequent since he'd acquired a ship that sailed to Bharat. He'd told her he was buying another vessel, and she thought that would bring him to town not three or four times a year, but rather make him consider moving his family to Saint Aeden altogether.

Catherine wasn't sure how that would affect their understanding, but she didn't think he came to her because he missed his wife. His wife probably had no idea of the things he liked to do with a woman. She'd given him his heir, and she probably sat at home all day in a pretty dress, surrounded by all the pretty things his money could buy, conversing congenially with her pretty friends. The woman was probably bored to death with life, while Brandner was living it up like there was no tomorrow, hooked on the things *she* gave him, things that would likely have pretty girls running from the house screaming bloody murder.

Catherine never tired of giving Brandner new and memorable moments every time he lay with her because she knew that was what kept him coming back to her, and she sure wasn't about to lose her best customer to boredom.

Hunkering down by the side of the bed with her back to the merchant, she pulled her long hair over her shoulder to the front, revealing the loosened tie-down fastening of the bodice to him. It was impractical, but of all the dresses she now owned, this was her finest, and she loved it the most.

"Help a woman out, would you?"

"And why should I do that?" he asked her coolly, rising from the bed to stand over her. A mischievous smirk tugged at his lips as he looked down at her. "I'm not your maid, you know, though sometimes I think you could use one."

She fixed her gaze to his. "But you do want me to go on being nice to you, don't you?"

The glint in his eyes had something dangerous and exciting. Any other woman might have been afraid of him in that moment because he was never gentle, kind or even nice when they were alone in the room together. He was anything but the gentleman who'd come to the hangman's house a year ago, but Catherine enjoyed his kind of game because she knew how to play it better than he did.

He laughed and eventually did as she asked. Then, he went to find his leather pouch in a pile of clothes on the chair by the window. He took a small silver coin from it and tossed it to her. She caught it easily in one hand.

"I won't be here next week," he told her. "Come back here on the first Wednesday of the new month."

This was unexpected. "I don't do house calls in the middle of the week."

"Except for me. You do want *me* to go on being nice to you, don't you?"

She laughed. "It'll cost you double."

"I don't think so, dear." He grinned, pulling on his pants. "It's not a Sunday – it's a *Wednesday*."

"I don't do house calls on Wednesdays any more than I do on Sundays."

He thought about it briefly before donning his shirt. "Alright. But be here."

"You know I will. What's the occasion?"

"I suppose you could say it's my divorce." His voice was completely even as he untied the leather straps from the bed posts.

"I'm sorry to hear that." She wasn't, really. She was mystified, but not sorry.

"Yes, well, it's been a few weeks, but I'm only now getting round to tying up some loose ends, and that calls for a small celebration. Particularly since it's the day the ship I bought yesterday is going to set sail for New Aberdon."

So he'd already struck the bargain and fulfilled another of his dreams, but his wife wasn't going to be a part of it. She asked herself if the two circumstances were connected.

"New Aberdon," she mused, passing over the other bit of information he'd given her on his wife. "How exciting. That's one of the biggest harbors in the Far East, isn't it?"

She could see he was pleased she knew what he was talking about. A few sailors who'd stranded in her bed had been there. Some claimed New Aberdon didn't smell one bit of fish, but only of the most exquisite spices and scented flowers.

He smiled. "Catherine, this is going to make me a very, *very* rich man."

"I'm so happy for you." He was a very, *very* rich man already.

He rolled up the cords around his hand and tied their ends together. "Wear something... dull. And respectable. I'm taking you for an outing."

She always wore *dull and respectable* over the *shameful and breathtaking* that she really wanted him to see when she went to meet him on Sundays, just like she always pulled the yellow ribbon from her hair the moment she'd rounded the street corner to the inn.

"An outing? That sounds... foolish."

He laughed, tucking the leather cords into a satchel along with a few other things he'd brought with him earlier. Then, he pulled her to him.

"Foolish?" he said in a low voice, his hands wandering over her lower back. "Really, dear? Do I strike you as the *foolish* kind of man?"

She studied him and decided he didn't. Never had. "What are you up to, William?"

He smirked. "I want to show you something. Business proposal. You'll love it. I promise."

He left the room a moment ahead of her, taking the front stairway while she went down the back.

She knew he'd order a measure of cider in the public room, as he always did. He'd made a habit of that so they wouldn't be seen leaving together. The innkeeper had a small crowd of Sunday drinkers he called *friends* and who knew to use the side entrance after Mass so the clergy couldn't say he was opening on the Lord's Day.

She made sure to take a look around as she stepped out into the alleyway behind the building, feeling the weight of Brandner's coin in the lining of her cloak. At this rate, she might be able to buy her own place soon. She was thinking of an alehouse somewhere on the outskirts of town, and she knew at least three girls who'd be willing to go along with that and work for her rather than stay with the hangman. Absorbed in her thoughts, she didn't notice the shadow that followed her.

Cold fingers closed about her shoulder and she spun around, ready to strike out at her assailant. There was no way she was going to surrender anything that belonged to her.

"Catherine, you have to help me." Desperation lined Bridget's voice. Tears had left dirty tracks on her dirty cheeks.

Catherine shoved the other woman away before she recognized her, and Bridget fell heavily against the wall of the building.

She wasn't in good shape. The eyes peering at Catherine from a face deathly pale were those of a woman double Bridget's age. She was missing several of those perfect white teeth of hers. The corset of her dress was in rags, and her tattered skirts couldn't conceal her swollen belly.

"You're a mess."

Bridget didn't reply. She fought for words that wouldn't come, training her gaze on the ground at her feet. Catherine thought she was going to collapse and kept some distance between them. She didn't want to catch anything.

"Look," she said, "just get rid of the brat and then go back to work. You'll be alright."

At that, Bridget looked up at her. Both anger and shame molded her expression. "That's easy for you to say. You never got pregnant."

Catherine sighed. "I suppose I'm just a bit cleverer than you, aren't I?"

She'd often wondered about that herself but couldn't explain it. There wasn't a doubt in her mind she would have dealt with it, though. She felt nothing when she looked at children, and she'd sooner drown one than have to nurse it between callers.

She had a sixth sense for when one of the hangman's girls got herself pregnant, and she knew a dozen ways to handle the problem. Few of them ever insisted on keeping their offspring, but Binns had brought Ellen to the poorhouse only last winter when she was a few days away from giving birth and no longer able to work after she'd refused to give it up.

Binns was a businessman, not a charity.

His house, his rules, Ellen's own recklessness.

"Look," Bridget said, kneading her boney hands, "you seem to be doing alright for yourself. I need help. Please."

Catherine wondered if Bridget had been watching her, perhaps followed her here from the hangman's house. "No."

Bridget didn't seem to have heard her. "I've been out on the street the last weeks. I'm afraid for my baby, and I don't have anywhere to go. You *have to* help me…"

"Stupid girl. You made your bed, and you'll have to lie in it." Catherine turned to walk away, but the other woman came after her, anger and shame turning to desperation once more.

"Please, Catherine, I'll pay you back."

"How would you *ever* do that?" She waited for a reply, but got none. "No."

"Catherine, I'm the one who helped you when you were new back on the road, remember? And I never said a word to anyone about your... *Talent.*"

Catherine stopped in her tracks.

"I do know what you are," Bridget went on. "I saw how you put some of your studs to sleep if they got out of line, and I never told *anyone.*"

But she was going to tell. Catherine knew that for certain.

"What's the trouble here?" Brandner's voice came from somewhere behind her before she had time to do anything reckless of her own. He must have passed up on the cider, and it was a good thing he had.

Bridget instantly stopped talking. Catherine felt her growing trepidation.

Catherine hesitated. "Nothing."

Brandner seemed to catch on that *nothing* was really more of a *something* than she let on, and she'd counted on that. He grabbed Bridget's arm and pushed her against the wall, glaring at her.

"Is that so?"

"I don't want any trouble," Bridget said, her voice trembling as much as her body was.

"Then why go look for it?" Brandner returned, letting go of her without backing away or taking his eyes off her. He pulled his coin pouch forth once again and counted some coppers into his palm so she could see. "Tell me your name, darling."

"Bridget, sir."

He shoved the coins into her hand. "Bridget, you take this, and you take yourself away from here as far and as fast as your feet will carry you. I don't want to see you again. Are we clear on that?"

Bridget nodded, looking at the ground with her fist closed around the money, but that wasn't enough for him. He slammed his hand against the wall right next to her face.

"I said, *are we clear on that?*"

"Yes," she wailed, "we're clear."

He retreated from her just enough so she could scuttle away, and she left the alley, looking back over her shoulder every few steps.

"What was that all about?" he asked Catherine.

Catherine had anticipated the question and readied the lie she knew would work in her advantage. "I think she's been following me. She knows who you are, and she tried to blackmail me."

Brandner's eyes widened for a second. "Well, that's too bad for her," he said. "What I gave her is not going to keep her quiet for long."

Catherine clasped her hand over her mouth and sighed. "Maybe I should talk to her again…"

"No. Don't. Let me deal with this."

"But how?"

"I have some very persuasive people working for me."

Wondering about that, she studied him intently, digging into his thoughts. What she saw there in his mind was a very permanent solution, and she had no objections to that.

Chapter Thirty

❧ Aeden ☙

Brandner's carriage stood in the backyard of the inn, still laden with baggage when Catherine arrived, thinking she was early. He'd probably just arrived in town and made this his first stop. She wondered if she was that important to him, or if there was another reason he was here already. She couldn't wait to see what big mystery he was keeping from her.

Their usual room was never locked when the innkeeper expected them, and she went in without knocking. The smile froze on her lips when she saw him sitting at the window, scowling at a small boy on the chair opposite him.

"Ah, there you are, my dear," he said, his face brightening considerably to what she'd seen a second before.

The youngster said nothing and just went back to staring at his hands. Brandner pulled him up.

"Catherine, this is Aeden."

Catherine didn't know his son's name and she couldn't say Aeden looked anything like Brandner with his soft brown eyes and mousy hair, but she assumed this would be his boy.

What on earth was he doing here? What was Brandner thinking?

"Pleased to meet you, Aeden," she said, bending down to him.

His jaw dropped. "Your eyes…" he began.

Brandner tugged at Aeden's arm gruffly, shaking him. "Stop that, now. I'll have no more of it!"

Catherine straightened, trying to work out what was going on here. "What about my eyes?"

"There's nothing wrong with your eyes, darling," Brandner said from between clenched teeth, cutting the boy off. "He has a very lively imagination. Likes to get attention that way."

Studying the lad and the way he looked at her, she doubted he'd just been trying to get attention. He didn't strike her as the type.

"Look," Brandner said then, "I need you to stay here with Aeden for me for just a few hours. I have a few things to take care of, but I'll be back as soon as I can."

She was about to ask what things, but they were none of her concern.

"Alright, I'll look after him." She faced Aeden. "Maybe we can get something to eat. Would you like that?"

The boy said nothing, but nodded slightly.

When Brandner was gone, she took the lad's hand and walked him to one of the smaller market places nearby in silence. They got some apples and a loaf of fresh bread, and the boy chewed slowly as they made a detour back to the inn, just so the time would pass.

"You're my father's new wife, aren't you?" he asked eventually.

She laughed. "No."

"Are you going to be?"

"I don't know." The thought hadn't crossed her mind. Well, not in a waking, rational moment. Brandner would never marry a whore.

Aeden seemed to accept that.

"Where's your mama, Aeden?"

He didn't answer.

"Not telling, are you?"

Perhaps he didn't know. When husbands cast out their wives, any children their marriage had brought forth remained in their charge, particularly when those children were sons. But, she wondered what had caused Brandner to take that step. Certainly not so he could be with her.

"My mother is dead," the boy mumbled eventually.

Catherine stopped in her tracks. "Dead?" This was getting better and better.

"Father said so." The lad wiped at a stray tear with his sleeve, sniffling.

Catherine hummed. She resumed walking, overgoing his misery. "Well, then it's a good thing you've still got him."

Again, silence as the boy kept her slow pace all the way back to the inn.

Brandner still wasn't there when they returned.

"About what you said earlier," she mused, looking out the window and down at the passers-by. "About my eyes? What did you see?"

Aeden sat down on his chair once again, the apple in his hand turning brown where he'd taken a bite out of it.

"I didn't see anything." He glanced at his feet.

She remembered what it had been like when she'd first learned that she had Talents that set her apart from other people. With that knowledge had come the instinct that she was better off hiding it from them. Perhaps he was one of her kind. Perhaps he saw the silver gleam Dean had spoken of.

Kneeling in front of him, Catherine gently made him look at her. "But we both know that's not true, love," she said quietly. "Your father isn't here. I just want to know, that's all. Tell me, what was it?"

Fixing her gaze firmly to his, she found herself confronted with a wall. It was thick and high and virtually impenetrable. She couldn't look into his mind at all. Not even a glimpse. He wasn't human, that much was sure, but she didn't think he was a Cine either.

"Don't do that," he said, trying to free himself of her. "I don't know what it was. Shiny. Like a polished coin in the light."

So he could see the silver she herself could not. Catherine knew he hadn't inherited the Gift from Brandner. Brandner was human through and through. Perhaps that was why the boy's mother was dead. Perhaps she'd been Tainted and Brandner had found out.

A hundred alarm signals shrilled in her head, but she didn't have the time to think it over before the door opened and the merchant reappeared.

"All set?" he said to the boy, and Aeden rose, paling. He nodded slowly.

"All set for what?" Catherine asked sharply. This day wasn't what she'd been hoping for, and it had the potential to get even worse still. She thought it might have been wiser to stay at home. This was why she didn't do house calls. It just got too damn personal.

"Aeden is going on a trip. The first of many," Brandner said far too brightly, grabbing the boy's shoulder and pulling the child to him. He may have been trying to convey some form of affection by the gesture, but Aeden didn't perceive it as such. Neither did she.

The smile on Brandner's face was both bitter and sweet as he looked at his son, and Aeden's eyes betrayed a deep-rooted sorrow Catherine could feel without having to invade his head.

"You didn't mention you were going on a trip, William," she said, trying to keep to a light and pleasant tone.

"Well, that's because *I'm* not." He motioned at the boy. "Aeden is. He'll be sailing to New Aberdon on the Ocean's Pride."

Catherine assumed that would be his new ship. "That sounds… *adventurous* for a little boy."

"He's almost seven. Time to stop babying him. Start at the bottom and work your way up, that's how you toughen up for what's to come. I was traveling the east-west Trading Road with a big caravan when I was five, cleaning boots and shoes, feeding horses and greasing their saddles. I had my own mount by the time I was nine, and I had my first cart before I was fourteen. I'm forty-five now, and I *own* that caravan and two others besides. I also own the Ocean's Pride and the Golden Dawn. Do you think that would have happened if I'd sat at home, starving by my mother's hearth or going down into the mines until I couldn't stand up straight anymore?"

Catherine wouldn't have guessed that about him, but she supposed there were a lot of things he might not guess about her, either. There was something wrong with this picture nonetheless.

"Come on, Aeden. Let's get you to that ship." He turned to Catherine, giving her that lop-sided smile of his that told her all was well between them. He was no threat to her. He was prepared to put his own small son aboard a ship to sail half way around the world, but harming her was the farthest thing from his mind. "Just a little more patience, love? I won't be long, and I still have a surprise for you. Order some wine for us, would you? I'll be right back."

Weighing her options, she decided she wanted to stay. She was curious where all of this was going.

Chapter Thirty-One

❦ The Duchess of Glasston ❧

When Brandner returned to the inn, he already smelled of drink. Anger and frustration twisted his otherwise so balanced features. In one swig, he downed a cup of the wine she'd ordered, and informed her the carriage was ready and that they were leaving.

It was almost evening by the time the vehicle rattled past the Fish Market.

"He's not my son, you know," Brandner said, staring out the window at the people they passed without seeing them.

"But you raised him."

He snorted a bitter laugh. "Not guessing he was someone else's bastard, silly me."

The coachman followed the water line, and Catherine wondered if Brandner could tell which of the two three-masters that were heading out of the harbor was the Ocean's Pride, and if he had any regrets.

"How did you find out?"

"I came home early from a trip a few months ago only to find my bed occupied by one of the stable boys." He shrugged, as though the memory of that moment couldn't touch him anymore.

"I had the lad whipped and I questioned him. He admitted to having slept with Amelie all the time in my absence for years. I had the bailiff's lieutenant come to take both of them away. I just couldn't have Amelie in the house anymore. She was tried a few days later for adultery and even admitted to having been pregnant already by some apprentice of her father's before we were married."

"I'm so sorry." That was what he wanted to hear.

He'd been within his rights to do what he'd done. But what, exactly, had he done? She knew he'd had Bridget silenced. She'd never seen her again after their argument in the alleyway.

"Aeden told me his mother is dead."

"She is. She was sentenced to twenty lashes and didn't survive them." He leaned forward, his bright blue eyes cold as ice. "I wasn't prepared to pay for leniency. No one makes a fool of me. *No one.*"

She didn't have any trouble believing that. Perhaps he did have regrets, but he wasn't going to let them overtake him. He was resolute to a fault. William Brandner would cut his own hand off if he thought it was going to steal from him. She liked that about him.

"You still have to tell me where we're going," she said after a while, when she saw they were leaving town.

Having told the hangman she was visiting a friend who'd fallen ill, she'd paid him for the day's losses, but he'd expect her to be home in the course of the evening. She was sure she'd have a few sorrows of her own to contend with in the morning if she wasn't.

Binns was a big oaf, but he knew when he was being lied to, and she hated dipping into his sick mind all too often because he also seemed to know when he was being fooled with, whether she did so by slipping him powders into his soup to keep him off her after the last of her callers had left, like she'd done with Cooper, or whether it was something more subtle like leaving an idea or an assumption in his head when she visited it.

Brandner's mien relaxed almost to a smile, and he patted her knee. "I've recently acquired a quaint little cottage in the country, and I thought you might like to see it."

"Binns is not going to be very happy with me."

He laughed. "Since when have you ever been afraid of Binns?"

She wasn't afraid. She was careful. There was a difference.

A country cottage didn't quite seem to fit Brandner. "Are you thinking of leaving Ironstone?"

"Good heavens, no." He seemed amused, and the coldness left his eyes at the prospect of making fun of her. "I'm the merchants' guild master there, and I have responsibilities."

"To all those people who make your money for you."

"You've hit the nail on the head. But I am growing tired of living in rented rooms in Saint Aeden, and it's time the both of us had a little more privacy."

She bit her lip. That was a delicious thought, but they were moving ever farther away from town.

"Privacy that's going to take me very far away from my workplace."

"Let me worry about that. I assure you, you have as much to gain from this as I do. I'd like to introduce you to someone tonight. Someone who's going to change your life – and mine."

Her brow creased involuntarily. She'd have to hurt him if he was planning on hawking her to one of his friends.

"And who would that be?"

A mischievous grin spread all over his face.

"You think too much. It's just a harmless little old lady I met some years ago in the Sudlands. She was one of my best customers. Her desire for fine cloths and good silken threads knew no boundaries. Her appetite for luxury on the whole knew no boundaries, but her husband was as much a fool for expensive things as she was, and they really knew how to celebrate life." He paused.

His use of the past tense didn't escape her. "And then their fortunes turned?"

"Sadly, yes. The good Duke of Glasston passed away about a year ago, and would you believe, Lady Glasston had to leave his ancestors' home last winter because she was so broke, she couldn't pay the king's steadily increasing taxes anymore?"

Catherine sighed. All well and good, but... "What has that got to do with me?"

"Nothing and everything, dear. The duchess and her unmarried daughter – whose name was *Katharina*, by the way – were traveling north with one of my caravans a few months ago. I *personally* arranged that so they'd get a passage from Saint Aeden to Walha, where they hoped distant relatives would take them in. But, robbers mounted a vicious attack on that caravan in the Northern Forest, and the young maiden was slain in the most grisly manner. Thirteen people were slain in all, and a dozen more injured. I also lost quite a few wagons with goods, ten horses, and a half a dozen donkeys."

"That must have been hard."

He nodded. "It was the second time this year, the fifth in the last two, despite a heavily armed guard, and all of the attacks took place on lands in Trondenburgh's charge. It won't ruin me, but it's damaging my reputation and it hurts financially, of course, especially in light of my most recent and largest ever investments and the new taxation laws that are bleeding me at every border and river my caravans cross."

She could imagine. He'd told her of his successes and new endeavors, but he hadn't so much as mentioned any of this before.

"One of the surviving guards I had accompanying the caravan showed up on my doorstep in Ironstone one day a few weeks after it happened. He brought the duchess. She was hurt and disorientated, but since I'd guaranteed her safety, she insisted on reimbursement, would you believe?"

His face told her he still couldn't. The carriage slowed as the roads became bumpier.

"I didn't know what to do with her at first," Brandner continued. "I had my own troubles with Amelie at that time, but something told me not to turn the old biddy away, so I had her brought here and promised her she could stay for as long as she wanted."

"That's charitable of you."

"Yes, but don't ask me why. I surprise myself, sometimes." His smirk told Catherine otherwise. He never did anything unless he saw a gain in it.

"And she recovered?"

He nodded. "Very well, considering. She still has… moments, but when she told me her story, it gave me an idea."

He broke off there because they'd come to a halt in front of a huge double-winged gate. It dissected a massive stone wall that was half-covered in ivy or some other kind of creeper. It still looked solid, but the gate seemed more decorative than resilient by the light of the keeper's torch when Catherine glanced out.

The keeper opened for them, and the carriage slowly pulled into a cobbled courtyard with stables on one end and a sizeable manor house on the other.

Darkness concealed much of the main building, but Catherine had the feeling they were so far from Saint Aeden, she'd be getting a tour of it in the morning anyway. They weren't going back to town tonight.

A servant hurried to unfasten the latch on her door and help her out of the vehicle. Brandner followed and led her into the Great Hall by the hand like a child, as though he was afraid she would lose her way, while the coachman tended to the horses.

Torches and candles immersed the Hall in warm yellow light and crawling shadows. A fire crackled in the hearth. An old lady sat in the chair next to it, poring over some embroidery work. Catherine assumed this would be the duchess Brandner had told her about. Her hearing couldn't be too good because she only became aware of them when they'd almost reached her. Setting her embroidery aside, she rose to greet them.

"William, how nice." A pleasant smile creased her aged face. "I wasn't expecting you just yet."

"But I *did* tell you I'd be back tonight, Lady Glasston."

The duchess looked confused.

Catherine's glance fell upon her sewing. It was a mess of threads and knots.

"That's alright," Brandner told the old woman, patting her hand. "It doesn't matter. I'd like you to meet Catherine."

"Oh, so this pretty young lady is your fiancée, then." Brittle bones embraced Catherine lightly, and the noblewoman breathed a kiss on each of her cheeks. "I'm so glad to finally meet you. Welcome to your new home, Catherine," she said.

Catherine gasped, ten questions on her lips, but darting Brandner a glance, she observed him placing a finger over his own to let her know now was not the time.

"Lady Glasston, we're both weary from the trip," he told the elderly woman. "I think we'll just retire now and see you at breakfast. We can talk about everything then."

The lady clung on to Catherine's hands for another moment, studying her. "She's a lovely girl, William," she told Brandner. "I'm certain we can remedy that neglectful upbringing in no time, and she'll fit in our circles just fine."

Brandner smiled. "I'm so glad to hear you say that, Lady Glasston. I know you'll do a wonderful job."

A servant informed them that a room had been readied for their guest. Brandner led Catherine up the stone stairway into the second floor to make sure she found it.

"William, what's going on?" she demanded once the door was closed firmly behind them. "What did she mean by *remedying my neglectful upbringing*, and why did you tell her we're to be married?"

He pulled her to him. "Don't get all excited, love. Enjoy the moment. I assure you, it'll be worth your while." Trailing kisses up and down her neck, he began undressing her, but for the first time since they'd met, she withdrew from him.

"Look, I've been very patient with you, but I do want to know what's going on now, or I'm leaving."

"No, you're not. You're not going anywhere." He backed her against the wall next to the wardrobe, cornering her, and held her there, covering her mouth with his own as his free hand began roaming her bodice.

"Stop," she said and pushed him away. "Seriously. You owe me an explanation."

He laughed, backed off, and plunked down on the bed, running his fingers through his thinning hair. The day had left him somewhat askew, she realized.

"You're right," he said, but didn't expand on that.

He just sat there, watching her.

It frustrated her.

"Why did you bring me here?"

"Because, my dear, it's time for some changes."

"What changes?" It appeared he was currently determined to make a lot of adjustments in his life.

"You have your troubles and I have mine, Catherine," he muttered, rubbing his chin. "What would you say if I told you we can help each other solve our problems once and for all?"

She sat down next to him. His problems and her problems hardly seemed related, and she wondered how he was going to make a connection between the two of them. This evening was turning out to be entertaining, at least.

"What are you up to, William?"

He planted a kiss on her knuckles. "I can make all your dreams come true, love. I can make a duchess of you. You'd have the finest of everything, and you'd live in a castle before the year is out. How does that sound?"

She chuckled. "I think you've had too much wine today. You're not making sense."

"Not at all." He stared into her eyes, and she was tempted to look deeper. He was wide open for her, and she couldn't resist. She saw he meant what he said, though he wasn't going to just *give* anything to her. Not without expecting something in return.

"Stop playing games with me, William."

"I'm not playing games. Not tonight." He cupped her cheek with his hand and stroked her skin with his thumb. There was affection in his voice, but she knew he was only acting. He wanted her to feel as though he cared for her, had an interest in what would become of her, but she knew all he really cared about was himself.

"What do you want from me?"

"I want you to become the young Duchess of Glasston," he told her. "I want you to take on the duchess' daughter's identity, and I want you to become King Lennard of Trondenburgh's mistress."

That was blunt and straightforward. She didn't know whether to believe him or write him off as insane. But... "Why on earth should I do that?"

"Because I happen to know you." He jabbed a finger in her direction. "You want out of the hangman's employ as badly as I want to see those caravans of mine get where they're going safely – and profitably. I need someone to get me information so I can better protect my interests, someone to whisper a few things in the king's ear, and who better than you, Catherine, the smart and beautiful Duchess of Glasston?"

"And how would you pull that off?" She rose and began pacing. Some part of her was still convinced he was jesting, playing with her, but she knew better because she'd seen outlines of the thoughts forming in his head.

"The question is: how would *we* pull that off? But if you trust me, it's not going to be too difficult." He got to his feet and put himself in her way, taking her hands in his own. "That little old lady downstairs is going to help you play your part perfectly. She's going to teach you to *be* a duchess. Lennard is going to believe anything you tell him."

Catherine didn't know whether to be shocked or delighted at what he was suggesting.

"And you've decided this without even asking me?"

He sat all the way up. "Catherine, you're not just beautiful. You're the smartest woman I know…"

"I'm a whore."

She didn't feel bitter about that. It was what she did. It was how she lived. She'd chosen this over scavenging in the forest, gutting fish by the docks, and dying in the poorhouse. She'd had no other options when she'd finally arrived in the real world.

"A whore, maybe, but a beautiful and a smart whore," he said. "I know you won't pass up an opportunity we both stand to gain from. What have you got to lose, Catherine?"

Nothing.

Nothing but her head, if this went wrong.

"Look, a little bird tells me Trondenburgh is going on a mission against the Unnaturals in a few weeks. He's going to be away from home, *away from his wife* for months, and I can get you into his camp, into his life, and into a position that will make you a woman of standing by the end of the year. A very *wealthy* woman of standing. All you have to do is get into his bed."

She remembered hearing that before somewhere, and she wasn't intent on falling for it again. She lived more comfortably now than she ever had, but she certainly hadn't become rich, and her existence depended on the mercy of a hangman.

She didn't want to go from one flesh peddler to the next when Binns got sick or died, and she had plans of her own. She'd put away a little something to make them happen. She could pay Binns a month's worth of losses *and* make a payment on a house of her own soon if she kept at it. Unless Binns decided he wasn't letting her go, but she could deal with him the way she'd always dealt with people who stood in her way.

"The hangman wouldn't be very happy with me about this."

Brandner laughed, his eyes dancing as though he'd never heard anything so funny. "That's the second time today you're pretending Binns has any influence on what you do with yourself. If I didn't know any better, I'd say you're either in love with him or afraid of your own courage."

She scoffed. "Neither. But you seem to forget – even if I was to impersonate a duchess, he and a whole lot of other people would always know who I really am."

He wrapped his arms around her, and this time, she let him. "Well, for one thing, Trondenburgh is far away from Saint Aeden, and for another, fate has already taken care of Matthew Binns and his household."

She frowned, rigidly wriggling out of his embrace. "What?"

"There was a fire at Master Binns' house this afternoon. Unfortunately, there were no survivors, I've been told. He's dead, and all of his girls are, too."

Searing anger took hold of her. She wanted to slap his face, she wanted to hurt him, kill him. He'd had no right to take this decision away from her. Her clothes, her money, everything she owned had been in that house.

She raised her hand to hit him, but he was quicker and grabbed her wrist, stopping her. She drew up her other arm, but he seized it, too.

She was in his mind instantly and saw the flames. She saw him paying the man who'd slit Bridget's throat and tossed her into the ocean, slit the hangman's throat and killed seven girls and a beggar woman in the house before he'd set fire to it. Then, she saw Brandner strangling the man from behind with a wire after he'd turned his back on him to count the silver. She saw herself through Brandner's eyes, and she felt his resolve wash over her, his determination to succeed at what he'd set out to do, and his desire to lie with her and prove the power he thought he held over her.

He pushed her hands behind her back and kissed her, and she let him.

He shoved her back on the bed, pinned her beneath him and tugged up her skirts, and she let him.

He tore off her undergarments and ripped open the cord fastening of his pants, and she let him.

He thrust himself inside her until she screamed for pleasure, and when he collapsed on her after he'd poured himself into her, she imagined how different her life was going to be from here on in.

He thought he was in control, but he was wrong. She had new plans of her own.

Chapter Thirty-Two

---

୧ Rocky Roads ୨

The matched team of black horses before Brandner's carriage set a quick pace despite the terrible roads between Saint Aeden and Ironstone. By the end of the fourth day, Catherine was sore in places she hadn't been aware of having, but she was still grateful to be underway.

She hadn't left the merchant's *quaint little country house* in weeks. She'd stayed behind when he returned to Ironstone. Lady Glasston, two servants, and the gatekeeper had been her only company, and she desperately missed being out and about, even if her *out and about* in Saint Aeden had never been far from the hangman's house, for the most part.

Lady Glasston had proven an impatient teacher, forgetful and irritable, but at least she'd never questioned Catherine, so Catherine had simply put up with her, knowing their arrangement was only temporary. She wondered what the old lady would do once she was gone.

Brandner had left instructions that she wasn't to leave the estate. Frail as she was, Catherine assumed she wouldn't venture outside the garden by herself anyway for fear of what lay beyond.

The duchess lived in her own world of make-believe. She'd talked herself into believing all was well, and none of what had happened to her over the past year was real. As far as she was concerned, her husband and daughter were safe and sound at their family home in the Sudlands, and she was just passing through on her way to visit relatives.

The old bird had written countless letters to her dead daughter, addressing them to *My Dearest* and *Sweet Child*, telling her how pleasant her stay at Councilman Brandner's house was. Catherine had burned the one that mentioned the guild master's beloved fiancée of low breeding, but she'd kept all the rest, as well as the Glasston signet ring the robbers had overlooked in the duchess' luggage.

Katharina of Glasston was very much alive.

The surviving guards who'd accompanied the caravan and knew better because they'd buried her by the roadside would soon find themselves with a passage to the New Tribelands never to return.

Catherine had already been savvy on the use of cutlery and how to eat at a proper table before her time with Lady Glasston – Cooper had found amusement in teaching her when she'd been his whore – but a hundred other big and small things made the difference between a lady and a whore, she'd come to realize just by watching the duchess. Observing Lady Glasston in and of itself had been a lesson she'd soaked up like a dry sponge.

Posture and countenance were her main and most obvious issues, followed directly by her ignorance of etiquette. Three weeks wasn't long to learn all of the things the old bird insisted she should know and practice, but by the time she was on her way to meet with Brandner, Catherine was convinced she could pull this off if she stayed on her toes.

The inn where they made halt in the late afternoon was already crowded with guests for the alewife's daughter's upcoming wedding, and Catherine was lucky to get a room. She was sure a lady of standing would never join in the merrymaking with the common folk when one of the bridesmaids invited her to come with them to a fair a little way from the inn. Still, the prospect of that was too tempting after the isolation of the last weeks. It would only be a short walk before dark, she told herself, so she decided to take a chance.

Her coachman and the servant were convinced she'd retreated early for the night when she snuck out right past them in a borrowed dark cloak over a dress that wasn't too telling of her new identity. She doubted they'd see her, but pulled the hood down low over her face as she followed the small group of women into the woods, listening to their giddy chatter and adding some of her own.

As promised, the fairground was barely a mile's walk away. It was on a clearing where wild flowers grew. Poppies, cuckoo flowers, and buttercups sprinkled the seemingly undisturbed high grass with color, and it didn't even occur to Catherine that this wasn't the time of year for the blooms she was seeing. The fragrance of the sun-kissed meadow was so inviting, so enticing, it didn't seem to matter.

She stopped just inside the tree line to take it all in. This place was beautiful.

The girl who'd invited her along smiled toothily at her, and when she smiled back, the bridesmaid grabbed her hand and pulled her with her onto the meadow. The air seemed to waver around them as they walked.

Catherine's breath caught in her throat, and she finally woke from her daze, startling at the magical surge all around them. It was so dense, she could feel it on her skin from the second she stepped out of the woods. She thought that the very air she was breathing was charged up with storm and lightning, almost to the point of hurting. The others didn't seem to notice anything and ambled on, babbling and cackling as though they were drunk on their excitement, while she fought to unclutter her mind from the questions and concerns that formed there.

For a moment, she considered turning back, but her curiosity defeated both the discomfort and the apprehension she felt, and she trailed behind as they crossed the line between what appeared to be one world and the other.

The first thing they saw was a soothsayer's yurt. The old woman sitting outside her tent balanced a thin wooden board with pieces of vellum on her lap, and she held a thin sliver of charcoal in her hand. Catherine could see she was blind, and she wondered what she did with the drawing equipment.

"A copper penny for your future," a younger woman offered, coming out of the tent behind the old Seer. "My grandmother can tell you what good things lie in wait."

The maiden who'd grabbed Catherine's hand regarded her skeptically, and she was about to move on when the bride herself squealed with delight and dug around in her purse for the coin.

"Yes, please, yes *please!*" she begged, "I want to know *everything.*"

"Well, then sit down close to me." The fortuneteller smiled, revealing that every other tooth in her mouth was missing. She reached for the girl's hand before her granddaughter could show her the stool to sit on.

Catherine watched the old woman's fingers wander over the girl's forehead, gently tracing the lines of her eyebrows and working their way downward from there. The girl giggled. When the soothsayer was done exploring the smooth features of the girl's face, she began drawing.

The semblance she committed to the parchment was astounding. It showed a mother with two small children in her arms. The girl was delighted when the old woman handed her the sketch.

"Their father is going to be so happy," she said, "and where there's two there'll be more!"

The old woman tilted her head and grinned. "You'll have to be patient a little while, though. You've not met the man who'll give them to you."

At that, the girl blushed and went silent, but she handed the soothsayer's granddaughter the copper penny.

"Now you," the bridesmaid told Catherine, nudging her toward the Seer.

"I'd rather not," she returned, wiggling out of the girl's arm, but the Seer had already risen and taken her hand.

The smile fell from the old woman's face in an instant, and she retreated, toppling the stool behind her. Her mouth worked, but she couldn't seem to find her voice. Groping around, she searched for her granddaughter.

"I don't feel well," she said to no one in particular. "Please take me inside."

The young woman complied, apologizing to them.

"Completely potty, she is," the bride remarked, and two of the girls giggled. "Come on, let's see what else they've got here."

The young women browsed through the busy sales stalls, stopping at various tables that sold every imaginable thing: jewelry made from semi-precious stones, drinking-horns with fine zinc rims, pointy-tipped shoes, scarves with glistening silver threads woven into the material, sweets made from honey and fruit, cakes that smelled of cinnamon, and packages of herbs and spices from all parts of the world.

This was nothing like the fish market or any other market or fair Catherine had been to on her travels with the harlots. She thought of the one Dean had described to her once. That would have been smaller, but looking around, she did see a big tent in the middle of the grounds. It matched the one Dean had described to her exactly. A cold shiver tickled her spine.

"Are you coming?" the bridesmaid asked when they were ready to move on with the crowd to where the shows were.

She shook her head, feigning interest in one of the booths selling glass beads with yellow and bluish casts. "Go ahead, I'll catch up with you later."

What if this was *The Fair*, and he was here?

She didn't think he would be, but…

What if he was?

She pulled her hood up over her head once again.

She didn't *expect* to find him here, even if this was *his* Fair, and she didn't *have to* go and look for him in this place or any other. She didn't have to invite the trouble that seeing him again would entail. She'd been doing fine without thinking of him for *years* now, and she didn't need that book anymore, did she? But...

What if he was here and he had it?

She let her gaze wander the market and what she could see of the encampment and the caravans, and she squinted at the booths and stalls around the Big Top, trying to block out the sounds around her.

Where would he be, if he was here? Would he recognize her? Did he really have her book? Would he tell her why he'd taken it, or would he lie and deny it?

Edging toward the Big Top, she warily peered about and startled every time she saw someone with Dean's hair color or whose build might match his as it would be now.

Would he have changed much? Would he tell her he'd been worried about her, searched for her? Would he know what she'd done with the years between then and now despite the new dress she wore beneath her cloak, the good shoes on feet that had always been bare when he'd known her, and the different way she wore her hair?

By the time she'd combed most of the fairground, there was no more than an hour of daylight left, and she knew she couldn't come back the next morning. She couldn't afford the delay.

The troupe of women she'd set out to enjoy the evening with had already doubled back in direction of the Seer's yurt. She saw them keeping an eye out for her and took down the hood, waving to tell them she was coming. Then, instead of looking where she was going, she glanced back over her shoulder for a second.

At that moment, a young man rounded one of the stalls, talking to a woman who'd hooked her arm under his. Catherine bumped into him so hard, she nearly fell over on her backside, and she was about to scold him for his clumsiness when she saw that it was *him*.

It was Dean.

Chapter Thirty-Three

Refusal

Her heart stopped, and her mouth went dry as it dropped open.

She wanted to talk to him – and she didn't.

She wanted to wrap her arms around him and feel him close – and she didn't.

She wanted to kill him for taking her property – and she didn't.

He was a man now, and a handsome one at that, and he had a pretty, if plain-looking woman on his arm.

She briefly looked away as if that would make her invisible to him and tucked a stray lock of hair behind her ear. She was convinced she was a complete mess, and she felt sure he'd know how many men she'd slept with the same way he could *feel* magic even if he didn't see the silver in her eyes. He'd know all the things she'd done with them, all the things she'd allowed Cooper to do with her. She tried to tell herself that was impossible, but hot shame stung in her chest as she felt his eyes on her, studying her silently.

She loved him, but she hated him for making her feel this way. How could he, who'd been a ghost in her heart for so long, have such a power over her and make her feel as though she was the one with the dirty secrets? *He* had betrayed *her*, not the other way around.

"Catherine," he finally said, unable to conceal the tremor in his voice.

She fixed her gaze to his, but she couldn't tell what he was thinking. He'd been so easy to read when they'd been friends. Her heart sank.

She smiled, but the smile on her lips hurt her cheeks. She wanted to recall the boy she'd met down by the river and his love for how tadpoles changed into toads, but the image wouldn't come.

"Dean."

More silence.

He didn't inquire how she'd been, but she was about to ask how life had treated him when his female companion interrupted them by tugging affectionately on his arm. Her curvy form molded snugly to him, and her happiness shone through her every fiber, even when she was puzzled at the situation and growing impatient with him.

"Dean, who is this?" she asked, her gaze wandering between him and Catherine.

Some of the happiness melted into a frown when he didn't answer right away.

His face flushed. "Margarete, this is someone I used to know… when we were children." He kissed Margarete's temple and then faced back to Catherine. "Catherine, this is my wife, Margarete."

Catherine felt as though he'd slapped her in the face. He was married to someone named for a flower, and she was nothing but a whore in fine clothes, *someone whom he used to know.*

Her world came unhinged, though she couldn't quite say why. What on earth had she expected? What had she been hoping for? Why had she stayed?

"Congratulations," she told him evenly, biting back the anger and the humiliation, still smiling as the hurricane inside of her gained momentum. "Would you mind…" *Of course he would!* "Can I talk to you for just a moment – alone?"

She was aware that her request was both inappropriate and presumptuous, but Margarete pretended to be unmoved. An accomplishment for a woman named after a common wayside weed, Catherine thought.

Dean squeezed his wife's hand before letting go of it, and Margarete reluctantly withdrew as Dean bade Catherine to walk with him.

"You look good," he said when they were out of earshot of his wife. "I'm glad things are working out for you."

A part of her was flattered to hear him say that.

"You don't seem to be doing badly yourself."

"No. All's well. I'm settled in here, and I'm happy. Have you seen any of the performances yet?"

She bit her lip. She wasn't interested in a juggling act or a knife thrower. He had to know that.

"You weren't sure you wanted to come back here last time we talked."

"And then *you* disappeared."

"I had no choice."

He hummed, turning that over in his head slowly, as though he hadn't considered the possibility. "I looked for you," he finally said, a hint of reproach in his voice.

She could hardly tell him the truth. She'd gone over this a hundred times in her head when she'd been living with Rebecca, yet she didn't know what to say to him now, so she chose to put one foot forward. "But instead of finding me, you found my book."

Again, he hummed, and again he made her wait. She hated it.

"I didn't want to leave it there," he finally said. "Catherine, it's a part of a set my grandfather wrote and my father spent a lifetime trying to finish to help protect this community. By all rights, it's *mine*. I'm now responsible for all of this—" He motioned around at the fairground. "I'm responsible for keeping *all of us* alive, for keeping our heritage alive."

"You?" That was hard to believe. He wasn't strong enough.

"It was what my father wanted," he replied firmly. "I didn't ask for it, but I *accepted* it. These people are all that's left of our kind, Catherine. My father spent his whole life building this community and protecting it, using the knowledge his father and father's father passed on through those three books. You just happened to find the one my grandfather hid at the Tierney castle before he had to flee my family's ancestral home."

Her jaw clenched and she stopped in her tracks. None of this could be true. It just couldn't be. *Three* books *his* father had owned...

Cooper had sold one of her two, so she guessed Dean had probably had the third all along.

He'd *known* all along...

But, he wasn't *better* than she. It was *her* name on that mosaic floor in front of the wall with the hidden nook, not his, and she'd died a hundred deaths for those books. He may have been the one born with the privileges, but she had a right to everything that had been in that chest, not he.

"Look," he went on more kindly after a moment's silence, "I just didn't tell you that day because I didn't want to take your illusion away from you and make it about me. I didn't want to ruin the moment."

Had he felt *sorry* for her? Had he merely indulged her, *tolerated* her presence?

"You didn't want to ruin the moment?" she repeated. "What moment was that, exactly? The one where I showed you how *real* magic works? Or the one where I showed you how to open *your* ancestors' book of spells?"

She didn't know what exactly the other Cine here could do, but she didn't think they'd even be here if they had just a fraction of the magic that humans feared so much. Dean certainly didn't have a thing on her. He didn't then, and he didn't now, and he knew it.

She glared at him defiantly, forcing him to look at her, and he began stuttering, stuttering like the fool he was and always had been.

"Catherine, I'm sorry, but you had no idea what you found. You had no idea of its value – to me *and* to this Fair – and yes, we *were* friends. Yes, I looked for you, but you left without a word, and I thought you were dead."

Simple as that. He'd abandoned every thought of her while she'd lain awake at night in Rebecca's cabin, dreaming of him, and later alone in the forest, cursing him.

"Well, I'm not, and I want my book back." She dug into his mind. He fought her without knowing what he was fighting against. She supposed it was a Cine thing. Humans never put up any resistance. They just weren't born with that kind of natural resilience. "Give it to me, and I'll go. You'll never see me again."

"No," he told her, struggling as she pitted herself against the wall he'd put up. "I can't do that. It belongs here, with me and with the *people*."

"Then let me stay here with you. Together, we could do anything…" She didn't finish voicing the absurd thought, and she didn't know why she'd even begun. The words had somehow slipped from her mouth like the dying breath of a child's hope for salvation before she'd been able to stop them.

"What?" He laughed at the notion, laughed at her. *"You? Here?"*

At that moment, her heart turned to stone in her chest, heavy, cold and unbeating. It was a challenge to keep breathing.

She focused on him with all her strength. No, he hadn't searched for her. She was convinced that even if things had gone differently with Cooper, she would have returned to the Tierney castle the next day to find the book gone and him along with it.

Clutching his arm so tightly that her nails pierced his skin, she burrowed deep into his thoughts, like a maggot into the soft tissue of his flesh, willing him to believe they were youths again, and he didn't have a chance against her. The new Dean may have been responsible for the fate of a community of jugglers and peddlers, but he was as weak as the old Dean, and the old Dean didn't have a friend in the world except for Catherine.

"Why did you *really* take it?" she asked quietly. She wanted to tell him what a liar he was, and what a cowardly fraud, but it was far more satisfying to hear him say it.

"I had the other two volumes before I went to the castle and got yours. I wanted it to complete the collection so I could understand my father better. That was more important to me than you were. All of those books together describe the workings of time, animate and inanimate matter in this world. They explain what makes our grasp on it different from the humans', but you need *all* of those books to understand. You need to be able to go back and forth between them."

He paused there, bewilderedly looking around for a second before she reined him in again. "Go on," she ordered.

"I'm not interested in potions or the nature of the different Talents of our people. What I really want is to learn how dimensions are layered. I want to perfect the art of traveling between them, maybe even travel back in time. I can complete my grandfather's work on that, I can be better than my father was, and I want to show him and everyone here I'm *everything* he was always looking for in others."

She hadn't expected so much bitter honesty in one chunk.

Never having heard him talk like this before, she wondered if the resentment he was nursing was new, or if she just hadn't noticed it when they'd spent their days together in the woods. One of their unspoken rules had been to avoid the topic of fathers in general, and maybe that was why she hadn't encountered this side of him then. There was more to him than she'd thought.

"Poor baby," she said. "Did your father spend more time on his dreams than on his family? Was he not there to tuck you in at night? Cut your vegetables? Wipe your arse?"

He didn't know how to react to that, but she wasn't looking for an answer. He was so weak, it was no wonder his father had rejected him. Dean Greenleaf could never in a lifetime imagine what other fathers did to their children. He wasn't the son of a gravedigger, and he'd never lain in a hole in the ground, dug by a man who buried the dead for a living. He would never know how it felt to have the insects and the mold beneath the rotten planks of a filthy floor in a filthy hovel claiming his body.

She hated him for it.

"So you *stole* my book, and then you came here?"

"I traveled for a while. I met Margarete."

She wasn't in the least bit interested in hearing his little love story.

All she wanted was those books – all three of them. They were *her* heritage. Neither he nor the homeless half-breeds who'd apparently voted him their king could make use of them, or they'd all be living in castles and not caravans, but she certainly could.

Leaning in to him, she whispered, "I want you to give me those books."

Again, he fought her, gritting his teeth. A sheen of sweat formed on his brow. "No…"

"Show me where they are."

Hesitantly, he turned about and started leading her toward the brightly colored wagons that stood a little way off from the main attractions. She assumed this was where he lived.

"How is this place protected?" she asked him as they walked.

"By my father's enchantments. I don't know exactly how he did it, but he created a pocket dimension and connected it to a Snow Globe that contains all of his magic."

"And those books explain how it's done?"

"Yes."

"Indeed they do, but I don't think this is something we should be discussing with strangers," a voice said from behind them, startling her.

She spun around and found herself faced with the dark-haired man it belonged to. He wasn't as tall as Dean and more slender, and he seemed strangely familiar as he scrutinized her, but she couldn't place him.

"Especially not with *whores*," he added then, recognition in his eyes, and it came back to her. She still had his black queen, and she had a feeling he knew exactly what she'd been up to.

"I'd advise you to be more cautious with the company you keep, my friend," he told Dean grimly. "She's taken the yellow ribbon out of her hair, but that doesn't make this woman a lady you'd want to be seen with."

Pulling her aside, he broke the contact she had with Dean. She stumbled and nearly fell. The expression on his face as he glared at her told her he was dangerous, and for a split second, she actually glimpsed a sliver of silver in his eyes. He was a man with real power and a will to use it.

Dean paled, but said nothing, his glance darting from her to his friend and back.

"I just want what's mine," she said.

The dark-haired man cast Dean a questioning glance, but Dean shook his head.

"There's nothing here for you, darling. Leave. Now."

She desperately wanted to get into his mind and do some damage, but he somehow seemed to sense her, and he was too strong. He was everything Dean was not. She'd never encountered anyone like him before, and she thought that he was probably one of the people Dean's father had chosen to spend more time on than his own son.

"Leave," he told her again calmly, and suddenly she found herself outside of the fairground, and outside of The Fair.

She was still on the clearing, and his voice rang in her ears, but the clearing was empty now. The tents and wagons, carts and stalls were all gone, and she was alone. She'd been evicted from Dean's adopted dream world, and she could do nothing about it. She was furious. Try as she might, she couldn't penetrate the protective enchantments that surrounded the fairground and get back inside. Whatever magic these enchantments were made of, they meant to keep her out.

Meanwhile, the bridesmaids got tired of waiting for her, and just as she was about to leave the outer perimeter of the site, the small troupe appeared next to her, laughing and joking, incessantly jabbering about unimportant things.

"Oh, there you are," one of them said, smiling at her. "Had a good time?"

Chapter Thirty-Four

❧ The King of Trondenburgh ❧

When she arrived in Ironstone, Catherine found Brandner impatient to leave. He'd already mapped out their journey in accordance with his newest reports on Trondenburgh's movements. The man he was paying for his updates had contacts in the king's camp, so Catherine guessed his information would be fairly accurate. At least she hoped so. She was growing tired of being tossed around in the merchant's high-class battering box already.

None of the mercenaries hired to escort them had any inkling of the true nature of her relationship with Brandner. Brandner himself didn't ride in the carriage with her most of the time. He covered the first ten days' distance on horseback, and they had separate rooms at the inns where they spent their nights.

He was adamant about not wanting any more loose ends to tie up than absolutely necessary, and she didn't insist on sharing his bed. She had other things on her mind, though she knew she should probably be worried. Or nervous, at least. She was going to meet the king of Trondenburgh, and if anything went wrong, they'd both end up in some dark, damp dungeon and never see the light of day again – if they were lucky.

"You aren't eating enough," the merchant told her over dinner at their last stop before they were due to meet up with Trondenburgh.

Catherine rolled her eyes. "And you're annoying me with your niggling."

"I think you're not taking this seriously, Milady." He kept his voice low and his face didn't match what he was saying.

They were surrounded by people, and although she didn't think any of them had an interest in their conversation, she played along.

"Oh, but I am." She smiled, pushing her plate away. "Mother would be proud of me, I'm sure."

Brandner left it at that, but took the inn's harlot to his room that night, and Catherine wished fungus and disease upon him.

Two days later, he began complaining. Three days later, he had trouble urinating, and four days later, he was in no state to meet the king, having refused to drink the tea or apply the ointment she'd obtained from the midwife she'd found for him along the way. His stubbornness played against him when they happened upon the king's camp a little earlier than expected.

Trondenburgh's army had set up base on a field near the river a good two hundred yards from the road. The bishop's colors were flying at half-mast next to the royal family standard, but Catherine recognized the papal crown in the center of the green and blue flag from all the way across the meadow. She briefly considered turning back in light of Brandner's condition, but then decided she was going to go through with this, no matter what. She hadn't come all this way for nothing.

Three armed cavalrymen stopped her envoy before he'd made it half way across the field, and she watched as the man was escorted to the camp perimeter.

A while later, a stocky, bearded steward met with her messenger there. The two men exchanged a few words, and the envoy handed the steward the scroll she'd given him.

He broke the wax seal she'd applied to it when she'd penned the note the previous day. She didn't know whether a steward from Trondenburgh would be familiar with the emblem imprinted on it, but she'd taken great care to make it recognizable.

She was the Duchess of Glasston, and she wanted him to know that.

He read the note and when he was done, he looked up at the carriage by the roadside for a time before he finally nodded and sent the envoy back to Catherine with his permission to come to the king's encampment.

"Now, what am I going to do with you?" she mumbled, studying Brandner from outside the carriage through the open door.

"I told you…" he said, spluttering, "I told you to give me a few days." He clawed at his sweaty hair with trembling fingers.

"A few days won't help you." She bent closer to him. "You might well be dead in a few days if you don't start drinking that tea."

"Witchcraft." Pain further distorted his handsome face. "Nothing but witchcraft, and I won't have it."

Leaning closer still, she stroked a damp lock from his temple as if she cared what became of him. "Well, then *it* will have *you*."

She decided to leave him where he was, and there was nothing he could do about it. She'd just have to do this on her own, and she wasn't afraid to.

She had two of the merchant's men accompany her as she crossed the field. Walking with her head held high and trying to manage the terrain with as much dignity as she could, she was aware of the steward's eyes on her.

He bowed when she'd reached him. "Alexander of Halesbridge, Milady. Will Master Brandner not be joining us?"

She held his gaze. By title, she was his better. "No, unfortunately Master Brandner is suffering from a colic. His Majesty will have to make do with my company for now."

She could see shadows of disapproval beneath his undaunted mien. "I'm sure the king will be pleased to receive you," he said and led the way.

As they headed toward the king's large square marquee in the center of the campsite, they passed a fletcher's tent. It was getting dark and she couldn't be sure, but she had the strangest feeling she knew the man looking up at her from where he was carving nocks into the arrow shafts he'd just finished. She couldn't quite place him, and when he returned his attention to his work, she trained her eyes on the steward's back until they'd reached the king's tent.

Long banners draped vertically along both sides of the veiled entrance displayed Trondenburgh's crest; a white steed in mid-leap on a red background, a crowned monarch on its back, holding his church's flag in one hand, a golden shield in the other, and his sword strapped to his saddle.

Halesbridge didn't make her wait, but led her straight through the curtain inside.

The marquee was spacious but gloomy. Its floor was lain with thick, fine carpets that smelled slightly of mold from the damp grass they covered. A man in his early thirties was seated at a table laden with fresh fruit and a heavy platter of cold turkey at the far back of the tent. He was tucking into his food whole-heartedly.

Halesbridge bowed, not going more than half way into the marquee. "Sire."

The king looked up and put his drumstick down as Catherine stepped out from behind the steward. He was a good-looking man, at least.

He wiped his hands on a fine linen napkin and rose, smiling. "Ah! Lady Glasston, I presume!"

"Your Highness," she returned, curtseying low as he moved around the table. To her surprise, he took her hand in his own and bade her to rise almost immediately.

"Won't you dine with me? It's been a while since I've had some civilized company out here. The turkey is cold, the bread is stale, but the wine is excellent."

Lifting her gaze to his, she could see he was a man who wouldn't take no for an answer, but she wouldn't have dreamt of refusing him. She knew nothing of kings other than what old Lady Glasston had taught her about making conversation with other nobles, but she guessed *no one* refused a king.

With a nod, Trondenburgh dismissed Halesbridge, and they were alone aside from the servant who hastened to place another silver plate and cup on the table opposite of the king's.

Silver, she thought. Not wood, not clay, not zinc or even glass.

Silver.

It was funny how things turned out, sometimes. Dean lay hiding among jugglers and jesters with some bland creature who had no idea what a coward and weakling he was. The hangman lay stiff in his earthen grave. The merchant lay rotting in his own rolling casket. *She* would soon be lying with the king in silken sheets, drinking wine from silver cups and laughing at them all.

The servant helped her out of her cloak and pulled a heavy oaken chair out for her so she could sit.

The king waited until she was comfortable before seating himself. "I gather Master Brandner is not coming?"

"No, Sire, I'm afraid he's been taken ill. I believe he's given himself an upset stomach."

"Would you like me to send someone for him so he can be taken care of here by my charlatan?"

She was momentarily confused. "Charlatan?"

The king laughed. "Oh, yes, I beg your pardon, Milady, my *physician*. Not worth the pennies I pay him for his services, but he can probably treat a case of the runs."

"Perhaps my traveling companion is best left where he is, Your Highness, lest he should contaminate your entire camp."

Again, the king laughed. "That's very considerate of you, Lady Glasston, but we're out here to fight the Unnaturals, so we're not afraid of a stomach flu. However, you're right. Perhaps I'll just send my man out to Master Brandner and save us some misery."

She smiled. "That would indeed be wiser, I believe."

She wondered if Brandner would accept a physician's help any more than he'd accepted the midwife's tea. Somehow she doubted it, but depending on how woeful he felt in the night, he might reconsider in the morning.

The servant piled her plate with meat and carrots, poured her a wine that was excellent indeed, and the king seemed content for a while to watch her eat. She didn't need to probe inside his mind to know what questions were forming in his head and what he was thinking. When the dishes had been cleared away, he leaned forward in his chair.

"Tell me, what important matter brings you and the councilman to me today, out here in the middle of nowhere?"

She inhaled deeply and cast her eyes downward, practiced grief and distress tugging at her features. She'd been over and over this with Brandner, so it wasn't hard, even though she was lacking his cues now.

"Your Highness, I'm here because I have a request to put forward. Master Brandner was so kind as to bring me this far, because he was concerned for my safety on the road."

His mien hardened slightly. "I see. Go on."

"Six months ago, my mother and I traveled through Trondenburgh lands via the Trading Road. We were with one of Master Brandner's caravans when the caravan was robbed."

"I'm sorry to hear that."

She pulled a delicate handkerchief from her sleeve and dabbed at her nose. "My mother was injured very badly trying to defend me and salvage what remained of the jewelry my deceased father had left her. Almost all of our belongings were either taken or destroyed, as was most of what the caravan was bringing north. Such senseless brutality." She paused, closing her eyes for a moment as though the memory overwhelmed her.

"Was your caravan not protected?" His voice sounded milder than before, and she fixed her eyes to his once more.

"Oh, but it was. A lot of brave men paid for by Master Brandner lost their lives to defend us. They were all slain save for the two who risked everything to bring my mother and myself to Ironstone alive."

The king sighed. "Well, I'm sorry to hear that this happened to you on my land. Did your mother recover from her injuries?"

She bit her lip. "No."

"My condolences." He let a moment pass. "I'm glad Master Brandner has been taking care of you."

"I'm grateful for the help he's offered, Your Majesty. My parents had dealings with him since I can remember, and I think he is a good man."

Leaning back, the king scratched his chin. "Well, he never struck me as someone with anything but his own interests at heart, but I'm happy to be informed otherwise."

"Sire, I'm not here to sing a song of praise for him. I gather he's a shrewd businessman, and he tells me you've had your differences, but he does think highly of you. He described you to me as a fair king, and man of integrity. Still, I had to convince him to bring me here, because he didn't believe you'd hear my request."

He smirked in a manner that would have shamed the merchant. "But you have my full attention now, Lady Glasston. What is it you request?"

"It's not for me, Your Highness. My mother is dead, and nothing can bring her back to me. My father's inheritance is gone, and that's hard, but I'll have to live with that. There is nothing you can do for me. You could, however, do something everyone in your kingdom would benefit from."

"And what would that be?" Amusement played around his eyes now, as though he guessed what was coming.

Did he guess? Had he heard this kind of thing a hundred times before? Probing in his mind she saw that he had. He was just wondering how she was going to package it. She also saw a twinge of regret form at the decision he'd already made, and the fact that he would have to send her away.

Taxes and tolls were what paid for his army and fed his family, and he was certainly not going to reduce either for the merchants so they'd hire more security to share the job of protecting his roads. He didn't want anyone Halesbridge hadn't chosen doing that because he was sure he'd never see a fraction of what they'd earn alongside. The knights he had patrolling the main trading routes couldn't be everywhere, but they were mostly loyal and they had principles. He was no more inclined to take any part of their livelihood away from them than he was to have Brandner's mercenaries running around his kingdom stating whatever they were up to was in the king's name.

Strangely, she could completely understand his attitude. She wouldn't trust Brandner, either. She needed a new strategy, and quick.

"I'm here to ask you to declare war on those criminals who go robbing the travelers on your roads, because after what I've seen, they're not what you think they are."

He raised an eyebrow at her. This, he obviously hadn't expected.

She looked at the servant, and when she did not go on, the king sent the young man away.

"I have reason to believe they are Unnaturals," she told him evenly.

"And how do you come to this conclusion?"

"It was in the way they stayed concealed to the guards protecting us until the very last moment before they attacked, and it was the precise and calculated way they did it. They knew we were coming, they were waiting for us. I believe they're systematically gathering resources by picking off the caravans carrying currency and precious metals."

He studied her. "Gathering resources?"

For the first time, she knew what listening to Brandner's eternal ramblings had been good for. "This is exactly what happened in the Sudlands before the Cine uprising. That's why my father supported King Harald in his last big campaign against the Tainted."

"So… you came to warn me?"

She nodded, then shyly lowered her eyes again. "I know this must seem strange to you, but I think you're… no, we're *all* in for a war."

He laughed. He didn't buy it – or did he? Was there any little huff of a doubt in the way he held himself? The way his hands tensed? "The Cine are almost extinct even here," he said.

"And I know they're not. There was a lot of confusion during the attack, but I overheard two of the men clearing out the wagon ahead of ours speaking of a place that harbors hundreds of Cine. They talked about a Sorcerer from the Tierney line–"

"What?" He sat bolt-upright.

All at once, she saw clearly. She knew that it was his own grandfather who had conquered the castle. The siege had cost the old man a brother, an arm, and his eldest son and heir. He'd been obsessed by the search for the Duke, obsessed with the thought of wiping out the Sorcerer and every last one of his descendants.

Trondenburgh himself bore no personal resentment or animosity against the Cine. He only did what the clergy asked of him, but he certainly wasn't going to ignore what she'd have to tell him about a Tierney or anyone else with hundreds in arms in connection with a rising.

She trained her eyes on his hands. They were milky white, and they seemed so unused. She didn't think they'd be capable of hard work, of heavy carrying, of inflicting pain - or wielding a sword the way his grandfather or father had, and he was aware of it.

"I heard them saying that things were going to be different after the revolution, and how they were going to wipe out the existing order with its own means."

The king rose and began pacing.

"Are you sure?"

She nodded. "I am."

"Well, then I thank you for your forthrightness, Milady." Again, he studied her. "Who else have you talked to about this?"

"Only Master Brandner."

He hummed, seemingly lost in thought for a moment. "I'd like you to be my guest here at the camp tonight. I'll have my servants ready a tent for you and make you comfortable."

"Your Majesty…"

"I insist. I will also have to insist that you keep what you've just told me to yourself."

She tilted her head. What was going on inside of him? Probing once more, she realized that he was completely overwhelmed. He was on his way to find a Dwarven settlement in the Winter Mountains, which he doubted would even exist, and now he'd just heard the Cine were planning a rising while he was away from home.

She rose, and he helped her with her chair. "Of course," she said. "Of course I will."

Chapter Thirty-Five

๛ Inviting the Devil ๏

Catherine hated sleeping in tents. Given the choice, she'd rather have slept out in the open. It was never one bit warmer inside of a tent than it was outside, and she couldn't see what was going on outside. That was what bothered her the most about tents.

The king's physician and Halesbridge had returned from where Brandner's men had set up their own camp by the time she was called to take breakfast with His Majesty. She hoped the merchant had had enough sense to play along or at least keep his mouth shut. She hadn't dared sneak out to him during the night, but she was fairly confident he hadn't betrayed them, or they'd both have been arrested.

Seating herself opposite Trondenburgh just like on the previous night, she smiled at him, but that didn't seem to ease his tension.

"Tell me about the nature of your relationship to the councilman," he said openly, picking a piece of fruit from a bowl the servant offered him. She guessed the charlatan had been smart enough to find out what ailed Brandner.

"As I told you, he helped my mother and me when we had nowhere else to go. I hope he's feeling better today."

"He helped you, and that's all?"

She nodded, pretending not to know what he was getting at. "He's been very kind, a man of honor at all times – toward *me*, at least. He never took advantage of me in any way, if that's what's troubling you."

The king nodded, still skeptical, but more relaxed. "Alright. Tell me about your parents."

"Your Majesty, I fear I'd bore you."

The servant poured him tea, and he blew on it before taking a cautious sip. "Not at all. I'm interested to hear."

She took a deep breath. "My father was a devoted husband to my dear mother. They both took great pleasure in socializing. They held many wonderful dinners and balls, and I love to remember the dancing lessons my mother gave me."

She paused, aware he was still taking measure of her. He'd undoubtedly spoken to his advisor as well as the physician. She wondered what council Halesbridge had offered him.

"Mother always worried about my lack of talent for languages, my unladylike posture, and she was concerned about my future because I hadn't married yet."

"That's understandable. Mothers always worry."

She laughed, wondering if he spoke out of experience with his own, or with the mother of his daughter.

"Perhaps. But the suitors she had in mind for me weren't anywhere near as dashing and as gallant as..." She paused, looking him in the eye. Scratching just below the surface, just deep enough to get underneath his skin, she left the essence of a lingering kiss behind in his thoughts, and his face flushed slightly at the notion of her lips on his. "... as dashing as I'd hoped they would be," she went on, giggling. "But, I was also more interested in other things, really."

"Other things?"

"Yes, Your Majesty. As much as I loved to dance..." she could see he was imagining it, picturing her in a ball gown of flowing silk, "... I also loved to go on hunting trips with my father. I was out and about more than would please my mother, I'm afraid."

He returned her smile. She could see that he was delighted, his gaze roaming over her form, as his mind went from the woman in a ball gown to the huntress on horseback with a quiver strapped to the saddle. It also answered at least one more of the questions that burned on his tongue. She'd never lost that outdoors-taint of hers, even in years of living mostly by night in Saint Aeden. He liked it. He liked it a lot more than he should, but she assured his heart that it was alright.

"You must accompany me some day, then," he said, possibly meaning it.

"That would be wonderful, Your Majesty."

She drank her tea, careful not to break eye contact with him, and she was aware that the tiny spark she'd lit in his imagination had set fire to a dry kindling in his heart. Whatever fears Halesbridge had instilled in him evaporated like dew on the fields in the morning sun.

"What are your plans for the future?" he asked.

"I believe I'll do what my mother had intended for us before... before..." she trailed off, thinking of her most miserable moment, which had to be the night she'd spent alone and afraid in the castle keep. Capturing the feeling, she bequeathed a rendering of it to him, and he understood what she meant him to before continuing. "I have distant relatives in Walha. Master Brandner has kindly offered to see me on my way once I've done what I set out to do, in the hopes they'll take me in."

"That's unfortunate."

"Pardon me?"

"*Unfortunate* that you still want to make the trip, Lady Glasston."

She replied nothing to that, but finished her tea and rose. "Having accomplished what I set out to, I believe it's time I said thank you for your hospitality."

"But you're not leaving just yet, are you, Milady? From what my physician says, Master Brandner should not be traveling at all in his state."

"Oh," she said, her brow creasing as he stood in front of her. "But I have no wish to impose on you any further than I already have, so…"

"Nonsense." He took her hand in his own. His skin felt as soft as it looked.

"My scouts are still in the Winter Mountains finding our paths, and I will have to insist on your staying under my protection for as long as the councilman is unable to personally guarantee your safety."

She looked down at her hand in his. "Alright. I'll stay until Master Brandner can travel."

With that, she left him, her fingers trailing his palm as he released her.

Chapter Thirty-Six

∝ The King's Lover ∾

Catherine took every meal with Lennard of Trondenburgh over the next days. He wasn't difficult to talk to, she discovered. They always found pleasant, innocuous topics of conversation. None of them involved the story she'd told him about the Cine rising, but she had a feeling he was discussing that at length with Halesbridge during the times when they'd sit in his tent, poring over maps for hours at a time, or when they'd ride out together.

She visited Brandner on one of those occasions and briefed him on the outcome of their plan. He would have scowled at her, she supposed, but he didn't much care for what she had to tell him in his present condition, so she left him to the reasonably comfortable straw bed Trondenburgh had had a few of his men deliver to him. He was such a proud fool, his stubborn unwillingness to let the physician burn out the disease that plagued him was going to leave him crippled or kill him, she was sure.

On her fourth night in the king's camp, Trondenburgh did not accompany her to her tent, but kissed her before she could leave his. She gently pushed him away.

"Your Majesty," she said, acting torn, "don't–"

"Don't what?" he whispered in her ear, gently drawing her back into his arms. "Don't care for you? Don't desire you? I can do a lot of things, but I couldn't *not* want you. Tell me you don't have a desire for me, too, and I'll let you go and never touch you again. Just say the word, if you can."

She hesitated, but didn't fight him. "Think of your wife."

One peek inside his mind told her he didn't want to. He didn't love Lillian, and she didn't love him. He hadn't insisted on his marital right to her body since the conception of their daughter. They both loved their only child, but that was all that kept their marriage together. The king of Trondenburgh was a lonely man, and he had been for too long.

She let him press his lips to hers once more and returned his affections, combing her fingers through his hair as he tasted her mouth with his tongue. She allowed his hands to wander over her back and hips, and she allowed him to lead her to his bed.

"Sire, forgive me, but I've never been with a man before," she lied more brazenly than she ever had in her entire life when he began undressing her, stroking the bodice off of her. She covered her bare breasts with her arms abashedly, adding a slight tremor to her voice.

She felt him startle; it was no more than a tiny flutter in his otherwise steady heartbeat, and he moved around to stand behind her. He kissed her shoulders and neck, and he snaked one arm around her, cupping her breast in his wonderful, soft hand while the fingers of his other hand found her most sensitive folds and caressed them, delving inside of her as though they'd find the truth there.

She could tell he didn't know whether to believe her, and he just held her, kissing and massaging her until she found herself yearning for more. He did not look at her face as he tried to decide whether or not he'd be a scoundrel for taking a maiden to his bed.

When she finally turned in his arms and fixed her eyes to his, he made up his mind that he was, but he didn't feel even a little bit guilty for it. He was in control of this, and she felt his resolve to have her all the more if she really was a maiden because that made her *his*, and she knew he liked the thought of that.

This was going just as she'd anticipated. He wanted her, no matter what the consequence, and if he took her now and liked what he got, he was certainly bringing her to Trondenburgh with him.

He lay her down on the warm, white sheepskins that covered the fine linen sheets on his bed, and lowered himself to her, by now firmly believing he was her first lover when he felt her tremble beneath him. She kept hold of his thoughts as he planted ravenous kisses on her throat and entered her, moving slowly and carefully at first. She clenched her teeth and let him think he was hurting her just enough to make him cautious, but he soon lost all restraint and indulged himself before he poured himself into her, gasping. He'd been alone too long, but that was going to change now.

The king was an awkward lover despite his efforts, Catherine realized – no wonder his wife hadn't felt pleasure when he'd slept with her, but Catherine thought this, too, could be remedied in no time.

"Are you alright?" he asked when he'd recovered, and she nodded but didn't reply as she molded herself to him.

"Have I hurt you?" He lifted her chin and studied her face.

A tear leaked from her eye, and he tenderly wiped it from her cheek with his thumb.

"No," she said, "it's just… it was just so much more beautiful than I'd expected."

At that, he kissed her again deeply, completely losing himself to her. When he was ready for her again, she set about teaching him how to make love to a woman properly so he'd be the lover she wanted him to be, and so it would never cross his mind to want any other woman in his bed but her.

Chapter Thirty-Seven

❧ Responsibilities ❧

The king of Trondenburgh was a busy man after his scouts returned and they broke camp to begin their march into the Winter Mountains.

He dispatched envoys to his liegemen throughout the kingdom with messages warning them of the new threat that had arisen. He issued orders for searches of the wooded areas where The Fair had been seen, and he informed the Inquisitor of his progress on finding the Dwarven settlement in daily reports. He spent hours discussing the mystery of the whereabouts of the Cine haven with Halesbridge and two other knights he trusted.

All that, and yet he still made time for Catherine. He insisted she remain with him for her own protection since Brandner was not recovering well, and she did not object. He took her to his bed every night, and to this, she did not object either.

Halesbridge's disapproval of her was obvious, but that didn't seem to bother the king. It bothered Catherine. It bothered her almost as much as Brandner's presence did.

Brandner was too sick to accompany them into rough territory. He tried to demand they take him along, but the king gladly ordered the merchant's escort to take him back to Ironstone when Catherine requested it. He protested, but Trondenburgh left him no choice in the matter.

Bidding the councilman a brief goodbye and a speedy recovery, she told him between the lines that all was going well, but secretly, she hoped he wouldn't make it home. With any luck, he'd die of his own stupidity and rot in hell, and she wouldn't have to worry that he'd become a liability.

Sitting opposite her new lover and enjoying a meal of vegetables and quails, she studied the man who now shared her bed, and she wondered if she'd have to kill the councilman when he came looking for her again at some stage. He undoubtedly would. If he didn't drop dead by himself, she was going to have to find a way to make sure he didn't ruin what she had.

She wore the new dress Lennard had bought for her in a town nearby – much more exquisite than anything Brandner had afforded her, and she saw how Lennard liked looking at her in it. He liked it so much, he sent away the servant and rose to retrieve something from the chest by his bed when the man had left. She knew it would go very well indeed with the new dress before he'd even returned to the table.

Moving around her, he adorned her with a gold necklace meant for his wife in a better moment that had never come and never would. She squealed with delight, hugging him, and he grinned mischievously. By the time she'd undressed him and they were making love, she was sure it wouldn't cost him a single sleepless night. Neither would the matching bracelet she knew was still sitting in that chest.

Wrapped in his arms and resting her head on his chest afterward, she admired the necklace and the diamond setting attached to it, but that wasn't the only thing on her mind.

"Tell me again why *you* are going to the Winter Mountains for the Inquisitor, and not Ironstone, when Ironstone is much closer to this no man's land? Cassandra could be sending her troops instead," she mumbled.

Depending on how long this campaign was going to last, she wouldn't be seeing Trondenburgh anytime soon, and she still hated tents, no matter how big or comfortable they were. She couldn't wait to hear how he was going to bring her into his home.

He snorted and got up to fetch them a drink. "Because my dear cousin doesn't trust Cassandra of Ironstone one little bit. He can't prove it, but he suspects she's got sympathies for the Tainted. Who knows? Maybe she's one of them – a Shapeshifter perhaps?" He laughed, but it was a thin, watery kind of fake amusement he didn't much enjoy.

Handing her a glass, he poured her some wine. It was the sweetest she'd ever tasted. He sat back down next to her and played with his own glass rather than drink from it.

"No, seriously, I think Terrence is... *obsessed.* It's completely absurd to think the Dwarven could be a danger. We all know they aren't. They won't last very long anyway, holed up in here in the mountains and cut off from the world – if there are any left alive. The Cine are a different matter, but I can't defeat them alone. I should be forging alliances to go after them instead."

"So why are you humoring Driesburgh, when you know the Cine are the much greater problem?"

Lennard reached for her hand. "You're really interested in what I do, aren't you?"

She smiled, training her eyes firmly on his. "Of course I am. You know that."

He returned her smile. "Well, then let me explain. Terrence of Driesburgh was my uncle's third son. He was the son that *didn't* inherit his father's lands, and *didn't* get to go into another nobleman's services. He was the son my uncle gave to God. As such, he doesn't get to make himself a name in the world any other way than to be a *warrior of God.*" Lennard said it with an extra pound of derisiveness, and Catherine chuckled. She loved his way of mocking everyone and everything that didn't convince him completely.

"I guess a warrior of God needs his missions."

"You could say that, yes."

"So, you're doing this as a favor to him? But, is this not going to upset the diplomatic relations to Ironstone? Queen Cassandra won't like you hunting in her woods, will she? Especially if you're going to have to ask for her help soon to defeat the Cine."

"No. She won't like it one little bit, but technically, I'm not hunting in *her* woods. The Winter Mountains are a no-man's-land. I'll just be close enough to Ironstone's borders to maybe cause her a hiccup or two." He released a lungful of air as he thought about it.

"No, I'm not doing this as a personal favor to my unfortunate, disadvantaged cousin. I'm doing this for *me*, because if I don't, my cousin is bound to go hunting in *my* woods again very soon, and that is going to cost me a fortune. You have no idea what he'll charge for putting a few farmers' wives on trial, and you can't imagine the people those old biddies will accuse of being Cine while Terrence has his torturers carving them up. I want to find that Fair, and I want to stomp it into the ground before the rats begin to scatter. I want to do this my way, without his church carrying off my silver to cover the expenses of their trials. No judge, no jury, no trials, no costs."

He pulled her to him, spooning with her. She closed her eyes when he started stroking her, and she could feel his desire for her building again. He couldn't get enough of her.

"One thing would lead to another if I didn't humor Driesburgh now," he said softly as he kissed his way up her neck, "and before you know it, I'd be too broke to make you any more gifts to underline your beauty, Milady."

He took her hand in his and slipped the bracelet around her wrist. How he'd snuck it into the bed, she didn't know, but it was perfect.

"I love it. I love the necklace and the bracelet, and I love you," she said, turning to look at him, making sure he lost himself in her eyes.

"And I love you, Katharina, more than you'll ever know. In another week or two, I'm simply going to tell Driesburgh we wiped those Dwarven out, whether we find them or not, and then I'm going to take you home with me."

Catherine swallowed hard, willing waves of what he would perceive as her sadness to wash over him. "How?" she asked weakly. "How could I ever be a part of your home or your life in Trondenburgh?"

She could tell he'd been thinking about this.

"The way I see it, I'm responsible for you. You should have been safe traveling the roads of my kingdom, and you lost everything only because I failed to do my duty."

She wanted to cut him off and tell him he was wrong, but he shushed her, laying a gentle finger on her lips.

"I couldn't possibly let you go now. As your king, I could send an escort to bring you to Walha, but in these uncertain times, everyone will agree that I really don't have any choice but to bring you back to Trondenburgh with me. Everyone *will* accept that. They'll have to."

"Are you sure, my love?" she asked in a small voice, and in answering her, he took her face in his hands, those wonderful, soft hands, and set about kissing her fears away.

Chapter Thirty-Eight

♋ Trondenburgh ♋

Trondenburgh was a rather remote place, but it wasn't hard to guess how they made a living here. Wheat, spelt, and oat fields blanketed the landscape as far as the eye could see. In between them, shepherds herded large flocks of sheep on vast, plane meadows.

The modest castle stood upon a tall mound rather than a hill. Hills were hard to come by here. Its defensive mechanisms were paltry in comparison to Ironstone, and instead of a town at the foot of the mound, farmhouses sprinkled the wider area. Catherine found all this a bit disappointing, but she was here, and she hadn't walked behind a donkey cart, carrying the tent she'd be working in tonight. She'd come in the king's carriage as the Duchess of Glasston, and she was sure she'd never work or worry again a single day in her life.

She was a lady of standing now, and she was in Trondenburgh by personal invitation of the king. That invitation was bound to expire sooner or later if she didn't use the time it gave her to make a place for herself, but that didn't make her nervous. She'd think of something. She always did. Catherine had decided that being the king's mistress certainly wasn't the end of her road, and without Brandner making demands of her, she was free to choose her own fate.

Lennard had told her he didn't love his wife, and his wife didn't love him, but a lot of marriages weren't built on love – they were built on the need to forge alliances. Smart decisions for the future never included love because *smart* had nothing to do with *love*. Catherine was aware that Lennard wouldn't give up his *smart decision* for a fling on the side, even if he swore his love for her would never end every time he lay in her arms, but it was the fling on the side he was sharing his bed with right now, and he was so easy to manipulate, it was almost ridiculous.

The queen and her daughter had come out into the courtyard to welcome the king home. They stood with some other men and women who might have been members of the court; councilmen, the child's nursemaids, ladies-in-waiting, stewards, and servants. A little off from the others stood the bishop himself with two priests whose function Catherine couldn't discern.

So this was the man she'd spent years of her life fearing. He was small, as everything here, and angular. The scars on his face marked him as a survivor of one of the plagues that had befallen parts of the Middlelands and the Northern Territories before she'd been born. A carefully trimmed mustache and anchor beard framed his narrow and unsmiling lips, but she found nothing else notable about him. He was just a man, and men were weak and vanquishable. It was an irony of fate that she should be dining with him tonight, and she wondered what kind of conversationalist he'd turn out to be.

Lennard dismounted from the horse he'd ridden ahead of the carriage by way of propriety. He greeted his wife with a chaste peck on the cheek. Catherine noted the couple's complete lack of interaction as she peeked out of the tiny window in the door of her carriage at Lennard and Lillian. The mousy woman's face revealed nothing in the way of emotion, although Lennard had told her she was a very sensitive person with a tendency toward both dramatics and melancholy. Catherine deemed her plain and pale both inside and out. Lillian matched the mental image she'd had of her exactly.

She watched the king sweep his child up into a hearty embrace. He swirled Lioba around and tickled her, and the girl's laughter filled the courtyard. Lennard's love for his boisterous daughter showed, and it was no wonder she was such a joy to him; the girl was radiant. Most of the adults present seemed to find the scene amusing. Even the queen's mien lost some of its lethargy.

Halesbridge's arrival was barely acknowledged. He'd been riding behind them for the last leg of their trip, and Catherine had tried to forget all about him. The king curtly nodded at him and the other men by way of a greeting, and then instructed one of the servants to open the door of the carriage for Catherine.

She stepped out into the daylight, dressed in the finest clothes Lennard's silver could buy, and he introduced her as Lady Katharina, Duchess of Glasston. The queen seemed somewhat bewildered.

Finally, Catherine thought, *a reaction*.

Lillian overplayed her initial surprise gracefully and dispatched one of her ladies-in-waiting to accompany the duchess to the guest quarters as they went inside.

Two servants carried Catherine's trunk with the clothes Brandner and Lennard had, each in their time, bought for her. The only personal things from her other life that she'd held on to were the things she carried with her wherever she went: she always wore the locket Rebecca had given, and the two coins from the chest at Tierney Castle, as well as the dark chess piece she'd stolen in Ironstone were in her coin pouch.

Twisting the locket in her fingers, she made up her mind this was the place she'd begin to make memories worth keeping inside of it. The Inquisitor was a pitiful, if powerful man, and the queen was no match for her.

Lillian remained at her husband's side, and the nursemaid went with the girl while Catherine climbed several flights of narrow stairs behind her new lady-in-waiting. Looking at the castle's rooms from the inside, she discovered Trondenburgh was less impressive in its state of good repair than the Tierney castle in ruins; it was a dark, damp cave, but she was its king's lover. She'd be his wife in the very near future, and she'd surely find a means of making this a fit place to live in.

Catherine decided she liked her new room. It was on the topmost floor of the building, one floor above the king's quarters, and hardly bigger than the one she'd rented at Binns' house. She had a good view of the courtyard, a bed with soft blankets, and a wardrobe in the corner by the door. The servants set her trunk down by the foot of her bed and left. The lady-in-waiting poured fresh water into a basin so she could wash, offering to help her.

She was about to refuse and send the woman away, but then she thought better of it.

"What's your name, dear?"

"Selene, Milady."

Milady. How that sounded. Real duchesses had people to help them with any little thing, and she had to appear as real as possible here, as if she was used to the attentiveness of personnel. No, she told herself; she *was* real. She was the descendant of a nobleman, a *Cine* Lord, but a nobleman nonetheless. She was nobility, and she deserved this.

She thought of Rebecca's story of her great-grandmother and saw some parallels. Only, she'd never allow anyone to send her away. She was here to stay.

Her only liability right now was Halesbridge. She was fairly certain Brandner wouldn't be a problem over the next weeks, but Halesbridge might be. She didn't trust the steward, he obviously didn't trust her.

When she was finished freshening up, she asked Selene to show her the castle, genuinely interested in getting a better feel for the place and the people who lived here.

From where he sat at the long table in the Great Hall, the bishop spotted her coming down the stairs behind her servant, and he beckoned her to join them.

"Lady Glasston, please give us the honor of your presence, since you did accompany the king on the last miles of his journey to the Winter Mountains," he said. "I'm so eager to hear every detail of that. Lord Halesbridge was just telling us of the difficult terrain you were faced with there."

Smiling shyly, she seated herself near Halesbridge. It was the only free chair.

Halesbridge ignored her completely and took a sip of his wine, while another servant poured a cupful for Catherine.

"I think we were barking up the wrong tree," the steward told Driesburgh. "There have always been rumors of a Dwarven settlement in those mountains, but no one has actually ever seen it. At least I've never met anyone claiming such a thing, and I spent a great deal of my youth near Ironstone. After the very thorough search we conducted, I'm convinced a rumor is all it ever was. The eighty-odd Dwarven our men disposed of were scattered across the entire mountain range, half-starved and confused, and they were the last of their kind, to be sure."

Catherine knew that stating the search as having been *very thorough* was something of a stretch – and they hadn't disposed of a sum total of eight men, never mind eighty. Neither the king nor Halesbridge had been particularly driven by the cause of their mission, and they'd made haste to get home in light of the information she'd fed Lennard. They'd hardly skimmed the western spurs of the mountains. The king had merely sent a few scouts and smaller troops farther in to make a quick survey.

Halesbridge had sent the troops off each within a day of the other, and he'd encouraged them not to hold back with their successes upon their return. The first to come back had reported encountering a party of ten Dwarven, none of which they could have taken back alive, apparently. The second boasted having fought and defeated twenty of the Unnaturals, and the final lot claimed to have tackled at least fifty armed Dwarven and a Shapeshifter.

Catherine was convinced the most any of them had killed was the occasional hare or mountain goat for a good supper and the blood on their leather armor. Halesbridge had commended them all for their bravery.

Observing the bishop, Catherine found he couldn't have looked more dissatisfied or unimpressed if he'd tried.

"Then tell me again why I lost an entire garrison of men in the forest east of Ironstone pursuing them after the new decree–"

"That was over four years ago," the king cut in. "Winters are cruel up there. Most of the old and the children wouldn't have made it past the first month of ground frost, I'd wager. As for the men you lost, well, maybe mine were just better equipped."

"Or maybe you should have done as I'd asked and gone *beyond* the mountains and into the woods after you were done with the Dwarven you *say* you apprehended and executed – if indeed you managed to solve that problem at all."

The king smiled indulgently. "Doing so would have been an outright declaration of war on Ironstone. I agreed to do you this service, ride under the episcopal flag and search that mountainside for you, but I also told you I wasn't taking an army that close to Ironstone. I have no quarrel with Cassandra. If you want to burn down that forest, you're going to have to find an excuse and a means of doing it yourself, *Your Excellency*."

"There are Fairyflies in those woods, and they're allied with the Dwarven. I've repeatedly requested Queen Cassandra incinerate that evil stretch of earth between the town and the moors. She's stubbornly refusing on the grounds of maintaining a few woodsmen's and hunters' livelihoods, but I'm telling you we have to take very seriously what's going on up there."

Catherine's stomach clenched. *Fairyflies!* If she'd known that, she would have insisted they go just to catch a glimpse of them.

The king sighed. "There hasn't been a sighting of Fairyflies in decades, and even assuming there *are* Fairyflies in that forest, why would a swarm of Errlights throw in with a bunch of outlawed Dwarven on the run? I've never heard of such a thing."

The Inquisitor's patience was wearing thin, and Catherine found watching his blood pressure rise most entertaining.

"Because, dear cousin, Fairyflies are cunning demons, and they're always the spearhead of disaster. They're just as evil as the *Dwarven*, the *Shapeshifters* and the *Cine*. They're the Devil's servants, as all of them are. They decimate the game, turn the weather against our hunters, and lead good men from their paths into the fog never to return. They devour human souls and turn human bodies into vile and despicable creatures of the night. Prince Eamon's disfiguration and his death less than a week after his birth was a *sign*."

The king rolled his eyes, sighing, and was about to speak when Driesburgh turned to Halesbridge and started in on him. "Rumors are always rooted in some manner of truth. You know that as well as I do, Alexander."

Halesbridge grunted. "Nonsense. Children die. *Many* children die."

Lennard shifted uncomfortably in his chair. "There can be no doubt that we need to protect ourselves and our kind against the Tainted. We have to act, but not against Ironstone, not against half a dozen starved Dwarven, and not against some mystical, probably non-existent insects buzzing around the uninhabited woodlands. We need Ironstone. We need all the help we can get if we're going to act against the uprising of the Cine."

Catherine supposed that every last one of the people at this table would have a heart attack if they knew whom they were sharing it with. A wicked, godless Cine sat right in their midst, drinking their wine, listening to the lies they were telling each other… she'd laugh at them all inwardly when next she bedded their king.

It never ceased to amaze her how it pleased humans to have someone to blame for their own insufficiencies. She'd always thought it an interesting notion that they actually believed the Tainted would be in liege with the Devil. She'd seen so many devils in human form, but the Beelzebub himself had failed to appear to her as yet. She might have remembered to ask someone at The Fair, but it was there she'd realized her own kind were no better than the humans; they lied and deceived and betrayed just as well.

The bishop's eyes were cold and dangerous when he directed them at Catherine. He reminded her of her councilman. She wondered how he liked his women – *if* it was women he liked at all. Men of the cloth were men nonetheless, and men were all the same beneath whatever cloth they chose to wear. She'd had her share of clergymen at the hangman's house.

"Milady, please accept my condolences for your loss. Your journeys over the past months must have been a terrible ordeal."

Breaking with his stare, she looked downward at her hands. "Yes, Your Excellency. It was difficult."

"Did you have to bear witness to your mother's death?"

"I did."

"And did you also have to bear witness to the king's soldiers slaying those Dwarven heathens in the mountains?"

She lifted her eyes first to Halesbridge, and then fixed them firmly to Driesburgh's piercing glare. "Yes, Your Grace," she lied, "I witnessed the executions of those brought back alive by the troops for questioning just outside of our camp."

He shifted his gaze from Catherine to Lennard and back, chewing on this. "I'll be praying for your mother's soul, Duchess."

Catherine was sure Maebh's soul would need every prayer it could get, wherever she was now. "Thank you, Your Grace."

The bishop rose from his chair. His secretaries followed his example.

"I'll be going back to Remulum this week to report to His Holiness that the Dwarven threat is... *stemmed* for now," he declared. "But mark my words: if the Tainted are planning a rising, they'll be gathering all manner of Unnaturals around them. They'll be knocking on the doors of the human vermin who are helping them, including Cassandra's, and I'm certain we're in for a long, dark night in the history of man."

Catherine was sure Driesburgh was, in any case.

Chapter Thirty-Nine

♋ Duties ♋

Strolling in the small walled gardens with her lady-in-waiting trailing behind them, Lillian pointedly avoided looking at Catherine.

"Tell me, Lady Glasston, was it hard for you to travel with my husband's army?"

Catherine wondered if Lillian had ever done so herself, but she doubted it. Though she knew some soldiers' and noblemen's families traveled with them when they went on longer campaigns, delicate little Lillian would probably rather stay home.

"It was taxing, yes. Sleeping in tents isn't very comfortable, and my traveling companion was taken ill."

"You mean Master Brandner?"

She nodded. "Do you know him?"

"Indeed." Lillian didn't elaborate, but Catherine knew from Brandner they had exchanged a few words on more than one occasion.

He'd told her Lillian didn't much care for politics, and she had no interest in the economics of her husband's kingdom beyond the walls of her home. Her presence at the formal dinners she organized wasn't always guaranteed, and she tended to excuse herself early when she did attend.

"Well, since Master Brandner had to be escorted back to Ironstone, I'm very grateful to be here, now," Catherine said, taking in the poor state of the flower beds as they walked. Weeds all but drowned the shrubs on one end of the enclosed yard.

"I can imagine. And when do you intend to continue your journey to Walha?"

Catherine couldn't help but admire Lillian's directness. Plain and delicate as she was, Lillian knew when to demonstrate that she had teeth.

"I haven't made plans yet. With the weather turning colder, your husband generously offered that I may spend the winter in Trondenburgh so I won't have to worry about stormy seas on the passage."

Lillian hummed. "I would have thought the seas would be calmer at this time of the year than in spring."

"I'm afraid I've never been to the sea." Catherine stooped to pick up a golden maple leaf, one of the first of the season. "I must confess I have no idea. But, I want you to know I do appreciate your hospitality."

Lillian's lips twitched into an empty smile that was there and gone in a flash. "My husband's duties are my obligations also, of course. I do hope you'll feel a welcome… *guest* in my house."

Catherine heard exactly what Lillian was saying. "I'm sure I will."

They'd reached the far wall. Among the weeds crawling along it were mohn flowers and white shierling plants. Catherine wondered if anyone here knew how poisonous the shierling plants were. They were among the first plants Rebecca had taught her to avoid when she'd been small. No one in the nameless village would have tolerated shierling growing in their yards for fear that the children would pick the flowers. The milk in their stems caused severe stomach cramps, and the roots, if ingested, would lead to death.

She smiled at Lillian. "I love your garden."

Lillian snorted a laugh. "Not much will grow here. The soil is weak."

The woman had no idea what strength could grow from weak soil. "I'm good with flowers, and with your permission, I'd like to tend to some of the flower beds in return for your hospitality. Perhaps I can work some magic here."

The other woman eyed her skeptically. "We have peasants to care for the gardens."

It didn't look as though they were doing a good job, but Lillian didn't notice these things, apparently, or didn't *want* to notice them. She didn't care for politics or economics, she let her home go to ruins, let her gardens grow wild – Catherine couldn't imagine how the woman managed to fill her days. The child was probably her only distraction from herself.

Catherine's smile widened, and the outlines that had been ghosting around her head gained dimension.

"My father employed gardeners, too, but it would give me something to do, with pleasing results, I hope."

When Lillian still seemed reluctant, Catherine fixed her gaze to the Queen Consort's and slipped a thought inside. It easily latched on to something that was already there.

It would be so nice if there were roses along that wall next summer. How Lioba would love them!

Seasons changed so fast, and Catherine made sure Lillian was aware that she would be long gone by the time they bloomed, leaving nothing but a scented reminder that she'd been there at all. Catherine was no danger to her. The Duchess of Glasston was just a girl from the Sudlands who liked to dig around in the dirt.

"Why not," she said finally. "Do as you please with the time you spend in my house."

Catherine thanked her and began going over where and how she was going to dry the shierling roots she'd dig up the next morning.

Chapter Forty

ᛢ God Save the Queen ᛒ

Lennard's physician was a charlatan indeed. He had no idea what was wrong with Lillian when he inspected her weary eyes and coated tongue. She was tired and nauseated all the time, and she'd lost weight. Halesbridge had finally decided to send for the healer, but Catherine was sure the whelp would never find out what he was dealing with. He couldn't tell his own head from a donkey's ass.

She was quite pleased with herself as she stood in the corner of the room along with the Queen Consort's lady-in-waiting, watching him listen to Lillian's heartbeat as if he knew what he was doing.

"It's a congestion of the juices," he finally proclaimed.

The lady-in-waiting breathed a sigh of relief. Catherine came to Lillian's side and squeezed her hand affectionately. A kind, carefully-placed thought here, a pleasant image snuck in there, and they'd become friends over the last weeks, even though Lillian had initially been quite determined to put Catherine in her place.

"See?" she said, smiling. "Nothing to be worried about." Then, she turned to the physician. "You can treat that easily, of course?"

The young man nodded and proceeded to give them instructions on the strict diet Lillian would need to keep over the next weeks. He left them some vile-smelling herbs for a tea and stayed to observe her drink the first cup.

Catherine had been careful about mixing the shierling in Lillian's soups and wine. She'd dried and ground the poisonous root, and she'd experimented with the dosage beforehand on two of the mongrels that ran around the castle grounds, as well as one of the squires.

The dogs had both died too fast because she'd put too much of the powder into the leftovers she'd fed them, but she'd done better with the squire. He had been roughly Lillian's size and weight, and he'd lasted over a fortnight. Lillian was in her third week now, and when she died, everyone would blame the physician.

The hard part was being patient. That, and staying away from Lennard.

A visit to his brother had taken the king south shortly after they'd returned from the Winter Mountains. The talks on their new strategies on tackling the Cine problem had lasted for weeks, and Halesbridge had kept him busy with his constant nagging about the state of affairs ever since his return.

He was fire and flame for her whenever they did manage to meet, but it was difficult for them to get away unnoticed. They'd only managed it twice in the whole time Catherine was here, but the good thing about this was that no one of importance had reason to voice doubts of the king's fidelity or Catherine's integrity.

She was thoroughly enjoying this game.

At first, there had been gossip of Lillian being with child. The talk of a new baby at the castle had lifted everyone's spirits except Lennard's. Despite Lillian's efforts to get his attention, he hadn't so much as touched her. As the weeks wore on, Lillian had taken to her bed, and Catherine was determined to make sure she never left it again. The only new baby in Trondenburgh over the next years would be hers when she was Lennard's wife. A little prince, perhaps, to help the king get over his loss.

Lillian beckoned the lady-in-waiting. "Go and tell my husband the healer prescribed some herbal tea."

When the servant was gone, Lillian sat on the edge of the mattress.

"As if he'd care," she muttered under her breath. "Help me up, please."

Catherine helped her find her wooden shoes, and she handed her a robe. Then, she cupped Lillian's cheek in her hands affectionately and looked her in the eyes.

"You're right, dear. He doesn't care about you. Not one little bit. He should be ashamed of himself. You'll have to let him know how much you need him right now. It's hard enough for you as it is. You're sick, and you're in pain. He should be by your side, helping you recover instead of traipsing around the woods with his friends."

Catherine knew Lennard was at the stables with Halesbridge and a small troop of soldiers, preparing to ride out to meet several of his knights. He'd been called upon to settle some land issues they'd been quarreling over. Feeble little Lillian was probably the last person he wanted to see right before he left.

Lillian considered what Catherine had said for a moment. "Help me find him."

"Oh, are you sure, dear? You're not up to it…"

"No, I really need to speak with Lennard. Please help me."

Catherine could barely hide her smile. This was almost too simple.

Together, they slowly tackled the narrow stairway. Catherine supported Lillian all the way to the main door on the ground floor, where they bumped into Lillian's lady-in-waiting. The servant was just coming back, and she obviously hadn't expected to find Lillian up and about.

"Did you find him – where is the king?" Lillian asked, but Catherine stumbled forward and yelped before the servant could answer. Clutching her ankle, she pulled a face.

"I'm sorry, Lillian. I think I twisted it."

Lillian let go of her shoulder, and the lady-in-waiting frowned, but took Catherine's place.

Catherine hobbled back to the stairs to sit down. She rubbed her ankle. "I don't think this is a good idea, my queen."

"Your Highness, the duchess is right," her servant agreed. "You should be in bed."

"Keep your weight off that foot," Lillian told Catherine absently, ignoring the other woman's advice. "I'll be fine."

A sheen of sweat covered the queen's pallid face, but she was determined to make a fool of herself. Catherine couldn't wait to hear what the king would have to say about it.

She waited until they'd left the building, and made haste to get back upstairs, fingering her locket. She'd stored the last of the powdered shierling inside. The tiny amount dissolved easily in the tea still sitting in its pot on the table in Lillian's room. She didn't think she'd have to make another batch. Lillian would drink her tea like a good girl and die.

From the window in her own quarters, Catherine could see the stables fairly well, and she wished she could hear all of little Lillian's arguments as she incessantly admonished her husband in front of Halesbridge and his men.

His face was red to the roots of his hair, and she looked like she was going to collapse. When she actually began swaying, he picked her up and carried her back inside, much to the amusement of the soldiers behind him. Halesbridge yelled something at the cavalrymen, and Catherine supposed he'd be having their hides.

After a while, she heard the queen's door slam, and hobbled back downstairs. She was just in time to catch the king on his way out. Their eyes met, and she could read him like a book. He was beyond annoyed with his *clever choice*.

Struggling with himself, he hesitated. Then, he mouthed the word *tonight*, and she nodded.

Tonight was the night, she repeated to herself several times over before she pasted her most complacent smile back on her face and knocked on Lillian's door before opening it.

Without warning, a cup came hurling toward her, missing her by mere inches as it shattered on the wall next to her head. Lillian's lady-in-waiting didn't dare intervene when Lillian lifted the pot and smashed it also. She darted an imploring glance at Catherine and hastily began cleaning up the mess when Catherine nodded at her reassuringly, growing impatient with her bothersome new best friend.

"What's all this?"

"I hate him!" Lillian spat, wringing her hands. Her blood-shot eyes protruded markedly from her sheet-white face. "I hate him!"

Taking Lillian in her arms and patting her back, Catherine wondered how she was going to replace the shierling. She'd left one plant growing in a peripheral part of the garden, but it had taken over a week to dry the last batch of thinly sliced roots properly.

"There, there, dear," she crooned. "Let's just simmer down, and we'll find a way to remedy all of what's amiss here. There, there."

Chapter Forty-One

‪ɑ Unexpected Friends ʂ‬

"Welcome to the game of kings and queens," the young Magician told his audience.

He was lean and pale, his eyes a deep earthen brown lined by the finest silver only his own kind could see if they knew how to look for it. The humans who'd gathered around the checkered floor portion of his square pavilion might have been frightened by the quality of its luminescence as he stepped out of the shadows and into the arena, but they'd come to see the remarkable carved wooden figures that were lined up in tidy rows facing each other, and not really the man who'd made them – or so they thought.

"This is a game for two people. Anyone can learn to play it," Lorcan continued, "but only thieves and scoundrels can learn to play it really well. That's why we sell so many sets to the nobility."

Hearty laughter rippled through the growing crowd.

"Let me explain the basics of the battlefield to you. You'll find yourself more familiar with it than you'd have thought, even if you've never had the misfortune to hold arms in times of war yourself."

He strode slowly over to the black king, his hands clasped behind his back as he directed his eyes first at several of the men nearest to him, and then absently at the three-foot-tall figure. "This is the dark ruler of the land on this side of the board." The king came to life and proudly lifted his head, casting a condescending glance at his subjects.

"Well, at least he *thinks* he's in charge. We all know that behind – or in this case *beside* – every powerful man stands a mighty woman, waiting to take control of his home, his social life, and his potency… his army, I mean, of course."

The queen brandished her scepter at the king, and he lifted both hands protectively over his head, ducking away from her, but not fast enough. She hit him over the head with it, and he let out a yelp of pain before both he and his better half went back to their still, rigid wooden forms.

More people gathered around to see what was going on.

Lorcan motioned at the black pawns, and they sprang to life, straightening as they saluted, eyes ahead.

"The king's infantry is made up of eight soldiers in all," he went on, and the pieces marched either two paces or one ahead. "That might not seem much, but these fellas are loyal to the end, and they'll fight to the last man."

The white pawns sprang to life and bowed before doing the same as their black adversaries.

"We've already seen that the queen can hold her own, so I think we should now have a little demonstration of the bishop's abilities, since it is common knowledge that most domestic squabbles in the royal household involve discussions about religion."

The black bishops moved out one after the other alternating with their white counter pieces. They defeated a large number of pawns easily as they went. The pawns limped to the sidelines, where they went back to being the wooden pieces they'd started out as. Lorcan watched the action and the onlookers, stroking his clean-shaven chin with the thumb of his right hand, his elbow resting in the other hand.

"And now the knights, please," he said eventually after the bishops had sufficiently decimated each other's armies. The board was now wide open and the status quo seemed clear. "Personally, I tend to place my hopes in the more heavily armed, better equipped people for the clean-up."

One of his remaining black pawns goaded a white bishop and was slain, upon which the Magician's black knight moved in on the bishop. Rubbing its backside, the white bishop limped to the side lines to join the rest of its army. That made for lots of room for the black knights and bishops to assume a better position, covering their queen as she moved out. One of the white rooks tried to start a maneuver, but was foiled by the last black pawn.

Between them, the black bishops and rooks took care of the white queen, while Lorcan's black queen and rooks cornered the white king.

"Check mate," Lorcan said quietly, letting the scene settle. When he was sure it had, he casually waved a hand over the board, and the white pieces shrank and turned to doves.

The birds rose gracefully and flew toward the ceiling of the tent. The tarp seemed to open up for them, fading completely away for an instant in the places where the birds exited. Then, it closed again, and they were gone from sight. Another flick of the Magician's hand turned the black pieces into bats, and they swirled upward after the doves, but the ceiling didn't appear quite as favorable toward them as it had been to the doves, and the bats scattered, eddying over the heads of the audience and causing some confusion until they'd found their way out through the side openings of the tent.

Smirking, Lorcan bent so it would look as though he was picking up the chess board by one of its corners. This was impossible, of course; everyone had been able to convince themselves that the checkered floor was made from solid wood planks with black and white squares painted on it, but Lorcan gathered it up all the same like a cloth and bundled it across his arm.

"Some assistance, please?" he asked, and one of the teenage boys watching volunteered. "Help me fold it nicely so I'll have a lovely, crinkle-free board for my next show, would you?"

The boy did as he was asked, and when they'd finished folding it to the size of one of the squares, Lorcan held it up for everyone to see. In another instant, however, it was gone.

Bowing, Lorcan received his applause, and pointed out where everyone could find smaller versions of the game for sale at the stall right next to the pavilion. He'd manned the stand with one of Freya's youngest boys, and the lad had already sold several of the less expensive sets even before the tent was empty. The more intricately carved ones would take a little longer, and there would be some bargaining.

He noticed that one of the men by the entrance of his tent didn't seem inclined to leave. He was well dressed, and a sword with an ornately crafted hilt was strapped to his belt.

"Can I help you?" Lorcan asked.

"That was very impressive."

Lorcan gave another small bow. "Thank you. I work hard on my illusions."

"And on your potions, hopefully."

"I don't practice magic," Lorcan replied. "This is a fair. I'm a craftsman and an Illusionist."

Again, the man smiled, but there was something painful in the way he did it. "I used to know the man who had the idea of creating a safe haven for everyone in need. I laughed at him because I didn't think it would work. From what I see here now, I can tell how well his memory has been honored, and I'm ashamed to say I had no part in it."

"You knew my father?" Dean asked, entering the pavilion. His glance darted back and forth between the stranger and Lorcan.

"I did. I'm Alexander of Halesbridge," he said, nodding curtly by way of a greeting. "Dean Greenleaf?"

"Yes. What is it you want here? I'm almost sure you didn't come for the entertainment."

"Just a minute ago, your friend here asked if he could help me. I'll answer that now: yes, I really do need your help."

Lorcan folded his arms across his chest. "Alright. We understand, but how did you find us?"

Halesbridge seemed reluctant to answer, but finally gazed at a woman who'd been standing by the stall next to the pavilion, admiring the artful chess sets. A boy of ten or eleven accompanied her. The lad saw Halesbridge looking over and nudged his mother. Lorcan thought she was one of the most beautiful women he'd ever seen. To him, her skin glowed. A recollection awoke. Before his mind's eye, he saw

Aoife and Cassandra, and he realized this woman was a Fairy.

She smiled. He found himself wondering what she perceived of him.

"She can open Portals," he told Dean softly, aware that Dean had no way of recognizing her for what she was.

Halesbridge's brow creased so deeply, Lorcan almost felt sorry for him with the headache he was in for. "Yes, she can," the steward said. "But how–"

Lorcan didn't feel like explaining himself. "And the boy?" The lad's skin wasn't quite as radiant as his mother's, and Lorcan guessed he was half human.

"He's my son, and we're keeping him out of this."

"You brought him here, so he's already right in the middle of it."

Halesbridge had to fight for composure. He shifted his weight from one foot to the other tensely.

"Look, the reason why I came here is because Lillian of Trondenburgh has fallen ill."

Dean snorted a laugh. "What's that got to do with us?"

"Not much perhaps, depending on your point of view, but you should be aware that not everyone is in agreement with what's going on. You do have friends in places you mightn't expect to find them."

"Are you trying to tell us Lillian of Trondenburgh is a friend of the Cine or the Dwarven?" Lorcan couldn't believe the nerve of the man.

He could see Dean was equally irritated. It was common knowledge that the house of Trondenburgh was an ally of the Inquisitor's cause. Driesburgh had orchestrated more trials on Trondenburgh's lands than in most other places.

Halesbridge took a deep breath. "The king has no more interest in the persecutions than you do, believe me. He isn't beyond reason. Neither is his wife. Trondenburgh is disinclined to continue actively supporting his cousin." He paused, waiting to see how this bit of news was going to settle.

Lorcan wondered if he was waiting for a pat on the back for statements yet unproven. He didn't really believe it. "Go on," he said patiently nonetheless.

"Recently, the king has acquired a mistress. I don't trust her. She has great influence on him, and I suspect she has a hand in Lillian's illness."

"Well, that's new!" Dean laughed. "The king's wife falls ill, and you suspect foul play by his whore. What do you think, is she a witch or is she a Cine, or just an overgrown Dwarve?"

Halesbridge was beside himself and began stuttering. "No… yes… but I wasn't trying to imply she's anything but a whore." He didn't know what to do with his hands anymore and began fidgeting, much to Lorcan's amusement. "I mean… you can never tell, but… the thing is, I can well imagine she's poisoning Lillian."

"Do you have proof of that?"

Halesbridge pulled Catherine's locket from the leather pouch tied to his belt, opened its catch so both halves came apart and handed the piece to Lorcan. Dean froze.

Lorcan examined the powdery residue inside, sniffed, and pulled a face.

"It's hers," Halesbridge said. "Do you know what was in it?"

Lorcan needed a moment to picture the plant that went with the root, and another to put a name with it.

"Shierling."

Dean took the locket from his hands. "Are you sure?"

Lorcan searched his friend's face. "I am. Have you seen this before?"

Dean shook his head and lowered his eyes, giving the locket back to Halesbridge. Something was very wrong here, but Lorcan couldn't say what, exactly.

"Shierling is deadly, isn't it?" Halesbridge asked.

Lorcan nodded. "But there is an antidote."

He motioned Halesbridge to wait for a moment while he took Dean aside.

"What is it? You look like you've seen a ghost."

"I thought I recognized that locket."

"But it isn't what you thought it was?"

Dean shook his head. "No. The woman I knew who had one like it would never poison anyone."

Lorcan thought that was more wishful thinking than certainty. *Want* made people do a lot of things. "One of our own?"

Dean hummed, but then seemed to regret having done so. "It can't be her."

"Want to make sure?"

"Let me think about it."

"Help him or not?" Lorcan briefly studied Halesbridge.

"What do you think?"

Under the circumstances, Lorcan believed it would be foolish not to. But, he was also curious about the king's mistress, and he asked himself how Dean came to know her – if this was indeed the same person Dean seemed so reluctant to name. "I'd say yes."

They walked back to rejoin Halesbridge.

"We'll help you. For a price."

The tension left Halesbridge's face and shoulders. "Anything you ask."

"Don't say that too loud," Lorcan mumbled. "We do have a lot of needs here, and I'm very confident you'll be seeing to one or two of them quite conscientiously."

He was already going over the ingredients for the antidote in his head before he'd finished speaking, and he decided he'd need one of the books because he wasn't entirely certain if he remembered everything correctly.

"Dean, I need your key and a little time."

Dean seemed a bit more himself as he handed him the key to the chest where he kept the brown book. As they parted ways, Lorcan made a mental note to continue their conversation later.

Chapter Forty-Two

☙ The Old Farm ❧

Mary sat in front of her caravan, so caught up in her pottery, she didn't hear him approach. He knew he'd startle her when he announced his presence, but that couldn't be helped. The bowl she'd been working on was ruined. She smiled at him all the same. There were five others sitting on the board next to her. The Sand Cat she couldn't perceive was curled up beneath it. He hadn't seen it in a few days now and asked himself where it went when it wasn't around The Fair.

"You're keeping busy. Don't overwork yourself," he told her, glancing briefly at her gout-ridden fingers.

"I get plenty of rest nowadays." She wiped her hands on a rag and got up to hug him, pressing a kiss to his cheek. It was seasoned with a gentle reminder that he hadn't been to see her in a while even though they were practically neighbors.

He'd been busy, too, and he would be preparing for his next trip to the Winter Mountains in a few weeks. He'd been playing with the thought of asking her to come, but something told him she wouldn't consider it.

"Mary, I need to go to the farmhouse."

She rubbed his arm affectionately and led the way into her caravan. There were too many humans about to open a Portal anywhere else.

He'd seen her do it countless times, but he'd never grown tired of watching her go through her clearly structured motions, and he loved the colors she created when she broke through from one world into the next, using those aged and stiff but still very capable fingers.

"It's time you started doing this for yourself, you know," she told him for the tenth time as she presented him with the gateway. "I'm old, but not stupid, and I know you could, if you wanted to."

He grinned at her crookedly, tapping his nose with the pad of his finger. "Do I look like I have Fairy blood?" He knew he didn't.

She grinned back. "Handsome fellow like yourself? I'd bet on it!"

He held her gaze, but refused to think about it. Only once had he attempted to create a Portal. Doing that had been so profoundly painful, he'd never ventured to try again. He remembered how the Master Sorcerer had asked him about it, and how he'd inquired about his mother. He hadn't known what to say, just as he didn't know what to tell Mary now. He didn't want to think about it. He just didn't. He was an Illusionist, and that was all.

There was a young man on the grounds with some recognizable Fairy lineage, but Lorcan hadn't spoken to him in detail about employing his Gift for the benefit of traveling between places as yet.

The Portals they needed had always been Mary's job, and unless there was an emergency, she'd always be the one he and Dean would consult with. The vast knowledge of places she'd collected in her life certainly couldn't be topped by any of them, and she was more than thorough and responsible whenever she opened a Portal, determining if it was safe by mirroring the other side before she let anyone pass through.

He couldn't bear the thought of her not feeling needed if he or Dean asked anyone else to take over her part, or even if he did it himself. She'd done so much for everyone here, for him in particular, it broke his heart to see how time was having its way with her in their growing community since Thaddeus had passed.

He hugged her.

"Watch yourself, dear," she said, and he promised he would before he crossed over into the other world through what resembled a doorway made of light and energy, the frame a tangle of glowing tendrils in soft gold and silver tones.

Nothing looked amiss at the abandoned house on the other side of the gate.

At times, he still wondered why Dean had chosen this of all places to hide the brown volume rather than just keep it with him, but Dean hadn't been willing to share on that. He'd merely told him he didn't think it wise to keep all three volumes together, and Lorcan hadn't argued.

Having spent a lot of time with those books since he'd returned to The Fair, he understood why Ortus had felt such a strong need to guard the one he'd had so well. He knew they had the potential to dismantle the Outer Haven's wards if they were to fall into the wrong hands. Those *wrong hands*, however, would have to know exactly what they were doing to accomplish that.

The house he found himself facing could have once belonged to a rather wealthy man, at least for these godforsaken parts. Blue painted shutters and carved hand rails on a porch that wrapped all the way around the building told of someone who could afford to buy good materials, someone who'd taken pride in his home before he'd left it, for whatever reason he'd done so.

The front door was in shambles. It had been smashed in years before Dean had brought him here. What remained of the back door hung by one hinge. There were stables behind the house, and there had been barrels, boards and picking baskets stored inside one of them up until a while ago, but those were all gone now. He supposed a neighbor had decided no one would miss them anymore.

The other stable had been used for livestock. Beside it was an old well that had run dry before the owner had dug another one closer to the house. Planks covered the hole in the ground. Lorcan quickly scanned the surrounding area before he labored to move them aside. A spell he himself had cast using the book he now sought protected the narrow side niche containing the box it lay in. He waved his hand over the nook, and the earth released the box. One turn of Dean's key opened the lid.

There was no need to bring the volume back to The Fair with him. He just had to look for the right potion, so he knelt and thumbed through the volume until he had what he was looking for. Bit by bit, he'd memorized what had seemed important over the last years, but sometimes, his memory needed a jolt.

It was just as well he was here, he thought as he packed the book back into its hiding place when he was done reading. The woods in this part of the land were good for every kind of thing he needed for the antidote, and freshly picked herbs were better than the dried ones he had in his caravan.

"Found the right potion?" Dean inquired from behind him unexpectedly.

Lorcan heaved the last plank back over the well and adjusted it with his foot to fit snugly against the other two.

"I'll need a few things from the woods, but I won't be long. Did you miss me already, or is

Halesbridge afraid Lillian might die while he's at The Fair?"

Dean smirked. "Bit of both, I think. Show me what to look for and I'll help you."

Lorcan projected some of the herbs from his mind onto the palm of his hand. The images that appeared were so real, Dean seemed to recognize them instantly and headed off in one direction past the little ash grove, while Lorcan went in the other.

When Lorcan returned to the house a short while later, Dean was already sitting on the steps leading up to the porch, his face in his hands, and a million miles away. There was a small pile of greens next to him, but Lorcan wasn't sure if even one of them was right.

This wasn't like Dean. Dean was always meticulous, and he knew his plants. Whatever it was that connected him to this house, it had to be something from the time after their trip to Ironstone, and it had to weigh heavily on him.

"Got everything?" he asked.

Dean nodded, blinking at the sun as he rose. "Let's go."

Lorcan touched the place where the Portal was with his fingertip in mid-air, and it rematerialized. They were back on the fairground in seconds.

Dean followed him to his caravan and, without paying much attention, silently sat with him while he made the antidote for Halesbridge. Lorcan found his friend's presence somewhat irritating. It was plain to see he wasn't interested in the potion as such.

"There's something you're not telling me, isn't there?" Lorcan finally asked outright.

A twitch of one corner of Dean's mouth told him he was right, but the prolonged stillness also conveyed that he wasn't going to get an answer.

He filled the last of the brown liquid into a small flagon and searched the shelf over his window for a cork. When he had it, he turned to look at Dean.

"Listen, I don't know what's eating you, but if it's something I should know about, I'd really appreciate some input."

"No," Dean answered decisively. "I'll be going with Halesbridge, though."

"Want me to come with you?"

"No. I don't think I'll be away for too long. I should be back in the morning."

Lorcan handed him the tiny flask. "Alright. But I *could* come with you. It's not a problem."

"No. Just… just look after things here."

Lorcan wasn't convinced, but Dean obviously had something to take care of, and he didn't think it would be very dangerous.

"Fine. Make sure the queen drinks all of it in one go, no matter what she may think it is. It's not very tasty, but it'll help with the symptoms, at least, and it'll prevent any further damage should she ingest more of the shierling over the next days. Tell Halesbridge to have someone keep an eye on her food and drink."

Dean nodded, but Lorcan wondered if he'd taken in all of what he'd told him.

Halesbridge was already waiting outside with his wife and son, and Lorcan watched them disappear around the corner of the caravan next to his own. When they didn't reemerge on the other side, he knew they were gone.

Chapter Forty-Three

❈ High Treason ❈

Catherine had searched everywhere for her locket, but it was gone. She believed she might have left it in the king's bedroom, but she didn't dare look for it there by day, so she tried to distract herself by reading to Lillian. She absently plowed through one of the books Driesburgh had officially approved, not taking in any of its content.

Having spent the night with Lennard, she felt somewhat more at peace with herself on the whole, but Lillian was still alive, and that was a problem. Catherine loathed the woman for having smashed the teapot and spilled her chance at happiness. She'd been *so* close. Between the thought of that and the missing locket, she was aching all over to hurt Lillian for standing in her way like she did.

Something had to give, *soon*, or she'd boil over.

When Lillian finally drifted off, she took a break and went to her room.

Pouring herself a cup of wine, she considered her options. Perhaps Lillian would break her neck when next she tried to leave her quarters; she was in bad shape, and a little accident on those steep stairs wouldn't incriminate anyone. Accidents happened. Lioba would be in sore need of a mother after the traumatic experiences of the last weeks, and after Lennard's declarations of love the previous night, she was quite certain he wouldn't wait longer than the appropriate mourning period to remarry.

Glancing out of her window by chance as she imagined Lillian falling to her death, she saw Halesbridge crossing the courtyard. He'd brought someone with him. She nearly choked on her drink when she saw that it was Dean Greenleaf.

Dean Greenleaf... What on earth was Dean Greenleaf doing here? A Cine at Trondenburgh!

Did Halesbridge know *what* Dean was?

What would Dean say if he saw her here? He'd ruin everything. But, she could destroy him just as easily as he could betray her. Whatever Halesbridge knew or didn't know about Greenleaf, she was sure the king wouldn't be very happy with him bringing a Cine to his castle. Lennard wouldn't take Dean's word over hers, she thought, but putty had a tendency to stick once it was thrown your way.

She had to think, but there was no time. The men were on their way to the keep.

She hadn't finished going through the first two possible scenarios yet when her maid knocked and entered the room behind her, carrying clean bedlinen.

"Milady, Her Highness requests your presence."

The thought of leaving her room made Catherine's stomach churn.

"I'll be right down," she said, observing the young woman putting the linen into the top shelf of her wardrobe. "Is anyone else with her?"

"Lord Halesbridge, but I didn't see him. I was told by Her Highness' chamber maid to ask you down." The servant turned fully to her, debating with herself before continuing. "Apparently, Lord Halesbridge has brought another healer to see her."

Catherine smiled. "Well, after yesterday's debacle, I hope this man is a little better at his craft than the one we had here already." Dean was no healer. Going by what she'd seen at The Fair, he wasn't much of anything besides an educated fool.

The servant hesitated, and her gaze wandered for a moment. It was then that Catherine noticed the similarities they shared. They both had dark hair, though the servant's was a little more brown than black, and they were both roughly the same height and build. The other woman wore a locket on a thin leather band around her neck. Its craftsmanship couldn't compare to the one Catherine had lost, but it gave her an idea. Sometimes, inspiration came from unexpected places.

"You're tired, aren't you?" she asked the girl, touching her arm.

The servant smiled timidly. "No, Milady…"

"Oh, but I know you have so much work. The same toiling every day. I do see your plight, believe me."

Catherine began searching for a way into the woman's mind. There wasn't much to stop her, and the thought she left behind there when she returned to herself had the servant feeling as though she'd slaved and labored non-stop the entire week without a rest.

"Please," she told the maid, "do have a little nap. No one will ever know – just you and I, and I'd never say anything."

The young woman yawned and rubbed her temple, then nodded.

Catherine led her to her bed, sat her down, helped her put her feet up, and all but tucked her in. Watching her intently for a moment, Catherine decided to take the locket. Something told her it might come in handy. There was a fine lock of hair inside, perhaps that of a child. She put the piece into the cavity beneath a loose board under her wardrobe, where she kept the coins from the Tierney castle and a wooden figure she'd had for longer than she remembered, and cast one last glance back at the sleeping form on her pillow.

Descending the stairs, she pictured the maid's rather plain face in every detail: a large nose, flat cheeks, and deep-set eyes of watery gray. Dean's defenses were weak, and he'd see exactly what she wanted him to when she entered Lillian's room.

The door opened quietly for her, and she was glad he was standing with his back to her. He and Halesbridge were making light conversation with Lillian. The mousy little wench seemed to have perked up considerably.

"Katharina," she called when she saw her, and Catherine smiled, not taking her eyes off of Dean as he turned around. For a moment, she was worried, but when he smiled back at her without recognition, she knew she had nothing to fear.

Halesbridge ignored her, as usual, but Dean gave a little bow. "Lady Glasston."

Lady Glasston – how that sounded coming from his mouth. How that *would* have sounded, had she been a Lady when they'd first met. He might have treated her with so much more respect. She didn't think he'd have stolen from her if she'd been a Lady then.

"I hear you've come to heal our dear Queen Consort's digestive problems," she said. "I'm glad Lord Halesbridge knows so many physicians. What a pity the last one nearly poisoned her with his wretched tea."

Halesbridge scoffed indignantly, but Lillian giggled.

"Master Greenleaf's elixir didn't taste much better, but I feel more like myself already," she said.

Dean seemed pleased. "Well, I'm hopeful you'll keep improving from here on in, Your Highness."

Halesbridge's mien told nothing. "The king is waiting down in the Hall," he finally told her. "I'd like a word in his presence, Duchess."

Catherine didn't think he wanted to talk about the weather. She felt a knot forming in her chest.

"Of course," she replied and followed the men out of the room.

On the stairs, she kept close behind Dean, trying to feel deeper inside of him, but she was too nervous and unfocused, and she worried she'd lose her connection to him altogether if she pushed too hard. After all these years, he still smelled the same of wood fire and grass.

She wanted to hurt him as much as she wanted to hurt Lillian.

Lennard waited for them in the Great Hall. Halesbridge lowered his eyes in keeping with good protocol, and Dean did the same. Catherine stood beside Halesbridge and curtseyed.

"I'd like to thank all of you for your efforts on behalf of my wife," the king told them. "I know each of you is trying to contribute to improving her condition in their own way." He fixed his eyes on Dean. "I don't believe I've ever seen you here before, Master Greenleaf."

Dean cleared his throat before answering. "I'm a traveling physician, Your Majesty."

"Well, I hope your experience will be of use in finding a cure for my wife's illness. Were you able to confirm the diagnosis that was made yesterday, or did you arrive at a different conclusion?"

"Sire, I did come to a different conclusion," he replied evenly. "The symptoms point to something more serious than mere congestion. I think your wife was poisoned."

The king paled.

"How?"

Halesbridge rummaged around for something in his pouch. "We believe someone poisoned her food or her drink, and we have proof."

Catherine caught a glimpse of the leather thong and knew that her locket would be at the end of it. She had to act instantly. She let go of Dean's perception and redirected her attention toward Lennard.

Halesbridge handed the king her great-grandmother's locket, but what Lennard held in his hand was, to his perception, a crude, square locket on a worn leather cord. Halesbridge glared triumphantly at Catherine as the king inspected the pendant. He didn't recognize it, and he opened it. There was still some of the powdery shierling residue inside.

Halesbridge looked more smug by the minute. "That's ground root of shierling, Your Majesty. It's lethal. It could have been given to her in small doses so the effect would not be immediate."

The king might not have been familiar with shierling, but Catherine could see he was making the connections. "Did you find out whom this belongs to?"

Halesbridge was obviously baffled. His glance darted back and forth between the king and Catherine.

"Well?" Lennard persisted.

He firmly believed he'd never seen the pendant in his hand before, and didn't even consider it could be Catherine's. She was glad she never wore it over her dress, so she didn't think anyone else would recognize it if he didn't.

"But, Your Majesty... it's the Duchess'. Surely you've seen her wearing it."

Of course he'd seen her wearing *a* locket, as well as a half a dozen necklaces he'd given her, but not this one. She inhaled sharply and was about to say something in her own defense when the king barked a laugh, and threw the locket back at Halesbridge.

"That old thing? I can't say I have. Katharina?"

Catherine acted utterly stricken and reestablished her link with Dean just in time to avoid catastrophe. "I don't know whom that belongs to, but it's certainly not mine, and I haven't the slightest clue what *sherling* is."

She knew the king would be relieved to hear he wasn't the only one with gaps in his knowledge.

Halesbridge turned to face her. "It's *shierling*, and I happen to know you own a locket very much like this one, Milady. Where do you keep it?"

"Yes, I own a locket, Lord Halesbridge, but I don't think I like what you're getting at," she answered. "I will show it to you, but I do have to wonder what makes you think I would try to poison Her Highness."

Lennard's brow creased as hope returned to Halesbridge's cold gaze. "I'm sure you can just show us *your* locket, then, and put our minds at ease."

The king's growing impatience resounded in his voice. "I don't think that will be necessary, Alexander."

Catherine folded her arms beneath her breasts. "Your Majesty, I have nothing to hide. The old piece Lord Halesbridge may mean is a keepsake, and I value it for personal reasons, but I rarely wear it. Perhaps we can go and take a look and set this… misunderstanding straight, and then concentrate on finding whoever is trying to harm Her Highness."

Lennard's eyebrows arched, and he rose. "Alright. Then let's do just that. Halesbridge?"

Dean was about to follow them out of the Hall, but the king had him wait. Catherine was thankful for that. She didn't think she could disguise the maid as well as herself for him in the same room.

Entering her room behind her, Halesbridge was appalled to see the woman lying on Catherine's bed. He barked at her to get up, slapping her so hard it left marks on her cheek. The frightened servant almost fell on her face scampering to her feet.

Catherine paid her no attention, and knelt to retrieve the locket she'd taken from the girl earlier.

"Now you all know where I keep my most personal treasures," she mumbled, and the king hummed amusedly.

"I suppose most women have one of those hidey-places," he said, and she thought of how Dean had raided the one she'd trusted him with.

The emotion this brought on made her fingers tremble as she pushed her hand into the hole, feeling around inside of it longer than necessary. She had to remind herself to keep breathing and concentrate on her real task. She wasn't sure she could pull this off, but she had *everything* to lose if she failed.

She'd never tried to influence several people at the same time like this, but she just had to keep it together, she told herself, she had to keep all of the threads in her hands and remember which one to tug on and which to loosen at the right moment.

She took the locket from the hollow beneath the plank and handed it to Lennard. He saw what she wanted him to see. Halesbridge saw the simpler piece of jewelry that belonged to the confused young woman cowering in the corner of the room.

He was seething, and Catherine could almost see the cogs in his head cracking under the strain. "Your Majesty, I don't understand…"

"Where did you find that anyway?" Catherine wanted to know, pointing at the pendant in Halesbridge's hand. Halesbridge clamped his mouth shut.

The king seemed interested in hearing his answer as much as Catherine was. "Lord Halesbridge?"

Halesbridge had a hard time finding his tongue. Eventually, glancing back and forth between Catherine and Lennard, he said, "In Your Majesty's private room."

"Whatever were you doing in my room? Have you taken to doing the cleaning, now that our maids are sleeping in our beds?" He turned around to the servant to show her his displeasure, and the girl's eyes widened at the sight of what she perceived as her own locket in Halesbridge's hand.

"That would be mine, Milord," she blurted unwittingly.

"Which? This one?" Halesbridge snapped. "Or the other?" Hope was again springing, but it was crushed as soon as it had arisen.

"The one you're holding, Milord."

The woman had no grasp of what she'd gotten herself into, though the implications were clear to everyone else present.

Lennard handed Catherine back the locket she'd given him, his eyes imploring her not to jump to conclusions. She found that quite comical.

Halesbridge bit down on his lip so hard, she thought he'd draw blood.

"So…" Catherine mused, addressing the maid and trying to sound as naïve as she could manage, "I suppose you lost it in the king's room while bringing fresh bedlinen. That's what you do here, isn't it?"

The woman blushed. She wasn't responsible for the king's room, and both Catherine and the king knew that.

"I don't know how it got there," she whined. "I swear I don't…"

Catherine could feel the servant's fear as Halesbridge glared at her.

"Well, it did. Can you explain why you kept shierling inside of it?"

"Shierling? Heavens! No!"

Catherine touched the king's arm, and they moved to one side of the room while Halesbridge proceeded questioning the maid.

"Please," she whispered, sobbing, "tell me the truth – are you sleeping with her?" A single tear spilled down the side of her face. "I mean, I was with you last night… I want nothing more than to make you happy, and I'm even nursing Lillian and helping her. Can't you see how much that takes out of me? Tell me, are you sleeping with her, and is that why *she's* poisoning Lillian?" She motioned toward the maid.

Lennard drew a deep breath, violently shaking his head. "No! I love you. What can I do so you'll believe me?"

She hesitated, swallowing hard, fidgeting. "Get *him* away from us," she finally said, "and *her* too. He hates me, I don't know why, but he does. You have no idea what I have to put up with from him *every day*. He was always touching me, saying things to me, and I keep refusing him, but I'm so afraid, and now *this*…"

Lennard's mouth dropped open.

"He's so mean to me *all the time. She* might be in on all this with him. Please, *I beg you,* have this over with before anything happens to Lillian or to me. The whole of Trondenburgh will find out about us."

The king looked like he'd been hit in the stomach with a war ax. She'd put so much hurt in her voice, she knew he couldn't possibly abandon her. Without another word, he gave her hand a quick squeeze and crossed the floor back to Halesbridge.

"Lord Halesbridge, I think we have our assassin," he said coldly. The maid paled and began to wail. "Take this woman to the dungeons, and have the hangman see me before he questions her."

Halesbridge's nostrils flared. "I don't believe that, Your Majesty. It's *her*." He motioned at Catherine, his jaw clenched. "I know it is. She's the *Devil*."

The king stared at him for a while, fighting for self-control. Catherine knew Halesbridge had been in her lover's employ for a long time, but she also knew he simply had to go. He was dangerous. Lennard had to understand this. Probing in the king's mind, she gave him one final push, putting words where there had been only rage.

"When you've done as I've ordered you, you'll leave my castle. You may take two horses for what I owe you for your services, and the grain they can carry on their backs. You and your family may stay on the land I've given you, but I don't want to see you here again."

Halesbridge was about to protest, but the king cut him off. "Have I made myself clear?"

Catherine thought the man was going to have a heart attack. Finally, he nodded and pulled the sniveling maid along with him from the room.

Catherine glimpsed her own locket on the floor by her bed and swiftly shoved it underneath the wooden frame with her foot before placing the maid's locket under her pillow. Lennard stood at her window, but he wasn't looking out.

She embraced him from behind and kissed his shoulder. "Thank you, my love," she said. "Thank you."

He sighed, putting his hands over hers, those lovely soft hands of his. She could feel his sadness through the warmth.

"Do you really think our little maid tried to kill Lillian?" he asked. "I'm not sure she'd have it in her."

"I don't know. I don't even know what was in that locket, or how she would have done it. Maybe it was all Halesbridge. I'm so sorry I'm no help. This is all my fault... He only did this to get rid of me..."

The king pulled her to him and held her, burying his face in her hair as she wept. "No, Katharina, don't you say that. None of this is on you, love."

At that moment, Dean appeared in the doorway. Catherine noticed him there too late. He recognized her. She thought he was going to be sick. He retreated and left quietly before she could say anything. The king felt her tense up, and he released her to turn around. He missed Dean by a second.

"What is it?"

"Nothing. I just thought I heard someone, but it was only the wind." She'd worry about Dean later. Somehow, she didn't think he was going to stick around for long.

"Don't worry," Lennard told her, reading her genuinely worried mien. "We'll fix this. I'll have the wench confess to high treason and executed by morning, and Halesbridge won't ever bother you again, I promise."

"Lillian will get well, and we'll find a way to be together," she added, entwining her fingers with his.

He pressed a tender kiss to her lips. "How do I deserve you?"

She smiled at him bravely. "I'd do anything for you," she told him, and he believed her.

Chapter Forty-Four

ೞ Regrets ಬು

It was impossible, Dean kept telling himself as he left the keep. Catherine couldn't possibly be here… but she was. He didn't know how she'd done it, but she had.

He wished he'd followed Halesbridge on his way out with the duchess instead of going upstairs to take his leave of the king. He didn't know why the duchess was now dressed in a maid's garbs, but he didn't care. He'd expected to find the king alone, but Catherine had been right there in his arms, and he couldn't make sense of it.

Whatever was afoot here, he wanted no part of it.

He found Halesbridge at the stables, having their horses saddled.

"What happened?" Dean asked. "Where's the duchess?"

Halesbridge snorted, his face a mask of contempt. "She's with the king."

"Didn't she just…?" Dean stopped short, thinking.

Catherine had manipulated him, just as she'd tried to manipulate him at The Fair. He'd had no idea of how to behave around her the day she'd turned up there, but he now knew he'd underestimated her in every way. The Fair's wards had picked up on the grudge she bore and the anger she'd harbored toward him, but it had been too late, and the damage had already been done. She'd developed her Abilities, and he'd been too busy with his own guilt to see that she'd moved way beyond the little girl he'd known.

She'd moved *way* beyond him.

When Halesbridge had come to him the previous day, he'd recognized the locket, but he'd wished he was wrong. They'd been friends. Hadn't they?

"What?" Halesbridge said sharply.

"Never mind. Are we leaving?"

Halesbridge nodded, throwing the saddle on his mount. "As soon as possible."

He left Dean for a while to pick out two good horses for himself from the pasture and arrange for the grain to be filled into sacks the horses could manage.

Catherine stepped out of the shadows as soon as he was gone, startling him. She was beautiful. She looked well-fed and taken care of for the first time since he'd known her.

He wasn't sure what role she was playing in the strange game he'd become involved in. She was wearing the duchess' clothes, and suddenly, it dawned on him that she had been wearing them all along.

"What are you doing, Catherine?" he asked, slowly shaking his head.

"The real question is: what are you *going* to do?" she returned quietly.

He looked around. The two squires mucking the stalls weren't paying them any heed. "Are you poisoning Lillian?"

Catherine gaped at him, bewilderment written all over her face. He felt guilty for having asked, but he had to know. It was her locket, he was sure of it.

"I don't believe this…" There was a tremor in her low, almost inaudible voice. "You never knew me *at all*, did you? What lies did Halesbridge tell you?"

He looked at his feet. Had Halesbridge been telling him lies, or was she playing him for a fool? Whose word was he going to take over that of the other? He felt her eyes burning into him.

"He said he suspected the *Duchess of Glasston* of meaning the king's wife harm. That's you, isn't it?" He didn't want to look at her, but he had to. "Catherine, tell me the truth."

"You never knew me at all," she repeated, and shame churned inside of him like a knife twisting in his gut. Her eyes were red from crying, and he was convinced he was a part of her misery.

"You said you were my friend," she went on, "and first you take the only thing of value that I own, and now you accuse me of trying to kill someone. What have *I* ever done to *you*?"

She'd kept secrets from him, but she was right; he'd never known her at all. The woman opposite him was a complete stranger, but she'd befriended him when he'd had no one.

He'd wanted to tell her he knew about Cooper all those years ago, and what the old farmer had been doing to her, but he'd never found the courage. He'd always been such a coward. He could have... well, what *could* he have done? He knew she'd kept going back to Cooper time and again, but he hadn't understood why, and he still didn't now. Why hadn't she just run off long before she finally had?

They could have gone away together – the thought had actually occurred to him on more than one occasion when he'd watched her hobble from the old farmer's cabin – but would he have wanted to make that commitment? He'd needed the time he'd spent at Caius' home to heal and learn, and dealing with this had been so difficult, he hadn't known how. Her burden would have been too heavy on top of his own.

He'd kept secrets from her, too. He was the Master Sorcerer's son, and he had responsibilities she couldn't possibly comprehend. Those books, hers and the other two, were important not just for him. They held the key to The Fair's survival. What would she have done with hers? Sold it for a week's food and shelter before she'd continued selling herself in Ironstone or wherever it was Lorcan had seen her?

"You're right. You've done nothing to me," he said. "But that doesn't make this any better. I don't know what's going on here, but Halesbridge is a man of honor."

"And what am I?" she whispered coldly. "A whore, like your friend said I was? Is that all you ever saw in me?"

"Halesbridge and his Fairywoman came to me, asking for help. He didn't trust you. The potion that cured Lillian was in one of my father's books." He instantly regretted what he'd told her, but it was too late. Why was he babbling?

Catherine looked stunned. "You mean *my* book? The one you stole from *me*?"

"I didn't *steal* anything. You left. I needed it more than you did." He looked around to make certain the squires were still going about their duties. "*The Fair* needs it more than you do. It's what saved the king's wife."

Catherine gave a bitter laugh. "Do you think she'd still be grateful if she knew what either of us really are?"

He felt his stomach tighten. "You have no idea what's at stake here. You don't understand."

"I think I do." She moved closer to him and reached for his arm, but he pulled back instinctively. He didn't want her to touch him. Last time she'd touched him, she'd done something with him. He hadn't been himself. He wasn't entirely himself now, and he realized he had to protect himself. They'd come a long way from sharing a meal of stolen bread and berries down by the river, where they'd spent days trying to catch the pike Catherine had been so determined to pull from the water.

"What's become of us?" she asked, and he couldn't say he knew.

All he did know was that she was a whore who was impersonating a duchess and had somehow become the king's mistress, and that he was to blame. He was a coward with next to no Talent aside from moving pictures and casting some thin cloaking spells and small shields anyone could penetrate, but he had responsibilities now.

Maybe she was telling him the truth, and Halesbridge was the liar. He wanted to believe Catherine was a victim of her circumstances because he owed her the benefit of the doubt. She was doing what she needed to do to survive. She'd *always* just been surviving, and he had no right to take that away from her, did he?

"You're leaving with Halesbridge now, aren't you?" she asked, wrapping her arms around herself.

He nodded. "I don't know what's going on with you and him, but don't worry. I'm not going to tell."

"That's good. It means I don't have to tell the king about you or Halesbridge's Fairywoman either."

Dean straightened briefly from his natural slouch and fixed his eyes to hers. "Lady Glasston."

She gave him a small nod. "Master Greenleaf."

Then, she turned and walked away.

He hoped he'd never see her again. He wanted to forget he'd ever met her.

Chapter Forty-Five

ભ Straw Dolls ৵৹

The air was crystal clear when Catherine stepped outside the keep. Frost coated the rooftops and cobblestones in the back courtyard a glistening silver-white. She trod carefully as she made her way toward the gardens. Most of the servants were already up and working, and there was a lot of movement about the stables out front because Lennard planned on joining the hunt today.

The beaters had left before dawn, and the king and his party were just about to depart the castle. Since Lillian had been feeling so much better, there was no reason for him to stay close by anymore, and Catherine knew he'd been aching to go. His restless soul wouldn't let him be, and a hunt was just the distraction he needed to get his mind off of all the trouble Halesbridge had stirred up.

Halesbridge... she'd been thinking about him a lot over the last week. She'd decided she had to find a way to discreetly do away with him soon, or she'd spend the rest of her life wondering what new scheme he'd be cooking up against her. Lennard had taken care of the maid – she'd been executed for treason as promised – and Halesbridge was away from the castle, but as far as she was concerned, he wasn't far enough away. He'd never be, as long as he lived.

She was just about to exit the courtyard via the narrow passageway between the servants' quarters and the kitchens to see Lennard off from the battlements of the rear gardens when a little girl bustled out through the doors of the kitchens. She was followed by her nursemaid. Catherine recognized the child's voice as she called to her. When she turned to face Lioba, she had her most pleasant smile in place.

The princess was delightful. For a child. She was bright and hardly ever annoying, never loud, and never out of place. The nursemaid, Veronica, raised her well.

The girl was carrying a small partially finished straw doll.

"Please can you help me with this, Katharina?"

Catherine always helped Lioba with her dolls. Rebecca had shown her how to make them when she'd been Lioba's age. The child loved each new one they completed together, and the little toys had become their common denominator.

She smiled until it hurt, despite being a bit irritated at not getting to wave to Lennard now after all. He'd look for her, and she took care to show him how much she'd miss him whenever he was heading out, no matter where he was going. It was only a glance from afar, but looks said more than words, and Lennard was a hopeless romantic – at least with her. Lioba was almost equally important though, because Lennard loved Lioba.

"Of course I can help you." She took the doll and scrutinized it, stepping to one side of the kitchen building where the walled well was.

Lioba had shaped and tied the body fairly well. It had legs and arms, but the head wasn't right yet. Catherine twisted the straw until it looked more like an egg. Then, she used the hemp string the child had brought to give it some stability, but it was strangely incomplete. Something was missing.

Ice splinters of different shapes and sizes covered the walled well, and Catherine soon found some inspiration there. One of the fragments had the shape of a heart.

"Oh, would you look at that," she said, showing it to the girl. Lioba was thrilled.

Catherine tucked it into the doll's chest.

"Won't it melt?"

"Only if you bring it inside for too long or leave it in the sun. Everything has its place and time, you know."

She looked up at the keep and wondered how Lillian's heart was doing. Would it be frail and fragile, in danger of melting in the sun, or would it be beating strong as ever after she'd had Dean's antidote? Another thing to hate him for.

She'd imagined killing Dean in the stables the day he'd intruded on her life in Trondenburgh, but that would have been too quick. She'd let him go for now, but she was going to have those books, and she was going to make him hand all three of them over to her personally. Moreover, she thought she might take pleasure in destroying his little dream. She hadn't figured out how she'd find The Fair again, or how she'd get around his pesky friend, but she thought Halesbridge might be of help with that. The fact that his wife was a Fairywoman was an invaluable snippet of knowledge. For the first time in her life, she appreciated Cooper's obsession with being informed.

"Would it melt even if I took it inside for a moment to show Mama?"

"Oh, I don't think so..."

She hadn't finished saying it when she saw Lillian at the window of her room. It was open, and Lillian was inspecting something closely by the light, unaware she was being observed.

Catherine wondered just what the queen was fumbling with, and began looking for a way into her head while pretending to listen to Lioba. The girl was prattling about the dress Veronica would sew from scraps for the new doll when it was finished.

She wasn't certain her intent would work at this distance because she'd never tried getting into anyone's mind when they weren't there right next to her before, but this appeared to be a whole week of *first times*. To her surprise, she discovered it wasn't so difficult.

For a moment, she saw the courtyard from above, and her locket in Lillian's hand. She couldn't help but admire the woman. She must have retrieved it from her room as soon as Catherine had left the building, but Catherine couldn't figure out how she'd known where to look for it.

She left just one thought in Lillian's head before returning her attention to Lioba's nursemaid. It was sparked by Lioba, and she loved the irony no one would ever see in it.

Up. Up on the window sill, my chilly heart, and don't move.

Lillian did exactly as she asked.

"Veronica, take Lioba upstairs. Lioba's beautiful work is bound to cheer her dear mama up." She leaned in to Veronica so the child would not hear and lowered her voice. "Her Highness has improved so much, but she's really not herself even still. A touch of melancholy after her long illness, perhaps."

Worry conquered the nursemaid's mien. "Do you think so, Milady? She seemed so happy after Lady Halesbridge came to see her last night."

Catherine nodded. *Of course. Halesbridge.*

Catherine had been to one of the hay barns outside the castle grounds with Lennard last night. Perhaps someone had been watching her or Lennard, or both of them, and tipped Halesbridge off.

Halesbridge definitely had to go, and so did his Fairywoman.

"We'll all take good care of Lady Lillian, won't we?" Catherine whispered, watching Lioba bob up and down on the soles of her feet in excitement.

The maid cast her a conspiratorial glance.

"Maybe she'd like to keep it," the girl said. "She could put it on her window sill so the heart won't melt."

Catherine feigned awe at her little friend's cleverness, and she hugged the child. "That's *such* a great idea, dear. I think I'll go up with you."

She followed the maid and the princess inside. Lioba darted up the stairs ahead of them and heaved the door open, but stopped just inside the room. The heart of ice slipped from the doll's chest and shattered on the floor.

"Mama?"

Catherine held tight to Lillian's will, although Lillian fought her with all she had. Entering behind Lioba, she directed her gaze straight at the confused woman kneeling on the window sill. Lillian's eyes were filled with terror, and Catherine thought that suited her extremely well.

It only took a second or two to plant another belief firmly in Lillian's mind while the maid tried to understand what she was seeing here.

No one loves you. No one cares for you.

Tears spilled down Lillian's cheeks.

Even Lioba won't come to you anymore unless the nursemaid or Katharina make her.

"Your Highness!" Catherine breathed.

You're a mess. You're completely useless.

"Lillian!" Catherine was sure Lillian didn't hear her voice or anyone else's over the din of her own wailing sorrow inside.

Why don't you just do yourself a favor and jump?

Lillian trembled like a leaf. Catherine asked herself if it was the fear of death, or the fear of surviving the impact.

Veronica was frantic, grasping Lioba far too tightly by the shoulders. "Your Highness, no!"

The girl began crying.

Jump.

And Lillian did.

The straw doll fell from Lioba's hands.

The sickening thud was followed by silence, and silence was all that remained in the castle.

Chapter Forty-Six

⳩ Meara ⳩

Catherine worried about someone finding the locket before she did, but no one knew it was there, so no one looked for it. She waited for a good moment later that evening and retrieved it from where it had fallen from Lillian's hands into the woodpile stacked against the wall of the keep.

While everyone knew Lillian had committed suicide, the king declared her fall an accident upon speaking with the distraught nursemaid. The wake was a silent affair, and on the following day, Lillian was buried in the family graveyard, bedded on straw and ashes next to Lennard's mother. Trondenburgh didn't have a mausoleum for its noble dead.

Catherine was quite pleased with the outcome, on the whole. She looked forward to the new life she'd be leading. There wasn't a doubt in her mind Lennard would want them to be married after a *short* mourning period – his daughter was, after all, lacking a mother – and Catherine was sure she'd have it all. She needed to take care of just one or two more things beforehand. The note she wrote and folded inside of the locket was going to help her remember that. A date and a place were still missing from the parchment, but she'd add them when she'd worked the last of it all out for herself.

January brought heavy snowfalls. Time itself seemed frozen at the castle as layers of thick snow blanketed the whole of the kingdom in white, bitter winter. There was no getting in or out of Trondenburgh by the only road leading there, so they had no visitors for over two weeks. Catherine spent a large part of her days with Lioba. The girl had been in shock after what she'd witnessed, but she was slowly recovering. Straw dolls no longer held a place in her life.

When the roads were manageable again toward the end of the month, Lennard left to follow an invitation to Ironstone to partake in what would undoubtedly be lengthy debates on issues of jurisdiction that may have had to do with his march to the Winter Mountains the previous year. Driesburgh was rumored to be on his way there also.

In his absence, the king left Catherine in charge of handling domestics at the castle. Most of the servants had no problems adjusting to the new situation, and she had no overlaps with the king's council. She was determined to make Trondenburgh hers as much as she could, within her rights, and outside of them.

Lennard was gone just over a week when the peasant she'd dispatched to keep an eye on Halesbridge's house came back telling her the king's former advisor had left after Lennard had, traveling north. The serf had a use for the silver coin Catherine reimbursed him with for his efforts.

She'd been eager to pay the Fairywoman a little visit. As a girl, she'd been fascinated by the various creatures of magic of which her books spoke, and she was curious to find out how the Fairywoman would be different to a human or a Cine, and what kind of personality she'd turn out to be.

Catherine knew which of Lennard's knights had been on Brandner's payroll, and had Steffen Stoker come to see her.

Stoker proved to be a man with foresight and ambition, and he had no liking for the old steward. He'd had his sights set on Halesbridge's post for a while now, but Lennard wasn't inclined to fill the vacancy yet. Catherine thought she'd have to speak to him about that when he got back.

To Stoker, she justified her visit to Lady Halesbridge with her hopes of bridging the rift between the king and his former advisor, at least well enough to maintain some sense of fealty toward the king in these uncertain times. Halesbridge wouldn't be coming back to Lennard's court, but they needed to make sure he stayed in line and knew his place, she told the knight, and he was in agreement with her arguments. It wouldn't do to alienate Halesbridge completely.

She'd assured Stoker his loyalty would be rewarded, and left an image in his head that showed him in the steward's seat to the right of the king in his council. Picturing himself there, Stoker was happy to gather a small guard of his men to take her to see Meara of Halesbridge. Catherine had never felt more self-assured than now, sitting in the king's carriage, with him riding along side.

When the conveyance reined to a stop in front of Halesbridge Manor, Stoker made haste to open the door and assist her. He treated her as though she was made of glass, and she thought Brandner had made an excellent choice by hiring him. She'd benefit from it for years to come if she played her cards right.

The manor was more of a big farmhouse than anything else, not extravagant or lavish by design, but comfortable and in good repair. It stood amid several acres of spelt fields on the outskirts of a tiny, grown settlement that probably accommodated the peasants. A few hovels huddled together by a lime and hazel grove remotely reminded Catherine of the place where she'd spent her childhood years.

The serfs and maids working about the functional buildings stopped what they were doing to stare at the royal visitors and gossip. A burly woman near the front door ducked inside to announce the retinue.

By the time Catherine had reached the entrance, Lady Halesbridge appeared to greet her. Not dressed for royal company, Meara was flushed, and her expression told of her irritation as her glance darted from Catherine to Stoker and back.

Catherine pasted a perfect smile on her face as the liegeman bowed to her before ordering his men to stand guard outside the house with him.

"Lady Glasston – what a pleasant surprise," Meara said, welcoming her into her home with the formal dignity due toward someone of high standing.

Catherine wondered if Alexander had told his wife of his suspicions about *Lady Glasston*. If he had, she wasn't letting on.

A servant took Catherine's wrap, and Meara led her into the homey-warm main room, where she bade her to sit by the fire and poured them each a cup of sweet wine.

Nipping at her drink, Catherine found it difficult to get an insight into the woman's thoughts. Perhaps this was the difference, or one of the differences between Fairypeople and humans. Meara was well protected in any case.

Chitchat wasn't Catherine's favorite way of passing the time, but she hated being denied something she wanted much more than she disliked idle conversation. She needed time to get to know how Meara's awareness functioned, so she told her of the king's trip to Ironstone and inquired if she knew the town, watching the other woman very carefully.

Meara told her she'd grown up there. Her sister was Queen Cassandra.

This was news. Ironstone, the seat of the latest wave of persecution against the Tainted, had an Unnatural ruling over it. There was a piece of truth at the core of all the little jokes Lennard had made. She tucked the information away for a later time and continued trying to find an inroad to Meara's mind as they talked on.

Finally, Meara lost her patience. "Milady, as dearly as I love visits, we both know you're not here to talk about family relations or the markets in Ironstone. To what do I owe this visit?"

Catherine smiled indulgently. "I think there have been misunderstandings between your husband and I, and I'm sorry to have missed him here." She took another sip of her wine and put the cup down. "I believe it's in all our best interests if relations between the king and Alexander were to return to a better level–"

Just then, a large hound romped by. Two boys of roughly twelve years of age hurried after him, both boisterous and armed with wooden training swords.

"Not in the house, Calum," Meara called after him, but not crossly.

Upon hearing his name, one of the boys turned, hazel eyes on his mother for a second. He was sidetracked long enough for his opponent to smack him squarely on the bottom with the flat of his blade. Howling as he reeled around, Calum retaliated, and the raucous play was back on.

Meara left her seat and pulled the boys apart, reprimanding them for their display in front of her guest.

Catherine seized upon the opportunity the distraction afforded. Quickly, she removed a small vial from her girdle. Uncapping it, she emptied the whole of its content into Meara's wine and reseated herself before her hostess sent the children to play in another part of the house.

"I'm sorry. It's been a long few weeks cooped up inside, and I'm afraid they tend to forget themselves," Meara said, picking up her cup.

Catherine laughed and shook her head, saluting Meara with her own. "That's children for you."

Meara raised an eyebrow. "Do you have any of your own?"

"Not yet, but I do think that's in my immediate future. I've grown so very attached to the princess. When the king and I are married in spring, he'll certainly want an heir."

Meara bit her tongue and drank deeply.

Catherine decided to offer no further explanation and let the news settle on the other woman as she waited for the mohn juice potion to take effect. Now, the game had begun in earnest.

"Tell me, were you and Lillian close?" she asked.

"We were. She was a good friend."

"I see." Catherine leaned toward her, lowering her voice. "And how close was your husband to Lillian?"

Lady Halesbridge bristled at the insinuation. "My husband was the king's advisor and trusted confidant. What you're implying is a *lie*."

Catherine sighed. "I only wish it was." Setting her own cup aside, she eased forward and gently probed the other woman's thoughts again. She smiled inwardly as she felt the growing cloudiness the mohn potion had begun to work on the Fairywoman's mind.

"I was often by her side in the days after her maid's treachery was discovered. Her illness made her reflective, and she told me she thought God was punishing her for her sins."

Meara looked stricken for an instant. "What sins?"

Catherine felt something twinge inside of her, a foreshadowing of an emotion that wasn't her own.

"She told me you'd been to see her. You were such a good friend to her. So concerned. She couldn't live with herself anymore, and she wondered how Alexander did."

Meara gazed at her in confusion. "I don't know what you're talking about."

"Well, between *you* being such a good friend and *her* sleeping with your husband..." Catherine paused. The other woman looked sick. "Her conscience bothered her day and night, you must know."

Meara's lips quivered, and as the accusation took root, the hold she had over her own thoughts slipped. She slowly began to accept the sordid accusation she would never have entertained otherwise.

He was always away for so long, so concerned about Lillian's welfare... what if this woman is right?

Catherine allowed herself a knowing grin, but Meara was determined to fight.

"I don't believe you." Her voice was low and warning, and her gaze wandered to the door.

Observing her eyes, Catherine discovered Meara's greatest fear about this conversation; she was afraid the boy would overhear it. He was right at the front of her mind all the time; knowing he was safe and lacked nothing was Meara's strength and anchor in life, but right now, the things they were talking about were shaking the foundations of her world – as they would his.

"I don't know why you're lying," Meara mumbled, trying to clear her vision by rubbing at her face with the heels of her hands. "You've already won, haven't you?"

"Not by a long shot," Catherine hissed, keeping her face as even as she could. She was walking out on a ledge, but it felt good. She knew she could pull this off. "I don't think you quite understand your husband's nature, or what's at stake here."

Alexander is always so concerned about others, about the king, about his lands... the only thing he's not concerned about is you, Meara.

"Lioba is a delightful child," Catherine plowed on. "She and Calum are so alike."

They could be twins, Meara. And Alexander would have kept this from you until the end of days. Has he got any more secrets?

Has he?

Catherine knelt on the floor next to Meara's chair and placed her hand on the Fairywoman's knee. The contact allowed her to move further past the waning barrier she'd been struggling with. "I wonder what the king would say if he were ever to find out. It would break his heart."

A tear tracked down Meara's cheek, and she tried to wipe it away but couldn't. "What do you want from me?"

Catherine pulled a handkerchief from her sleeve and gently dabbed the moisture from Meara's face. "I hear Alexander has been to see mutual friends of ours recently. I have business with Dean Greenleaf, but I seem to have lost track of him. I want you to take me to The Fair."

"No."

It's such a small price... so little to ask, and then you can start sorting out this mess.

"No."

Just be done with it.

Meara fought her tooth and nail. "I don't know where to find The Fair."

Catherine could feel the lie. Meara was a strong character, she had to leave her that. She was thoroughly enjoying the challenge. "Are you sure, dear?"

Meara didn't reply, at first.

Such a small thing to do in return for time to think... time to find a way to sort this mess.

Meara shook her head miserably, and Catherine knew her instincts were telling her there was something wrong. Something was burrowing into her thoughts... a creature that didn't belong there like a maggot on her face, biting its way through her skin and into the flesh. Meara was afraid, but still brave enough to want to defy her. Catherine nearly laughed as the Fairywoman sought fortification in her wine and drained the remainder of her drink from the cup.

Leaning forward, she drew her lips to Meara's ear and whispered, "I wonder what the king would do if he knew what you really are? What *your son* really is? Meara, I *do* hope he never finds out."

Meara paled even further, and her mouth worked, but it took her a moment to find words. The mohn juice had laid bare her soul, the threat of disclosure hung over her, and she was defeated.

By the look she gave her, Catherine realized the noble lady now also saw her for what *she* really was.

"Alright," Meara whined, "I'll take you there."

She folded her arms across her chest first one way, then the other, agitated and not knowing what to do with herself. Her eyes brimmed with tears of anger and of shame. Catherine recognized both emotions instantly because they were so familiar to her from another time.

"That is *such* a good decision, dear," she told the Fairywoman as though she was talking to a child.

Meara awkwardly rose, wobbly on her feet. "I want your word this'll be the end of it. I'll take you there, but you'll never threaten me or ask anything of me again."

"Your secret is safe with me." Catherine walked over to the window. Leaden clouds brought forth thick, sticky snowflakes and rain. "I'll have arrangements made to have you picked up first thing in the morning."

She hoped the weather wouldn't thwart those plans, and that their trip wouldn't be too long.

Meara brushed another stray tear off her cheek. "No need. We can leave right now."

Catherine spun around. "What, now?" she asked testily.

Meara looked her up and down, swaying as she shook her head. She wiped her runny nose on the back of her hand, sniffing. "What the hell *are* you that you don't know these things?"

Catherine wanted to teach her a lesson that really hurt, but she needed her alive for a while. "You know *exactly* what I am and what I can do."

At that, Meara pulled herself together and left the room for a few minutes, calling one of the servants for their coats. When she came back with them, she closed and bolted the door behind her.

"I want this over with," she said firmly. "But it's much too far from here to go by carriage, so I'm going to open a Portal."

She threw Catherine's cloak at her and set about closing the window shutters. Then, she donned her own coat before turning her back on Catherine and bending down so her hands touched the floor.

At first, Catherine thought she was looking for something, but when she saw the light emanating from the other woman's fingertips, she realized there were still a lot of things she didn't understand. She didn't like that feeling one bit, but...

A Portal.

She knew what that was from the green book, but she'd never imagined she'd see one, much less travel by it.

She watched Meara patiently raising what looked like a doorway made of light from the floor as far up as her fingers could reach into the air.

When she was done, Meara turned back to face her.

"Is that it?" Catherine asked, despite her firm resolve to appear as unimpressed as possible.

Meara nodded disdainfully. "Your way into The Fair, *Milady*," she said, inviting her to enter the glowing Passageway.

Chapter Forty-Seven

❧ Revenge ❧

"After you," Meara told her.

Catherine wasn't afraid. She envied Meara for her Gift, but she didn't trust her. "What makes you think I'm going to go in there ahead of you?"

Meara sighed. "I have to close this portal behind us so no one will stumble across it by chance," she said. "It's either that or two weeks in the back of a coach across country. It's winter, in case you haven't noticed. But this is your choice, of course."

The coach trip wasn't an option. She could never explain a long absence like that to Lennard. He'd want to know where she was if he returned to find her gone.

Still, Catherine hesitated, digging deeper into Meara's mind than she'd ever been in anyone else's, but she didn't find anything there except for fear and images of the boy and herself standing at what looked like a market stall. And, she saw the dark-haired man she'd encountered in Ironstone. He stood beside a dark queen.

"You know what will happen if Stoker finds me gone or hurt, Lady Halesbridge?"

Meara tried to straighten her back. "I do, but you can choose to trust me or leave it be."

Catherine caught a fleeting thought from the back of her mind. It involved escape, but there was the boy to consider. Always the boy. Catherine knew she'd have to break this woman beyond repair to keep her from doing something they'd both regret, but she was going to make time for that later.

She gave Meara one last cold look and stepped forward.

Transiting the Passageway reminded her loosely of what she'd felt when she'd passed through The Fair's protective wards. It was bright on the inside, and louder than a roaring waterfall. Her skin tingled, a thousand tiny explosions beneath the first layers.

She didn't know what to expect on the other side, but when she emerged, she found herself on the edge of a clearing much like the one where The Fair had been the last time she'd seen it. This time, however, a mantle of snow covered the site.

The white plain was immaculate. There wasn't a single footprint anywhere, no sign of anyone having been here recently. She couldn't see any of the brightly colored wagons or tents she remembered, but she knew they were there. She could *feel* the magic and the buzz of the protective enchantments that surrounded the grounds.

Exiting the Portal in her wake, Meara obviously saw the wagons and the marketplace. Her ashen face spoke volumes. "Just follow me," she said, not realizing Catherine couldn't perceive what she did.

The Fairywoman trudged through the knee-high snow into the meadow until Catherine stopped her.

"Wait," she said. "I can't follow." She wanted to smash something or hurt someone.

Meara was momentarily at a loss. "What's wrong?"

"I can't go in there."

Meara briefly contemplated the fairground, and then faced back to Catherine. Eventually, realization sank in. "You can't see it, can you? The magic that protects it won't *allow* you inside."

Catherine exhaled, and a cloud of mist formed near her mouth. "Tell me why."

She'd been expelled from this place once before, but she'd blamed Dean's vigilant friend then, whoever and whatever he was. Surely he wasn't there on the other side of the invisible barrier, laughing at her? That couldn't be it. He wasn't one for hiding behind walls, whether visible or invisible. He just happened to be in the wrong place at the wrong time and probably didn't belong there any more than she did.

"The enchantments won't let anyone bearing ill will toward The Fair or its people to find it or enter the grounds. Greenleaf told me it's how his father designed the protections."

Catherine hummed, intrigued by the notion that a magic like this existed. So many new discoveries on just one day. The spell protecting The Fair was a perfect shield. She wondered exactly how it worked, but guessed she'd have found out, had she not lost the books that held all these secrets… the secrets of the Cine living on the other side of that shield, hiding like rats in the sewer when they could be ruling the world. They were cowards, the lot of them – with the exception of one, maybe: the Master Sorcerer who was helping the biggest coward of them all be king of his pitiful little realm.

She turned away from the clearing and toward the forest, just in case any of the sewer rats might happen to look her way.

She was hurting all over – just like on the day when she'd suddenly found herself outside with no means of returning to finish her little talk with Dean – and so she motioned Meara to come with her into the woods. The more distance she put between herself and The Fair's protections, the better she felt.

At a safe distance within the tree line, she stood staring at nothing in particular for a while and thought about her predicament. Finally, things clarified.

She might not be allowed inside The Fair, but if Meara could see it, then the Fairywoman would be. Catherine didn't have to be on the fairgrounds herself to deliver her message.

"You're going to help me, dear," she mumbled, clutching both of Meara's arms.

She looked into the Fairywoman's eyes, and it took a little time to find the right level of awareness, but when she did, tapping into it was child's play.

"Listen to me, the reason why I'm here is because Dean Greenleaf, *your* Alexander's new best friend, is a very dangerous man. He put him up to his cheating and his lying and God knows what else."

The words she whispered into both Meara's ear and subconscious transformed smoothly into images, and Meara pictured her husband with Greenleaf, talking in their house about this and that, but she couldn't quite hear what they were saying. She hadn't listened well enough the day Alexander brought Greenleaf back with him from the castle. Now she was almost sure Alexander had been telling a complete stranger their best-kept secrets, but she reeled as Catherine spun this new idea in her head, her thoughts at war between visions of betrayal and what she'd assumed to be true.

"Alexander told Dean Greenleaf *everything* there is to know about you," Catherine went on. "I don't think he realizes the damage he's caused because Greenleaf has him fooled. Greenleaf is *totally* indifferent toward you or your kind... all he cares about is his Fair. Other people, the other Talented, don't matter to him one bit."

Meara didn't seem to want to believe it, but Catherine made her look at her.

"I happen to know the Inquisitor is looking for The Fair. That's why he sent Lennard to the Winter Mountains. He thought the Dwarven settlement would lead him to the Cine as well. Now Greenleaf is planning to point him elsewhere to take the pressure off. He will give him you and Calum, and you know what that means. Driesburgh would gut your boy alive to find out if you know the whereabouts of any other Fairypeople, and he's going to be so distracted, he's going to lose sight of The Fair long enough for Greenleaf to find out who's been feeding Driesburgh information."

"That's why Driesburgh is heading to Ironstone too, isn't it?" Meara was in tears again.

The woman did nothing but cry, and Catherine resented her for it.

"He knows about Cassandra – he could just never build a case before," the Fairywoman continued, trembling all over. "What if he's already coming for Calum? We have to go back to the house! We have to make sure my son is alright!"

Catherine had to shake her to get her to refocus. "He's fine, for now, don't worry. My men are there, and they'll look after him."

"Katharina, what are we going to do?"

"We need to work together. I'm so glad I confided in you. Maybe it's not too late to save Calum and Cassandra if we make sure Greenleaf understands who he's up against."

Meara was still sobbing when Catherine stepped back from her without letting go of her completely. "If we play our cards right, things could go back to the way they were. You want everything back the way it was, don't you?"

"Yes, of course I do. But how?"

"I need you to find Greenleaf's wife and give her something from me. I know her well, and I think I can talk some sense into her."

"That shouldn't be a problem," the Fairywoman said, perking up. "I met her last time I was here."

"Good." That meant Margarete would have no cause to distrust her. "I'm so glad we're on the same side, you and I. You're a *mother*. You understand how important this is. You're the only one who can save Calum now. He's relying on you."

Firm resolve burned in Meara's blood-shot eyes. "I'd do anything."

"I know that." Catherine caressed the other woman's cheek affectionately. "I need to be able to trust you completely – I want you to promise me you'll talk to no one but Margarete, and only then if you're absolutely sure no one else is listening."

"Alright. I can do that."

"Good." Catherine pulled her locket out from under the collar of her dress, took out the coin and handed it to Meara. "Give her this and tell her it's from a friend who believes in Dean's dreams and can help fund them. She's to come alone. If she asks why, tell her it's a friend Dean would be much too proud to see."

Meara smiled bravely. "I'll bring her here."

"Alright. Now go. I know you'll do well."

When Meara had gone, Catherine pulled the hood of her cloak tighter around her and pressed back into the silence of the pine forest. She hoped the potion and the lies she'd planted in the Fairywoman's mind would hold long enough for her to get what she wanted. Then, she remembered that her note for Dean was still incomplete, pulled the scrap of parchment forth and ran her fingers over the words she'd inked. If Dean could make the lines he'd drawn shift, then she could, too. She pictured how they would move on the vellum, and they did. They stretched and thinned, and new letters formed beside the ones already there. When she was finally satisfied with the result, she tucked the note back into the locket and waited.

Her thoughts tumbled with fragments from Meara's perception behind the barrier she herself couldn't cross, as well as her own memories of Dean and their time together. Both sets of recollections were painful. Long minutes passed as she shivered under the frozen evergreens, and she almost began to doubt her scheme's feasibility when she saw Meara emerging from the pocket dimension, Dean's *Love* following her. A powerful hate welled up so intensely at the sight of the woman, she had trouble breathing.

Removing another vial from her girdle, she tried to steady herself, listening for the crunch of footfalls in the snow behind her as the two neared. She only revealed herself when they were within touching-distance of her.

"Margarete, I'm so glad to see you," she said in her most pleasant voice.

Margarete didn't recognize her immediately. Her bewilderment was written all over her face when she realized who was behind the Tierney coin Meara had brought her, and she froze for just the second it took Catherine to lunge at her, grab a fistful of her hair and bash her head against the closest tree trunk while Meara shrieked, looking on in confusion.

Moving quickly, Catherine flicked the cork from the opening of the vial and forced the brown liquid inside between the dazed woman's lips. Closing her hand over Margarete's mouth and nose, she forced her to swallow the bitter sleeping potion.

Margarete coughed and clawed at the firm hand holding her until the liquid coated her throat. Almost gently, Catherine aided her as she slid to her knees and lay down in the snow, bedazzled from her head injury and already suffering the effects of the potion. The warm blood dripping from her temple painted crimson flowers onto the white ground beneath her.

"Open that Portal," Catherine ordered Meara.

Meara shuffled from one foot to the other, murmuring to herself somewhere between panic and mad hysterics, and Catherine had to repeat what she'd said, but the Fairywoman eventually got to work.

Margarete moaned.

"Hush," Catherine hissed into her ear, tucking the vial away, "or I'll finish what I started right here."

"Why?" Margarete whimpered, slowly slipping into oblivion.

"Interesting question, isn't it?"

Catherine took her locket off and opened it once more. She unfolded the parchment and reread her own words. Pleased with what she'd inked, she replaced the note in the locket and placed it in the snow, next to the pooling blood.

"You know, your husband never answered me when I asked him *why*, but I'm going to tell you my secret even if he couldn't share his: it's because I deserve *better* than he gave me, and I'm going to get it. I'm going to make sure he remembers *why* for the rest of his life."

She looked at the Fairywoman, who struggled to maintain the light in her hands. "Are you done yet?" she yelled before she realized she was making too much noise.

Meara nodded, tears leaking down her face again when the Gate was ready.

"Well, then come here and help me get her home!"

Catherine hauled Margarete to her feet, hooked one arm over her shoulder and motioned Meara to go around her and take her other arm.

By the time one of the patrolmen Dean had issued to walk the perimeter of The Fair at regular intervals found the blood and the note, Margarete was safely imprisoned in Stoker's dungeon, Meara was frantically scrubbing Margarete's blood off her face and hands with a nailbrush far too hard for her skin, and Catherine lay between Lillian's embroidered sheets in her bed, satisfied with the day's accomplishments.

Chapter Forty-Eight

ଔ Little Talks ଓ

Halesbridge paced by the little fire he'd lit for himself on the barren slope. Shaking his head, Lorcan decided the king's man couldn't have chosen a worse place to set up camp. There was no protection whatsoever. Granted, he could see fairly well in all directions, but he'd managed to miss Lorcan anyway.

"Did no one ever teach you how to build a blaze?" Lorcan said casually, startling the other man, coming from behind.

Halesbridge spun around, drawing his sword.

Lorcan frowned. "Please put that away."

Halesbridge breathed a sigh of relief. "I didn't think you'd come."

Smirking, Lorcan gathered up what wood Halesbridge had piled a little way from the fire and crouched down to arrange it around the waning glow. "This is wet," he remarked. "It won't warm you. It'll just draw attention, and I don't think you need a lot of attention out here."

Halesbridge huffed a laugh. "Well, it got yours."

"I do tend to keep my word. *You,* however, are late."

Halesbridge shrugged. "We were snowed in."

Lorcan spread his arms, motioning at the winterscape. "*We* still are."

"So I've noticed." He came closer to the fire and rubbed his hands. The horse snorted beside the tent, and Lorcan wondered if Halesbridge had anything to feed it.

"Your message said you needed to speak to me urgently."

"Well – I do." Oddly, he didn't continue right away. Lorcan hated when people didn't get on with it.

"Has your king's spouse recovered?"

"No."

"I'm sorry to hear that. Did the potion not work?"

"It wasn't that."

Lorcan tilted his head and rose, crossing his arms. "Look, what is it you want of me? I believe you had an arrangement with my friend, Master Greenleaf, but you didn't honor it. You didn't pay for what you got, and now you're here, wasting my time, but you won't tell me why."

"It's you I needed to speak with because I can't shake the feeling your friend knows the king's mistress. I believe she murdered Lillian."

Lorcan inhaled sharply. His patience was waning. "That's a strong accusation. Are you saying you think Master Greenleaf was in on it? Is that what you're trying to tell me, because if it is–"

Halesbridge shook his head frantically, rising also. "No, you don't understand – that came out wrong."

"Then enlighten me. If the potion worked, how did she do it, and how does Master Greenleaf tie in to it?"

Halesbridge shifted his weight uncomfortably. "She… I don't know. I really don't, but I'm sure that she did, somehow. Maybe by some form of magic. I'm very sure your friend had nothing to do with it, but one of the stable boys told me he saw them talking the day he came to the castle. The boy couldn't hear what they were saying, but he told me neither one of them seemed very happy."

Lorcan thought of the way Dean had looked at the locket. "Well, then let's start at the beginning. How did Lady Lillian die, if not by poisoning?"

"She fell from the tower."

"Did you see her fall?"

"No. I was… I'm no longer in the king's services. I accused the Duchess of Glasston of attempted murder the day Master Greenleaf gave Lillian the antidote. Needless to say that didn't strike a chord with His Majesty, and I couldn't prove it. Lady Glasston denied the locket was hers and produced one from her room he recognized, apparently. The king was so angry, he discharged me immediately. That's why I wasn't there when Lillian fell from the tower."

"She *fell* from the tower, she *jumped* from the tower, or she was *pushed* from the tower?"

"I really think she was *pushed*, but not physically."

"Do you know where Lady Glasston was when this happened?"

"Nowhere near her, I hear. But I think she's guilty all the same."

Lorcan hummed, but he didn't quite understand. Halesbridge's dislike for the duchess was palpable, and he wondered if the man wasn't imagining things. Humans had a tendency to obsess over things they were powerless to change, and they often resorted to trying to explain them with evil doings or magic. Nonetheless, it wasn't entirely unthinkable the duchess had played some part in the death of her lover's wife.

"Did you find out whose locket that was?"

Halesbridge nodded. "One of the maids admitted it was hers. The king had her executed. Point is, she had no reason to poison Lillian, and I *know* that locket belonged to the duchess because I took it from the king's room right after she'd left it."

"Okay. So it was hers, but the king didn't recognize it."

That was strange. Lorcan was convinced he'd have recognized a piece of jewelry he'd taken off a woman he'd just slept with.

"No, he claims he'd never seen it before."

"Funny thing about love: it tends to obscure the eyesight, the insight, and the foresight." Perhaps the king hadn't wanted to recognize it. Perhaps Dean hadn't, either. What was Dean keeping from him?

"Look," he told Halesbridge, "I have no idea why I should be helping you, but I'll be heading back to The Fair by the end of the week, and I'll try to find out about that locket."

Halesbridge seemed satisfied. "Will you contact me?"

"I'll send a dovelen. Your wife seems to know her way around those."

For a moment, he thought about asking Halesbridge to accompany him to the Winter Haven so he wouldn't lose a few toes in the night, but then he reconsidered. Halesbridge was desperate, but Lorcan wasn't sure he was trustworthy. He may have married a Fairywoman, but Lorcan suspected Halesbridge's love for his particular woman didn't extend toward any other kinds of Unnaturals. Halesbridge was protective of what was his. He suffered from hurt pride, and he'd be lacking the king's wages now. Perhaps he was beyond caring what he set in motion to reinstate himself.

Trudging back to the horse he'd left some distance away, he thought about the locket some more and it occurred to him it hadn't been particularly valuable. It might have belonged to a maid, but the maid would have needed a lot of nerve, a bit of know-how, and the right incentive to poison someone with powdered shierling.

Perhaps the duchess had put her up to it, promising her wealth if she succeeded. But how had the duchess gotten Lillian to throw herself from a tower?

There might have been magic involved, but more likely than not, Halesbridge had some unresolved personal issue with the Duchess of Glasston, and he'd have no qualms ridding the kingdom of her to prove his loyalty to crown and church.

Humans and their grudges, he thought. No disease claimed more lives than human resentfulness, and he hoped Dean didn't have any part in this.

Chapter Forty-Nine

❦ The Locket ❧

Dean saw the blood – *so much blood* – and thought his world was going to wither away. Fingering Catherine's locket, he tried to imagine if anyone could have survived what must have happened here, if his delicate, little *Margarete* could have survived what must have happened here.

Catherine had hurt or killed Margarete, but he didn't understand why. There wasn't a doubt in his mind now that she'd poisoned the queen. She'd lied to him, and he didn't recognize her as the girl he'd known – or the person he thought he'd known.

He'd been wrong to take her book, he'd been wrong to keep it from her, and he knew he should have reacted differently when she'd come to The Fair, but nothing he'd done justified her hurting or killing anyone, least of all Margarete.

Margarete had nothing to do with the books or whatever lies Catherine had spun around herself. Whatever world she was living in, it wasn't his, or Margarete's. Catherine was a Cine, but she had no idea what that meant. Perhaps she never had, and maybe that was on him, too. He should have looked for her and brought her to The Fair, but he'd turned his back on her, and now Margarete was going to pay for his mistakes.

"We've searched the grounds," one of his sentries breathlessly informed him, pushing his hands in his sides and bending over. "She's not there. Someone saw her leaving with a stranger."

"What stranger?"

The young man shrugged.

"What stranger?" Dean repeated, his voice a growl, because he knew Catherine couldn't have entered the grounds. Someone was helping her, but who*?*

He put his hand in the crimson snow, as if that would tell him where his wife had gone. It would be dark soon, and they had no hopes of finding her out here once the light was gone – if she was really still somewhere in these woods, but he doubted it.

"Master Greenleaf, I'm sorry. The woman seemed familiar to Dorian, maybe from one of the shows, but he couldn't place her."

"Alright." Dean tried to simmer down and nodded. "Alright. You go back and get five search parties of three men together and start swarming out."

The watchman hesitated briefly, his gaze on the locket in Dean's hand, but then did as he was told.

When he was gone, Dean opened the pendant, and a parchment fell out. He looked around to make sure he was alone before unfolding it. Whatever Catherine had inked was for his eyes only, he was sure.

Dreams are so easily destroyed. Bring me back my dream so I can give you back yours. Come alone. The old Tierney castle in five days.

The old Tierney castle was almost a week's ride from here. He could ask Mary. He *could*. Or he could try to make the trip on his own and not have to answer any of the questions she'd ask. If he left right now, he might make it. Mary wouldn't think twice about opening a Portal so he could fetch Catherine's book from its hiding place, but he couldn't tell her he needed to go to the castle. He couldn't tell Mary what he'd done to provoke this. She wouldn't see him the same way ever again.

When he came to Mary's caravan, she hadn't even heard the news yet. She'd been napping, but she was happy to help him. He retrieved the green leather volume and was back before anyone had missed him. Knowing the guardsmen were out on a wild goose chase didn't particularly bother him. Not tonight. The end would justify the means. He'd decided he'd send them out again at first light, and head off toward his forefathers' home while they were combing the woods. There would be no harm in it for them.

He barely noticed he was clasping the locket so tight, the tiny metal hinges tore into his hand and drew blood.

Chapter Fifty

❦ Saving Calum ❧

Meara was frantic. Opening the Portal to Cassandra's room after Catherine had left was a challenge. She had to make several attempts to raise the Passageway from the earth's elements and the old magic in its soil. Calum watched her anxiously, and she knew she was upsetting him, but it couldn't be helped.

She knew it was late, and she hoped to find Cassandra alone in her room. A glance through the first layers of the Lightgate told her she was safe. She hadn't done this in years – not since Cassandra had married Henric. Henric was human, and he'd never have understood.

Her sister startled at the sight of them in the mirror behind her. Meara could see she'd been getting ready for bed; Cassandra dropped the brush she'd worked through her long brown hair and quickly rose from her chair in front of the vanity, nearly toppling it.

There was a knock on the door. "Your Majesty?"

"It's alright, Nellie," Cassandra called out, hurrying to make sure the chamber maid didn't open it. She leaned against the frame and slid the bolt into the lock. "I just dropped my brush. I have no need for you. Goodnight."

They heard footsteps, and Meara realized the risk she was taking – the risk she was putting Cassandra at.

"What are you doing here?" Cassandra whispered, wrapping her arms first around Meara and then the boy. "What's going on?"

Meara retreated from her, placing her hands on Calum's shoulder. She had to be careful, but she didn't think she had much time. "I need your help."

Cassandra led her to a stool and made her sit, hunkering down in front of her. The boy sat on the floor next to her.

"Go slow and tell me what's happened."

She just couldn't answer that in front of Calum. She couldn't answer that at all. Her head was awash with all the things Catherine and she had been speaking about and all the pictures and images that were real, unreal, and something in between. She knew she shouldn't be here at all, but she felt a desperate need to protect her son, and if nothing else seemed clear anymore, the fact that she couldn't do that on her own was.

"I'm sorry, but I can't." A tear tracked down the side of her face, and she wiped it away. "I need you to trust me, *please*. I wouldn't ask if I had any other options."

For a moment, Meara thought Cassandra was going to insist on being the older sister again, stubborn and wise, but then Cassandra stroked her hand and firmly returned her gaze. "Tell me what I can do for you."

"You have to take Calum somewhere he'll be safe."

Calum jumped up, eyes wide in alarm. "What? I'm not going anywhere without you!"

Cassandra reached for his arm with her free hand. "Calm down and lower your voice." Looking at Meara, she said, "I don't understand. He's safe with you and Alexander."

"No, he isn't." Meara couldn't believe she was hearing herself say this, but it was the truth. "Something terrible is going to happen, and he will never be safe with me again."

Cassandra slowly shook her head. "Meara, where *is* Alexander?"

"He went north on business, but he didn't want to tell me where he's going."

"Do you want me to have someone look for him?"

"No." That wouldn't help one bit. It would just speed up what was to come.

"Mama, why are you acting so strange?" Calum insisted.

She was glad she hadn't taken the time to talk to him beforehand. She mightn't have had the strength to leave him here if she had. Pushing back a stray lock of hair from his forehead, she smiled. "I love you. I know you don't understand right now, but you will."

Then, she looked at Cassandra. "Promise me you'll take him to a safe place this very night! I know he can't stay here." There would be too many questions if he suddenly appeared in the Great Hall for breakfast the next day.

"Where do you want me to take him, dear?"

"As far away from me as you can. Don't tell me or *anyone* else who might be looking for him where he is, no matter what happens."

Cassandra clasped her chest, as though she needed to calm her heart. "What about Alexander?"

"Not even him." She was sure Cassandra would never see Alexander again, but she couldn't tell her that.

She should be at home, waiting for him right now. There wasn't much time; he could be back any moment, and what would he do if he found Calum gone? Her head hurt so badly, she felt like it was going to burst.

"Alright," Cassandra said, "I'll do as you ask."

"Mama, for how long?" Calum was fighting his tears, and she rose, hugging him to her.

"Not long," she lied, hoping he'd forgive her one day.

With that, she left him in Cassandra's charge. She didn't look back for fear she wouldn't be able to leave him then. She'd take him to hell with her if she didn't make sure he was elsewhere when next the Devil came calling, because hell was where she was certainly heading.

Chapter Fifty-One

ᥱ The Storm ᥲ

Meara of Halesbridge watched the sun rise from her bedroom window. She'd stood vigil there throughout the endless night. It had been five days, and she'd barely eaten or slept or left her room since she'd closed the Portal on her sister and on her son. Five days of waiting, and there was still no sign of Alexander, no hope of help, though she doubted there was anything even Alexander could do to help them out of this.

Katharina was probably already on her way, her demon, Stoker, in her wake.

The sky was ablaze as if the whole firmament had been ignited with every shade of crimson. She remembered what Alexander's mother had always said: "Red sky in the morning, shepherd's warning." But, neither warmth nor storm touched the world below. The lands were covered in snow and barren winter. A white mist marked the rhythm of her breathing. It was all that told her she was still alive – that, and the dull thud of a heart that had stopped feeling anything at all.

She was still standing at the window when the carriage finally drew up just after noon. As she'd predicted, Katharina was accompanied by Stoker and his black-clad soldiers on their black-clad horses. Everything about Stoker was black, and he fit Katharina perfectly.

She couldn't see if they'd brought the unfortunate woman they'd taken from The Fair with them, but perhaps Margarete was in the carriage. Who knows what they'd done to her.

Quickly, Meara dressed and attempted to run a comb through her tangled hair. There was no time for a wash anymore. One of her servants knocked and announced Lady Glasston, and she went downstairs to meet her unwelcome guest.

"Meara, how nice to see you," Katharina sang, embracing her and touching cheeks as if they were old friends. "I trust we're not too early…?"

Meara couldn't bring herself to reply, but offered a painful smile that wouldn't stay on for longer than a second, and she shook her head.

Stoker brought in Margarete Greenleaf, and Meara curtly dismissed a servant who'd been hovering, wondering if she should fetch wine or food. Meara declined both and ordered her to get out of the house and keep away.

Margarete didn't look well. The wound on her head had been dressed, but she was sickly gray in the face. Her pupils were strangely dilated. She was physically there, but the rest of her was absent as

Stoker sat her on a chair and left them, closing the door behind him.

Again, Meara bolted it, and again, she closed the window shutters, wondering what Katharina had given Margarete and how much damage she'd done.

"Where to?" she asked, closing her eyes to the younger woman's smugness for a moment.

"The old Tierney castle. I told you that last week."

Meara thought about it. She was almost afraid to admit it, but her head was so cluttered, she really couldn't say if she'd find the right place. "I'm not sure I know it…"

Katharina grabbed both her hands. "Well, then let me help you."

She fought her. Every instinct told her to.

"Don't," Katharina hissed. "You'll just make this so much harder for yourself."

It was difficult to let go, but once she had, she saw the forest as Katharina saw it. She saw the ruins up on the hill, and she knew how to get them there.

When Katharina released her, she felt sick, but she immediately set about opening the Portal. If she did this, maybe Katharina would leave her alone, and things would go back to how they'd been. Maybe.

She'd only seen the Tierney castle from afar once, and she'd never been inside it, but when she emerged from the Lightgate behind Katharina and Margarete, she was awed at the size of the compound.

The size, and the shadows that lived here. She could feel the presence of the souls that had perished in this place, and they frightened her.

Katharina maneuvered Margarete to a spot where she could sit down, and Meara went to join the lethargic woman when she'd closed the Portal. They waited together in silence as Katharina paced, but no one came. The day wore on endlessly, and Meara felt the blood in her veins slowly turn to ice. Margarete slumped against her shoulder and went to sleep at some stage, and she let her, trying in vain to keep them both warm.

Leaden clouds promised fresh snow and hurried along the dusk. Finally, Katharina lost her patience.

She shook Margarete awake. "Looks like you weren't it," she told her, blue lips thin and pulled into a sneer.

Margarete obviously had no idea what the woman was talking about.

Meara felt her mouth go dry.

"Not *what?*" Margarete replied, still half asleep and slurring the words.

"His dream, dear." Katharina stroked her cheek as she would an unwitting child's. "His dream."

Meara couldn't tell what was going on inside of Katharina, but she realized by the way the *fine duchess* was trembling – not with cold, but with rage – that things were about to get nasty.

Katharina pulled Margarete to her feet. She could hardly stand, but Katharina shoved her toward the keep. Its entrance was blocked by the debris of the tower that had toppled next to it. The rubble was blanketed in snow. Meara followed the women a little way, unsure of what to do with herself. She watched as Katharina shoved and dragged Margarete to the top of the stone pile, slipping and sliding and panting with the effort. She didn't understand what was going on, and so she stayed at the bottom, looking up.

Then, Katharina pulled a half-sized dagger from the girdle beneath her wrap and thrust the blade into Margarete's stomach without hesitation and before her victim had even seen the weapon properly.

At first, Meara didn't comprehend what she was witnessing, but when Katharina twisted the knife upward, a small gasp escaped Margarete. It was no more than a tiny little sound, almost completely lacking of voice, but to Meara, the fragmented silent scream filled the frozen courtyard, and it stopped not just Margarete's, but her own breath dead in her lungs.

Katharina caught Margarete as she stumbled forward and carefully sat her down. She pulled her legs about, and laboriously pushed her through the hole into the keep. The wind had freshened up and brought a blizzard of thick snowflakes with it. It muffled the thud of the dying woman's body hitting the ground inside. Katharina tucked the dagger away before starting her descent. More sliding than climbing back down, she didn't seem to notice the bloody tracks her hands left in the snow. Meara knew they'd soon vanish beneath this night's horrifying cold white shroud.

"Let's go," Katharina told her. "We're done here."

It was morning before Dean Greenleaf arrived. He'd driven his exhausted mare without rest through the snow storm only to find the castle grounds deserted.

Chapter Fifty-Two

⍒ The Downfall ⍓

There was movement far afield, up on the road that led to the house. Meara watched for a while as the distant speck came closer, realizing somewhere in the back of her mind that the rider would have passed Trondenburgh and the spies Lennard's mistress had stationed south of the fields. As he got closer, she recognized Alexander.

Hurriedly, she went inside and stripped off the gray work dress she'd put on that morning, washed her face and hands and slipped into a dinner gown of pale blue. It was completely unsuitable to the weather, to the time of day, and to the occasion she found herself in, but it was her husband's favorite. She wore it as a tribute to the love they'd shared these past fourteen years, and to the trust that had stood between them when they'd started their family. There wasn't much left of that trust now with the doubts Katharina had sown in her mind, but ultimately, he was the man she'd married, and no matter what he'd done or failed to do in the past, she was sure he'd stand by her now because that was who he was.

His face was lined and weary when he dismounted in the yard, but his eyes brightened upon seeing her in the door. She fell into his embrace, absorbing the chill that clung to his clothes, his cold face pressing against her neck as she welcomed him home.

"I love you," she told him.

Alexander cupped her cheek with his hand and she put her fingers over his.

"Did anything happen while I was away?" he asked.

She nodded slowly. "Lady Glasston came to see me. Let's go inside. We have to talk."

Alexander sat by the fireplace and listened patiently as she told him what had been going on in his absence. She left out nothing.

He looked stricken when she got to how Katharina had killed Margarete.

"So she knew about The Fair, about Greenleaf, and she knows what you are and what *Calum* is... but how? *Why?*"

"Alexander, I think it's because she's a Cine, and I believe she knows Greenleaf from before. It's not just that he could connect her to Lillian's death. There's got to be more to it." The truth of everything she said hung in the air like a bad smell.

"Meara, where *is* Calum?"

"Safe for now," she told him quietly, rising from her own chair to kneel beside him, taking his hands in her own. She needed to touch him. "Alexander, I think we have to leave, and we have to do it fast. We should go and fetch him, and we shouldn't ever come back."

She knew what she was asking of him. This was the house his father had built. These were the lands he'd worked so hard all his life to keep. This was his home. She'd followed him here from Ironstone for love, but would he follow her advice now, or would he insist on trying to take on his liege lord? She was certain this was a battle they couldn't win.

He only had to think about it for a moment. Then, he rose, pulling her up with him. "Pack a few things. I'll get someone to ready the horses."

Shrill screams sounded from outside in the hallway. A heartbeat later, two soldiers rushed through the door, swords drawn. Pushing Meara behind him, Alexander drew his own sword and glared at the intruders. Meara recognized them by their black leather armor.

"What is the meaning of this?" Alexander demanded.

"Stand down, Milord," Stoker said as he stepped into the room, calmly tugging off his gloves. "The king wishes a word with you."

Casting a quick glance at Meara, Alexander nodded and yielded his sword to the young soldier holding him in check. "Of course, I am at His Majesty's disposal. Lennard of Trondenburgh is always welcome here."

Meara didn't think the king would send Stoker, if indeed Lennard was already home from Ironstone. She knew it had to have been Katharina. Fear pricked at her insides.

Stoker smiled. He walked to a side table and poured himself a glass of wine from the decanter Meara had set there earlier.

"I'm afraid the king is a bit behind me, Milord. He is coming to take you and Lady Halesbridge to the castle. I'm here to prepare for his arrival." He paused, and then spoke to his men. "Make sure the rest of the servants have all been rounded up in the courtyard."

Meara could see the shock in Alexander's eyes as his gaze darted between her and Stoker. Lennard had *never* ordered this.

She heard screams from every corner of the house and the other buildings as her people were seized and forced out into the cold.

"What *is* going on here?" Alexander asked. "Am I the king's enemy that he would dishonor me in this way?"

Stoker laughed, relaxing his stance as if he had made some joke at a feast. "You, sir, are under arrest."

"On what charge?"

"Treason."

Meara watched her husband's face redden with rage, his jaw set. "Who dares to bring such nonsense up against me?"

"Our dear departed late Lady Lillian," Stoker answered smugly. "She confessed to adultery before her unfortunate fall, and she named you as her lover."

Meara felt her chest close up. Katharina had tried to plant that idea in her mind, and she'd made good on her threat to use the lie against them. The shock on her husband's face told her all she needed to know about his fidelity, but the king would listen to Katharina, and there was no doubt that Alexander, that *they* were ruined. His holdings, his life, all would be forfeit to the crown.

He squeezed her hand almost unperceptively. His eyes locked on hers for a moment. She knew he was up to something as he shifted slowly toward the door, drawing the attention of the king's emissary away from her.

"Have you lost your mind, Stoker? Who on earth would believe these lies? I demand to know who is spreading them!"

Stoker took the bait and picked up the argument.

Meara knew it for what it was: a show. She wouldn't need long to create a Portal, and they could make their escape. It would betray her Gift to the knight, but she and Alexander could get Calum and go someplace where they'd be safe, someplace where no one would ever find them.

Before she could do anything, however, the door crashed open again, and with a bellow, Calum's young friend Rob burst into the room. His face was a mask of determination. Armed with a short sword, a real one made of metal and not of wood, he lunged at the knight. Stoker yelped in surprise, backpedaling as the boy hacked the air toward him. The tall man fell against the table as Rob bore down on him, wielding his weapon with enough force to cut into the table as Stoker rolled out of his way. The blade lodged, and he couldn't yank it free. Rob's only ever opponent had been Calum, and nothing about their training or the games they'd played could have prepared him for this.

It only took seconds for Stoker to recover. He punched Rob in the face so hard that he sent him reeling into Meara's arms.

Enraged, the knight pulled his sword from its sheath and started toward them, only to be challenged by Alexander, who'd grabbed his father's old sword from the wall above the hearth. He swung the blade at the younger man, but missed him. Stoker jumped back. Alexander pressed his advantage, maneuvering his opponent away from the woman and child. The room rang with the sound of steel on steel as each man fought for control.

Meara held tight to Rob as the boy struggled to rejoin the fray. One of his eyes was already swelling shut, and she was sure his cheekbone was shattered. She had no idea what had possessed him to come to their defense, but she admired his ill-timed courage. Orphaned at three by the milk maid who'd given him life, he'd been Calum's playmate for all the years the two boys could remember. They were inseparable, and Meara realized there was no way she could leave him behind.

"Do as I say no matter what happens. Stay with me," she whispered. He was confused. She shook him harder than she'd intended. *"Promise me you'll do as I say!"*

Finally, he nodded, and she released him.

Stoker lagged under Alexander's onslaught. Meara knew her husband was stronger than he looked, and his eyes told her he was prepared to kill Stoker. He wouldn't think twice about doing away with the man who threatened their family, regardless of the consequence. There would be no coming back from this, but it didn't matter anymore. Only staying alive did.

A few more strokes of Alexander's blade pushed the knight against the window casement, and Alexander disarmed him.

"You're done!" he spat, ramming the pommel of his sword into Stoker's head.

The younger man crumpled to his knees and fell forward. Rob ducked in from the side and picked up the knight's sword. He dragged it away to a far corner.

Meanwhile, Meara wasn't wasting any time. Kneeling on the floor, she drew energy from the elements around her. Light emanated from her fingertips as the magic came to her, and it grew as she rose, her hands tracing the outline of a doorway. Rob gasped, and when she turned, she saw the boy gaping in wonder at the display, but in a good way. She was sure he wasn't afraid.

"Let's go, Rob," Alexander said, moving toward the Portal. "Meara—"

All at once, he stiffened. His eyes widened in a mix of surprise and agony as Stoker's dagger lodged beneath his shoulder blade with a dull thud. Meara could see blood spilling from her husband's mouth as he tried to reach back at the knife, but his fingers couldn't get a hold of it.

Scrambling to his feet, Stoker quickly pulled the blade from Alexander's back. He came around the stunned nobleman and plunged it into his neck. Instinctively, Alexander grabbed first his neck, and then at the knight for support as he stumbled downward. The sickening sounds he made in fighting for his last breaths shook Meara to the core.

Stoker smirked as he detached Alexander's hands from his arm. "You hit like a girl, and now you're going to die like one."

Meara screamed and lunged across the room to help her husband as his blood soaked into the rug beneath him. She clutched at him, dread weighing her limbs as she tried to gather him into her arms, aware he was dying and that there was nothing she could do about it.

"Alexander!" she screamed, begging him to stay with her, "Alexander, no!"

From the corner of her eye, she saw Rob picking up the knight's sword, but she didn't have the strength to call him back. He couldn't handle the weapon even with both hands on the hilt, but he launched himself at Stoker all the same, blade in the air ahead of him. Stoker got out of his way and tried to grab his sword back, but Rob got a hold of the dagger. Meara didn't see exactly what happened then, but a strangled cry broke, and Rob doubled over and sank to the floor, the knife in his chest. Stoker seemed worried, all of a sudden. He pulled it out of the boy's stilling form and tossed it aside, but Meara could see there was nothing anyone could do for the lad.

Rob died quickly.

Stoker sighed, briefly closing his eyes, but he wasn't mourning the boy. Meara guessed he had other reasons to regret Rob's death. "Ah, well," was all he said before he rose and stepped over the body toward her.

"You have an interesting talent, Milady," he said after a moment, gesturing to the Portal still flickering in the middle of the room as though they'd been having tea together. His voice was muffled by a deafening gush in her ears, and she could barely hear him when he stopped and stooped over her. "I can see why the duchess has taken such an interest in you. You might come in quite handy yet."

"You killed them," she stuttered. "The king wanted to – he wanted to talk to Alexander…"

"Yes, well, he probably did," Stoker said, "but I had my orders from Lady Glasston. She wanted the Lord of Halesbridge dispatched before the king got here. Shame about the boy."

It took her a moment to comprehend that he thought he'd killed Calum.

"You bastard! You're the traitor here, Stoker, you're a *monster*!"

He smiled indulgently. "Milady, Katharina of Glasston controls Trondenburgh in all but name, and when she has her titles, I'll also have mine." He pulled her up without warning. "I must confess, I had no idea how special you were when she ordered me to bring you to her, but it seems the duchess is full of surprises, and I'm sure it's going to be very beneficial to be on her right side. I'd consider being *very* cooperative from here on in, if I were you."

She felt faint, and he took her elbow to steady her as he led her toward the door. Turning the last few minutes over in her mind, she realized how easily Katharina had brought death to her house. It had only taken the witch moments to wipe her family out, and she hadn't even needed any kind of potion or magic to do it.

But, Calum was safe. Cassandra wouldn't let any harm come to him, but Katharina didn't strike her as one who let something pass without checking on the results herself. Stoker had never seen her son before, but Katharina had, and Lennard knew Calum... If

Lennard really was on his way here, or if Katharina ever found out he was still alive, she'd search for him until she'd found him.

Meara decided she couldn't let that happen.

With all her strength, she pushed against the man holding her up, throwing him off balance long enough to pull away. She ran for the waning Portal, but stopped halfway between it and Stoker, who was struggling to his feet. Stretching her hands toward the Gate, she willed it to come to her. It responded to the summons and rippled liquidly through the room, following the sway of her arms as she arched them toward the furious knight. The light's energy slammed into him, sucking him inside, and it deposited him in the forest nearby, where she and Alexander should have been now. She could see him turning in an attempt to pass back through into her house, but she snapped the Portal shut.

The room was engulfed in a stunning silence for a moment. She ordered herself to keep breathing. This was the calm in the eye of the storm, and she needed to stay clear and focused now so Calum would survive the hurricane.

Sounds from the courtyard outside announced the king's arrival.

"Too late," she mumbled, "too late, too late, too late."

The House of Halesbridge had fallen, and she had to make Katharina believe not one of them was left. She bolted the door. Grabbing the edge of the rug

Alexander had fallen on, she labored to pull it over to the blazing hearth, and then gathered up the boy several feet away. Laying him gently beside her husband, she spared a moment to dab the blood away from his pale face with the hem of her skirt. Smoothing back his hair from his brow, she placed a tender kiss on his cool temple. "You will always be in my heart," she whispered. "Peace be with you, my sweet Calum."

Horses' hooves clattered outside on the cobblestones, and shouts hailed the king. It would be mere minutes before he discovered the carnage, and found out who'd survived it. Quickly, she fetched a woolen blanket and a jug of lamp oil. She threw the blanket over the two bodies, emptied the oil over it and pulled one end of the fabric into the flames. It caught fire immediately.

Taking a candle from a nearby stand, she lit it and circled the room, touching tapestries and curtains and parchments that lay upon the table. She was confident that the men already knocking on the door and rattling it would be too late even if they broke it down. Flames leaped into being, spreading to the furniture. They hungrily devoured whatever they could reach, and thick smoke fanned out, choking her. Ignoring the heat with grim determination, she made her way back to the chair her husband had sat in less than an hour before. Along the way, she picked up the dagger Stoker had dropped. Smiling triumphantly, she seated herself, stabbing at the armrest with the tip of the blade as she waited. Her dress caught fire. She didn't panic. She wanted to burn for all of the mistakes she'd made over these past days and weeks – she wanted the pain. Her last coherent thought before it consumed her was that Katharina wasn't so smart after all.

Chapter Fifty-Three

⟨ふ The Letter ♥⟩

Dean looked around, but he found no sign of Catherine or Margarete or anyone else at the castle. The storm would have wiped away any trace of them, if they'd ever been here. He was too late. A day for a laming horse in the blizzard had cost him his wife.

He wanted to go to Trondenburgh and tear Catherine's heart out. He wanted to make her bleed like she'd made Margarete bleed, but he feared that if Catherine hadn't already killed Margarete, she might do it then. She could well be capable of that.

No, he'd have to wait. The best he could do was to write a message for her and find an envoy to take it to Trondenburgh for him.

The nameless little village where he'd spent the summer after his father's death didn't have an alehouse anymore, so he rode to the nearest town, and there he found a place that served food and a man who'd take his letter to Trondenburgh. Catherine knew nothing of dovelens, he was sure, and he paid the man a stately sum to convey the parchment.

He wasn't sure if the envoy could be trusted, so he wrote:

> *My Lady Duchess of Glasston,*
> *I implore you to forgive my tardiness in the matter you forwarded to my attention. I realize that my carelessness was inexcusable and beg another chance to prove my willingness to comply with your request.*
> *I humbly await your answer with the object you desire at my father's home where you met my wife, and beseech you to remember our friendship for what it once was.*
> *Yours sincerely,*
> *D.*

She'd surely respond, he told himself. She had to.

Chapter Fifty-Four

❧ The Survivor ❧

The king of Trondenburgh looked troubled when he returned home.

Standing out in the courtyard next to the clergyman with Lioba in front of her, Catherine could read him like a book as he dismounted, throwing his gloves at one of the squires waiting to take the men's horses. A mixture of sadness, anger, and disgust lined his face.

She hoped everything had gone according to plan. Her spy had been quicker than he, and the little man confirmed that he'd been to Halesbridge Manor on his way back from Ironstone, but she didn't know what, exactly, Lennard had seen there. She was dying to find out.

The biting smell of smoke on his clothes hit her as he closed the distance between them, and she had to wonder if Stoker had done something stupid. Straining, she could see him skulking way back in the entourage behind a horse-drawn cart, and he did not look happy.

In keeping with protocol, Lennard should have greeted the clergyman first. Instead, he hunkered down in front of Lioba and intently studied her face. The child tried to hook her arms around his neck, but he pushed her gently away and held her at arms' length, fixing his eyes to hers as though he was searching them for something, or trying to commit them to his memory.

The clergyman smiled. He mistook the king's behavior for a display of affection. When Driesburgh wasn't around, he wasn't inclined to take himself or his role too seriously, and he was just as fond of the child as everyone else here was, but he didn't know Lennard as well as Catherine did. Delightful little Lioba had them all firmly in hand, but something about the way Lennard looked at her told Catherine a little bird had whispered things in his ear he didn't want to believe.

A commotion reared up about the cart when it stopped close by. Servants came running and stood around it to look on as three soldiers carefully lifted a body off the back of it on a blanket so they could carry it. The woman was so badly burned, she barely recognized her, but Meara was still alive.

The clergyman inhaled sharply at the sight of her. "Your Majesty, what happened?"

"There was a fire at the Halesbridge farm," Lennard told them, straightening. "I suggest you go and offer a prayer for the only survivor." He turned to face Catherine. "We need to put Meara up someplace where she'll be comfortable. Send for a healer – but one we're familiar with – so he'll ease her pains, please, and then join me for a word in the Hall."

"Papa?" Lioba whimpered, clinging to him.

He picked the child up and balanced her on his hip, turning her away from the scene unfolding as the men lugged Meara up the steps to the keep's entrance. Lennard's arm brushed against Catherine, and she placed her hand on it affectionately, to let him know she was with him. This had to be hard for him. She was sure this was going to be hard on all of them for a while. Especially Stoker, when she got him alone.

Lioba couldn't help staring at the woman being maneuvered carefully into the building. Tears leaked down her pale face.

Catherine planted a kiss on her cheek. "It'll be alright, child," she said. "Don't worry." This was going to be another valuable life lesson for the girl, she thought, and you could never get enough of those. Growing up was not all sweetness and pretty rhymes, no matter which side of the castle walls you were born on, and she was sure Lioba would do well to learn that.

"Up the stairs," she told the soldiers, going after them. "Take her to my room. It's at the very top, but it's the most comfortable." That wasn't entirely true, but she had a supply of mohn juice there, and a few other things besides that might help her keep the Fairywoman alive.

"Your Majesty, what of Alexander of Halesbridge?" she heard the clergyman inquire behind her.

He hadn't set his feet in motion yet, and she didn't think he would. Not until Meara's burns had been covered.

"As I told you," Lennard replied, "Alexander is dead, and his son is, too."

At least Stoker hadn't messed that up, she thought. On the other hand, if the boy had still been alive, she wouldn't have needed to bother much with Meara. Not if he'd inherited her Gift. She could just have had the knight bring her poor orphaned little Calum, and she'd have convinced Lennard to give him a place in his home.

When the soldiers had lain Meara on Catherine's bed, Catherine ordered her lady-in-waiting and two other servants to boil as many clean bandages as they had in water and bring them. They'd have to keep the severely damaged skin clean and covered or she'd lose her Portalmaker, though she couldn't say for sure if the woman would survive even so.

She could feel Meara's eyes on her as she moved about the room, and there was nothing but hate in them. It didn't really bother her, but having Lady Halesbridge here instead of in Stoker's dungeon, as planned, was going to be tricky to handle.

"I'm guessing you brought this on yourself," she told her as she poured some mohn juice from a small flagon into a cup and filled it up with wine.

Meara said nothing, but refused the drink when Catherine propped her up and held it to her blistered lips.

"Don't be stupid," Catherine said. "It'll take the edge off the pain."

Meara's labored breathing irritated her, but the Fairywoman stayed stubborn.

"Suit yourself, but believe me, when my maid comes back and starts cleaning you up, you'll wish you were dead."

Perhaps she already did. By the looks of her, she was in for weeks and months of agony – if she survived. She was certainly going to be a burden.

The lady-in-waiting returned with the first of the bandages in a basin much faster than expected, one of the younger maids in tow.

Catherine rose from the edge of the bed. "Have you really boiled those?" she asked, and when the woman didn't reply right away, she slapped her across the face. "Go and do as I say, you silly goose! I want them *clean*!" To the other girl, she said, "I'll be downstairs if you need me. Make sure Lady Halesbridge gets plenty to drink." She handed her the cup, almost sure Meara would take the wine from someone else. Once the first few doses were in, it wouldn't be a problem keeping Meara in a daze.

The servant nodded eagerly. "Of course."

Lennard was seated at the table in the Great Hall alone, downing his own measure of wine when Catherine got there.

"We couldn't help them," he told her quietly as she closed first one door, then the other. She sat next to him, picked up his cup and took a sip before she put her hand over his.

"Don't torture yourself."

He drew closer to her. "When we got to the house, Meara locked herself in with Alexander and Calum. I had my men break down the door, but she'd already set fire to the room. The only one they could save was her – Alexander and Calum were already dead."

"But how…?"

"I think she killed them both."

"What?" Catherine did her best to look shocked. She was, a little, and she desperately wanted to talk to Stoker.

Lennard hesitated. "They were alone in the room, and when my men broke down the door, they found her holding a bloody dagger. I just can't explain this any other way, since she was the only one left alive."

This was interesting. Catherine had assumed Stoker had something to do with the fire for some reason, perhaps to disguise Alexander's death as an accident.

"I sent Stoker there earlier to ask Alexander and Meara to come to dinner tonight. I thought… I thought it would be good if we could fix this mess."

"Well, I had much the same idea," Lennard said, caressing her hand. "But, apparently Alexander threatened Stoker and sent him packing minutes before I arrived. Perhaps Stoker wasn't such a good choice of man to send, but Alexander is a stubborn man. *Was* a stubborn man."

He'd sent Stoker packing? Perhaps she'd overestimated her new friend. No wonder the knight hadn't been particularly eager to show himself.

"Did Stoker say anything?"

"Only that Meara was convinced Alexander was the reason Lillian killed herself."

"Why would Alexander have anything to do with that? He tried to find a cure–"

Lennard brusquely cut her off. "For Meara's poison, I'd say. She knew they were having an affair."

"So you think the maid was in Meara's employ?"

He nodded. "I do. And, when my men pulled her from the burning room, she was ranting on about the healer Alexander brought into my house – that man, Master Greenleaf – being a Cine from The Fair, and that he would certainly soon bring death and destruction to Trondenburgh."

Catherine waited for him to continue, but he took his time and poured himself more wine.

Eventually, uncomfortable curiosity got the better of her. "Did she say anything else?"

Lennard thought about it, studying her. "She lost consciousness quickly, but before she did, she pulled me close and told me you were a witch, too."

Catherine exhaled loudly, and then chortled a laugh. "In league with Greenleaf, no doubt."

Shaking his head sadly as he reclaimed her hands, Lennard scoffed. "No doubt. I'm glad no one else heard." She could see he didn't believe it.

"I just don't understand. Why the boy?"

Could it be she'd killed him to stop her from using him against her? Was Meara that kind of woman? She thought not. More likely that fool Stoker hadn't followed her orders for some reason. Perhaps the lad had been too much for him to handle. She was looking forward to the conversation she'd be having with the knight about that.

Lennard rose. "I don't know. I wish I did. I'm going to find out, though. If she lives, I'm going to make her tell me everything, and after she does, I'm going to have her burned all over again." The resolve in his eyes made Catherine shudder, but he saw that and pulled her into a tender embrace. "No one is to speak to Lady Halesbridge but me, not even the priest. See to that, my love. She's not going to bring harm to another member of this household or pull my name further into the dirt."

Catherine nodded, pressing a kiss to the corner of his mouth. This she would certainly make sure of. Meara wasn't going to talk to *anyone* ever again. The human voice was a gift, and a gift could be taken away.

"Share my bed tonight," he told her then. "Come to me when you've tended to our guest – come as my betrothed, Katharina. I need you at my side as my wife so I can rest easy."

Her breath caught, and she pushed away from him weakly, but barely able to contain herself or feign reserve. "Now? Are you *sure*?"

She'd left hints of many variations of the idea in his head over the past weeks, but she hadn't forced the issue. He'd made his decision freely, and she'd wanted him to – it was the only way to ensure he'd stand by it.

"I've never loved anyone as much as I love you," he said, not letting her go, "and I want to know you're safe and beyond doubt, holding my house together while I make provisions and smoke out the Cine haven. I want you to raise Lioba. The girl might not be of my blood, but she knows no other father. She's not to blame, and I won't abandon her."

"You know how attached I've grown to the child," Catherine assured him.

He stroked her face affectionately. "I do. It'll be forty days after Lillian's death next week. Just say the word."

She smiled tensely, making him suspect an insecurity about her that she did not feel. He bent and kissed her lips. "Say yes," he repeated softly as he wrapped himself around her.

She wouldn't have dreamt of refusing him.

Chapter Fifty-Five

❧ Vanishings ❧

Lorcan didn't bother with greetings or chitchat when Geraldine emerged from the back door of Ember's house. He didn't care why half the roof had fallen down without anyone bothering about it, or why the yard was in such a shabby, untended state. All he cared about was finding out why someone else was living in Brandner's house, and where the Peacock had taken his son. He thought Geraldine, who always knew everything, would certainly be able to help him with this.

"Don't scream, or I'll give you a reason to," he breathed into her ear, pushing the frightened woman against the wall beside the door.

He'd secretly been looking in on Aeden in Ironstone every time he'd been to the Winter Mountains, save for the previous year. Dean had gone instead with Margarete, leaving Lorcan to manage The Fair. They'd had busy times.

Dean didn't know about Aeden, and Lorcan hated himself for not having insisted to make the trip. It wasn't that he hadn't wanted to see Aeden – he just hadn't found an excuse to leave The Fair and hadn't made it happen. Now he was going to pay the price, and Aeden was, too.

Geraldine dropped her pail and it clattered on the cobblestones as she struggled, but he was much stronger than she. He held her firmly in place and clamped one hand over her mouth until she stopped fighting him.

"Good girl."

He waited another few seconds, using that time to envision the iron bolt on the other side of the door sliding smoothly into place. With the door locked from the inside, no one could come out and surprise them, and she had nowhere to run.

"I'm going to take my hand off your mouth now, and you're going to tell me where my son is," he said.

Her eyes narrowed and filled with tears. He loosened his grip, and she tried to find her voice while avoiding his stare, but he made her look at him.

"He's gone," she finally told him, sniffling. "Amelie is dead. Brandner found out Aeden isn't his, and he took him away from Ironstone."

Lorcan's stomach lurched. Why hadn't he just asked Mary to open a Portal for him and not question him? She would have done him that favor without losing a word over it.

He let go of Geraldine and backed away, noticing how poorly she looked herself. "How did Amelie die?"

"Brandner accused her of adultery and… and… she was found guilty." She couldn't go on, shaken as she was, but he could imagine the rest.

"Where did Brandner take Aeden?" He knew he'd be lucky if the boy was still alive.

"You're not going to find him," she sobbed. "That was almost a year ago."

"Where did he take him?" he repeated in clipped tones, watching her cower down on the unswept ground. She was afraid of him, and he wanted her to be. "Where is my son?"

"I don't know. All I know is that he took him north. I swear I don't know anything more." A new wave of sobs beset her. "I couldn't offer to take him in – I have so many mouths to feed on no income with Father and Frederic dead," she wailed, "and the scandal of it all!"

He felt his heart pounding in his head, and he wanted to shake her. Hands clenched to fists, he did his best to stay calm. "Do you know where I can find Brandner?"

"He isn't here. He's away on business, but I don't know where. For God's sake, have pity and don't hurt me! Think of the children!"

It took a lot of restraint to keep himself from boiling over. "What about *my* son? Who's going to have pity on *him*?"

Who indeed? A Cine boy among humans all alone… What if his Gift had emerged? What if

Brandner knew? Had he strangled him and thrown him in some ditch by the roadside, or had he just sold the child? Lorcan realized it wouldn't help to turn that over in his mind any further, and he tried to shut down the line of thinking. He had to keep a clear head.

Leaving Geraldine to her self-pity, he revisited some of his old haunts. They were places where he was bound to be recognized, but he didn't care. He needed information. Several people told him Brandner had rented his house to a friend and embarked on a journey on the southbound Trading Route to make new contacts. Others claimed he'd acquired two ships and was sailing for Sutrailia. What they all agreed on was that Brandner had it made, that unfortunate business with his second wife aside, and what none of them could tell him was what had become of the boy.

Returning to The Fair seemed like a waste of time after this, but Lorcan felt that he had to tell Dean he was leaving, and he had to do it personally. He owed him that, so he drove his horse hard across the icy countryside to get there faster, debating with himself on whether to take the southbound road from there or double back and go north.

The horse shied at the sensation of crossing over into the Outer Haven, but he didn't think the mare had gotten squeamish; it was his own nerves lying bare that made the exhausted creature nervous. Slowing as he wove his mount between the wagons, he noticed there wasn't as much activity on the grounds as there should have been. The Big Top wasn't lit. It was still winter and it was already dark, but that never deterred people from preparing and taking their meals together outside or rehearsing in the arena.

Dean and Margarete's wagon was dimly illuminated. He tethered the horse's reins to the handrails beside the treads leading up to the door and knocked.

When he didn't get an answer after the second knock, he called out, "Dean? Margarete? Anyone home?"

The door wasn't locked, and when he cautiously entered, he found his friend sitting by the window with his head in his hands, the weight of the world bearing him down.

"Dean – everything alright?" he asked.

Dean slowly looked up at him. He was pale and drawn, his eyes shadowed from lack of sleep. "No."

Lorcan took off his leather gloves. He was dusty and dirty and all kinds of agitated and tired, but he saw a need to sit with his friend for a while and keep his own news to himself.

"Where's Margarete?"

"She's gone."

"What do mean *she's gone*? I don't understand."

"Missing. Gone. She was seen leaving the fairground with a woman. We found a lot of blood just outside the perimeter, and a locket of hers."

Lorcan rubbed his stubbly chin, at a momentary loss. "Dean, did you find her body?"

The other man shook his head. "No. We had search parties out all these past weeks, but we didn't find any trace of her."

"How far did you go? Did you go into the towns and villages? Maybe someone saw something…"

Dean rose, and Lorcan could see he'd asked too many questions all at once.

"*Of course* we did! We covered *every* possibility," the Sorcerer's son snarled, looking twice his age.

"I don't know what to say, my friend. Tell me how I can help you."

"Where were you when we needed you? You should have been here a week ago."

Lorcan wasn't sure what Dean was getting at. "I was at the Winter Haven," he replied firmly, although the glass he'd meant to take back from there was still packed in crates and in the wagon where he'd left it. He'd been in such a hurry, he'd abandoned all thought of returning for the wagon as he'd intended to.

"Mary tried to find you there. Abhac told her you'd left days ago when she asked him. So, where were you?"

Lorcan felt as though he'd taken a punch in the gut. "I had business to see to in Ironstone."

"Business…" Dean raked his hand through his hair. "I needed you here, and you were *on business* in

Ironstone? What were you doing there? Drinking and gambling like your father? Or playing hide and seek with the Inquisitor's soldiers?"

Lorcan realized Dean wasn't looking for logic tonight. He was looking for a punching ball.

"I'm sorry I wasn't here," he said evenly.

"You should have been – but you're never around when you're needed, are you?"

There was more truth in that than Dean could ever guess – or maybe he *did* guess.

Lorcan stood with his feet rooted to the ground. He'd failed Ortus and he'd run from The Fair instead of staying and trying to work through what had happened with Dean, but he'd been no more than a boy then.

He'd failed Aeden now, too.

Amelie was dead, and his son was likely lost, and he needed to go look for him, he needed certainty. Dean might have understood that before – if he'd known – but no matter what Lorcan said now, he knew Dean wouldn't want to hear it because he felt Lorcan had failed him again, and this time, he might not so readily forgive. Margarete was missing, perhaps dead, and he didn't even know how Dean might have expected him to fix that beyond being there to help him look, but perhaps that was all it would have taken. Just being there might have sufficed.

"I'm sorry, Dean. I'm sorry I wasn't here. I'm going to go to my wagon now and we'll talk in the morning."

"I don't think I want to talk to you in the morning."

"I'd say we'll see about that, then." He turned to leave.

"I was wrong about you," Dean said to his back. "I thought we were friends, but if you're not honest with me and I can't rely on you. Who's to say I need you here?"

Lorcan couldn't believe he was taking the bait, but he shut the door he'd just opened without exiting and faced Dean.

"Your father did," he informed him. "This is as bad a time as it'll get for you, and we don't need a conversation about your father right now, but I'm going to tell you this anyway: Ortus wanted me here to be your sword and shield, and I'm aware that I've failed both him and you. Now, as it turns out – we may *both* have failed the people we love, because I also happen to know you're keeping things from me and everyone in this Haven, too. You're hurting like you've never done before, which is why I'm not going to knock you on your butt right now, but I'm telling you, don't tempt me any further tonight, *friend*."

Dean looked at his feet. He didn't reply.

Lorcan lingered for a moment. He realized he'd have to sit this out. He wasn't going anywhere anytime soon. He couldn't just leave Dean with this. Aeden was out there, but what was he going to do?

One more day, he told himself then, just one night's sleep and he'd find a way to fix this. He'd see where they stood when they were both less tired, and after that, he'd go search for his son.

"I'll see you in the morning, and we'll talk," he repeated. Still there was no reply, but he hadn't expected one.

Chapter Fifty-Six

☞ Katharina of Trondenburgh ☜

The date on Dean's letter told Catherine it had taken over three weeks to reach her. Its seal had been broken and very amateurishly fixed back in place. She didn't believe the envoy who'd delivered it deserved to be reimbursed for his efforts, and she wondered whom he'd shown that note to. There were a number of possibilities.

The messenger could have made the trip to Trondenburgh in less than half the time if Dean had hired him anywhere near her home village. She didn't doubt her old friend had paid him well, and he wouldn't have failed to stress the importance of haste. After all, his little wife's life had been at stake. Not that it mattered. Catherine assumed Margarete had probably bled to death within hours after she'd shoved the knife into her stomach.

Stoker was still extremely anxious to make up for his blunderings at Halesbridge Manor, so she didn't think twice about sending him to have a little chat with the messenger about that broken seal and his work ethics. It was her wedding day, and she didn't want any incalculable worries to burden that.

Unfolding the parchment, she discovered that the words penned upon it were as pitiful as everything about Dean, although she was glad to hear he was willing to bargain. She thought about this before she climbed the stairs to her old room in the keep, and she already had a plan when she unlocked the door.

"How are we feeling today, dear?" she asked without looking at the Fairywoman, opening the curtains.

She didn't expect an answer. Meara would never speak again. Catherine had given her an extra dose of mohn juice and used a sharp knife to sever her vocal cords the night after Lennard had brought her to Trondenburgh. She knew how because the hangman had taught her. So many of the lessons she'd learned from Binns and Rebecca served her well. No one would ever know what had really happened to Alexander and poor little Calum.

The widowed, orphaned mother lay on her side, staring at her. Catherine could see she was in pain and waiting for what she thought of as her medicine. The merciful haze it induced got her through. There were no more infections, but the scars on her damaged skin were pulling and tearing at her day and night. Her hair would never grow back, her nose was destroyed, her right hand was almost useless, and so much of her face had been burned, she was lucky she could close her eyes at night. Leaning in to get a closer glimpse of those eyes, Catherine confirmed what she'd already known: they were brown, just like Margarete's.

She poured a small cup of wine and measured a generous amount of mohn juice into the drink. Meara grabbed at the cup, but Catherine withheld it for a moment before giving it to her.

"Go slowly," she said. "I won't be back today. The king and I are to be married in a few hours."

Meara didn't give her reason to suspect she cared. All she cared about was how quickly the effects of the potion would set in so she'd find relief.

Catherine was pleased.

***

Dean Greenleaf sat at his window that day like he did every day; unwashed, unshaven and wearing the same clothes as he had the entire week.

When Lorcan entered, he wished he could tell him about Margarete. He'd almost lost hope that she'd still be alive now, but if she was, he couldn't risk it. Lorcan would do what he always did if he told him. He'd take charge, and he'd look at him *that way*, like he always did when he'd done something that wasn't good enough – it was much the same way his father had looked at him all the time. No matter what he did, he just wasn't good enough, skilled enough, fast enough, brave enough or clever enough.

But, enough was enough.

He didn't need Lorcan to tell him he'd ruined his own life by forfeiting Margarete's, and he didn't need Lorcan to rescue his wife. If Catherine hadn't already killed her, he'd save Margarete himself, somehow. He didn't need Lorcan or *anyone*.

Catherine would answer his letter, he'd hand over that wretched book, and that would be the end of it. The Fair might never need it again. He'd find some way of compensating its loss. It wasn't important. He'd make the exchange and take Margarete home, and he'd never think back on this again.

But who was he trying to fool?

Giving Catherine one book wouldn't be the end of *anything*. Catherine was after something else entirely, and she wasn't going to stop until she got it. He knew he'd set this upon himself, and Catherine was just warming up.

"Dean, you should eat something."

He ignored the plate of eggs Lorcan put down in front of him. "Just go away and leave me alone."

"Alright then, suit yourself," Lorcan replied, and walked back the way he'd come, but stopped when he'd reached the door, turning on his heel.

"No. You know what? I haven't got time for this. I don't know what's really going on here, and I don't even know if I care. I care for Margarete, yes, but you're making it very hard for me to like *you* right now, and I don't understand why."

Dean felt his anger take control, and he wiped the plate off the table with his arm. The earthenware that looked like a part of the set Mary had given them for a present when he and Margarete had been married shattered on the floorboards.

He simply couldn't take *that look* anymore.

"For the last time: get the hell out of here and don't come back."

Lorcan just stood there. "If that's what you really want," he said. "I was going to tell you last night that I have to leave The Fair. Something happened, and I won't be back for a while. I couldn't sleep wondering how best to help you, but now I know. Good luck, Dean."

Dean did not reply, and he felt nothing when Lorcan closed the door quietly behind himself.

***

Catherine wore a dress three seamstresses had worked on the entire week. Walking up the aisle, she felt the cool swish of the silken skirt like a gentle caress on her legs, and she knew the tiny sparkling beads sewn to the bodice would catch and reflect the light from the stained glass window behind Driesburgh at the altar.

For a few seconds, she imagined she was at the Tierney castle, and from the corner of her eye, she could see the other Catherine peeping out from behind one of the columns that held the church's vaulted ceiling. The girl was pale and in rags, but she smiled, baring rotten teeth. Catherine looked the other way.

The king was waiting for her.

***

Dean stepped out of his caravan in time to see Lorcan depart. He watched him bend to kiss Mary's cheek, holding her hands and making a silent promise, perhaps, as he fixed his gaze to the old Fairywoman's. The Snake Sisters were there with their families to say goodbye. He hugged Freya and shook each of the boys' hands in turn. Then, he mounted his horse and took one last look around. Their eyes met, and despite himself, Dean nodded at Lorcan. Lorcan returned the gesture, and set the horse in motion.

Dean stood on his little porch until his friend – if he still *was* his friend – disappeared from sight.

"Wake up to yourself," Mary told him in passing. "You're not the only one with worries, and time is not our friend."

Dean scoffed. "Then why does he ride when he could be opening Portals?"

Mary raised an eyebrow at him in surprise. Had she really thought he wouldn't know?

"Because it's not smart when you're looking for someone and you don't know where to begin," she told him, "as opposed to when you *do* know where that someone you're looking for is."

His jaw clenched, and he could feel her probing gaze reaching into his heart.

"Dean, do you know where Margarete is?"

***_

Driesburgh's ceremony was a trial. The man's voice was monotonous and too high-pitched to be pleasant, and he had eyes so cold they'd shame the Devil. Sometimes, Catherine wondered if they saw more than he let on. She wasn't really listening to him, though. The other Catherine stood beside her, and the sickly-sweet stench of the child was overwhelming. It was as though she'd come straight from the grave to be her grisly bridesmaid. Catherine kept smiling nonetheless. This was her big day, and she wasn't going to let anything spoil it.

***

"Dean, do you know where Margarete is?" Mary repeated.

He briefly considered admitting that he thought he did, but he wasn't that weak, whatever she thought of him. He was going to do this *his* way.

"No, I don't. But you're right. I do need to find a way back to myself, and I have a place to be. Would you open a Portal for me?"

"What, now?"

He nodded. "Yes."

***

When the bishop was finally done talking and blessing their marriage, Catherine bore the title *Princess Katharina of Trondenburgh*, and a warm feeling spread inside of her. As such, she was Queen Consort.

She'd made it.

She was where she wanted to be, but her breath caught and bile rose in her throat as she turned around to face the congregation that had gathered to witness their king's vows. They were all there: Cooper, Laura Shearer, Caleb, Rebecca, Binns, the girls Brandner had killed in her name, Lord Halesbridge, and a boy she didn't even know, all of them a gruesome sight to behold; burned, bloody and in rags, half-eaten by maggots, missing limbs, missing parts of their faces, but all of them very much recognizable. Her smile derailed. She nearly screamed. It took everything she had to keep herself on her feet, but she swayed, and Lennard grabbed her arm to support her, mumbling about her corset being too tight and the excitement of the day when Stoker came to his aid.

She'd made it, and this was the bed she'd have to lie in, she told herself. Voices and shadows were only small pieces of reality, fleeting moments and nothing that could harm her. She'd done away with these people, and if she closed her eyes, she could be rid of them once again. They were the past. If she wanted to step into the future, she was going to have to walk by them and never look back.

***

Exiting the Lightgate Mary had opened for him, Dean found himself in the stables of Trondenburgh. He looked around as he walked to the wide doors and discovered he was alone. There was a huge commotion going on in the courtyard, a festivity of some sort. Pulling the hood of his cloak as far over his face as possible, he left the stable, making sure to keep his head down, and mingled with the crowd of people cheering and drinking to the king and his new wife.

New wife... Of course he knew who that would be.

He made his way toward the church just in time to see them: Lennard and Catherine. She was a picture to behold, but she was surrounded by an aura so black, he recoiled in horror. The moving shadows shrouded her like a dense fog one minute and flocked out from her like an angry murder of crows the next. They rose into the sky, and he followed them with his eyes. Just then, a hag clutched at him, a creature burned beyond recognition. He struggled to free himself from her grasp, disgusted by the woman's appearance. For a split second, he thought he recognized her eyes. His hood slipped back.

***

Catherine breathed a sigh of relief when the shadows dispersed into the air. Standing on the topmost tread of the steps leading up to the church entrance, she made herself smile and wave to the people. They were cheering for Lennard and for her, and she was determined to enjoy the moment until her gaze caught on the monstrosity that had once been Meara of Halesbridge right next to a familiar face in the crowd, one of many, but unmistakable.

Panic almost immobilized her. Both Dean and Meara looked straight at her.

Lennard squeezed her hand. "Katharina, how did *she* get out? And isn't that–"

"I don't know!" She couldn't make sense of it. She'd locked the door. "And, yes, that's Halesbridge's *healer*." She shuddered at the thought of Dean escaping with Meara every bit as much as him being captured. She couldn't allow either to happen.

"Get the woman, and kill *him*," she hissed at Stoker. The knight was close behind her, his sword already drawn.

"The red-haired man?"

She nodded. "Don't let him get away–"

"No, bring him to me alive," Lennard cut her off, putting himself in Stoker's way, but Catherine knew whose orders the knight would follow.

"Just go," she mouthed to him, burrowing into his thoughts and leaving an image of Dean's dead body there.

Stoker took four of his men and swiftly dug his way through the masses toward Dean.

Dean tugged at Meara, but Meara didn't seem to know what to do and kept shaking her head, turning first this way, then that, and finally, he abandoned her. He raised his hood, and within an instant, he disappeared from sight, leaving Meara behind.

The soldiers combed the courtyard and searched all the buildings, but they couldn't find him. All they came back with once Stoker had safely reinstalled Lady Halesbridge in her room was the book Catherine had so longed for.

"Burn it," the king ordered, recognizing the symbols on its cover.

Catherine bit down on her tongue until she could taste the blood, unable to find a reason to object, but Driesburgh surprised her.

"Your Majesty," he whispered. "Give it to me. I'd like to take a look at it. Perhaps this book is the key that will help us understand how we so quickly managed to slip into the dark."

Dies Irae Series

If you enjoyed this book, visit the author's homepage at www.lisahofmann.net for background and details on the Dies Irae Series and other upcoming publications.

Short stories available for e-book readers:

Fairyflies

Fire

Fairypeople

Available for e-book readers and in paperback:

Stealing the Light – Dies Irae Book 1

Coming soon:

Gates of Eventide – Dies Irae Book 3

Other works

Trading Darkness